The highest praise for
Thomas Gifford's classic thrillers

THE ASSASSINI

When lawyer Ben Driskill's sister, an outspoken nun, is
murdered at her prayers, Ben sets out to find her
killer—and uncovers an explosive secret. *The assassini.* An
age-old brotherhood of killers. Once they were hired by
princes of the church to protect it in dangerous times. But
whose orders do they obey now?

Please turn the page for more about
Thomas Gifford's novels. . . .

PRAETORIAN

London, 1941. American radio correspondent Rodger Godwin has been chosen by Prime Minister Churchill to cover the story of a lifetime: a daring raid to assassinate Field Marshal Rommel. But the mission, code-named Praetorian, is a disaster, and now, a gravely wounded Godwin wants only one thing: revenge against the traitor who leaked the plan to the Nazis.

"Filled with excitement, passion, and drama . . . I didn't want it to end."—*The Washington Post*

"[A] superior international thriller . . . told in a taut, cinematic style à la Graham Greene."
—*The Denver Post*

"By far Gifford's best . . . a tough book to put down."—*Daily News*, New York

"A thriller of enormous breadth."
—*The Tampa Tribune and Times*

"Stirring . . . Brimming with bold action and characters: Chalk up another likely big hit for Gifford."
—*Kirkus Reviews* (starred review)

"Keep[s] the reader guessing right up to the surprising denouement."—*USA Today*

SAINTS REST

Thomas Gifford

BANTAM BOOKS
New York Toronto London Sydney Auckland

This edition contains the complete text
of the original hardcover edition.
NOT ONE WORD HAS BEEN OMITTED.

Saints Rest
A Bantam Book

PUBLISHING HISTORY
Bantam hardcover edition published October 1996
Bantam paperback edition/September 1997

ISBN: 0-553-57226-1

Published simultaneously in the United States and Canada

Bantam Books are published by Bantam Books, a division of Bantam
Doubleday Dell Publishing Group, Inc. Its trademark, consisting of the
words "Bantam Books" and the portrayal of a rooster, is Registered in
U.S. Patent and Trademark Office and in other countries. Marca
Registrada. Bantam Books,
1540 Broadway, New York, New York 10036.

PRINTED IN THE UNITED STATES OF AMERICA

OPM   10 9 8 7 6 5 4 3 2 1

for CARLY

I never fail to be astonished at how much I am at the mercy of television directors and editors, at how my public image depends far more on them than it does on myself. I know politicians who have learned to see themselves only as the television camera does. Television had thus expropriated their personalities, and made them into something like television shadows of their former selves. I sometimes wonder whether they even sleep in a way that will look good on television.

—VACLAV HAVEL

For TV purposes, the ideal world is one in which whatever is on the screen at this moment is entirely engrossing. One event is not necessarily more important than another, because they all are supposed to claim our attention in the brief *now* during which they exist. It could be the NBA finals. It could be live scenes from the explosion in Oklahoma. It could be Kato Kaelin's first network interview. It could be the election returns that give us a new president. . . . The O. J. Simpson trial symbolized the convergence of "news" and "entertainment," but the convergence was inevitable as long as athletes, politicians, movie stars, and murderers had to compete for space in the same small box.

—JAMES FALLOWS IN HIS BOOK
BREAKING THE NEWS

We push on, we heal the American people, we build a great second term for Charles Bonner—and we do our best to keep the past from growing sick and diseased and infecting the present. We are political men. . . . It's show business— you must see that. We are like everything else, just another branch of show business. It's enough to make a man laugh, isn't it? We take ourselves so seriously. On your way, Ben. Go live your life and be well.

—ELLERY DUNSTAN LARKSPUR

Author's Note

This novel really could not have been written without the cooperation of selfless people who had nothing to gain from my writing it. The administration of President Bill Clinton was unfailingly helpful and kind and tolerant of the poking and prodding I did wherever I went, from the offices and corridors of the West Wing of the White House on through the halls of Congress and the Justice Department. I therefore owe a debt of very real gratitude to the following:

President Bill Clinton

Carl Stern, Caroline Aronovitz, and Dan Hamilton, all of the Department of Public Affairs at the Department of Justice

Theodore J. "Tade" Sullivan from the office of Senator Daniel P. Moynihan

Karen Finney of the White House Visitors Bureau

Jim Hewes, The Round Robin Bar, Hotel Willard

Noreen O'Dowd, Manager at the Latham Hotel

Gene Foley

Chris Warneke

Jim Beem

Ann Stock, Social Secretary for President Clinton

Lisa Caputo, Press Secretary for Hillary Clinton

Christine Maloy

The late Reid Beddow, of the *Washington Post*, a lifelong friend

And I owe particular thanks to Marc Hoberman of the White House Visitors Bureau who tirelessly supervised our time in the West Wing and rode herd on us, never ran out of breath answering the endless questions, and was good enough to take some snapshots with which I could prove to friend and foe alike that I'd been there, done that.

There were many other folks who stood still for interviews and shared pizzas at Gepetto's and sumptuous dinners at Citronelle and some very long and pleasant evenings at the Four Seasons and Red Sage and the Jockey Club at the Ritz and Duke Siebert's. And at the end of the day it was always politics. Washington is indeed a company town and the company is Politics, Inc. I can only hope that some of the experiences and some of the fears they expressed to me are reflected in SAINTS REST. If not, I have failed, because they were very successful communicators.

Charles Hartman, as he was during the course of writing my previous novel THE ASSASSINI, was the most steadfast of friends and sounding boards throughout this entire undertaking. His sense of storytelling is as good as anyone I've ever known and, for better or worse, he will not give up until he makes his point. That he came through in one piece is testament to his resilience.

My editor, Beverly Lewis, made immense contributions and survived a very daunting task which I seldom made any easier for her though I swear my heart was in the right place. And my agent, Kathy Robbins, went above and beyond the call of simple duty in seeing me through some very rough patches. And my Saturday Morning Political Seminar leader, Tom Adcock, tried to keep me up to the mark politics-wise, encouraging me to match him rant for rant in the manner of Everett True though it was clear I was out of my league. And finally I owe a debt of gratitude to all of the folks at Bantam who helped in every way they could.

They all have my thanks and appreciation.

This novel would never have seen the light of day without Carly Wickler's faith in me and in the task. Her wisdom and humor and beliefs have completely changed my life. Here—to everyone's relief—words fail me.

—Thomas Gifford
Dubuque
24 April 1996

Prologue

He stood in the well of the House of Representatives looking out over the assembled joint session of Congress, over the assorted honored guests, looking out at the television cameras that carried his words into every corner of the United States of America and around the world. It was the night of January 19, and he might well be delivering his final State of the Union Address. Entering the fourth year of his presidency, Charles Bonner looked fit and strong and determined. There were those who thought he must have stopped reading the polls long ago.

They were wrong.

He'd been reading the polls all right. He had seen where Americans were going. To the right. Fear over jobs lost in the nineties, fear over the standard of living and fear for their children, fear of old age and fear of competition, fear of crime and drugs, but growing most quickly of all, a fear of maintaining their own borders and losing strength and independence in terms of the nation's security. And now the outbreak of civil war in Mexico and the rise of a powerful ultrareactionary government in China were threatening American borders and national security, respectively, and Americans were getting nervous looking out for number one. His polls had been slipping for months—down to 42 percent approval and falling. There was no end in sight.

And Charlie Bonner knew something else. He knew that he had been getting misinformation about the Mexican situation and the China outbreak from his intelligence sources. Independent tests had been run by the National Security Agency, disinformation had been plugged into the system, and three men had died as a result. The intelligence community was a sieve—and not only that, a sieve that was for sale. Or so it seemed. His director at NSA had told him there was nothing they could do about it, that it would take too long to fix before the election.

Well, there was something he could do about it. He had a year. He had kept his own counsel. He wouldn't go quietly. There was still time to raise a little hell.

He had been speaking for thirty-one minutes when he departed from his printed text. In the press gallery Anson Dameron of the *Los Angeles Times* jerked out of a brief doze, looked around, and wondered why the hell the President wasn't talking. Brenda Halliday of the *St. Paul Pioneer Press* elbowed him and told him he'd been snoring. "What's going on?" Dameron said, yawning. She gave him a look.

The President leaned on the lectern and the tone of his voice changed; his entire demeanor seemed to reshape itself, and he was suddenly the same man who had three autumns before campaigned across the nation, ridden trains and buses and stood amid great throngs in open squares and sat on hay bales beneath the harvest moon with fifty people gathered to listen to him. He was the same man who had shared his innermost thoughts about why he wanted to be president and why he might deserve your vote. He wasn't reading a speech anymore. He was just Charlie Bonner, a man you could trust. Or not. It was up to you.

"During the campaign we waged nearly four years ago, as we prepared for the New England primaries I found myself speaking at Fort Ticonderoga and I was deeply moved by that place and its history. And Ticonderoga has been much on my mind lately.

"Where in 1775 a young nation took its first steps to fight for its freedom. America was forming back then. Word of the engagements at Lexington and Concord had reached Colonel Ethan Allen not far from there, and he knew that the time had come to begin the fight for liberty . . . to go on the attack for the first time against King George. It was time for that rabble in arms, as they were called, to rise and make its case with musket and pike . . . and that is what Ethan Allen and his Green Mountain Boys did."

In the old pressroom, smoking a short fat cigar with his feet up on a scarred tabletop, watching the speech on television, Walter Peterson, who often recounted his career as having been spent with "the AP, the UP, and every other goddam P," turned to Mike Fulton of *Newsday* and said, "What the hell has this got to do with anything? Am I going to have to do a new lead? Jesus, politicians." Fulton said, "Listen," and pointed at the screen. The President was continuing.

"Ethan Allen knew that all-out war was at hand and that the redcoats were coming down from Canada in great numbers, coming down the length of Lake Champlain to muster with their fellow soldiers of the king at Fort Ticonderoga, which was known then as the Gibraltar of America. . . . So, early one morning, Ethan Allen in his coat of green, with the epaulets of gold, led a band of eighty men who arrived in small boats from out of the foggy dawn that lay across the lake, and they struck the first blow of the American Revolution. As he stood on the beach before the fort, he spoke some words which echo down through the corridors of time until tonight, when we hear them anew and afresh. . . .

" 'We must this morning either quit our pretensions to valor, or possess ourselves of this fortress . . . and inasmuch as it is a desperate attempt, which none but the bravest of men dare undertake, I do not urge it on any contrary to his will. You that will undertake voluntarily—now poise your fire-locks.'

"And when the sun finally rose that morning Ethan Allen and his boys were in possession of the fort, and he wrote in his diary that he and his followers passed around the flowing bowl—they'd worked up a thirst, I suppose—

and wished success to Congress and the liberty and freedom of America."

"Pass the flowing bowl this way," Bill Steinberg, producer of *The Evening News* with Phillip Carmichael at CBS, remarked to one of his researchers. They were watching at the West Fifty-seventh Street operation in New York. "Look at that son of a bitch lapping it up." Steinberg was a handsome man. He believed he would have made a fine president. You needed plenty of ego.

The President was smiling at the crowd. He was a handsome man himself, once a football player. Quarterback at Notre Dame. He had been known to inspire people.

"Tonight I invoke the name and memory of Ethan Allen, and the battle at Ticonderoga, with good reason. Tonight I am here to tell you, my friends, and to tell the world that an army is descending upon us again. From out of the fog. Only this time it is an army from within our own ranks and—for that reason—all the more deadly. This time it is a secret army representing our own secret government . . . composed of those who would stop us from pursuing our goals and realizing our destiny as the greatest, freest, most open society on earth."

There was just a bit of rustling among those in the chamber. A frisson of unease. In the old pressroom Walter Peterson swallowed a great cloud of cigar smoke and coughed: "What the hell is this? What's he saying? I *am* going to have to write a new lead. . . . I can feel it in my bones."

"And I want to reassure you all," the President continued, "that the second American revolution is already under way. . . .

"That nothing, not even this secret government, can withstand our determination to save this nation. I want to remind you that Ethan Allen confronted treachery as well as redcoats. And it is of treachery that I must speak to you tonight—treachery and its consequences. This . . . is a very solemn night.

"I ask you to listen very carefully, because the rest of

your lives and the lives of your children and their children will depend on how you respond to what I have to say.

"In recent weeks it has come to my attention, through the efforts of certain deeply committed public servants such as our attorney general, that various of our intelligence services have been engaging in what I can only describe as policies—foreign and domestic—of their own, not those of your elected leaders. These agencies which operate with funds that they are not required to account for . . . which operate without the consultation of the executive or legislative branches of the government . . . which operate and have operated for many years on their own initiative . . . have committed new and critical security breaches in our intelligence community . . . breaches and thefts that may be designed to affect our policy and decision making in Mexico, our neighbor to the south, and throughout the world."

Anson Dameron whispered, "Looks to me like he's about to put his foot into a veritable mountain of it. He'll never get his shoes clean—you can't screw around with these boys—"

Brenda Halliday shrugged. "Sounds like it could be fun to me. Reign of terror at Langley? Good story."

"For reasons involving the safety of Americans in harm's way," the President intoned, "I can be no more specific at this time.

"But the message I bring you tonight is this: For too long our lives—your life, my life, all of our lives—have been controlled by this secret government which you did not elect, which cannot be seen, which is not answerable to any of us, and which until now has held this great nation of ours in its grip. So many of us have fought, and so many others have died, for this secret government without knowing it even existed.

"Well, it's time we stopped fighting and dying for the secret government!"

The chamber was still except for nervous coughing and muttering between observers, but the members of the press were darting glances at one another, making surprised faces, raising eyebrows. This was all news to them.

Pudge Buchanan of the *Chicago Sun-Times* jotted on a pad: *Thin ice.* He passed it to Sally Ledbetter of PBS. She nodded, wrote: *He's already broken through.*

"I mean a secret government," the President said, "composed of forces within the intelligence-gathering community, the military, and our greatest industries. And be sure of this—I am not speaking metaphorically. I am speaking of a real, live, functioning secret government . . . which is why there have been no advance copies of this part of my remarks this evening, why no one on my staff has been informed about the subject of this speech, why there could be no risk whatsoever of a leak. . . . The secret government is hearing these remarks—and their own death knell—as I speak these words."

"Jesus Christ," Fulton breathed softly.

The President spoke with feeling. "This secret government depends on these agencies which now operate in a cloak of inviolable secrecy. You don't know what they're doing . . . your elected representatives in the Congress don't know what these agencies are up to . . . and, trust me, your President has only just begun to discover the truth. They have become rogue agencies, carrying out their own national and international policies for their own benefit and the benefit of their supporters and suppliers.

"Since I am not dealing in platitudes or generalities this evening, let me tell you what I intend—with your help—to accomplish.

"As of yesterday, I have by executive order officially ended the charter of the Central Intelligence Agency. The power of the old intelligence community must be broken and exposed. This will be accomplished in part by making public the budgets of their agencies . . . the National Reconnaissance Office, the Independent Supply Audit, and others. But let me return specifically to this area in a moment."

Dameron said quite audibly, "I don't fucking believe this!"

Halliday answered, "I really don't think he's kidding, Anson."

In the pressroom Walter Peterson rolled his chair back and stamped his feet on the floor. "Sunny Jim," he said to Fulton, calling him by the name he used for anyone who hadn't won a Pulitzer, "we got ourselves a real shitkicker of a story here. You know what? They'll kill him before they let him make those budgets public! I kid you not, mark my words. Jesus, he's living in a dream world!"

"I wish you wouldn't say things like that, Walt."

The President was going on.

"As of tomorrow, Samuel Aiken Lord, director of the CIA, will be relieved of his post, though I blame none of these specific transgressions on Director Lord. He will immediately serve as joint chairman of a special peace mission to Mexico City.

"And I have already put in place at CIA headquarters in Langley, Virginia, one of my most trusted appointees.

"As of today the dismantling of the old CIA and the laying of the groundwork for the new intelligence-gathering organization and its oversight committee—the National Security Executive, answerable to Congress, the president, and the people—has been placed in the immensely capable hands of Attorney General Teresa Rowan, the first director of the National Security Executive."

There were loud groans from the Republican side of the aisle. The Democrats were trying to work up some applause but were caught so far off balance the attempt was anemic. Dameron's mouth was ajar in pure astonishment. "Can he do this?"

Brenda Halliday said: "He's the President, idiot! He's the commander in chief. Try and stop him."

On West Fifty-seventh in New York, Bill Steinberg stopped daydreaming about his own qualifications for the White House and began tapping notes into his computer. The researcher had been sent to research and be bloody quick about it.

Pudge Buchanan scribbled: *We are watching the shit hit the fan.*

Sally Ledbetter scrawled: *Remember—it's the budgets, stupid. They've got to stop him or close the candy store.*

The President was going on: "This will be a long and painful process for all of us. But necessary. These agencies must still function even as they are restructured, reorganized, and made accountable. Attorney General Rowan will in due time name new appointees to take on crucially important roles. All of our best wishes go with her. Believe me—the second American revolution has begun!

"And I pledge this to you," President Bonner continued, "you, the people, will be kept informed by me personally as this great new revolution continues.

"I pledge also that our unprecedented peace initiatives throughout the world—beginning with an all-out mediation effort in the tragic civil war south of our border in Mexico—will continue. The recent assassinations and the terrible bloodshed among the civilian population have all led me to this decision. We will begin a renewed and strengthened peace initiative in Mexico.

"My fellow Americans, I close with this thought. The old order passeth away . . . and the new order dawns. We stand at that dawn . . . we greet it proudly with a clear vision of our future and a belief that we must be the good neighbor to the world.

"And now it is time to say good night.

"As we enter this new era in our nation's history, I ask for your prayers. May God bless you all. And may God bless America."

"In a daring and historic State of the Union Address to the American people Tuesday night, President Charles Bonner may have played his trump card in an attempt to regain some momentum with Democratic delegates and succeed in his hard-fought quest for a second presidential nomination. Speaking in the well of the House to a joint session of Congress, Bonner announced that the intelligence community is the source of the internal corruption behind what he termed 'the secret government,' which he has now identified as the nation's true enemy.

He has cast himself as St. George off on his steed to slay this dragon bedeviling America, and nothing less than unconditional victory will suffice."

—Phillip Carmichael, CBS-TV

"Tonight, invoking the name of Ethan Allen and the Green Mountain Boys and their capture of Fort Ticonderoga from the British, President Charles Bonner, sinking ever lower in the approval polls, rolled the dice, double or nothing, by abolishing the CIA as we know it, putting its re-creation in the hands of Attorney General Teresa Rowan, and setting the agenda for a second American revolution. . . ."

—Hugh Macklowe, BBC

"In a desperate, last-ditch attempt to salvage what appears to be a failed presidency which has run aground on the rocks of voter apathy, Charles Bonner may have committed treason tonight by dismantling America's first line of defense, the intelligence community. . . ."

—Arnaldo LaSalle, *On Deadline*

"In the most idealistic speech made by an American president since John Kennedy urged Americans to ask not what their country could do for them but what they could do for their country, Charles Bonner asked the American people and the world to follow him down a long, difficult road which includes rebuilding the intelligence community, allying ourselves long term with the Russians, and pursuing a series of peace initiatives beginning with an attempt to end the civil war in Mexico. . . ."

—Arthur Ryder, *The New York Times*

"Tonight, while a snowstorm descended on Washington, beleaguered President Charles Bonner dropped a bombshell of stunning proportions and it landed squarely on the intelligence community, blowing it to smithereens. Whether Mr. Bonner's cohorts can put it all back together in a new and responsible manner may decide the

issue of a second term for the President. With the Republicans set to offer not former president Sherman Taylor but his bland vice-president Price Quarles, America goes to sleep wondering if anyone will challenge Bonner for the Democratic nomination. The bet here is that this speech will produce an alternative candidate who will stand up for the strength and power of the nation against Bonner's willingness to diminish it."

—Ballard Niles, *World Financial Outlook*

"Hey, is this guy asking for trouble? Whooooheeee, baby, you can say that again! Come and get it, y'all. And remember all you Longhorns, Notre Dame with Charlie Bonner at QB had no mercy on Texas that time in the Cotton Bowl! Forty-eight to six. Well, you can get a piece o' him now! Selling the good old US of A down the river!"

—Jim Bob Sterling, Dallas Drive-Time DJ

Chapter 1

It was a dream or a memory and it came to him in the night again and again. He was a boy, maybe ten or twelve, or so it seemed. Walking down a long corridor past display windows full of small figures to which he paid no attention. He was walking toward a glowing kind of window that wasn't like other windows. There was something special about it, a magic he couldn't resist, and he felt his pace quicken.

As he drew closer he saw that the window was actually a kind of bubble, a head-sized bubble intruding through a flat window, a bubble that was just plain irresistible. He was thrusting his head into the bubble, his eyes wide; he couldn't wait, knowing what he was going to see.

And there it was.

The soldiers spread out over the blankets and bedspread were advancing toward him. He was a small boy with the covers pulled up to his chin, watching them come with their rifles and their sabers, he could almost hear the pop-pop-pop of the guns going off, smell the puffs of smoke in his bedroom. . . . There was General Lee down by his foot and over there Sam Grant marshaling his troops. . . . They were coming and the little boy with the war on his bed was wide-eyed in rapt excitement. . . .

Then, in his dream, or memory, he wasn't a child anymore and the sounds of the battlefield were fading and somebody was saying something, he strained to hear it.

"Back when politicians were soldiers, they meant something. Now the goddam politicians don't mean a damn thing, they send men to their deaths, they use other men to do their killing for them. . . . You can't trust 'em, son, they're nothing but fakes and rabble-rousers and most of 'em send somebody else to do the hard things. . . ."

And then that voice was fading and the view of the soldiers was fading and then it was all gone. . . . Had it been his father speaking to him across the years? Or someone he'd followed into battle. . . . Who was it?

When the man finished dressing he was the paradigm of the perfect scholarly type, an immaculately realized cliché: horn-rimmed glasses, straight grayish-brown hair cut long enough in back to touch the collar of his blue oxford-cloth button-down shirt with its brown- and green-striped rep tie. His trim mustache was also a mix of gray and brown. He wore slacks that bagged slightly at the knees and a somewhat wrinkled seersucker jacket. A leather thong was pulled through the buttonhole on his lapel, and a small gold watch hung down into the breast pocket of the jacket. He wore pebble-grain brown walking brogans and subtle argyle socks. Over his arm he carried an inexpensive tan raincoat.

His name, according to his driver's license, was Curtis Westerberg. Full professor in the English department at the University of Missouri. He was forty-seven years old and resided at 311 Elm Drive in Columbia. The papers were of the very best quality. No one could have guessed he was Thomas Bohannon, who, a check of records in Washington would inform you, had died years ago in the service of his country. His records in the Military Index had been almost completely scrubbed: no fingerprints, no mention of the many decorations he'd been awarded, no history of any kind. There were perhaps no more than ten such severely sanitized records in the Index, and they were kept in a file of their own, open to almost no one.

He had driven from Chicago the day before. In Saints Rest he had navigated his way up the alarmingly steep and narrow switchbacks from Bluff Street and checked into one of the Victorian mansions that had been turned into exquisite bed-and-breakfasts. He would be checking out tomorrow.

That first night he'd driven over to Fever River in Illinois and dined on superb sauerbraten at the Kingston Inn. The next morning he slept in, then left the shining antiques and the smell of lemon polish and the pervasive fragrance of potpourri and walked down the hillside for a leisurely breakfast with the *Des Moines Register,* the *Chicago Tribune,* and *USA Today.* There was little news capable of making him proud to be a member of the human race. But, then, that was always the case. No point in dwelling on it.

His postlunch stroll took him to the Toy Soldier Shop near Saints Rest's Town Clock Square. The sky had grown purple, threatening. The heat and humidity on this July day were both over ninety; the air reminded him of the year he'd spent in the tiger cage, an animal on exhibit, trying to ignore the sharpened sticks the kids and the women jabbed through the bars. The old wood-framed glass cases in the only slightly air-conditioned shop held battalions, regiments, and armies an inch or two high, carefully hand-painted warriors dating from ancient Egypt through Vietnam and the Persian Gulf, thousands of tiny soldiers, fierce and armed to the teeth, all in perfectly replicated battle dress. Highlanders in their kilts. French Foreign Legionnaires. Indians on their fleet ponies. Settlers gathered round their wagons. Quantrill and his raiders. He saw his own reflection in the glass, eager as a kid's, as he stared at the superb figures of the Civil War. The Blue and the Gray. Honest Abe in his stovepipe hat with one hand holding his lapel. Robert E. Lee, the glory of the South. And of course the great man—Grant. He was considering the figure of Grant when he saw, in the reflection, the man coming up behind him.

"What can I do you for? I can open up these cabinets if you'd like a closer look." He was a big beefy guy stretching his T-shirt, sweating in the heat. His fingers and hands were flecked with paint. Thunder was pounding outside. The first of the rain was bouncing off the sidewalk, streaking the plate-glass window. "Let's see . . . I take you for a Civil War man. Am I right?"

"As a boy, yes, I was. Now I'm wondering—do you have any Hessian mercenaries from the Revolution? Green and white . . ."

"Ah, let me see." He pushed his glasses up his broad perspiring nose. "Not many calls for those. Only the real collectors. You're a man who knows what he wants."

"Yes, I guess you could say that."

"Soldier, were you?"

"Long time ago."

The beefy man in his too-tight shirt was slowly passing the cases, peering intently, pushing his glasses up again and again. "Well, the Hessians should be right here. And they're not. You could order some, how about that? I could do up a few, send 'em out to you next weekend. I've got 'em, you see, they're just not painted. I'll pay the postage since I should've had some on hand for you. How's that for service with a smile?"

"That's wonderful, but I'm afraid I can't have you send them. I'm not sure where I'm going to be. Traveling the country."

"Well, take along one of our catalogs. You can always give me a ring. Hessians. I'll remember you. I'm Mike." He held out one of the big moist hands.

"Curtis," the man said. He shook the hand.

"Now I can't let you leave without a soldier. You were looking at General Grant back there."

"Yes, I was. My first set of soldiers was from the Civil War. My grandfather gave them to me. They'd been passed on to him by a man who'd fought at Chickamauga."

"Think of that," the fat man said, eyes getting dreamy for a moment.

"First thing I ever owned that was worth more than a nickel."

"Where are they now?"

"Oh, you know . . . ," Westerberg shrugged.

"I know, you were a kid, you lost 'em." Mike smiled with his mouth and all of his chins. He'd heard the stories before. "Or your mom threw 'em away when you went to college."

"Well, not exactly. Not quite like that." He looked at the perfect figure of Ulysses Simpson Grant. The great man. He remembered watching it fly across the room and bounce off the wall, he heard his mother's voice, *"Not the boy's soldiers, Frank, not the Civil War soldiers,"* and he saw the figure of Grant landing, bouncing on the linoleum floor, and his father was staring down at him, his face a mask of mindless rage. Slowly, afraid to take his eyes off his father, he reached out across the floor for General Grant and suddenly his father's booted foot was raised and the boy drew his hand back, knowing what was coming, and the boot smashed down on the figure of the great man. . . .

It no longer made any difference why. His old man was a prick who made a point of beating up his wife and his son and in the end he got his and then some. He didn't like to make a big sob story out of it; that was the trouble with people nowadays, they put in a little hard time and for the rest of their lives they had this big, all-purpose sob story, this perfect excuse for fucking up their own lives. He'd stopped worrying about all that a long time ago, and he hadn't thought much about Grant, either, for that matter. Not until now, not until he'd made his way across the world from the Congo, from Beirut, from the tiger cage he'd lived in for that endless year before they made the mistake of letting him out so they could execute him properly, from the years of Special Services jobs, from the little house nestled back in the countryside above the Grand Corniche where they let him go to rest up, sometimes for a year or two until they needed him for a job, until he got to Iowa and happened to run into Sam Grant again.

"I'll take a couple of Grants," he said at last. "One for me, one in memory of my old man." He smiled at Mike.

"Now that's real nice." Mike jumped at a particularly wicked blast of thunder. "Dad got you started, did he?" He was taking the two figures from the case. Bohannon was thinking about Mike, wondering what difference it might make if Mike remembered him. He'd sure as hell remember all this talk about Grant and the Hessians.

"Yes, I guess you could say Dad got me started. In his own way."

Mike saw him to the door. The rain had stopped and the sun was peeking through, drenching the clock tower and the plaza in a kind of molten gold, but there were mountain ranges of purple clouds piled up off to the west above the bluffs. "You be sure to give me a call about those Hessians, hear? And it's been real nice talking to you."

The man took a long look at Mike, then around the little jewel of a shop.

"You're a lucky man, Mike."

"Oh, I know that."

"No, no, you don't." Westerberg smiled at him. He felt the weight of the killing knife in the spring-loaded harness strapped to his right arm beneath his shirt. "You really have no idea."

President Charles Bonner sat in the dimmed study aboard *Air Force One,* leaning back in the leather chair, hardly aware of the throbbing jets, sipping a Ketel One martini and staring out the window. He supposed they were somewhere over Tennessee or Kentucky, on the way back from his meeting with the opposing generals in the Mexican civil war. Nothing had gone well. The government and the rebels, who now controlled more than a quarter of the country and were fighting in the outskirts of Mexico City and threatening Acapulco and the garrisons along the Texas border, were intransigent. The former felt they had survived the worst of it; the latter believed their rise was irresistible. Bonner and Hubert Lassiter, his secretary of state, had gone to Mexico City seeking a face-saving compromise for all and were coming home empty-handed. The polls were killing him. He swirled the icy vodka on his tongue and thought about the inevitable reaction in the media.

BONNER MISSION FAILS. Mexican Civil War Rages.

Hazlitt Charges Weakness. No Solution in Sight. It was going to be another nightmare.

He had reaffirmed his message of January 19 with action, reaffirmed that foreign policy was going in the wrong direction, and had taken his stand, staked his claim again, dramatically.

The night sky was checkered with clouds, a hazy moon and lightning flickering along the horizon. He turned his attention back to the movie on the VCR. Humphrey Bogart in *Beat the Devil*. There had to be a lesson for him in the dark, eccentric comedy, if only he could find it.

Linda Bonner, the First Lady, was sleeping. She'd had a trip as demanding as his, visiting children's hospitals, trying to give hope to the wounded and dying where in fact there was little hope to give. Using her formidable clout to arrange for more doctors, more supplies, more hospital flights heading in and out of battle zones. She'd collapsed into bed five minutes after boarding the plane. He envied her ability to sleep.

The latest newspaper reports lay on the desk along with Ellen Thorn's analysis of the last of the primaries, the brand-new "New England Mega-Primary," which was now ancient history. TV demanded an explosive end to the primary season, a nice buildup for the coming conventions. All the New England states in one day, a week ago. The sitting president bending though not quite breaking as he was challenged for the Democratic nomination by *Time* magazine's "second richest man in the United States," Bob Hazlitt of Iowa, "the Emperor of Information," as the *World Financial Outlook* dubbed him when he announced his challenge a month after the State of the Union speech. Both campaigns had poured tens of millions of dollars into those primaries, and Bonner had, at least for the moment, stemmed the rising tide of Hazlitt support, battling him to a draw—an exact draw in delegates with only the convention remaining. But the worsening situation in Mexico would cost him a point or two more in the polls, and that was perception. And that perception might cost him a wavering delegate here and there. In the end it was all perception.

Charlie Bonner had finished with the breakdowns provided by Ellen Thorn and her polling staff and now he was wondering why God had singled him out for such a fate. On the desk before him the front pages blared the two views that were cracking him like a Christmas walnut: the rising objections, on one hand, to U.S. involvement of any kind in Mexico, and on the other, the hoarse cries to go in with a huge show of force from those citing the administration's unwillingness to unleash its awesome power. Charlie Bonner knew where he stood. And that was the problem. Bob Hazlitt was doing a Teddy Roosevelt, waving a big stick and an arsenal of tactical missiles, and making hay.

Inevitably the President's mind kept returning to Hazlitt, to the convention up ahead, and to the fight that was bound to be vicious.

How in the name of all that was holy had it come to this?

The economy had continued to work against him. People had grown pinched and afraid and sometimes meanspirited. They were resentful and angry. They felt weakened, forsaken, almost powerless before the steamroller of history. And Bob Hazlitt could point to his guns-and-ammo approach to foreign policy as conservative, on one side, and yet point to the veritable welfare state he'd created in Heartland, Iowa, where nobody had ever lost his or her job and the kids were all smart and healthy and unfailingly polite, as liberal and beneficial on the other. It was quite a political conundrum for Charlie to solve.

In the State of the Union speech Bonner had tried to give the people some hope that they could revolt and take their country back. Had they believed him? Had they cared? Or had it all been too abstract? Too far from their daily lives? He hadn't made their jobs more secure. He'd tried to give them a rallying cry. A common enemy to fight against. But had it been enough? Well, he had to content himself with the knowledge that it had all needed saying more than anything else he might have said. It was something he actually could *control* . . . and in some quarters, he'd drilled right into a nerve. It was a start.

A multibillionaire communications tycoon from Iowa had decided he knew what was best for the people. Naturally, given his overweening ego, he wanted to be president. Bob Hazlitt. Flying Bob Hazlitt with his collection of great old war planes. Flying Bob of the flowing white silk scarf and the scuffed helmet and leather jacket, like one of those legendary mail carriers of the twenties and thirties. Like one of those dashing, heroic barnstormers. The Great Fucking Waldo Pepper.

And for the past four months the techniques Bonner would have expected from the Republicans had been brought to bear on the sitting president by a growing number of his fellow Democrats. It wasn't really a nightmare. More like an apocalypse, he thought wryly. Death, Fame, and Pestilence—that was the firm handling Bob Hazlitt's irresistible rise. And they were beating him to death with a club called the Mexican civil war, as the cartoon had it in the *Post* the other day. Bonner was selling America into slavery, was the way they were telling it.

And now a new scandal among top government officials had broken in Mexico followed by a string of assassinations, and Hazlitt was making it all work for him. For months he hadn't even thought of the Republicans and their certain candidate, Price Quarles, who had been VP to President Sherman Taylor, the man Bonner had unseated. It was the goddam Democrats, his own party, who were out to get him. . . . They'd been eating his lunch all winter and spring and now on into summer.

The Secret Service man acting as midnight steward came back to the study and tapped on the door. The President looked up wearily and smiled. "Little lonely up here tonight," he said.

"Would you like another drink, Mr. President? Or sandwiches?"

"No, I don't think so. I'll finish this one down to the last drop. I could do with a couple of Advil, though."

"Very quiet tonight, sir."

The President looked at the young man, crisp and fresh. He tried to know the staff personally. But he'd never noticed that Bill was from Iowa. Now he noticed it on his name tag.

"Iowa," he said. "Iowa is much on my mind these days."

"Yes, sir, I can imagine it must be. I remember when you came there during your first campaign."

"Twice."

"Yes, sir. For the caucuses and then during the general election campaign. My folks went to see you both times."

"Bob Hazlitt was *supporting* me then. Seems like a helluva long time ago. What part of Iowa you from, Bill?"

"Do you remember *Field of Dreams,* sir?"

"I've cried every time I've seen it."

"Well, that's in Dyersville. Not far from Saints Rest which is the biggest town nearby. I'm from a little town in between the two. Epworth. Dad used to be superintendent of schools in West Saints."

"I'll never forget that line in the movie . . . *Is this Heaven? No, it's Iowa.*" The President leaned back and felt himself relaxing. "I made a speech at the diamond in Dyersville. Right by that cornfield. They had a bunch of guys in old-time baseball uniforms standing out there at the edge of the corn. . . . Well, it's something worth remembering." He sipped the martini. "Iowa's a mighty handsome place, Bill. You must be proud to be a Hawkeye."

"Yes, I am, sir. Closest thing to Heaven I've seen yet, sir."

"Well, you must have me give your folks a call when I'm out there campaigning in the fall. I mean it. Remind me. I'd be pleased to meet 'em."

"Thank you, sir. They'd enjoy that."

"Well, Bill, do you think you could rustle me up some Advil?"

"Yes, sir. I'll get some for you."

"Atta boy, Bill. Thanks a million."

Iowa again. Field of dreams . . . Flying Bob Hazlitt . . .

Who the hell had ever told Bob Hazlitt to run for president? After all, Howard Hughes never ran for president. But Flying Bob had contracted the bug. Nowadays he would come out of the blue in one of those World War II planes, maybe a P-51 Mustang with the tiger's jaws painted on it, and tell the folks out at the airport that he'd had a vision, a vision of a new America that would never be afraid of anything again, would never take orders from anyone again, wouldn't need the damn UN, an America that would use the power at its command to make a better world for people everywhere. . . . But for Americans first. The rubes ate it up and Bob Hazlitt was counting on their appetite for bullshit to continue unabated.

It was clear that Hazlitt had recognized what the President himself had characterized as "the Balkanizing of America." Almost every interest group in the land had mysteriously acted in unison over the past decade to destroy the idea of rational compromise, of civil and reasoned debate, of the concept of the greater good. Now the true believers had taken over. *My* cause, *my* demand, *my* need—they were the only causes, demands, and needs that existed anymore. The hell with everybody else. *The Great I* had to be number one with its fist in the air. It was the triumph of the barbarians.

Bob Hazlitt, the Pride of the Tall Corn State, had put together those Democrats who feared that America had grown weak and indecisive and was letting the rest of the world push it around, put them together with all the poor souls who longed for the old days when there were families worthy of the name, when the unwritten contract between company and employee meant something. And now they had found their issue: a threat to the nation's vital interests in Bonner's move against the intelligence community . . . and his refusal to solve the Mexican problem with firepower. And they decided—by the millions—that Bob Hazlitt, of all things, spoke for them. They believed he would be at home at their kitchen tables. If they still had kitchen tables anymore.

Charlie Bonner had no idea what the man was *really* saying. It was just a whine of white noise crackling across the land. Too simplistic to be believed. The thing was, the message certainly went well beyond the literal words he spoke.

People were out there, they were listening to him, and they were hearing between the lines.

But what were they hearing?

There was a tap at the door and it opened.

"Mr. President? Charlie?" It was Bob McDermott, chief of staff.

"Yes, Mac . . . I was a million miles away. What can I do for you?"

"Charlie, we just received some pictures and text. Honest to God, it's just awful . . . there's been a hellish earthquake in Mexico." He was holding several sheets of glossy photo paper and pages of text.

The President took the sheets, tried to make sense of them as Mac's voice went on.

"Damn thing is a seven-point-two, it looks like, the first word and photos are just coming in now. Charlie, it hit along the Tijuana/Chula Vista fault—"

"Christ!" the President exploded. "That means Americans! Any American casualties? Is that what you're saying?"

"Some, not a lot so far." Mac was leading the way into the working office and lounge area of the plane where a laser printer was pumping out pages. "We've got twelve dead on our side of the border. But, holy shit, they're up to fifteen hundred and counting on the Mexican side. It hit one of the big government army garrisons, an armaments depot blew up. The freedom fighters are moving into some of the villages, lots of looting, massacres of progovernment civilians . . . Charlie, this is big. They're estimating three, four thousand or more dead from the quake, God only knows how many more in the looting and fighting."

"Y'know, Mac, it makes me feel like I should go back down there and go back to work on the peace proposals—"

Mac shook his head forcefully. "Over my dead body! You've risked enough—your going down there was a security nightmare in the first place, and in the second place everybody told you that putting your prestige on the line was dangerous—"

"Well, Mac, there's danger and there's danger. My political risk doesn't weigh much in the scales of all those lives."

Mac frowned, shaking his head. "Not a chance, no going back there."

The President was standing beside the humming printer, looking at the pictures of rubble, of limbs sticking out from bricks and adobe and mortar, bloodied bodies, an American border guard whose uniform was soaked with blood. . . . On a direct transmission monitor live TV footage was coming in, streaked and picking up electricity in the atmosphere, but he saw the camera panning across shantytowns flattened, mothers screaming into the camera while holding their babies up like evidence of what had happened. God, he was so tired, and now there was this new horror to deal with.

And then he saw the photograph of the little girl in her bloody dress, an indescribably beautiful child, huge eyes so overwhelmed with shock and sadness, her dress torn and blood running down her arms and legs, appealing to the still camera with her slender arms at her sides with the palms turned out, beseeching . . . pleading for someone to understand what had happened . . . to help . . .

"Yeah," Mac nodded, "that's a tough one, Charlie."

Tears were welling up in the President's eyes.

On the horizon first light was dawning gray like an abstract painting. "Good morning, Mr. President. We're beginning our descent, sir." The voice of the copilot came softly across the sound system. "It's raining at dawn in Washington. The temperature is seventy-six and the high for today will be ninety-five. We'll be touching down at Andrews in thirty-one minutes. I'll update you again, sir."

The President wasn't really listening.

The commuter plane caught an updraft and lurched ahead, engines throbbing, the clouds dark and purple just beyond the tiny window. They were crossing the Mississippi. Oddly enough Hayes Tarlow had never seen it before. He'd flown coast to coast, but at thirty-seven thousand feet you didn't see much of the planet below. At about, oh, maybe a hundred feet you saw too goddam much of it. Rain was lashing the twenty-seater, but it was the fucking wind . . . Up and down, this way and that, back and forth . . . Then a blaze of lightning arced through the clouds off the wing-tip and simultaneously a downdraft pulled them earth-ward. Christ, was this the end of Hayes Tarlow?

Hayes Tarlow was miserable. Stuffed into a wrinkled, sweat-stained, cream-colored linen suit, his tie loosened, sweat streaming from the sloping dome of forehead down his pink face, soaking his gray eyebrows, burning his eyes, then dripping down into the salt-and-pepper mustache that hooked down around the corners of his wide mouth. The pink was draining out of his face, leaving him increasingly putty-colored. He was sure he was going to throw up and he couldn't seem to locate the little bag normally supplied for just that calamity. His knees were crammed up against the seat in front of him, which some son of a bitch had pushed as far back as possible before falling into an infuri-atingly deep sleep. Throwing up on him might be a very good idea if it came to that. Who'd have thought Hayes Tarlow would hand in his lunch pail like this, the veteran of a thousand sticky situations, trapped and helpless, stom-ach in turmoil . . . ?

He'd come from New York in the morning, then laid over at O'Hare where he'd fallen asleep in the sun, which had been a mistake, wakened feeling like the dog's break-fast, and then gone down the steps and straggled with his shoulder bag out across the tarmac to this little plane, which reminded him of some of the Air America cans of bolts he'd been dragged around in a few years before, when he'd been trying to get a diplomat in deep shit out of Bang-kok. He'd jumped out of a plane a lot like this one once, a long time ago, over jungle so dense it looked solid, and he'd puked all the way down and then sprained his ankle upon landing.

There weren't many men who could have sweet-talked him into this job, but wouldn't you know, one of the few had asked him. Saints Rest, Iowa. It was politics, of course, and it was flattering to be the one doing the job. He'd been doing the political clog dance for a long time, but now he was closer to the top of the heap than he'd ever been before ... which showed you what kind of shape the country was in, calling in Hayes Tarlow to save the world out in the sticks. Well, it was a mess, there were no goddam standards anymore, it was whatever you could get away with ... and he wasn't even thinking about the politicians. Hell, politicians had always been the same, from Julius Caesar's time until today. It was the press—the *media,* as they said now—that had changed. It was that first taste of blood in the water, the roiling of the waves, the ripping and tearing and the explosions of blood that drew ever more people calling themselves journalists to the scene of another floundering officeholder who need never have left the family insurance business or the law firm or the tenured chair at dear old Siwash State or the farm back home ... People had, in his view, gone crazy.

Charlie Bonner was finding out what it was like. No fucking fun, and how did you know whom to trust? Could you trust anybody?

What had made him want to be President in the first place? That was the question. What was it that made a man offer up his life and the lives of his family on the altar of public service only to become a defendant in a court where you always lost? Crazy.

The plane banked sharply through what seemed to be yet another field of lightning, slashing away at them like a buzz saw. It sounded to Hayes Tarlow as if the wings were going to just vibrate the hell off.

Suddenly the plowed furrows of a field rose up like a muddy fist and he gasped for breath with his stomach in his mouth and the plane was struggling to pull its nose up, struggling to flatten out, and then somehow the wings were level again and the fields with the fledgling cornstalks were drawing them down to eye level and then the reassuring clunk of wheels kissing the runway and he realized he'd forgotten to puke, you should pardon the expression. The plane shimmied in the standing water, the props blowing the oily rain back along the windows; then it slowed down and rolled toward the small terminal.

First thing, he'd call Nick Wardell to come out and pick him up. Then he'd get down to work. This was urgent. No horsing around, that's what the old man had told him. *Go hear what he's got to say and report back and don't dally, Hayes. We're getting low on time. . . .*

He was smiling behind the mustache as he nearly fell down the rickety steps from the passenger compartment. With his weathered bag over one shoulder he clomped through the puddles, feeling the rain sprinkling on his face. No, he'd come through again.

It wasn't Hayes Tarlow's time quite yet.

As Nick Wardell was picking Hayes Tarlow up at the Saints Rest airport and driving him into the office, Herb Varringer put on a dark blue summer suit and a straw Borsalino and in late afternoon went out and sat in a big wicker chair on the front porch of the great old house that sat on one of the seven hills looming over Bluff Street and downtown Saints Rest. The huge house gleamed, white with green trim. People sometimes said that his house, viewed from the park down in front of the post office, gave the impression that its owner must in fact own the town. And he always replied no, that was the fellow in the house next door. He was a long way from owning the town, but it was a fancy-looking house, all right. Big devil. He'd bought it on the cheap when he made his first pile and real estate happened to be in a downturn. Cost a fortune to heat in the winter and air-condition in the summer.

The flag was whipping itself on top of his flagpole. It was breezy, but the afternoon was another real scorcher and enough humidity to drown a cat. A quick-moving thunderstorm with plenty of lightning had just moved through. Nothing changed the temperature. It was ninety and the humidity had to be close to saturation point. He smelled his bay rum cologne blossoming in the heat. And he smelled more rain coming, too. He finished reading the morning paper while he waited for his guest. He owned the morning paper. He wasn't all that crazy about the morning paper. But he hewed to the rule that when you tinkered with things you didn't really understand, like the editorial content of a newspaper, you got just what you deserved.

The youthful editor was smitten by the Iowa billionaire—that's the Iowa *populist* billionaire, pardon me—who had decided to duke it out with President Charles Bonner for the Democratic nomination. Flying Bob Hazlitt.

Herb Varringer and Bob Hazlitt went back together to the years when they were both breaking into the electronics business and they knew that transistors and high-powered chips and personal computers were only a few years over the horizon. In the techno-boom they had both prospered, Bob out in the middle of the state not far from the town they now called Heartland, Herb right in Saints Rest on the Mississippi. It was a time of lots of government contracts, what with the Cold War reaching critical mass. But Herb lacked the visionary nature of Bob Hazlitt: For Herb the name of the game was the electronics he and his engineers dreamed up, had fun with, developed, and then sold off for advantageous royalties. For Bob Hazlitt the electronics was only half of the game. The other half was the partnership with the United States government. In time, Herb Varringer had agreed to meld Varringer Electronics into Hazlitt's much larger firm in exchange for a stock position in the parent company, which came to be called Heartland Industries, as well as a large amount of cash. Herb Varringer had taken a prominent place on the Heartland board and life had gone on.

He put the newspaper aside as he heard the AAA #1 taxi pull up in the street below. He heard the door slam and then somebody swearing as the taxi drove away.

The man laboring up the long flight of stairs from the sidewalk came into view one step at a time. His face was red with exertion, mouth open and sucking in the humid air like a fish on a dock. He was wearing a linen suit that looked like a cry for help. You didn't see many of those anymore. Lots of wrinkles. Coat hanging open like a worn-out memory of other adventures, red suspenders showing against the white shirt. The man was sweating rivers, wiping his red face with a big handkerchief. He was slowing down as he neared the top of the driveway. He stopped and looked upward at his host.

"Mr. Tarlow, I assume?"

"Yeah, and if you ask me if it's hot enough for me, you'll be the sixth person so far today, and so help me God I'm turning around and walking back down that stairway and if I have to walk to the fucking airport then that's just what—"

"I take it that means it is hot enough for you. The trick, I find, is to move real slow when it gets like this. Come and sit down, there's a pitcher of iced tea ready for us. Don't want you having a heart attack, do we?"

"You're right. I don't want to die in this godforsaken place."

"Oh, it's not so godforsaken, Mr. Tarlow. Just a little sultry today. Fact is, I been everywhere you can go and Saints Rest is the most beautiful spot I've ever seen. I've been to Monterey and Cape Town and Sydney and the Côte d'Azur and Biarritz in the season and New York City on a perfect fall day. . . . I've smelled the burning leaves on the banks of the river in Cambridge and I've rowed on the lake in the Black Forest. . . . This is best. Course it's home and that might have something to do with my feelings. You have to love the river and the bluffs and all the greenery . . . if you do, you'll never find better than Saints Rest."

Tarlow passed the time of day on the front porch of Herb Varringer's grand old house, put back his share of iced tea and ate the cucumber and cold chicken sandwiches, and got his blood pressure under control. "You know who sent me, of course."

"Yes. He called to tell me you were coming. Very thoughtful. I've never actually met him but it was nice to have my concerns taken seriously by a man like that."

"Oh, he takes you very seriously. That and more."

Varringer put on his beautiful straw hat, his shining blue eyes somehow complementing the hatband. He smelled good: Tarlow got a whiff of the bay rum and found it oddly reassuring. His grandfather had worn bay rum.

"Now, would you care to take a little walk? I'm going to take a big chance with you, Mr. Tarlow, I'm going to tell you a story. It's costing me a great deal in terms of money and more importantly in terms of peace of mind. But it must be done and now's the time to do it. I'd like you to see my world, though, Mr. Tarlow. I'd like you to understand a little about my values . . . why I mourn the passing of one age and dread the coming of a new one, a thousand times more terrible than anything we've ever imagined possible. I want you to know why I'm taking the risk of telling you."

Tarlow said, "Jesus. Sounds like fun."

Varringer smiled. "I'll try not to make it too painful. Look upon it as a trip down memory lane."

Varringer walked with a polished stick capped off with the head of a bulldog. Somehow it worked. He struck Tarlow as a bit of an old aristocrat, though in fact he was a self-made man.

"Are you sure this is what I came out to Saints Rest to hear?"

"We'll get to that later, Mr. Tarlow. First, the big picture, the context."

"Call me Hayes."

Herb Varringer smiled and nodded and they set off down the street, in the shade.

"Real piece of Americana here," Varringer said. "This elevator was always considered the fastest way a man could make it from the flats to the top of the hill. Short of marrying the right girl." They were standing on a little wooden observation deck atop one of the bluffs looking down across the town, down the length of the shortest narrow-gauge railway in the world, which climbed the face of the bluff. "Rich folks always lived on top of the hills, what they used to call the working class down on the flats. Always made sure I knew a lot of the folks who lived down in the flats. You never know, you might be living down in the flats someday and you might need a friend. We were sort of all in it together, the flats and the hills, it was like we really respected one another. Well, hell, that's all gone now. Nobody respects much of anybody. You're just more likely to get flooded living down on the flats."

Hayes Tarlow looked out across what seemed like dozens of church steeples, lots of them black with the same white gingerbreading painted around the steeple about halfway up. New one on him. Far away he saw the reservoir at the point of what Herb said was the most beautiful park he'd ever seen. Herb seemed to think everything about Saints Rest was the most this or that he'd ever seen. Still, looking upriver or across at Illinois and Wisconsin, Hayes Tarlow had to admit it was a fine-looking part of the world. There were some barges heading upstream on the Mississippi, and a section of what looked like a railroad bridge was turning on its axis to open the river and let them through. Another bridge with a back arched up like some big damn dinosaur crossed over to East Saints, which was in Illinois.

"Down there," Varringer said, extending his long arm, waving with a flick of long bony fingers, "between the business district proper and the river, down there I had my first electronic works . . . we actually built Hawkeye radio sets down there, high-end items, some great portable radios in real leather cases, big antennas telescoping out of 'em. I was a teenager then, in business with my older brother. Then the river got him, bad storm that was, and I went to college, picked up some engineering . . ." His voice trailed off, then he said, "People forget but we built some television sets and sold 'em all over the Midwest, had a pitchman on the local TV stations in Chicago and Cincinnati and Cleveland and Detroit . . . 'the Sharpest Picture is by Hawkeye'. . ." He turned with a quick smile.

"Pretty good slogan, Herb."

Varringer nodded. "Not bad, if you like 'em perfect." He snorted, remembering he was supposed to be a tough old businessman. "Well, it's all gone now. Progress, you know. They cleared the old one-story works out of the way, put in a warehouse that looks like a shoe box. We were right down there by the Fourth Street ballpark."

"I don't see a ballpark."

"That's right. You don't. But there used to be a ballpark right there. This side of the shot tower. Now the shot tower—that's pure Civil War. They'd heat the slugs, then drop 'em the length of the tower to cool 'em off. Something like that. Before my time. Shot tower's sort of a lonely place, down there by the floodwall. See that train trestle, right to the side of the tower? Saints Rest has always had a lot of train whistles in the night, grew up with them, probably die hearing one. Lonely sound—kind of sounds like a poet's idea of forever." He chuckled dryly. "Let's take a ride."

They waited for a gaggle of little girls in shorts with ice cream cones to get off the miniature tramway car. Varringer bought the tickets and they pushed on through the turnstile and climbed into the tiny cab with its sharply raked seats. It was a slightly rocky ride a few hundred feet down the side of the bluff, steep enough to be in the shade all the way.

At the bottom of the hill they disembarked to let a group of white-haired tourists on. "How about an ice cream, Hayes? Humor me on my valedictory tour."

With waffle cones wrapped in napkins, they crossed through the once bustling business district and Varringer said, "Big mall out on the highway took quite a bite out of the downtown area. Jesus, they just rolled over and died in the face of the malls. Happened all over the country, course. Over there, there's the newspaper. That's mine. And the TV station. Sold Hawkeye to Heartland and they eventually got out of Saints Rest altogether. But I had the paper and the station to putter around with."

Hayes Tarlow nodded in agreement. Herb Varringer's soft, homey voice was hypnotizing him. Hayes was seeing things in what was for him a new perspective. He'd never been much of one for small towns, had liked to be where the action was, and only as he'd passed through his fifties had he begun to realize that there was action everywhere.

He'd just been too stupid to see it. Varringer was opening a window, showing him a town and its past for just a moment in time.

"Oh, sure," Varringer said, "some social inequities have been fixed a little—some of the bad things aren't as bad as they once were but they're a helluva long way from well. You live longer, there's more medicine. But we're going to wind up warehousing all the old farts because there are just too damn many of them. Like me." His smile was wintry. Listening to him made Hayes Tarlow feel like more of a thinker. "Used to have a mighty fine train. You could catch it in the morning, have breakfast with real linen and that heavy silverware, read the papers, get to Union Station in Chicago, do some business, catch the Pump Room for a bite of lunch, take the evening train back and have a good steak and some coffee and apple pie and you were back in Saints." He shook his head. "No, it was a better world."

Hayes Tarlow said, "Is that what you want me to take back east with me? Is that the report you want me to make to our mutual friend?"

"That? Hell, no, I told you, that's the preamble. He knows all that. That's just me setting the scene for you, for what I've got to tell you. If you don't understand the past, you can't imagine what I'm going to tell you about the future. There are worse things, my friend, than toxic waste, and they're on the way. *That's* what I want to talk to you about. That's what I want you to take back with you."

"When do you think that's likely to happen, Mr. Varringer?"

"Well, I'm going to show you something right now. I want you to take a look at it—it's important." He pointed out a park bench across from the post office. They sat down and Varringer took a folded sheet of paper from his suit-coat pocket, handed it to Tarlow, who smoothed it out on his knee.

"What's this? This is just a scribble—"

"No, by gosh, it's not just a scribble. It's the key to the whole damn thing—what do you think of that?"

"You'd better tell me what it is, then."

A cardinal flickered through the tree before them, disappeared in the mass of limbs and leaves. "All in due time. But I want you to learn that scribble, as you call it."

"I can't *learn* that—can I have it?"

"No, but . . . oh, hell, sure, you can have it."

"Let me keep it safe, then. I flew out here on the damnedest plane you ever saw. I don't want it going down with me on the way back." He looked up and surveyed the situation. "Let's go over to the post office for a second."

"All right, Mr. Tarlow. You know, you impress me. A man who takes infinite pains when it's an important matter."

"Well, I learned a few things as I went down life's trail." The two men smiled at one another, understanding what was going on. They went to the post office and about five minutes later they emerged.

They were standing in the shade. "We'll walk down to the brew pub, have a sandwich and a nice local beer or two as the sun goes down and I'll show you this river up close, you can throw a stone in the mighty Mississippi . . . and I'm gonna proceed, if you'll pardon my French, to scare the living shit out of you."

The sky had darkened with another set of huge purple gray clouds piling up over the bluffs, and the first drops of another warm shower had begun spotting the dusty street down by the floodwall.

He'd followed them on foot. A single tail is tough to do but it's made easier when the subjects don't know they're being followed. His old colonel in Special Services—that was back in Uganda in the very bad old days when he was very young and the dictator was eating people who crossed him—his old colonel said he was the best ghost he'd ever seen. The colonel meant he was someone who could be there but not be seen.

He watched them stop in at the post office, watched them visit the brew pub. After forty-five minutes, Varringer stood up to stretch his legs and Tarlow took a look at the side of the Heartland warehouse and at the huge billboard of Flying Bob Hazlitt looking back toward town. It would be impossible to miss as you drove into town on 52 from the west. Hazlitt was smiling, thumbs up, and his pilot's scarf billowed out behind him.

Tom Bohannon, who was calling himself Westerberg, shifted positions in the covered bus stop. In the old days, Tarlow would have noticed the man at the bus stop, how he'd still been there after the bus had come and gone. Back in Beirut, Tarlow would have made him in a heartbeat. But Saints Rest wasn't Beirut and Tarlow didn't do wet work anymore. And he sure as hell didn't think he was being stalked today. Not in Saints Rest, Iowa.

Varringer led the way through the intermittent sprinkles across the street and through the railroad underpass and they were out of sight. Varringer would be over there showing Tarlow the old shot tower, which he could see against the deep purple sky, rising up like a memory of war demanding attention.

They came back into view, strolled across the far opening of the railroad underpass, and began to climb the steps leading up to the top of the floodwall. Going to show his visitor the Mississippi. There was a sudden crack of thunder and a flash of lightning that flickered like luminous yellow paint flung across the clouds. The wind was picking up. The rain was coming again. Thunder clapped, impatient and demanding. He stepped out of the shadows and moved quickly through the dark underpass. There was a single light burning just above the door on the side of a grain storage elevator. Above it, Bob Hazlitt gazed down benevolently from the billboard.

The parking lot along the floodwall was empty. He climbed the steps and sure enough, down near the water to the right, the two men were making their way carefully along the boulders that formed the basis for the wall. He felt a very slight adrenaline rush, enough to sharpen his senses. He smelled the river, the coming rain, the water slapping on the rocks, the fishiness and the mud. He heard the wind rustling in the trees growing all around the pub, he heard the far-off wail of a train coming behind him. Coming from the west. He moved along the top of the wall, tracking them. He felt the raindrops warm on his face. From the top of the wall he could hear the rainstorm marching down the street toward him. In the scrub brush growing along the floodwall and around the trees over on the pub lawn he saw the tiny yellow flares of the lightning bugs. Off and on, off and on, some enduring code of their own. The train was drawing closer but hadn't come into view.

The rain was almost upon them, and they were going to take shelter beneath the underpinnings of the railway bridge that flung itself out over the great river toward Illinois. He began climbing down toward the water. Which was when the rain hit again. It came in a vast emptying out, he saw them reach the shelter of the bridge and he kept on going. One of them waved to him, called something, and then, slipping and holding on to the steel supports of the bridge, he was with them.

"Any port in a storm," he said, out of breath, just someone else out for a walk on the floodwall.

"Good place to wait out the rain," Varringer said. Tarlow was shaking himself like a big wet dog. Varringer was inspecting his straw hat, brushing the rain away. He was carrying a walking stick with the carved head of a dog at the top.

"Well, you know these summer storms," the man said. "They come and go before you know it. Sounds like the river's really running." The wind was swirling along the rocks, blowing rain at them, whipping the river.

Tarlow had walked toward the other side of the bridgework and was staring out into the night. The train whistle was louder now. The trestle overhead was beginning to shake and clatter. Thunder cracked almost steadily.

The man made a move past Herb Varringer, and as he drew even, Tarlow's back still turned to look out at the night, he released the knife in his sleeve into the middle of the older man's chest cavity, just below the breastbone, made one quick sawing motion. He felt Varringer die in his arms. With a quick, immensely powerful jerk of his arms, like a man hoisting a sack of cement, he thrust the body down into the water where it bobbed silently in the eddying pools. The stick with the dog's head floated beside the body. He armed the knife again, felt some of the sticky blood against the inside of his forearm.

Tarlow finally turned away from watching the storm and shouted, "It looks like the end of the world out there. . . . Herb? Where did he go?"

"He was here, I guess he left the other way."

"He wouldn't leave without me." Tarlow was coming back and damned if he didn't catch sight of the straw hat floating, bumping against the rocks. "What the hell's going on?"

The man was scrambling down the wet stone surface. Tarlow called: "Jesus, pal, he fell in—didn't you see him fall? Jesus, he's facedown. . . ."

The man was almost upon him as Tarlow turned, seeming to sense that this was all wrong. He stood up, a bulky character, staring at the man, and a moment of recognition crossed his face. The knife was coming at him and he felt it going into his flesh, cutting through the fatty part of his arm and driving with great force into his left side, but suddenly the stranger with the knife slipped and fell backwards on the wet rocks and then noise exploded overhead in a rattling, banging fury as the train reached the bridge and shook the foundations and the rocks, and Tarlow struggled away, knowing his lung had taken the hit and was collapsing, tasting blood in the back of his mouth, knowing his chances weren't so hot, and the stranger rolled down toward the slapping water, hit his head on one of the stones, his hand flailing out and touching the hat, touching Herb Varringer's head. . . .

Hayes Tarlow couldn't breathe very well, felt a god-awful pain in his chest, slipped and slid along the goddam cement and rocks, not knowing just where he was going but hoping to hide in the arms of the dark, somehow reached the top of the wall, stumbled down the steps he'd climbed, surprised he'd gotten so far, then heard the son of a bitch behind him breathing hard, coming, he knew the sonuvabitch, *knew* him, and Tarlow believed he was running but that was only for a moment before he realized he was crawling and ahead of him he saw the tower rising darkly, like some strange church, a place of salvation, and he was soaking wet and the thunder was crashing like incoming fire in the old days and the train was roaring and he thought, fuck it, if this is the production number closing the Hayes Tarlow Show it's pretty fucking impressive, and he was half smiling when he reached the shot tower and sagged back against it as if he'd reached home after a long time on the road. . . .

He looked up at the huge billboard.

America's Favorite Son . . . Iowa's Bob Hazlitt.

The handsome face, the blue eyes and the silvery hair and the goddamned white scarf . . . the old plane soaring in the background . . . Bob Hazlitt . . .

Tarlow knew his vision was fading. The man loomed over him. He looked up into the familiar face from long ago. The man was looking down at him, just standing there panting, dripping on him.

Tarlow gasped softly: "Jesus Christ, it's *you* . . . of all people. . . . I remember you from Beirut. That cruddy little bar . . . What the . . . hell are you . . . doing here?"

"I wish I didn't have to do this. It's just a job, that's all. Nothing personal, Hayes."

Tarlow gulped, tried to laugh. "*You* wish . . . that's a good one. . . ."

The man was dropping down to one knee. "Let go, friend. Just let go." He was pressing his right hand directly over Tarlow's heart.

Hayes Tarlow felt as if somehow this familiar man was his savior about to gently withdraw the life from his dying body and set it free in the night. He liked the thought. He looked up, trying to focus past Bohannon, locking eyes with the giant face of Bob Hazlitt, feeling himself drawn into the smile and the eyes. . . . A friendly face welcoming him. . . . It was the last thing he ever saw.

He felt nothing more than the tap of a fingertip as the knife drove all the way through his heart.

Chapter 2

Ben Driskill was reading the *New York Times* and he was not amused.

His displeasure wore a variety of guises. In the first place, the *Times*'s front page was devoted almost entirely to national politics, dissecting last weekend's final explosion of primaries in New England and beginning to beat the drums for the upcoming national conventions. The same thing was true of the National News pages, the Op-Ed page columnists, the editorials themselves. . . . It was an avalanche of politics. Too much. An endless conflagration of anger and conflicting versions and bellicose lies. It wasn't politics as he remembered it—this was all hate-driven and it sickened him. Everything existed only as directly partisan contradictions, and the partisans had their knives out. After dealing up close with his father Hugh Driskill's life and death in politics and, finally, his own immersion in the politics of the Vatican—well, Ben Driskill felt he'd had enough politics to last a lifetime.

He was the last man to claim to be an intellectual or, for that matter, morally above the battle, but the level of political discourse was seeking new low ground each day. It wasn't the same as somebody calling Lincoln a yellow-bellied scum-sucking murderer back in the 1860s. Now everybody in the world got to watch it on TV as it happened. It was media-driven and media-exploited. Fun was fun but this was something else. He wanted no part of it.

And wanting no part of it brought him to his second cause for concern. His old college friend Charlie Bonner had been elected President of these United States three and a half years ago. That had required a certain limited involvement in the campaign on Ben's part—either that or an irreparable breach with his longtime friend. Charlie had asked him to take on some fund-raising duties. There had been occasional campaign road trips with Charlie, who was governor of Vermont at the time, and his family and his inner circle. Ben had inevitably become a kind of sounding board for Charlie, and he had felt powerless to step away during the heat of the battle.

But now, his friend had made a huge, courageous, but equally controversial State of the Union speech six months ago. Charlie had taken his stand, and Ben Driskill respected him for it. And it had cost Charlie. His approval rating still hung at about thirty, but he'd brought a new candidate pawing and snorting into the race for the nomination. At the core, a red-meat issue. National security. People were worried about a lot of things and they blamed some of them on Charlie, but they were really worried about America's power and prestige, and that they blamed squarely on Charlie. A hell of a lot of them were deciding that the machismo was all Bob Hazlitt's. But Charlie believed in what he had done. He saw it as a position of moral bedrock. Lose on this one, then winning no longer mattered. He'd made that clear to Ben at the same time he'd asked Ben to come down and strategize with him on the reelection campaign in March.

Charlie had known him longer than anyone else on the scene: It wasn't surprising, Ben supposed, that Charlie would turn to him late at night for a drink and an analysis of the way things were going. But he was reluctant to lend a hand because he was dubious about politics and the accompanying sideshow. They had played football together in the ever more distant past at Notre Dame. The fact that Charlie had been the one drawn to politics and ultimately voted into the White House indicated that handsome quarterbacks are bound to fare better than hulking linebackers in the beauty contest that politics more than occasionally became. Which was fine with Ben Driskill. He had never developed the ability to embrace easy compromise, the fluidity of mind to see the most sophisticated routes to what might be called the public good. He wasn't enough of a bullshitter to be a politician. As a lawyer he'd been a negotiator, a bringer together, and a bad man to tangle with. The ways in which he moved to work his wonders lacked the stealth and legerdemain required of politics at any level.

Charlie Bonner had once said, "Ben, you're the least deceitful Irishman I've ever known. As president I'm going to need a friend who can give me perspective and tell me I'm an asshole—in the unlikely event that description ever fits me. I want one guy up close and personal who can tell me to kiss his behind and walk away—in other words, someone I can't do anything for. Somebody who doesn't need me in any way at all. It's a very short list, pal. You're going to be my trusted outsider."

It never seemed to cross Charlie's mind that that made Ben an insider, inevitably surrounded by jealous rivals. There were those who'd have said Ben had been too successful in the political maneuvering within the Bascomb office to plead distaste for politics in general, and they might have had a point. Clearly he was the heir to Drew Summerhays's place within the firm. But he seldom spared people's feelings or let his attitudes go unknown, and he'd been clear on what he felt about further involvement once Charlie had, rather to Ben's surprise, been elected president. He'd even turned down White House dinner invitations to make his point. However, by a kind of peculiar power osmosis, Ben found that he could never entirely successfully evade the subject of politics, simply because of his friendship with the President. And if the going ever got tough enough, Ben Driskill knew that man in the White House would never hesitate to play the old football chums–at–Notre Dame card. But that wasn't all that was bothering Ben Driskill as he read the *Times*.

The third cause of his concern—as he sat at his elegant antique desk in the corner office on the fortieth floor of the

Wall Street tower that housed the venerable firm of Bascomb, Lufkin, and Summerhays—could be found in the very heart and soul of that firm. The Bascomb office had long been a force behind the scenes in Democratic Party politics. No one had been more illustrious in his service to the party and to the nation than the reigning head of the firm, the great Drew Summerhays, who, in his nineties, remained "of counsel" and was a daily participant in the firm's activities . . . as well as the Democratic National Committee's honorary chairman emeritus. Which would have been no particular concern of Ben's if fate had not also cast Drew Summerhays in the role of his surrogate father. With the unhappy passing of his own tycoonish father as well as his beloved little sister who had been a nun, Ben had turned for the security of family to the firm. Even his marriage to Elizabeth had not affected that bond. For wisdom and support and counsel he had—for many years—turned to Drew Summerhays, who had, in fact, provided him with salvation of a kind. He quite simply loved and revered the man as he never had his father. All of which necessarily involved Drew's continuing efforts to draw him into the great game. Politics.

Drew was a hard man to ignore, and Driskill frequently felt that he'd been a disappointment to the old man by steadfastly refusing to involve himself in the game, great or not. And that morning Drew had dropped a word in his ear when they'd passed outside the partners room. He would be stopping by Ben's office after lunch for a chat. When Drew wanted a private little chat there wasn't much doubt about the subject.

It was funny the way things turned out sometimes. It was Ben's wife whom Drew doted on when it came to politics. They were at one on the subject. It was not only the great game, it was the only game. When Ben met her, Elizabeth had been a nun, a dear friend and colleague of his murdered sister. Elizabeth had worked in Rome covering the Vatican for the Order's influential newspaper. It was natural that Ben had turned to her for advice on that labyrinthine world, and she had been nothing less than the mother

lode of information. They had played out their developing
friendship against the background of the Church's intrigues, and when they had fallen in love and she had made
the decision to leave the Order to marry him, it was natural
that she would continue to follow the same occupation.
As Mrs. Ben Driskill, Elizabeth had parlayed her extreme
intelligence and good connections, such as Drew Summerhays, first into a job at the Columbia School of Journalism
and subsequently into the PBS television show, *Opposites
Attract,* which she cohosted with a partisan of the political
right, Ballard Niles, the much read columnist of the *World
Financial Outlook.* When the opportunity had arisen to
join the Europa News Syndicate as their "American political analyst," she had debated back and forth, discussed it
with Ben, who told her that any job that did not involve
Ballard Niles was a step in the right direction, and had finally taken it. The syndicate had sold her column to two
hundred newspapers from the British Isles to Turkey, from
the Arctic Circle to the Mediterranean.

The downside to all that was simply that she was gone
much of the time, and he missed her. At times he was jealous of the job that took her away from him, angry when
he felt the job was more important to her than their life
together. He knew how solid that life was, how strong the
foundation, but he couldn't ignore the constant separa-
tions, the feelings that at times they were losing touch. By
leaping into the political world, he could have reached out
to her. Maybe his need to stay out of politics was as strong
as hers to stay in and report what was going on, what it all
meant. What it meant for them, he didn't quite know.

President Charles Bonner was in heap big trouble these
days and that was why Ben was praying the call from the
White House asking him to help out, to get down to Washington, wouldn't come. The trouble kept getting worse, it
seemed, with each passing day. The Republicans had lately
been joined by a far more bloodthirsty truckload of Democrats out to eviscerate the President.

He hadn't heard from Charlie in nearly a month. During
those weeks things had been going from bad to worse in

Bonner's battle with the Iowan, Bob Hazlitt. And, here they were, only two weeks from the Democratic convention in Chicago. You couldn't avoid hearing the rumor of impending ruin for the Bonner administration. At the center of it all was the administration's foreign policy—most specifically in Mexico now—which the conservative wings of both parties characterized as "peace at any cost" and "a great lost opportunity"—for what exactly they didn't say but implied that anything up to and including the annexation of Mexico was a grand idea. It made for a constant din emanating from Washington.

Drew Summerhays appeared almost as if by magic at the half-open door, gently tapping. He was not a tall man but so excessively slender and so elegantly tailored that he appeared tall and graceful and far younger than his years. He had passed ninety without so much as a backward glance. He maintained his usual schedule, counseled his longtime clients, lunched two or three times a week at the Four Seasons or the Harvard Club, and was the man to whom the Bonner administration always turned first for advice and insight. If there was a politically gifted successor among the present crew of East Coast Democrats, the smart money was on Ellery Dunstan Larkspur, whose only drawback was that he had never picked up a law degree. Larkspur was, instead, a public relations genius who knew Washington inside and out. Otherwise, with an admittedly different style from Drew's, he seemed to have the inside track to become Drew's successor. But for now Drew was still the Keeper of the Keys. No one held him in higher regard than Larkspur, no one but Ben Driskill, whose relationship with the old man was like no one else's.

"Ben, I'm sorry to interrupt you—"

"Drew, I'm standing at the window staring into space. Nothing going on here."

"I need a word with you." He raised his snow-white eyebrows as if they were question marks. "It's important."

"Look, it's Washington . . . right? Something wrong?" He had a feeling.

"That's a good one, Benjamin. When wasn't there, may

I ask?" He stroked his chin for a moment, staring out the window, then made a decision and turned back to Driskill. "The President is back from Mexico. I understand it was pretty rough down there, dealing with the warring factions—the assassinations, the whole bloody mess. And now there's the earthquake." He shook his head, almost as if he couldn't bear to remember the images. Finally he turned away, lost for a moment in thought. "First the assassination of the director of intelligence and the chief of police of Mexico City—what, two days ago?—and Charlie visiting both sides in the civil war. He took a hell of a risk, Ben. I was just reading that seventy percent of the American people were against their President exposing himself to that kind of danger. But, then, sixty percent approved of his personal bravery. The real problem is that fifty-four percent think his policy there has taken a wrong turn. Enter . . . Citizen Hazlitt."

"I sense a Jacobean jab there, Drew."

"It's all up for grabs at this point. I don't like it, not any of it."

"Charlie knew what he was doing in his State of the Union Address. He decided and that was that."

"It was a gamble, Ben. And Hazlitt's been the one taking advantage of it . . . to make himself sound all the more forceful. He's saying, don't send one man to do an American army's job."

"Well, Charlie can get pretty stubborn—"

"Yes, and maybe Hazlitt is right, maybe we should go in there and put the lid on—but who are we kidding, it's never that easy, is it?"

"Hazlitt," Driskill said, "is a fascist—"

"Careful, don't get wrapped up in campaign rhetoric." Summerhays was smiling at him. "Charlie's numbers are going to take a hit but he may fight his way back. It'll get bloody, though. Can you meet me in my office in an hour or so?" He leaned casually against the frame of the door, one hand in his trouser pocket. He wore a gray suit with a subtle flicker of red-and-blue windowpane pattern in it.

You never thought about his age when you were with him. It seemed preposterous.

"It's my unhappy job to tell you that I've got a meeting with the surviving children of the Brogan trust. . . . Liam and Carol Brogan are trying very hard to get their hands on the money again. They're due in half an hour and you know what that means." He hated putting Drew off for any reason.

"Yes, I'm afraid I do. The original Brogan, so to speak, was Emmett, and he was a client of mine. My fingerprints are all over the creation of that trust. I'm afraid they're out of luck on the money front." He smiled thinly. "Emmett quite rightly feared the profligacy of later generations who lacked his strength of character. So I dotted every *i* and crossed every *t* to keep this item intact. My goodness, Liam and Carol must have twenty million of their own, surely."

"Brace yourself. Liam wants to be a movie producer and knows nothing about how to go about doing it—"

"You might point out to him that the first rule is never to use your own money. The man's a goof. So, you're tied up."

"Give me a hint—what's up?"

"There are a few things I need to go over with you. Whether you like it or not."

"Which means our friend—"

"In the White House, yes. I won't accept a hard time from you about it, Ben, so save your breath. *This* time I need you to take an oar and row."

"That bad?" Driskill heard in the tone of Summerhays's voice the sound of distant alarm bells.

"But you have the Brogans. . . ." Drew was ignoring the question. "Well, we can do it Monday, I suppose. First thing. Breakfast at the Harvard Club?"

"I'll be there. On my best behavior."

"What a relief," he said dryly. "Eight o'clock. I'll have the chopper bring me in at six-thirty."

"You're spending the weekend at Big Ram?"

"It's a bit cooler out there and they say there's a nice storm blowing in. Perfect for thinking. And I'm reading a

wonderful biography of Evelyn Waugh." The thought
seemed to please him. "I'm going out to the cottage to read
and think things over. Maybe it's *best* we meet on Monday
actually. I'll have had time to digest my thoughts. Maybe
I'll have a plan . . . it's a tricky business, this one."

"What business, Drew?"

"I'll take you into my confidence on Monday. I'll have
more to tell you then, in any case."

"All right, Drew."

"May God bless you and keep you, my son." There was
always a slight chill when Drew Summerhays sought God's
blessing for you. It always sounded as if he thought you
might need it rather badly. He was gone from the doorway
and his voice floated back. "Love to Elizabeth."

Once he'd finished with Liam and Carol, Driskill noticed
that his office windows were spattered with raindrops, and
far below, the awnings at the tables of the outdoor cafés
were blowing in the wind and people were scurrying inside.
The clouds had moved in. He hoped the temperature had
dropped. He threw some weekend reading into his briefcase and grabbed his Blackwatch raincoat and the door-
man-size umbrella Elizabeth had given him and when he
left the building discovered that it was still hot, just wetter.

He stopped for some cigars at J & R, then decided the
heat in the subway would be just too damn much. He
waited for a cab in Park Row, thankful for the extra-large
umbrella. It had grown abnormally dark and the cabs had
their lights on as they hissed through the puddles. He finally got one and sank damply into its clutches. It took half
an hour to reach the upper East Side. He rode with the
window open, the rain spraying his face from time to time.
He was trying hard not to think about Drew, not to wonder what was going wrong in Washington. But there was
no avoiding it.

The radio was tuned to a drive-time talk show. The host
was ruminating on the subject of the day. "In view of the
earthquake hitting along the border with Mexico, it may

sound cynical to speculate—but just how is this going to impact on President Bonner's policy of helping to establish a successful compromise government that would end the civil war? We've got our own national security to think about—this is Mexico, not Hindustan. Now this earthquake leads to looting and reprisals and who knows what else and Americans have been caught in it and are dying. . . . Let's see, punch line one, there . . . Hello, caller, you're on the air. . . ."

The racket went on and on. Driskill was struck anew by the mess Charlie was in. The cabdriver lowered the volume, glanced back over his shoulder. "Can you imagine if you had relatives down there? My wife's got a cousin who works in Arizona and she says he's scared shitless, got the family down there. She says he wishes we'd just do something but, y'know, like what? Right?"

He entered the black wrought-iron gate at street level, unlocked the heavy door, and went into his front hallway on the lowest of the four floors, stuck his umbrella in the brass boot, went down the hall to the kitchen, and carefully constructed a large vodka and tonic, lots of ice, lots of lime. The empty house made its little noises. The refrigerator, the air-conditioning on low, the dehumidifiers humming, a radio turned to a classical station with the volume low, the ticking of the grandfather clock at the top of the first set of stairs. He wished Elizabeth were coming home for the weekend, but unless he had mixed up her schedule, she was on the road. It might be California taking the pulse of the voters. It might be somewhere else. He missed her. He always missed her.

He took his drink out onto the back patio with the three trees towering overhead and stood watching the rain dripping off the awning that was reputed to be waterproof. He sat down at one of the metal tables and closed his eyes, trying to drain the day away. The sound of the rain lulled him. Drew was on his way by helicopter out to his cottage. Elizabeth off somewhere checking out the politicians and figuring out how to explain them to the people of Europe. Damn, he wished he hadn't had to put Drew off the way he had. He felt guilty about making him wait. He also felt the slight tugs of anxiety that came from the Washington tentacles. All the stuff in the *Times* had set him off, then Drew's request for the little chat: He felt the tension building subtly.

The ringing telephone burrowed into his consciousness and he went back into the kitchen to answer it. There was a Hazlitt attack ad on the small television, something to do with the earthquake and its results. They were so damn fast! He was thinking the call might be from Elizabeth. But it wasn't. Ellery Larkspur, instead.

"Ben, you sound like you're underwater."

"You're not far off, Larkie." It was the call from Washington he'd been dreading. It was almost a relief now it was here. "Raining up here. What can I do for you?"

"Any momentous plans for the weekend? Foxhunting, hang gliding—?"

"I'm not coming down there if that's what you're after. I have no answers to any of your questions. No, I don't know how Charlie can pull this off. No, I haven't got the goods on Bob Hazlitt. Is he Elvis's love child? Maybe, maybe not—not enough to go on. Anything else?"

"You underestimate yourself. Still, I respect and understand your unwillingness to blah-blah-blah. I've heard it all before. So, for the love of God, spare me your whining." Larkspur spoke with affection and a peculiar mid-Atlantic drawl. He'd been a Rhodes scholar, had learned much of his public relations wizardry among English masters who'd had a certain style. That had all been a long time ago. But still there was the slight English manner of speech with the drawl of Savannah from which he'd come. He was a great devotee of his fellow Savannahian, the great songwriter Jimmy Mercer. In fact it was Ellery Larkspur who had convinced Charlie Bonner to use the Mercer classic "In the Cool, Cool, Cool of the Evening" as a personal campaign theme song. He even resembled slightly photographs Ben had seen of Mercer: a balding dome with a few hairs combed straight back, curious, mischievous eyes, a cigarette in one hand and a glass of bourbon in the other, suits from London's Savile Row.

Ben was smiling as he listened to Larkie. The vodka and tonic was watery, and while he heard Larkie's report on the full horror of the Bonner campaign's present state he splashed a touch more vodka and a lot of tonic into the glass, dropped in cubes. He was perspiring. It wasn't the heat, it was the humidity. "Get to it, Larkie. What do you want?"

"Well, it's Drew. I admit I'm a little worried about our friend Drew. Last time I saw him he was looking a little shaky, a little fragile—"

"He's in his nineties, you may recall."

"No, it was more than that. Hesitant. Tentative. Slow to make connections. He called me late this afternoon, said he wanted to talk to me . . . but said he'd wait until I could get up to New York. He said that everything had gone too far. He seemed upset by the reports of the earthquake. Well, damn all, here I am in Washington, I'm in the middle of what looks more like a lynching party than a reelection campaign. . . . I'm just about spun out with these reporters. It's like holding court at the deathbed—"

"That bad?"

"Well, not quite. We'll pull it out."

"You don't have to put the spin on with me."

"Sorry. Occupational hazard. Moving on . . . Anyway, Drew—I just wanted to get your thinking on him. I wish he lived in town like a normal person—I don't like the idea of him being all by his lonesome out there on Big Ram. And there's some damn storm on its way up from Cape Hatteras. Going like a sonuvabitch. He putters around out there all by himself—what if the electricity goes out and he falls down the stairs or slips in the tub? Call me an old woman—"

"You're an old woman."

"Ah, I knew you could be counted on to take the mature approach."

"Actually, it worries me too—it's the storm that's got me thinking. I'm not at all sure *I'd* want to be out there alone in one of those things. Elizabeth isn't here, of course; it's not like we were going to have a wonderful weekend together—"

"I wish you and she would get your scheduling problems straightened out—talk about ships that pass in the night! I know she wants to." Ben heard him sipping at his bourbon.

"I do, too. The truth is, I'm a little down this evening."

"Benjamin, she'll be home in a day or two."

"I know, Larkie."

"Don't call me, I'll call you." Their little game.

Sitting alone in the rainy backyard, Driskill realized his catnap had perked him up considerably. He picked up the phone and dialed Drew's number. As he waited, he thought about Drew's good Scotch and how much he loved to drink with his senior partner. There was no answer. Maybe Drew had dozed off, too.

He cleaned up the drink mixings, went upstairs, and threw some clothes into an overnight bag. Why wait until Monday morning? Might as well drive out tonight just in case he could be of some help to Drew if the storm hit bigtime. He called Elizabeth's number at the apartment just off Dupont Circle in Washington. The answering machine came on and he waited for the beep.

"This is your late lamented husband, Ben—you remember. I'll be out at Drew's place for the weekend. It's Friday, past eight o'clock. I'm just leaving. Give us a jingle if you can—you know how much Drew would love to speak with you. I wouldn't mind it, myself. Love, my darling." He was trying to take the sting out of their last conversation. It hadn't been an argument, but he'd made clear he was tired of missing her, tired of the half life, weekends alone, all the rest of it. She'd promised they would talk. They'd parted with a hurried kiss that felt more like a handshake.

Once he was out on the Long Island Expressway, the rain thickened and occasional gusts of wind felt their way along the side of the car with fingers like sledgehammers. Whatever was coming up from Hatteras couldn't be far off.

The wind hurled itself with increasing abandon at the big Buick Roadmaster as it clung fast to the rain-blown Long Island Expressway. The beams of the headlights bounced off the driven sheets of rain. The wind threatened to rip the wipers from the windshield. It was a perfect night for this kind of errand, and the thought of the old "cottage" with all its fireplaces and overstuffed furniture waiting for him at the end was all that brightened his mood. If Drew had gone to bed he'd make himself a drink and read a book until he fell asleep in one of the guest rooms. The rain made the going slower than usual but there was a nearly complete absence of traffic. Maybe he'd be there in time for a nightcap with Drew, a time for talking things over and outlining the big picture. He'd even talk politics with him. Whatever, they had all weekend.

As he drove he listened to a call-in radio show, which was about all there was on radio anymore. A politically conservative host was playing skillfully into the prejudices and hatreds of his followers. Everyone was using President Bonner as a representative of the moral decay that was eating through the society. This one was saying that President Bonner was not doing enough to protect the country from nefarious forces beyond our borders and that in the end he would be held accountable and would suffer for it. The guy made it sound like a personal threat. "Thank you, Eddie from Brooklyn, I'm sure you've put into words what most of us are thinking." On and on it went. Know the enemy.

It had become a kind of national radio game of late: Why the medium had spawned so few hosts of a more centrist or liberal persuasion baffled him. He had mentioned to Elizabeth that he supposed it made for "good radio," something to get your dander up, something to talk about the next day. Conservatives seemed better at that kind of exercise. Elizabeth said that in the first place people still talked about David Letterman's stupid pet tricks the next day and in the second place it was merely that conservative causes produced shriller, more hateful fanatics. "Conservatives want to keep people *from*," she had written in one of her columns a couple of months ago, "while liberals want to empower people *to*."

Ben Driskill's political disaffection from so many of his liberal views stemmed from the fact that most of what he'd once espoused had misfired or been corrupted or had come to grief through neglect or, conversely, too much attention. The credo everywhere was the opposite of what had been intended by do-gooders of his generation. No one was responsible anymore for his or her own behavior. There was always a way out of facing up to reality, a way you could paint yourself as the victim. There was always someone else to blame for whatever you didn't like about your life. *Not my fault,* that was the cry heard from every corner. And he believed that his kind of liberal had to haul around their share of the blame, which was substantial. More than anything, in recent times, he had responded to the liberal dogma of his earlier years as he had responded to the ultra-conservative dogmatic practices of the Church. He rejected them. Received wisdom, imperishable, immutable doctrine . . . He'd have said that doctrine, immutable doctrine, the absolute belief that you were right—all that was the mug's game.

Drew Summerhays had been responsible for teaching politics to both Ben Driskill and Ellery Larkspur, one within the law firm, the other within the convoluted ways of the Democratic Party. Drew had always concentrated on getting the best he could out of a situation. Best for the nation, best for the most people. Lyndon Johnson, master of the art of the possible, had said Drew Summerhays was the only man he'd ever met who was Sam Rayburn's equal when it came to understanding the true nature and purpose of politics. The best Drew got out of Ben Driskill wasn't much, when it came to politics, but he always said Ellery Larkspur was his greatest achievement, the quickest learner he'd ever encountered.

The ferry to Shelter Island from Greenport was loading up. His was the sixth car in line, just another car, just another driver. They were packed in tight and the kid collecting the fare never looked at the faces, his head ducked back under the hood of his anorak. The storm was blowing hard and the water kept giving and rolling as they struggled toward the dim lights of the opposite landing. Nobody was paying any attention to anybody else. The idea was to get home, batten down the hatches, hunker down. The ferry banged into the wooden pilings and settled against the dock, emptied its cargo, picked up a couple of cars heading for the mainland, and hastened off into the night.

Ben swung the Roadmaster to the left, circling up past the clutch of grocery stores and gas stations, past the golf course, heading for the tip of the island. The wind was stronger on the island. A couple of small trees had blown down and jutted a few feet out into the road just as you came around a corner. He felt like a man in a commercial for tires you could trust your family to. Headlights occasionally flared out behind him in the blowing gloom. Patches of wet mud had slid across the road, and little rivers flowed down from the rises at the passenger side.

The headlights picked out the causeway up ahead. He'd come down to sea level from the hump of the island. The thin strip of land connecting Shelter Island to Big Ram appeared on the verge of sinking beneath the water. It was always littered with ground-up clamshells. Nature at work. The gulls that lived in considerable numbers in the vicinity had put their tiny bird brains to work as soon as the causeway was built. They would swoop down, pick up the clams in their shells, swirl back up into the sky, and then dive-bomb the hard road, dropping the shells with amazing accuracy. The shells would splinter open, revealing the morsel of clam within, and the gulls would zoom down again and pluck it out. There was always a lesson in stuff like that.

It was no night for gulls but the shells were grinding beneath the tires. The car sent up plumes of water spewing into the darkness and then the road was climbing up the hill and past the Ram's Head Inn. Its lights glowed through the sheets of rain, and the windows looked inviting. The house was only minutes away.

Then, around a dark turn hugged by shrubs and trees, he saw the twin gatehouses where the gate hadn't been closed since the Second World War. The gate itself, like something from *Citizen Kane,* swept back with vines and shrubbery grown up through and virtually obscuring its vertical iron bars. The black driveway shone wetly in the headlights, and up ahead the house loomed, three stories with gabled roof and several chimneys and lights on in several windows across the main floor. Drew had always called it the cottage. Lights also under the roof of the porte cochere where he eventually stopped the car.

No one answered the door chimes. The door was unlocked. He pushed it open. Immediately the sound of Mozart's *Requiem* reached him faintly, from the study.

He called out a few times, expecting to see Drew come from the library or the study where lights burned, but there was no answer. You could smell the wood burning in the fireplaces. It was hot, but the very old were always chilled, or so Drew had told him. Drew employed a husband and wife who lived off-island to come in most days, attend to the house, endlessly polish and dust and keep it perfect, arrange the mail that might have arrived, lay the fires for him to light when he got home, make sure there was something to eat, turn down the bed and plump the pillows. If he needed more, they could always stay the night. There were fourteen bedrooms, Ben seemed to recall.

Well, Drew must have fallen asleep, left the lights burning. He liked to think of himself as pretty much on his own when he was on the island. In town he had a live-in couple for his exquisite little mews house at the foot of Fifth Avenue; out here he liked to think he was still capable of making it on his own. Ben quickly ducked into the library, the study, the billiard room, and the shining black-and-white kitchen. Empty. With Mozart following him he climbed the heavy, meticulously carved staircase and went to Drew's bedroom. The light was on beside the bed. The bed was turned down. Pajamas and robe laid out. But no sign of

Drew. The rain was rattling at the window and blowing in on the sill. Below, another light caught his eye. It was the greenhouse, which lay off to one side of the main house, and it seemed like an odd time to be working at the potting bench. The metal-framed glass door stood open; light fell out across the crushed-rock path leading into the darkness between the house and the greenhouse. A gust of wind moved the door to and fro. The light was a constant, nobody moving around inside making shadows.

Why the greenhouse? Fingers were running along his spine, the hair on his arms rising.

He was down the stairs and outside in seconds. The wind was blowing harder, the rain stinging his face. He was soaked with sweat. He bent into the gale and watched the greenhouse coming closer and closer, the door squeaking as the wind tore at it. He was imagining what had happened. Drew had heard the door banging, he'd gone out to fix it, he'd had a stroke or a heart attack, he'd gotten into the greenhouse, turned on the light and collapsed. That had to be it. . . .

The breakers were exploding on the rocks at the foot of the cliff bordering his property. The smell of salt blew in on the wind. Somewhere off the shore was the south fork of Long Island. It might as well have been the Crab Nebula.

Drew was in the greenhouse.

Ben saw his legs first, the trousers of his suit, the highly polished black shoes soiled with rain and mud. He went around the bench, saw him stretched out on his side. He was wearing a dark blue cashmere cardigan, his white shirt open at the neck. "Drew, for chrissakes," he shouted over the noise of the wind and the water crashing against the cliff and the gale rattling the panes of glass overhead. He knelt beside him and then, in the dim light of the shadow cast by the bench, he saw that it hadn't been a stroke.

There was an entry wound, small and scorched, on his right temple. At the end of his extended right arm, half concealed by the bench, was the gun. It lay a few inches from his relaxed right hand. A Smith & Wesson .22 revolver.

He looked so fragile, so terribly breakable, stretched out in death. So small, not merely lean and fit as he'd appeared in life but pathetically small. The soul of the man, the life force, had left the body, and it made you realize just how fucking big a man's soul can be.

Kneeling beside him, breathless from the shock, Ben Driskill began sobbing, feeling his whole body cramp in emotional distress, his tears running down his face and dripping on the body of Drew Summerhays. He was mourning the end of such a remarkable life, mourning the simple passage of time—forget the means of his life's ending—that had consumed him and had a pretty damn good start on Ben himself. He was mourning for himself, for the hope of youth and the endless vistas of prospects, as well as for Drew—sorrowing over what it all comes down to in the end when it's time for us to go. You go and for that moment, while your being hangs suspended between one place and the other, even if that other is the Great Nowhere, there must be the momentary sense of its all adding up to nothing, that you might never have lived, that it was all just a question of killing time and smoke drifting away on the wind. You were Drew Summerhays, a giant among the mightiest of your time, and then—you were gone.

Ben said good-bye to the remains of his old friend, the man who had played the role of his father through so much of his life. He felt rather foolish until he got the tears stopped. Drew would have been taking a somewhat jaundiced view of such carrying on. What, Ben asked himself as he stood up, would Drew do in this situation? For one thing, he wouldn't touch the body, the gun, or anything else in the greenhouse. And he would think of the Democratic Party.

Ben went back to the house through the storm, almost blown off his feet, leaving the door as he'd found it, open and being pushed around by the wind.

Tom Bohannon drove off the ferry with a wave to the toll collector.

"You guys really do get through, whatever the weather."

"Beats the post office, I guess," Bohannon said, pulling the brown UPS van off onto not-so-dry land. He would ditch the van in Jamesport and pick up the car waiting there for him. A lime-green '79 Olds four-door. He knew it would be there.

The old man had been easy. He sighed heavily. Poor old bastard.

Not like his father. Not like old Frank . . . He'd taken some killing but that was all a long time ago and there was no point in dwelling on it now. It had come to mind because his father would have still been younger than the old man tonight. He didn't like thinking about his father but he was never that far from his cortex of memory. There was just no forgetting big, old Frank. He'd been a good hater, consumed by his various hatreds . . . queers and mongrels and niggers and wops and spics, the Commies and the Russkies and the fucking Jews and . . . His father had hated them and he'd beaten the same hatreds into his son. But the son had discovered there was more to the world while the father just went on marinating in his own hatreds and when he discovered that his boy had some ideas of his own he'd taken the strap to him, which had been a mistake.

They'd never found his father's remains because, when you got right down to it, there hadn't been any. It was as if the son of a bitch had never existed. He could still see the warm, sweet blood spurting from the carotid artery and the jugular vein, blood squirting across his own shirt and hands as the bastard had fought, he could still see him disappearing into the Everglades swamp that sucked him down, a big old gator racing to claim the prize. He was the first and last man he had ever killed in anger and, no, nobody ever found his father.

When he had heard Charles Bonner's State of the Union message, he had felt the same anger. Outrage. Then the call had come, he mused.

Suddenly the cellular phone in his coverall pocket gave

its little chirp and he dug it out, answered it as the wipers kept slashing across the rain-blown windshield.

"Everything went off like clockwork." That was how he answered. Only one person had the number.

The wind-whipped waves were sloshing across the causeway and the road was dark, trees whimpering in the wind as they bent, bounced off telephone wires, sometimes split and cracked and fell across somebody's driveway. Driskill passed the Ram's Head Inn again going the other way and circled down into the town where a couple of advertising lights were still lit and some streetlights were casting swinging, eerie shadows against the rain. There was a telephone booth stuck on the side of the gas station, which was closed.

He pulled the Buick up as close to the telephone as possible and huddled beneath his umbrella as he used his MCI card and called a long-distance number, area code 202. "Yes?" The voice was just short of digitalized. It was a number so private that writing it down was forbidden. He disliked the game. It made him feel like he was back at school.

"This is Archangel."

"Yes, Archangel—read any good books lately?"

"John Steinbeck. *East of Eden*." Another code.

"What can I do for you, Archangel?"

"Fishercat. Get him on the line. Immediately."

"He's retired for the evening, Archangel."

"Then get him the hell up. Or your next job will be as underconsulate assistant in Tierra del Fuego."

"I'll see what I can do."

There was a series of clicks and pauses.

"Archangel, what the hell's going on?" It was the President of the United States. "It's eleven o'clock."

"Drew Summerhays is dead." Driskill was trying vainly to catch his breath. "Shot. Suicide or murder, hard to tell." His own voice sounded unreal, as if some of the circuitry was shutting down. "It looks like suicide, but why would he kill himself? Still, it *looks* like suicide. . . ."

There was a brief pause, and he heard the President swallowing hard.

"Well, hell, Ben . . . I loved that old man." His voice was shaking. To hell with code names, he was the President of the United States. "And I know what he meant to you. Believe me. What can you tell me?"

Ben gave him the quick essentials. The rain was spitting in under the umbrella. The rain was heavier all the time. Jesus. It wasn't a hurricane but it was a hell of a night. "Ben, where are you?" It was Larkspur.

"Out in the middle of some gale-force winds. It's a mess here. What's going on—are you in bed with Charlie and Linda?"

"We're in the study," Charlie said. "Have you reported any of this to the authorities?"

"I'm not going to do a damn thing before we talk. That's why I'm calling. I don't want to involve you in any way, and once the papers get hold of this, Ben Driskill and a dead Drew Summerhays—well, you'll be in over your head. The point is, what do you want me to do—?"

"Your instincts are absolutely right, Ben." The President had broken back in. "What do you say, Larkie?"

"Not a word, Ben."

The President said, "Can you handle that for me?"

"Of course."

"You're not happy with the suicide option?"

"It's just that I can't imagine a less suicidal man. That's all. Why? Why would he do it?"

"I don't know, Ben, but you heard me say a few hours ago that I was worried about him." It was Larkspur again. "Things happen in the brain of a man of his age."

"Look, I can't get off this goddam island until morning. Then I'll be just another car on the ferry."

"Ben, are we clear on this? I'm asking you not to tell anyone. We've got to talk first. I've got to figure out how to handle it." The President broke off and was murmuring something to the others.

"You know there's always the chance it could get a little tricky," Driskill said, letting it sink in for a moment. "I want to make that clear to you."

"You don't agree with me?"

"No, no, Charlie. I'm just being a lawyer. But my gut tells me you're right."

"Ben, I want you down here." The President's voice still sounded strained, on the point of cracking. He was an emotional man and he'd revered Drew Summerhays. "I want a report face-to-face. This is a terrible thing. We've got to deal with it in the best possible way."

"Okay, okay. I'll come down tomorrow—" It was no time to get shirty about going to Washington. In the President's mind Ben Driskill was on the team when the chips were down. The crisis management team. And Ben didn't want to be alone either, thinking about Drew and what might have happened.

"First thing."

"Okay. This storm might screw up the shuttle flights. I'll get the Metroliner out of Penn Station. I'll be there by noon."

"Good-bye, Ben. And, Ben . . . I'm so damn sorry." The line went dead.

So, Ben reflected as he pulled out of the deserted hub of the village, the cover-up begins.

Still, Drew would have endorsed the path taken. His death would certainly bring the President's name into things but nothing like what would ring the bells if it came out that Ben Driskill was at the scene. He could imagine the stories now, all the leading questions with all their devastating implications. Why was Ben Driskill out there in the middle of a stormy night? And what did it have to do with the party? What had been so important that it couldn't wait until the next day? Was it yet another presidential crisis?

There was always the chance that it might be found out—the fact that he hadn't reported a suicide—but the chance seemed slim. It was worth taking the risk to keep the President's name out of the guts of the story. He wasn't obstructing justice; he certainly wouldn't adjust, move, or remove anything. Somebody would have to look hard to see even the hint of a cover-up. Covering up what? A suicide? Nobody was ever going to know he was there. It was what Drew would have wanted.

He headed back through the driving rain, across the dark island with the waves smashing across the bays, washing across the causeway. Back in the house he took off his coat, draped it over the couch in the study, went into the kitchen, and made a cup of coffee. Cup in hand, he went back into the study where the fire still burned. Too damn hot. Jesus. He spread the wood out with a poker, knocked it apart, watched the flames dying. He wiped the sweat beaded on his forehead. Don't think of Drew's body out in the greenhouse, you mustn't think of it, it's not Drew, Drew is gone now. . . .

Drew's briefcase—a green-and-brown leather affair from Madler on Park Avenue, three thousand dollars years ago, a gift from a client—sat by one of the leather wing chairs. Half of a Macanudo Churchill lay in a cut-glass ashtray with a two-inch cylinder of grayish-white ash. It was still warm. A big cigar would stay warm a long time. An hour, maybe even two.

He poked at the logs again, trying to extinguish them. A beetle scuttled out from within a log and was fried in his own juice. Only an oracle could explain why the hell Drew had killed himself. Could he have heard someone outside, a burglar, and gone with his old Smith & Wesson to investigate? Could he have fallen, could the gun have gone off? Could it possibly have been an accident?

With his handkerchief in his hand he opened the elegant German briefcase, careful not to leave fingerprints. He'd take care of the coffee cup and the kitchen surfaces later. There wasn't much in the briefcase, just a couple of file folders. One contained several sheets of computer printouts, mostly numbers, as if it were a code waiting to be fed into an electronic deciphering machine. It meant nothing to Ben.

The other folder was fatter, secured with a rubber band, corners of some loose pages sticking out at hasty angles. Obviously it was a file of clippings and notes and reports devoted to the most logical of all subjects—the man who was challenging President Bonner for the nomination. Flying Bob Hazlitt. Father of the World's Third Largest Communications Empire. Iowa's Favorite Son. The Man with an Answer. The Man Who Would Be King. Ben was sick of Flying Bob Hazlitt. He leafed through the file folder. It was a standard campaign folder. Drew had been planning to review it, maybe let it jog his creative juices in hopes of seeing something he could discuss with the President, some kind of response to Hazlitt's continuing attack.

There was a folded sheet of fax paper on the desktop, an advance copy of the coming Monday's *World Financial Outlook,* the great journal of politics and economics and finance that was read as avidly in Washington and New York as the *Post* or the *Times* and that, nationwide, had a larger circulation than either. It had the look of something left over from another age, a newspaper from a Dickens novel: few photographs, endless columns of unbroken type, pages of graphs and stock market prices, impenetrable to some, to others as necessary to sustain life as blood and oxygen. Its outlook was fiscally conservative and politically right wing. Its editorial board had never met a Republican they didn't like, unless of course the Republican, as in the case of President George Bush, began to drift toward the center. Democrats were normally placed somewhere along a kind of ideological yardstick ranging from good ol' down-home rascals to modern incarnations of the Antichrist. The President was about 75 percent of the way toward Antichrist at the moment, in this long season of Charles Bonner's discontent.

With the unflagging rise of Bob Hazlitt, speaking out for "Common Sense and the Common Man," one man—the man who was the soul of the *WFO* to all intents and purposes, Ballard Niles—had taken up the crusade against

Bonner and was providing his own cudgels. The Republican National Committee were a bunch of pantywaists, bound by good manners and a sense of fear at what the other guys might say about them and their own weak candidate, Price Quarles: that was the view of Ballard Niles, who appeared not to be afraid of anyone, so violently did he flail at the administration.

It was all reminiscent of the attacks launched against Franklin Roosevelt or, in more recent years, Bill Clinton. At the real Gridiron Dinner a while back, the President had actually joked about Niles in a sketch, calling him "the Big Shark, a one-fish feeding frenzy." There had been tunes adapted from Sondheim's bloody musical, *Sweeney Todd, The Demon Barber of Fleet Street,* and behind and beneath the roars of laughter there were many in the crowd put off by the depiction of the President going into Ballard Niles's barbershop and settling down for a shave, the light playing on Niles's gleaming straight razor. Clint Spencer of the *Washington Post* had remarked in print, "The sketch cut a little close to the bone, even for this shebang, but the President apparently found it amusing. Art imitating life. Bonner's administration is already bleeding like a stuck pig. But the President was cool, a good sport—and maybe that's his problem. Maybe it's time to get out the heavy artillery and go after those in his own party who are betraying him—go after them breathing fire."

And now somebody had faxed Drew Summerhays advance copies of Ballard Niles's next column. Curiouser and curiouser. Through the looking glass. Who could do such a thing?

Niles wrote three times a week, and for months he'd been scoring off the administration, but the attacks had increased during the last three or four weeks. As the President had remarked to one of the anchormen in an interview the week before, "The foam around Ballard's muzzle is not really all that attractive, do you think?" Someone— presumably Drew—had marked this faxed column with a yellow Hi-Liter. The standard title of the column was *Niles to Go.* Ben Driskill felt the bottom falling out of his stomach as he read it.

> ... *The rumors of impending disaster swirling about the White House and the administration of President Charles Bonner are, to quote that late great estimable elder statesman Ross Perot, creating a very great "sucking sound" as the ethical well runs dry and the still-beating ethical heart is ripped from the breast of the rotting host. Perception becomes reality, more so in Washington than anywhere else. And I might add reveals reality, as well. Somebody—or perhaps somebodies—has been very naughty. Both in the past and present. We have word that it is only a matter of a day or two before a major scandal erupts, gaseous clouds emitted from this particularly fetid political swamp. Their shapes are not yet clear and you can't make out their name tags yet but they are inevitable. They reek of Charles Bonner's destiny.*
>
> *We hear rumors of illegal campaign financing (so what else is new? Admittedly, the Democrats have no patent on this transgression), under-the-table deals with Mexico and Japan and Russia on environment, trade, and human rights, unseemly involvement in laundering vast amounts of drug money—you name it. And then there are all the stories of the love nests in Virginia and on the Maryland shore and who knows where else. The rumors are all being discussed quite openly over dinners in private homes and at Duke Siebert's and Citronelle and the Jockey Club and, believe it or not, yesterday I was offered the opportunity to gaze upon a candid snapshot or two! No, not the spicy ones, none of the naughty bits.*
>
> *Rather, I was told, shots of no less a player than the Ultimate Gray Eminence, Drew Summerhays, rising ninety and dapper as ever, deep in conversation with Nestor "Tony" Sarrabian at the latter's Virginia estate. For those who may have forgotten, Tony Sarrabian, who started out as a "sales associate" to a prominent Arab princeling known for running down youths in the streets*

of Washington and escaping prosecution by way of the old diplomatic status gambit, is what used to be called "a fixer." He has, indeed, made a good thing out of being useful. Say you want to arm an insurrection or, conversely, put one down, stop by and see Tony at Sarrabian Associates . . . and bring money. Or say you want to help somebody get a broadcast license from the FCC, meet our boy Tony . . . and bring money. Need an indictment quashed (or "squashed," as we hear in our postliterate society), want those perfect, impossible-to-get Redskins play-off tickets, want to lay off some nuclear warheads that have never been used and are cluttering up the place . . . go with cap in hand to Tony Sarrabian and by all means, bring money. Or, should you want to help finance the political ambitions of Charles Bonner and his merry men, Tony's your boy, your guaranteed access to the White House.

But where does Tony's influence come from, you ask? From his connection to the biggest dogs in the pack, the dogs who intimidate so mightily that they never have to fight—dogs, you should pardon the expression, like Charlie Bonner and his gang, dogs like Drew Summerhays, who in his dotage is still "of counsel" to the President of these United States.

So, did I look at those snapshots? Of course, I did. I didn't pick them up from the table where my informant had placed them but there they were, Summerhays and Sarrabian. It's bad enough just to imagine a pillar of the Establishment sharing a moment with Tony Sarrabian. But what, one wonders, might they have been discussing in the seclusion of Tony's country house in the Blue Ridge Mountains? Or were they taken at the monstrosity he calls home along the Potomac?

I didn't pick them up, mind you. But I suggested that my informant might want to have those photos delivered to our offices, and if we were in the proper mood we might just run them next to my column. Proof that you can trust me, friends.

Never fear, Gentle Reader. It won't be long before we

hear the other shoe dropping. It's as certain as Death, Taxes, and the political fall of Charlie Bonner. But what, I ask myself, has Drew Summerhays come to at the end of the day? If you run into him in New York at the Harvard Club or the Four Seasons—he's rarely seen anywhere else—you might ask him.

That was what Drew had been reading just before he put a bullet in his head. Ballard Niles had another notch in his six-shooter. At just that moment, Ben Driskill would have gladly killed Ballard Niles with his own two hands. What he was doing—the destruction of men with innuendo and rumor—was in Ben's view an offense punishable by death.

In a rare exception to the newspaper's normal makeup, there were two black-and-white photographs in a sidebar to Niles's column. The lighting wasn't perfect and the resolution left something to be desired, but they did reveal Drew Summerhays and Tony Sarrabian. One depicted them standing at the rail of Sarrabian's yacht on the Potomac, leaning forward with elbows on the rail, smiling out at the picture taker. The other showed them in a more private moment, sitting on what seemed to be a stone parapet that probably offered a view of the river behind them. Their heads were inclined toward one another, and Sarrabian seemed to be doing the talking while Summerhays listened. Sarrabian was wearing a polo shirt open at the neck in both pictures. Summerhays was wearing a double-breasted blazer with a white shirt and tie. Ben would have bet he was wearing white wing-tip shoes, as well, just as his father had when Ben was a boy. And the natural question arose unaided: What in the world had they been talking about? What was the occasion? Who took the pictures? And most important of all . . . who had given the pictures to Ballard Niles? Who had sent the fax to Drew? There was no identifying number, just the generic G-3 at the top of the page.

Funny, the way things could sneak up on you and before you knew it you'd stepped off dry land and were stumbling out into the gap where everything was smoking and indistinct, like the immediate aftermath of a plane crash, where you could feel a scream building up inside of you, where there were other rules and you had no idea what they were. . . . That was Driskill's prevailing view of the world as the rain and the wind and the dense humidity swept the island through the night.

It was a long night, sleeping in the house of the dead. He finally dozed at about four o'clock. The driving rain changed to a blowing mist, and dawn came gray and limp with the temperature going up at an ungodly rate. He drove back across the deserted causeway, avoiding the limbs and occasional tree trunks littering the road. No traffic. He parked within view of the ferry and on the third load he left Shelter Island.

Chapter 3

The heat was stifling as Ben Driskill stepped off the Metroliner and made his way down the platform toward the interior of Union Station. He hadn't been able to sleep on the train, had stared out at the passing scene with his mind trying to cope with the death of Drew Summerhays. He wanted to talk to somebody, and he couldn't until he got to the White House. He was hot, tired, and frustrated as he entered the magnificent old beaux arts building that had been saved and refurbished and was now one of the great public spaces in the capital. There was a thick lunchtime crowd overflowing the restaurants, tourists and shoppers doing the boutiques, kids out of school, all the faces with that shine of perspiration that would last through the summer and on into the fall in Washington. He was just leaving the shopping area when he saw the welcoming committee.

Ellery Dunstan Larkspur was the only man in the station who wasn't sweating. He was always crisp, shirt collar starched to within an inch of its life, bow tie knotted, cuffs unwrinkled, creases razor sharp. He brushed his hand back over the strands of hair combed straight back from his high forehead and waved as he approached. "Honest to God, what I do for love of my fellow man." He had a slight lisp, a trademark. "I've brought a car and driver, laddie. Can't have the great Ben Driskill standing around all damp waiting for a cab." There was something somehow endearing about the lisp. All the television interviews and sound bites had made his lisp famous.

Now the joviality was falling away like a mask. "I am so terribly sorry, Ben. You know how I felt about him." His voice had dropped to a whisper and his hand rested briefly on Driskill's arm. "Here, give me that." He took Driskill's briefcase, a gesture of welcome. He was a tall, stoop-shouldered man, who gave the impression of viewing from on high, whatever the object of his gaze. His face was pinkish, his eyelashes pale, his eyes a warm blue.

"Nice of you to meet me, Larkie. Don't tell me it's out of sheer good fellowship."

"You holding up all right, Ben?"

"No, now that I think of it. I wish Drew were here."

"So do I, Benjamin. So do I. He'd be of great help."

They had turned and were walking toward the vast entrance where taxis seemed to shift their shapes and quiver in the waves of heat writhing upward from the sidewalk. At the far end of the line of cabs, a black limo waited in a pool of shade. Huge, billowing white clouds were piling up over Washington. A man was standing in the median, staring at them malevolently. He didn't look like a voter. More like an assassin. He wore a T-shirt with a legend written across it.

**It's Not the Heat.
It's the Stupidity.**

Larkspur was moving on. "Well, one is always working, isn't one? Two weeks to go." He smiled distantly. "What we have on our hands, besides a terrible personal tragedy, is a political PR problem."

"It's a mess."

"You don't know the half of it, young Ben. Not the half of it." His pink jowls draped for a moment over his brightly flowered bow tie. It resembled a small, very exotic bouquet. He had a quick, ready smile, and it was always a surprise when his face collapsed into concern.

"What's that supposed to mean? I hate it when you're elliptical."

Larkspur waved to the driver to stay in the car and opened the door for Driskill himself. The sun was desperately bright, something vengeful, and even in the shade the doorframe was painful to the touch as Ben climbed into the car. The windows were tinted, the leather cool, the air-conditioning throbbing, and he took a deep breath while Larkspur settled himself and tapped on the window partition to let the driver know it was time to go.

"I can't steal the President's thunder. He wants to orchestrate this meeting. He's going to put you in the big picture in his own way. The polls are not going up. But the campaign was in trouble enough before, Ben, and now this . . ." He plucked absentmindedly at his tie and cupped his chin in his hand, a characteristic pose when he was thinking. He was tapping his fingers along his jawline. "Dammit, I'm trying to stop smoking. It's a bitch. I've got one of these nicotine patches. I know it's going to work— and I'll be damned if I'll let some quack hypnotize me. No, sir, it's the patch for me. I can do it. Anybody can." He often presented his thoughts as if he were back pitching a PR account in the old days, before Larkspur & Company had straddled the English-speaking world. He was a salesman who specialized in ideas. His genius, his stature in the world—everything stemmed from his ability to make the abstract real and palpable. He always argued that what he did was simply educate people. Make them see the situation in the correct way, turn the facts carefully so that they might be seen from all the telling angles, and the rest would follow. He did it all very well. He had helped Ben at the time of Hugh Driskill's violent death, and they had been friends ever since. They didn't slobber all over each other, but both acknowledged the bond of affection that had begun growing with the passing of the elder Driskill. Only Larkspur and Drew Summerhays, from among his friends, had been invited to attend Ben and Elizabeth's wedding in the little family chapel on the Driskill estate in Princeton. "Things are bad, Ben . . . but"—he recovered with a less than robust smile—"we'll be equal to it in the end, I pray God."

What Driskill was hearing in the back of the limo was the concern that Larkspur guarded jealously and would never reveal in public. Even alone with the President, he was careful to expend no more unpleasant truths than need be. Of all people, the President needed to be shielded from some of life's harsher realities. His spirits must not be allowed to flag as the great cannons began to hammer away in the final stages of the campaign. Ellery Larkspur would be the last voice to admit defeat. The private slogan of the Larkspur office, as it was called in the manner of a law firm, was his credo: *You will fight until the last dog is dead . . . and if you're not the last dog, you'll answer to me.*

"You're not going to tell me . . ."

"Oh, hell, you'll get the whole thing soon enough. I just wanted to give you some breathing room. I don't want you taken by surprise. The President puts so much stock in your thoughts and reactions—I don't want him to see you drop your jaw and begin to wail and chew the snappy new carpet with the seal on it. But things *are* worse than you know. And be prepared for your audience. Landesmann's going to be there. You, me, Landesmann, the President."

"That's a thrill. What about Mac?"

"Don't mention Mac. He's somewhat out of favor—Charlie doesn't seem to have quite the unqualified trust in him that he once did. It may stem from Mac's affair with Ellen Thorn—shifting their priorities, cutting into the time Charlie wants them to spend on him but, you understand, that's tricky ground. They couldn't spend more time on him if they were celibate. No, Ben, I don't know where it comes from but Charlie is getting a little—dare I say it?—paranoid, these days. Of course, who wouldn't in his position? Hazlitt is feasting on him three days out of four. Maybe Mac is just an unfortunate victim. Anyway, just let it go. I want you to balance the gloom and doom the President keeps getting from Ollie and Ellen. They drive me nuts. Just when he needs all the bolstering he can get."

The limousine veered slowly off Pennsylvania Avenue

and passed through the guard post and moved slowly along the path beneath the arching trees toward the entrance to the West Wing of the White House. To the left, in their accustomed spots, were the correspondents for all the networks and cable services, standing in the burning shade, worn down by the heat. Their lights and reflective umbrellas and sound equipment gave the passing impression of a safari that had made camp and settled in for a long stay. They watched the limo with quizzical expressions. Who was sitting behind the tinted glass? As the car rolled up to the portico and the uniforms came out to hold the door the correspondents peered from their compound, cataloged the arrival of Larkspur, which was hardly news, and Ben Driskill, presidential friend, which probably wasn't, either. Clearly the news of Drew's death had not broken.

Larkspur nodded in the direction of the press, but the heat rendered them unresponsive. He whispered to Ben as they slipped through the moment during which they were visible: "Ah, if they only knew . . ."

"They'll know soon enough," Driskill said.

"Yes, well, let's go figure out what we're going to do."

There was no sense of the outside world once you'd entered the West Wing of the White House. Year-round it was always springtime with vases full of fresh flowers. The functionaries who okayed your arrival as you passed through the scanners were always smiling and making small talk as if they hadn't a care in the world. The smiling black man who passed you through was said to be the strongest man in Washington, a quality that had come into play with one or two obstreperous guests in the past. A guide and a secretary were standing with a famous actress who'd come for a quick hello with the President.

Charlie Bonner had once said that it was very peculiar, knowing that you were standing at the center of the world and yet life seemed to be going on calmly and even happily. "It's an office, that's all, and it's hard to remember that sometimes. There's this tendency to think everything's okay just because everybody's so civil, nobody's killing anybody on the stairway . . . but the truth is you're always hanging by a thread just above the dumper."

Larkspur led the way down the hall and up the stairs, occasionally nodding to someone, murmuring a quick hello. Down the carpeted hallway. Cream-colored walls, paintings of glorious and bloody battles, courageous men charging into the fray. The guards were like pieces of the furniture, like the potted palms. The air-conditioning hummed faintly behind the walls. The Cabinet Room on the left was roped off, the big table visible through the open door, one chair taller and more equal than the others.

Larkspur stopped just short of the doors leading into the Oval Office. "I always check my zipper before going in," he said. He smiled at Driskill. "Went in once with my zipper down and the laundry ticket on my shirttail sticking out. Mrs. Colfax, who was ambassador to the UN at the time, was kind enough not to mention it, but I thought Charlie was having an attack of Saint Vitus's dance." He turned and spoke with the guard. Their names were noted in what the President referred to as the book of the dead, and the guard stepped forward and opened the door.

The President was sitting on the edge of the huge dark rectangle of desk that Teddy Roosevelt had once sat behind. He was in his shirtsleeves with the cuffs rolled up on his forearms. He launched himself off the desk, came toward Driskill with his hand out, and if you didn't look too closely he might have been the kid who'd played football at Notre Dame back when the wheel was being invented and they'd inflated a pig bladder for a ball. His blond hair was now barely streaked with gray and it was due to be colored before the last siege of campaigning. There were crow's-feet at the corners of his eyes and mouth. He always had a tan, either from skiing or golf. He was six feet two, weighed about two-thirty, and looked like he could whip any man in the house with one hand tied behind him. He wore a knee brace beneath his trousers, just in case the old football souvenir acted up on him. If the knee ever gave out on camera and he fell down, he didn't want to have to deal with the ensuing stock market crash.

"Good of you to come, Ben." The telephone on the historic desk rang and Bonner reached back and grabbed it. "What, goddammit?" He listened for a moment. "Oh, all right, all right. But I want updates on American casualties every hour." He looked at his watch. "Later, later. Okay." He dropped the phone back into the cradle and stood up.

"Ben, you know you're top of the list today, but with this situation in Mexico . . . we're also having the daily campaign analysis in a couple of minutes, and I want you both to stay right where you are. I'm counting on you. Now don't get into the Summerhays thing though—I'll tell Mac and Ellen later."

There was a knock at the door.

On his way to let them in personally, Charles Bonner said, "Wait till you hear this stuff."

Bob McDermott had known and worked with Charlie Bonner all the way back to the Vermont days when he'd run a small, aggressive ad agency that handled the Bonner family bank, founded in the 1860's by a previous Charles Bonner, the President's great-great-grandfather. When Charlie entered Congress, then became governor of Vermont, and finally President, he'd always kept McDermott at his side. There had been a natural affinity between them, and thus far it had survived the stresses of Charlie Bonner's rise to the presidency. Now, when Ben stood up and shook hands, he was struck by the bags under McDermott's eyes and the weariness he was battling to keep out of his voice. McDermott always liked to give the optimistic impression that he was on top of everything and loving every minute of it. At the moment, the facade was slipping. His gray hair was drooping across his forehead and the freckles across his nose no longer gave him a youthful look. He looked angry.

"Ben, it's good to see you. Bringing some sunshine, I hope."

"Don't count on it," Driskill said.

McDermott smiled reflexively, but it was obvious his

heart wasn't in it. "It's been so long since we've had any good news, I wouldn't know it if it bit me on my nether regions." His eyes were bloodshot from lack of sleep. He was wearing gray slacks, a blue blazer, blue shirt with a dark red foulard tie, and tasseled black loafers so shiny they looked almost like patent leather. Hands down, the White House contained the shiniest shoes in the known universe, shinier even than the shoes at Bascomb, Lufkin, and Summerhays where they had someone come to every partner's office every morning to administer the requisite polish.

"We're having the last council of war before Ellen hits the road tomorrow. She won't be back in Washington until after the convention. Boston's next for us all." He was a smooth-featured man, always perfectly turned out, his clothing fresh as a daisy, no matter how tired he was. The only flaw was the faint whiff of cigarette smoke he carried with him, impervious to cologne. His voice, too, bore the distinctive crack of a heavy smoker. A seeker of company, a man who enjoyed long bull sessions when there was an opportunity, he'd been known to do justice to single malts and small-batch bourbons, as well as playing a sound hand of poker with a treacherous ability to bluff you out of a big pot when the going got tough.

With him came Ellen Thorn. She was a political strategist from Stanford and Harvard who'd been a newspaper columnist, a consultant to lobbyists, and finally a gun for hire in the business of getting folks elected. She had made a name for herself with a string of upset victories for her clients, including three senators who were facing what seemed like sure defeat and a would-be governor who came from behind to win going away. She had come aboard Bonner's team in his last run for governor and played a key role in his successful presidential campaign against the incumbent Republican, Sherman Taylor. She may have been the only person in the room with a truly ruthless flair for politics, the killer instinct: She was no gentleman, as her opponents were always saying. She was nearly forty, trim, with short black hair, piercing black eyes, and a sexy, lopsided grin. She wore heavy tortoise-framed glasses that made a great prop. Today her red suit was reminiscent of Chanel.

Ellery Larkspur was speaking with her in the moment's interval as they were reconstituting themselves in a semicircle around the President's desk. The afternoon beyond the tall windows had darkened. The rain that was beating up on the East Coast looked like it was about to begin again. Larkspur was ticking off items on his fingers. Ellen had a reputation for being much at home with unpleasant news. Larkspur did not: He was the spin doctor, the man who could see rays of hope in any situation. He believed that if the messenger was going to get it in the neck for bringing bad news, he—Ellery Larkspur—was sure as hell going to see things through a different lens. At the moment Driskill was quite sure he was encouraging her to calm down her rhetoric. "You have to keep the candidate hopeful," he'd often said. "Otherwise, he'll just drift away and never be seen again. They get to despairing and their egos are so huge and so fragile, they just die on you." Ellen Thorn, on the other hand, had a reputation for figuring that they were big boys and they had better learn to take the bitter with the sweet.

Driskill just wanted to keep himself distanced from the campaign conversation. It was all part of his not wanting to give in to Charlie's urging. The rain was now running down the long windows and the thunder claps came powerfully and there were spindly shafts of lightning in the purple sky.

They had begun analyzing Ellen Thorn's overnight poll numbers and adjusting the coming week's schedule to accommodate the less-than-promising results. They were arranging a tour of buses, the equivalent of a whistle-stop campaign, which would trek across the country to Chicago, featuring prominent national Democratic figures and the President himself when he could hit the trail. It would produce a lot of TV coverage. It struck Driskill as desperation planning.

"I think we have to face the music," Ellen Thorn said

in her tight-lipped manner. Larkspur was frowning, hand cupping chin. "The best-case scenario at this point is that we're going to make some history this summer. Best case, we'll be going to Chicago with the nomination still up for grabs. It's been more than half a century since there's been an open convention. Our polling figures show that since New England there's lots of movement in the polls, nothing too big—we've got to start landing some haymakers or Hazlitt's momentum with the delegates is going to win it for him. We did what we had to do in New England, we denied him the prize . . . and now we have to reach deep down inside and take it away from him in the horse-trading and arm-twisting at Chicago."

Charlie looked as if he weren't appreciating her disquisition much, but she kept boring in. "We've got to be prepared for him to come at us as dirty as he can—he *is* winning. He's been winning ever since he announced and we have refused to take him as seriously as we should." She meant that Charlie hadn't taken Hazlitt seriously enough. "Charlie has always had a strong following in Pennsylvania, Massachusetts, and New York, and we got the tie in the New England primaries. But all of Hazlitt's poll numbers are going up, and ours are going down. We're going to have to fight for every delegation, every vote, delegate by delegate." She sighed. She'd gone through all this before with the same students, but she believed it would be irresponsible to let up. Without her, they might refuse to acknowledge just how drastic the situation was. They might suck up the relative hopefulness Larkspur was dribbling on them and if they did, they were lost. "I bring it up again so it won't come as a surprise. There's no point in worrying about it—"

The President smiled and made a face, said, "What? Me worry?"

Everybody chuckled but Ellen. She didn't give the slightest damn about presidential horsing around. You horsed around once you were reelected.

"You're going to have to do something decisive, maybe

in Mexico. Your policy doesn't seem to be working with the people, all our figures show that."

"What do you suggest, Ellen? Would you like to see me leap in and turn it into something more than a civil war?"

"The electorate is very much up in the air about your visit to Mexico and the chaos down there." She stared back at him. "Maybe Hazlitt's right on this one. Lots of people like his position—"

"Like hell he's right," the President fired back. "He's a trigger-happy cowboy—"

"It would have been a good idea if you had shared the State of the Union Address with us." It was an argument that had been going on for months.

"Not that again . . . I knew you were opposed to it."

"That may be, Mr. President, but you're not going to carry out any policies at all if you're not reelected. Then we *will* be in a war."

"Well, thank you for that small gem of wisdom, Ellen."

"I'm very serious, Mr. President."

"Oh, you needn't remind me. You're always very serious, Ellen."

"I'm not saying you're dead yet, Mr. President."

"Ah," he said, "a ray of light from the lady with the blowtorch."

He couldn't scare her off. She ignored him. "These figures haven't been turned into delegate voting results, not yet. There's avalanche potential for Hazlitt, but there's also the chance we can squeak out a win. That's what we've got to aim for and . . . you *are* the President. That's our best card. That alone will control some delegates."

McDermott looked up from a clipboard full of computer printouts and handwritten notes. "Hazlitt and you, Mr. President, are both going to try to beat each other to the punch now—the polls are going to be very volatile. All we can do is our best . . . we've got a good strategy." He looked pointedly at the President. "It had better be, I should say."

"You think so, do you, Mac?" The President was almost grinning.

Ellen Thorn was boring in again. "Given these poll numbers and the downward trend, you have got to develop some momentum going into Chicago. A speech about the World Bank or even the war in Mexico won't do it, toxic waste won't do it, forget another crime or welfare or drug plan—nobody believes any of that crap anymore, no matter who's president—"

The President slammed his open hand down on the desk and everybody jumped but Ellen. "Jesus, Ellen . . . I'm not an idiot, I have some vague idea of what I'm doing! Christ! We're way beyond speeches at this point! We've got to twist arms and I've got to make people see Hazlitt for what he is!"

Ellen Thorn wouldn't back off. It wasn't in her nature. Driskill figured that the death wish inside her was too strong for her own good. "Mr. President, you can yell at me all you want, but the electorate knows they're going to be fucked by the government—that's a given. They're just deciding which fucker they like best." Larkspur winced. Driskill fought off a smile and looked down at his shoes. "You either give these delegates something to get 'em to the polls, something that'll make 'em say, Well, that Bonner's one smart or tough or exciting son of a bitch and maybe we oughta make sure our delegation votes his way, or the next day you're finished. That's the brutal truth."

The President had turned in his high-backed chair to watch the rain and lightning. He was fiddling with a presidential seal ballpoint pen. Ellen Thorn wasn't finished.

"In the end, you can listen to us all day and night and I can strategize and Mac can schedule airplanes, trains, and buses until he throws himself under one of them. Ellery can fret about rumors and Oliver can shut his eyes to the whole thing and be avuncular . . . but at the end of the day, it's up to you. If everything goes right, you've got a chance. You have to make them *love* you. Some politicians can dazzle them with their footwork and brilliance, but you're more like a movie star, it's all emotional, they have got to *love* you, plain and simple."

Driskill had seen Charlie Bonner lose his temper. He

wondered if they were now in for one of his explosions. He let his eyes move away from the President's tightly clenched jaw, began surveying the portraits on the walls, the President's personal choices. Ulysses S. Grant dominated the room, the President's personal hero. Great general, mediocre president; historian and writer of genius. And Franklin Roosevelt, a large black-and-white photograph with his cigarette holder at a jaunty angle. On the desk, alongside photographs of his wife Linda and the two kids, was a picture of Joe DiMaggio and Ted Williams, flanking the then-governor of Vermont, Charles Bonner, and inscribed by both of the long-retired baseball greats. "Presidents are a dime a dozen for the most part," Bonner had once said, "ordinary men with a hunger for power, but DiMaggio and Williams, they're for your whole lifetime. Their greatness is forever. Which is the rarer talent, Ben? Getting some votes or doing what they did? Case closed, amigo."

The explosion didn't come. The President stood up and nodded to Ellen and Mac. "Very bracing, as always. Keep me up to date on all the polling numbers, Ellen. But leave the speechifying to me, please. Mac . . . no need to keep you two here any longer. I've got some things I want to speak with Ben and Larkie about." He was seeing them to the door. They looked somewhat relieved at his reaction to Ellen's remarks.

By the time he'd returned to the desk his face had lost its tone and he looked his age. He turned to them, voice cracking as he spoke.

"Thank God, that's over. But . . . I don't know what to say about Drew. It's hard to take it in." He turned away for a moment, as if giving in to deeper feelings, then turned back and threw his long arm around Driskill's shoulders, shepherded him to the bulletproof windows looking out onto the Rose Garden. "We knew he wouldn't last forever, but this . . . We've got something real nasty, real hundred-proof nasty. I need your help, Ben. Understand?"

Driskill nodded. Already Charlie was laying the trap, calling on his old friend.

"This is for Drew, Ben." He paused. Ben willed him to stop, but it didn't do any good. "That's what it comes down to."

He picked up the phone and said, "Mary Lou, tell Ollie to get his ass in here."

Ben felt himself bristling. "What's Landesmann got to do with my making a report to you?"

"Well, hell, Ben, we need a lawyer in on this—"

"I know it's hard to keep everything straight, Mr. President, but think back—I'm a lawyer. Law degree, everything, the works."

"Don't get your shorts in a bunch, Ben. You're *involved.* Ollie's—"

"*Involved.* That sounds ominous."

"Well, you were there, you left the scene of a violent death. Technically this is a cover-up, if you see what I mean. Ollie's distanced. Objective."

"The President of the United States told me to get the hell out of there. Told me not to tell anybody. Seems to me like there are two of us involved." He hated this part of it. The jockeying, the covering your ass. "Three . . . Larkie was there. And, hell, four with Linda." He and the President had known each other for more than thirty years, but the point was, one of them was President and the other had left the scene of a violent death. Bonner was always the President, and the person he was dealing with was always a potential human sacrifice. It just came with the job.

"Nobody's trying to hang you from a lamp pole, Ben. It's just that we've got a problem and I think the White House counsel ought to be in on it. Relax. We're going to handle it."

They'd been talking about the death of Drew Summerhays, and after a moment of emotion and sorrow it had become a problem, something to be *handled.* He felt the President's hand on his sleeve. He was both repelled and flattered. He knew he was being seduced and part of him liked it. He hated that.

Oliver Landesmann came into the Oval Office from the cubbyhole where Mary Lou Daniels, the President's secretary, reigned more or less supreme. Landesmann was the White House counsel—that is, the counsel to the office of the presidency—whereas Drew Summerhays had been Charles Bonner's personal legal representative. Landesmann was a Washington insider of imposing credentials. He was short and rotund with tight curly gray hair. He usually sat motionless like a little Buddha with his hands clasped across his tummy and habitually let his eyelids flutter shut. You'd swear he was asleep but he never, ever was. He had a smooth voice full of the lubricant of persuasion. He wore half-glasses on a chain around his neck. He positively loved making evildoers squirm with his questions. During what came to be known as the Alabaster Industries hearings it was said that he had "publicly executed, in a courtroom, four self-aggrandizing gentlemen of the Reagan revolution and the go-go eighties." Thereafter he had been known not merely as a legendary insider but as a man who'd appeared on the cover of *Time*. A mighty hero of the liberals. One of the Law's celebrities. He knew, however, that the job of counsel to the President had been offered first to Ben Driskill, who had turned it down. Only then had it passed to Landesmann. And Oliver Landesmann was not accustomed to feasting off the leavings of others. Inevitably the relationship between them was never much more than civil.

"Ben," he said. Landesmann's small, well-manicured hand was lost in Driskill's huge paw.

"You're well, I hope, Ollie."

"I've been better. Politically speaking. Otherwise my bad cholesterol is down, blood glucose down, and the prostate medicine is working. I was only up twice last night." His sleepy eyes flickered across Driskill's face. "But I'm sure the only thing you ever worry about is maxing out those testosterone and adrenaline levels."

"All I have to do is come to Washington. Always makes me want to grab somebody by the throat and beat hell out of them."

The President laughed softly. "You guys kill me." An aide appeared with a pitcher of iced tea, tall glasses with ice cubes and a sprig of mint in each one. There was a faint taste of raspberry as Ben replaced some of the fluids he'd lost on the steamy train.

The President called the meeting to order. "Ollie, I've kept you in the dark because I want you to hear the story from the horse's mouth. Namely, Ben. I want your fresh reaction because we need some legal advice, some options. We don't want to get caught with our pants down but— well, I'm getting ahead of myself." They were all seated, the President in an armchair upholstered in hunter green with gold piping, Larkspur and Landesmann on the print couch with leaves and vines intertwined with some kind of goldish pillars, Driskill in a chair more or less matching the President's. The seal of the presidency was woven into the new beige and dark green rug. Abe Lincoln and Harry Truman and FDR were watching from their pedestals. Over the fireplace hung a large portrait of a naval battle dating from the Second World War. The Battle of the Coral Sea. The President had found it in storage and brought it up. His father, Thomas Bonner, as a young lieutenant (j.g.), had survived the battle, and the picture, with a small engraved oval beneath it mentioning that fact, had been resurrected in his memory. "Ben, you go ahead and tell us the tale."

Driskill, for the first time, recounted the whole business, from his inability to meet with Summerhays the previous afternoon, through Larkspur's call of concern over the old man's health, through the finding of Drew's body, the call from the pay phone to the White House and the discussion with the President and Larkspur, on through finding the advance copy of Ballard Niles's vicious column, and his leaving the island in the morning.

Landesmann opened his eyes when the story was finished. His hands remained clasped across his tummy, which rose and fell slightly as he breathed. "Well, Benjamin, was he murdered or did he kill himself?" Otherwise he showed no concern about Summerhays's fate, though he'd known him all his professional life. Ollie Landesmann carried the concept of the poker face to almost ludicrous extremes, as if to show emotion might somehow weaken his powers of reason.

"It *looked* like suicide. But . . . that doesn't hold together for me."

"And you touched nothing?"

"Nothing in the greenhouse. I wiped everything I touched in the house. Which wasn't much."

"I'm confused by your reasoning. It looked like a suicide. You found the Niles column with the photographs which might have upset Drew a great deal—it was a scurrilous attack, Drew was very old, Larkspur says he was exhibiting some worrisome behavior . . . whatever. Drew was shocked when he read it, feared for his reputation, wandered out to the greenhouse so as not to make a mess in the house, and shot himself." He paused for effect, as if he were trying to win the case with his summation. "It looked like a suicide. It smelled like a suicide. It walked like a suicide. I'm baffled as to why you seem to think it could have been . . . murder."

"Frankly, I think we'd have trouble arguing it was an accident, Ollie."

Landesmann ignored the observation. "It seems to me you're looking for trouble where, yes, there is trouble but not the kind you're proposing. What makes it murder?"

"Because only a few hours before he was perfectly normal, his mind was occupied with something he wanted to talk to me about, something having to do with 'our friend in the White House,' as he put it, which he thought was very important. We made plans to meet for breakfast Monday. He was in no mood to kill himself. That's the way it seems to me."

"But let me submit," Landesmann said, eyes drifting to half-mast, "that when you spoke with him at your office he had not yet read Niles's column, and it seems not unreasonable to assume that the column so distressed him that he did what would seem the unthinkable. That's how it appears to me."

"We differ, Ollie. He wouldn't let a shit like Niles do him in."

Landesmann smiled. "Now we come to your leaving the scene. I must tell you, Benjamin, I am not overjoyed to hear this."

"Well, my God, that *is* a blow, Ollie." From the corner of his eye Driskill saw the President frowning, shaking his head at the squabbling children. "Look, it was the best thing to do. Nobody could have known I was there—"

"Please, no absolutes. Never absolutes."

"That's an absolute, Ollie."

"Well, it's the only good one. If it comes out . . ." He shrugged. "Get out the hip waders because you'll be in the deep and smelly, my boy."

"Right along with Charlie. And Larkie. I'm getting just a wee bit tired of being the patsy here, y'know what I mean? They told me to tell no one and agreed I should get the hell off the island."

"In a hypothetical sense," Landesmann murmured, "that would be very difficult to prove. In any case, they're not lawyers . . . you are a lawyer. For God's sake, didn't you have even a doubt or two?"

"Oliver," Driskill flared up, "open your goddam eyes, will you?" They popped open. "I know what the law requires me to do in that situation. I also know that a man closely connected to the President had just died violently. I had found the body and I too am connected to the President. I did what I thought it was best for me to do. And I had to think about the President's interests. I chose to protect a president who's having a real tough time of it in a brutal campaign. Now there's no point in going on about—"

"Well, my friend," Landesmann interrupted, blinking, "there *is* a point. You have now told us that you've done something you shouldn't have done for purely political reasons, *partisan* political reasons. I don't like to think what either the Hazlitt wing of our own party or our Republican friends might do with that tidbit. You have also told the President. Under oath, should there be an investigation of this suicide, if there's anything untoward, we would all be forced to tell the truth. You should have considered that. Now we have a problem."

"So many George Washingtons in one room! Amazing. And it's all bullshit!" Driskill knew he was in danger of going over the top. Landesmann, after all, was making a valid point. Which was exactly why Ben hated hearing it. "I left no evidence that I'd been there, and you're so damn sure it's a suicide, an obvious suicide, not a homicide, what's the big problem? You're beginning to piss me off, Ollie."

"Am I really? Furthest thing from my mind, Benjamin." Landesmann clucked and closed his eyes, folding his hands across his Phi Beta Kappa key and chain. "I think you're on testosterone overload—better be careful or you'll pop an artery. I'm merely pointing out the facts. Whether or not they piss you off, Benjamin, is of little concern to me. What you did could be interpreted with considerable validity as the beginning of a cover-up. Plain and simple. I'll say no more."

"In the nick of time," Driskill said.

"You boys getting all the crap out of your systems?" The President was staring at them, and his face had lost any touch of humor.

"I don't understand," Larkspur said thoughtfully, turning the problem, looking at another facet. "No note. If Drew had decided to kill himself he'd have left a note. If only for those of us who were close to him. He would have wanted us to understand. He was no more of a candidate for suicide than I am. Egomania keeps all of us going. Once you get through your fifties and sixties you begin to think in terms of living rather a long time. Drew was looking forward to the campaign, the conventions, the election—he thought in terms of the future. . . ." He shook his head, stood up, walked slowly to the window.

The President had been rereading the fax of Niles's column that they'd passed around as Ben told the story. He wiped his eyes with a fresh white handkerchief and cleared his throat. "Ben, I appreciate your thinking of what might be best for me, for this office. And I acknowledge Oliver's point but . . ." He shrugged. "Your heart was in the right place, Ben."

Driskill didn't like Bonner's tone of voice, as if he were forgiving his pal for a lapse in judgment, but he knew Charlie was just trying to placate Landesmann. Driskill said, "I think we'd better take a pretty close look at those photographs in the fax. Oliver, if you think you'll be compromised any further by taking part in this discussion, why don't you go away—"

Landesmann laughed softly. "Now, don't be that way, Ben. I'm not the enemy. As counsel to the President, I've got a job to do, too. And it's not myself I'm worried about being compromised. There's only one person in this room who matters a tinker's damn, if you see my point. I've had my say. Plunge ahead. The damage—if any—is done." His little round eyes, well open, were twinkling.

"But you're such a pain in the ass."

"Please, counselor, go ahead."

"These photographs. Drew with Tony Sarrabian. Does any of us know what he was doing with Sarrabian? The meeting between them was the point of Niles's column. Sarrabian lives over in Virginia in those mansions he stuck together. When was Drew here? Larkie? Did he see you? Call you? Was there a meeting with you, Charlie?"

"No," the President answered, "no meeting with me. He hadn't actually been down to see me in months. We did our business over the phone. I think he'd come to realize that too much traveling didn't do him any good. Larkie?"

Larkspur shook his head. "Maybe they were old photographs? Niles is the kind of mongrel who would use anything . . . dredge up old shots . . . fake 'em for all we know."

The President said, "But why would Drew have been talking to Sarrabian at any time? He's not exactly Drew's style. And who would give the photos to Niles? There's something going on here and we are just seeing the fluffy tail going out the door. Who the hell faxed this thing to Drew? There's no indication of the sender."

"I must say," Landesmann murmured, "I am quite taken

aback by the piece. The virulence was extreme even for
Niles. But that same virulence is everywhere, Mr. President. Arnaldo LaSalle, what passes for a television journalist these days, is running all over town saying that he's
going to make the sky fall on you this weekend. The rumor
is absolutely everywhere but nobody seems to have a hint
as to what it concerns—"

"So what else is new?" the President responded wearily.
"That bastard has been after my hide for six months—
honest to God, I think he just makes stuff up."

"But surprising numbers of people believe him," Landesmann said softly. He turned back to the subject at hand:
"And I am disturbed by those photographs of Drew and
Sarrabian. Of course this is just a fax, and they *could* be
doctored. . . ."

"There were no clues about LaSalle's rumors?" The
President couldn't quite get past Landesmann's remark.

Larkspur said, "Don't pay any attention, Mr. President.
There are always rumors and there's not a damn thing anybody can do about them. They come and go—"

"More often than not," Landesmann interjected, "they
stick. At least in part. Merely my observation."

"Anything these bastards say, Niles or LaSalle or anybody else, it always seems to stick." The President shook
his head. "Go on, Ollie."

"Back to Drew, then. I probably knew him least well of
anyone here, so don't start screaming at me—but what if
Niles's accusations, vague as they were, weren't lies?" He
held up his small hand as if to cut off any dissent. "If Drew
was up to something, something none of us knew about
. . . well, maybe Niles was cutting too close to the bone.
And Drew took his own life rather than face disgrace or
worse. Is that possible? Of course it's *possible*. And I'm
only suggesting that we consider all options, that we not
be blinded by our affection for the man."

Larkspur set his empty iced tea glass on the table and
came back and stood looking down at the others. "But
what is Niles accusing Drew of here? Of having his picture
taken at Sarrabian's estate? So what? I've been out there

half a dozen times what with one thing and another. The President and First Lady have attended Sarrabian's spring garden party. We've all been guests at one time or another."

"Damned if I have," Driskill interjected. "I just don't move in the right circles, I guess."

The President said, "And I say good for you, Ben . . . but let's face it, you're not part of the hurly-burly down here. People in Washington need money, Sarrabian is a conduit for money. American money, foreign money—and he gets it into the campaigns more or less legally. Maybe less, on the whole." The President was making a point. "Take out the slimeballs in this town and the social life would be cut in half. And campaigns would be running on credit cards. I've been seen with lots of people . . . that's all Niles is accusing Drew of here. No, it must be something else—and I say, bottom line, Drew just wouldn't kill himself. No way. Not Drew Summerhays. In the first place, Niles couldn't have had anything on him because there wasn't anything to have. Drew *never* left footprints. He was too careful. Ben—I think you're right on the money."

"You're saying he was murdered?"

"That's *exactly* what I'm saying."

The President went to the drinks table, took ice out of the refrigerator beneath the table. "Anyone for a bracer?" Landesmann had departed for another meeting. Only Driskill and Larkspur remained. They both assented and he plunked ice cubes into leaded-crystal glasses, splashed Bombay gin over them, added tonic and lime wedges. "*This* is what's going to happen to us on the weekend. *This* is what Ollie's rumor was about. Drew Summerhays, my personal lawyer, the head of the DNC. The Sunday papers tomorrow and all the TV shows will be full of it." He sighed, sipped, rattled the ice. "What's that going to do to Mr. and Mrs. Undecided Delegate?"

"The problem," Ellery Larkspur said, "is that there won't be time for a dead-cat bounce. We'll still be going down in the polls if there are big investigative pieces in the Sunday papers. Or series investigations during the week. And you can count on the *Times* and the *Washington Post* to do it big and prominently. There'll be no time to rebound."

"Wait a minute," the President said. "How can LaSalle's rumor be true? How could anyone know this was going to happen? They're not psychics out there—"

"You've got a helluva point," Larkspur said. "*If* this is the weekend disaster they've been predicting the last day or two . . . then they must have known Drew was going to die. And you're right, Mr. President, that's impossible. Isn't it?"

The President looked up slowly. "Unless they killed him. It's not impossible—if they were going to *make sure* we had a problem this weekend." He shook his head. "Am I nuts or did I just suggest something totally crazy? We haven't come to killing each other in the name of the two-party system, have we?" He waited. "Still, somebody killed him."

They sat silently, watching rain streak the windows. The air in the Oval Office was clammy. But cool.

The President was switching subjects. "Ellen Thorn is getting on my nerves, folks. Bright but a little too straightforward. Sometimes I need to be . . . shall we say *handled*? She's like a goddam cancer diagnosis. We're going to survive, that's my opinion, but if we don't, if we get to the convention and our head counting shows we're whipped, we're going to have to pack it in."

"Please, Mr. President, let's not bury you so quick."

"It's disaster management, Ellery. Nothing should come as a surprise. Ellen's right about that. When we're surprised, the other guys have a huge advantage. That's all. Now . . . what do I say about Drew?"

"The usual. Distinguished service to his country, a dear friend, we shall not see his like again."

The President was recovering his energy. "There'll be a big funeral as soon as they release the body. I'll attend. There'll be some sympathy in that, I suppose. Drew's last gift to the party. Ellery, you may have to eulogize him. I don't want to put myself through that. I don't want to start blubbering on TV. And what about his will? Does he have any family? Is there an executor? Ellery, will you check out all that for us? Or, Ben, what am I thinking about? That's really your bailiwick at the Bascomb office. Look, we've got to hit the ground running tomorrow. I'll be in Florida—the delegation is up for grabs." Where did he get the reserves of energy? Maybe it all came from the well of ego that made him believe he should be president.

The President looked at Larkspur. "Go on, Ellery."

"Hazlitt has a big rally at Faneuil Hall in Boston, then goes to New York for a fund-raiser tomorrow. You're going to Boston for the first of the week, then up to Sugar Bush. Then we regroup in Washington, then it's on to Chicago . . . that's about it, Mr. President."

The mood had gone from depression to determined optimism, and Driskill didn't quite understand how the trick had been managed. It was politics, getting the scent in your nostrils and going with it. Laying back your ears and charging, the hell with the civilians. It was the politics of the underdog. Ben was not a political animal, he didn't have the instincts, but he'd picked up a bit along the way. And even he felt the adrenaline starting to pump.

Charlie had taken three very large cigars from the humidor and clipped them. Larkspur turned down the cigar while the other two lit up, filling the room with the heady blue smoke and the rich aroma. He'd put the bottle of gin and the ice bucket on the desk where they all could reach it and the drinks had been freshened. Beyond the windows the clouds had further darkened and the streetlights were on, as were the lights on the White House grounds. The rain was pelting the windows. Ben and the President sat at opposite ends of the long couch, their feet up on the coffee table. Ellery Larkspur had slipped off his jacket, pulled his tie loose, and it dangled limply. His collar was open. He seemed supernaturally calm, but that was his style.

"Ben," the President said, "I'll bet you thought I was going to drag you down to Washington and sink you into this mess of ours. Isn't that about right? Now tell me the truth."

"The thought had crossed my mind, yes."

"Well, pal, you can relax. This isn't a little campaign advice I need. I have to clean up a mess, and you can be the biggest help to me by going back to New York, taking over at Bascomb, Lufkin, and Summerhays. You know where the firm has always fit in the overall idea of the party. We need you to go back there and stabilize things now that Drew is gone. You're going to be running that place now, one way or another."

Charlie Bonner got up, steadying himself on his bad knee, and grabbed his hand. Charlie was a great hand-shaker, always had been. Sometimes in college he'd see you walking across campus, half an hour since he'd last seen you, and he'd grab your hand, pump away. Just for the hell of it. Driskill was never sure if the human touch was giving power to you, or drawing power to him. Maybe it worked both ways. That football team would have run through the proverbial brick wall for Charlie Bonner because they all knew there was no quit in him, so there couldn't be any in them. "Old friends are best friends, Ben. I promise you, I've got no secrets from you. You're not going into battle with a broken lance. You know what I know."

"Well, let's keep it that way," Ben said. "One thing bothers me. You seemed awfully damned sure Drew didn't kill himself. Where's that coming from?"

The President tapped his head and then his heart. "Just makes sense to me, I guess. But with you in New York, you'll be able to liaise with the cops, who are certainly going to want to talk to you. You're Drew's successor, you had an appointment with him for breakfast Monday. Keep your ear to the ground, pick up anything you can. You can find out if they're treating it as murder. We'll be in constant touch, if you don't mind."

"All right, Charlie." The President had been right: He was surprised that he was going back to New York. Surprised and relieved. He'd be reading about the campaign, not putting his foot in it.

"You're a pit bull, Ben. Good for you!" He looked at his watch. "I've gotta put Mac in the picture on Summerhays or he'll spontaneously combust. Have a good trip back, Ben. Larkie, I want you to hang around and take the heat off me if Mac has one of his fits. In fact, why don't you go get him and bring him in, soften him up." The President, having accomplished his mission, was moving on, the telephone to his ear. He waved as Larkspur and Ben Driskill left the Oval Office.

"I just don't believe it," Driskill said softly. "I've escaped. Free at last."

"Well, don't be too sure. Washington has a way of sticking a hand up out of the grave and grabbing you." Larkspur was chuckling. "And he's not kidding, he wants you to keep us current on what's going on up there with the Summerhays investigation. Frankly, I would hate to entrust our intelligence gathering to Ollie Landesmann."

Chapter 4

I n the hallway outside the Oval, Larkspur turned to Driskill. "After the President does poor Mac, I'm going to work on a eulogy that Charlie—or I, if I have to—can give at the funeral. If you need me, or just want to talk, give me a call."

"Where?"

"At my house in Virginia. I'm worn out. We were pretty much up all night after your call. I caught a little nap about six this morning. And Charlie's worn out from the flight from Mexico City—"

"How big a mess is that down there?"

"Couldn't be much bigger, Ben. I didn't go, mind you. But I've talked to Linda—she visited all the hospitals, she's lobbying now for more medical aid, more doctors. I can't believe the committees will turn her down but they'll wrangle for a while. Charlie met with the president of Mexico and his military people and some of the other Central American leaders—we've backed the peace process. Charlie is worried that maybe we backed the *wrong* process, that there's no way we can get a handle on what's happening down there." Larkspur shrugged. "I'd kill my sainted grandmother for a cigarette. Dammit, it's all in my mind."

Bob McDermott came around the corner from his own office tucked back behind the Oval and stopped abruptly. He was slipping back into his blazer.

Larkspur shook his head. "Not so fast, me young bucko.

Greatness awaits you in the Oval Office. I was dispatched to bring you personally."

McDermott cocked his head. "No hints, I suppose? Gimme a minute, Larkie, I'd like a word with Ben."

Larkspur nodded and leaned against the wall next to the doors to the Oval. He was humming one of Mercer's songs, "Laura." Not many people knew he was a fine jazz pianist. He stuck his right hand into his trouser pocket, tinkling the change. "Don't go far, boys. Use the Roosevelt Room."

McDermott turned to Driskill: "I just got a call from the attorney general. She wants you to call her back. Here's the private number. She's over at Justice." Mac was pulling Driskill into the empty Roosevelt Room, out of earshot of anyone who might be passing.

"Thanks, Mac. I'll take care of it."

"I got the idea she's upset. Something she saw on TV. Look, Ben . . . there's something I need to talk to you about. Can we have a drink later? Where are you staying?"

"I'm trying to get home, Mac."

"Look, this is serious. What about seven o'clock over at the Willard? You can still catch a train."

Driskill didn't want to meet Mac or anybody else for drinks. McDermott could see it in his face.

"This is *very* serious," Mac said. "For me, for Charlie, for Ellen . . . I have to get this off my chest." He whistled a long sigh, bloodshot eyes flickering back and forth. "He's waiting for me . . . look, just one drink. I'll look for you. Seven o'clock, Ben."

"Okay, okay—you'd better get in there."

He nodded. "I wonder what the hell he wants." Larkspur opened the door and ushered the chief of staff into the inner sanctum.

Driskill imagined the conversation, the President telling him that Summerhays was dead. Mac was in for an earful. He turned and headed down the hallway toward Mac's office and asked his secretary if he could use the phone. She said, "Certainly, Mr. Driskill," and pointed to the privacy of Mac's office. The door was wide open. The desk and the floor were stacked with towers of papers, folders, notebooks, newspapers, magazines, and books. A forest of paper. He punched in the numbers and the telephone was answered almost immediately. "Yes?"

"Hi, pard, it's me. Ben."

"Oh, Ben . . ." She sounded as if she had a cold. "I've been crying—I just heard a news flash about Drew. Did you hear it?"

"I know he's dead." He hadn't expected the news so quickly.

"Is that why you're in town? Somebody told me today that you had a sudden meeting scheduled with the President."

"Yeah, that's why I'm here." What did you have to do to keep a secret in this town, anyway?

"Are you free now?" He had always loved the soft, sinewy voice of Teresa Rowan, formerly of Bascomb, Lufkin, and Summerhays, now attorney general of the United States. She was a daunting woman: had been a successful fashion model while she was in college, the first African American partner at the Summerhays office, and the first of her race and only the second woman to be attorney general.

"For a couple hours," he said.

"It's so awful about Drew . . . isn't it, Ben? Such a shock."

"Bad news."

"Are you finished with the President?"

"Yeah, finished."

"Why don't you come over to Justice—I need to talk to you. This has hit me really hard."

"Can you warn the crew downstairs I'm coming? Last time I came over there, they did everything but proctoscope me before they'd let me in."

"Because you're such an asshole," she whispered.

"Noel Coward would be so proud of you—"

"I'll tell them to be on the lookout for New York's most distinguished lawyer."

"Actually . . . he died last night."

Larkspur had made sure the car waited for Driskill. The rain was drumming down, bouncing off the parking-lot tarmac and the long black car. The press corps had gone to hide in the press briefing room. The heat had not abated. He lounged tiredly in the cool leather of the backseat, watching the sweeping of the wipers moving through rain that clung to the glass like sludge.

Would Charlie make it, could he pull one out of the hat again? Driskill couldn't really read the signs, take the pulse and blood pressure of the electorate the way Ellen Thorn could. It had seemed almost as if she cared more than Charlie did. It was just that they had different styles. Ellen Thorn was going at it the wrong way.

Teresa Rowan was waiting for him in the long room on the fifth floor, the one Bobby Kennedy had used for his office. In the years since Kennedy, succeeding attorneys general had used it as a conference room. It had a certain grandeur in its proportions, which tended to intimidate even the most egomaniacal holder of the office; and all had been aware of its place in history, almost as if it somehow now belonged forever to the martyred brother of the martyred president. Upon her appointment and confirmation, Teresa Rowan had wasted no time in making the room her office, precisely because it had once been Robert F. Kennedy's. He was one of her heroes, maybe her first hero. And she wasn't the kind to forget.

Her stature within those corridors of power stemmed not only from her gender and color and the acuity of her brain and the canniness of her judgment—it stemmed from the fact that Drew Summerhays simply adored her. He respected her, he was impressed by her, he enjoyed working with her, and by God he was enchanted by her.

She was small, the color of *café au lait*, with elfin mischief in her features and in her glittering obsidian eyes. Her hair was always cut short like a bathing cap of black points across her forehead. She was trim and precise and perfectly organized and exquisitely put together. She could be a brat and get away with it because she was black and beautiful and too smart and too funny and too stinging in her attacks: None of her potential critics wanted to take her on *mano a mano,* and that number included some people Driskill would never have climbed into the ring with himself.

When she was tapped for attorney general, it surprised her that the press made such a big deal out of her race. She was a distinguished attorney who had worked in a few of Drew's very sensitive areas—the government and, specifically, the intelligence community. Her record and background made her a logical candidate for the Department of Justice. She even had supporters who wanted her on the Supreme Court. And yet it was her race that had put her on the cover of *Time* and *Newsweek* and *The New York Times Magazine.*

She hadn't married. Career had come first: The demands had been intense and enjoyable. She had fancied herself in love with Ben Driskill a long time ago at the Bascomb office. And, really, who more likely than one of Drew Summerhays's protégés, one from a different generation? They were both single and conventional enough to find the black-white thing intrinsically thrilling. Driskill became her confidant, a second mentor after Drew himself, an ally in her career climb. And after a year of overwhelming work, the relationship metamorphosed into a deep friendship. They both acknowledged that marriage was unlikely—he had not yet begun his final struggle with the Church, had not yet lost his dear little sister, had not yet met Sister Elizabeth. They were both incredibly busy, more often than not exhausted by the demands of work, and quite unable to perform the care and tending of a romantic relationship.

So, they chose to be friends.

All of it was flashing through his mind as he walked across the vast office and saw her coming toward him. It had all been a long time ago. When he put his arms around her for the customary hug, he felt her firm body rising on tiptoes, felt the small high breasts and the delicate bones of her shoulders and back. Desire flared in his mind and she looked up, her grin slow and impish, her eyes so shiny. She was thinking what he was thinking. And then she was letting go, the smile slowly fading. She sighed: "What a day, what a day!"

She led him back across the crimson-figured carpet to her desk, a long table where she sat with her back to the bulletproof windows and the large fireplace to the left. The soiled spots, just noticeable in the pattern of the carpet, had been left years ago by Bobby Kennedy's dogs, who'd go to work with him and the kids on Saturday and sometimes didn't get walked when they needed it most. Looking at the fireplace, he could imagine the picnics Bobby would have in the office with his kids on those weekends. They'd make hamburgers over the fire and you could smell the cooking all the way down the halls outside. A long time ago . . . history. The players long gone from the front pages, from the stage.

"I'm trying to deal with Drew's death as best I can," she said. "I had to see you, there are things . . . we need to talk about. How is the President taking it?"

"Well, he's got a helluva lot to worry about at the moment."

"You're telling me—you don't know how much he's got to worry about."

"What are you talking about?"

"Ben, the *campaign* . . . If I'm burned out, think what it feels like to be the President. And my work out at Langley. This has been brutal." She sighed.

She led him into the little room behind the big office. It had served as Janet Reno's office during the Clinton administration, and Teresa had left it much the same, except that it was now a kind of reading room. The carpet was the same creamy off-white that had to be shampooed every two weeks. All the pictures from Reno's term—so many of them taken in the countryside, with friends and with her mother out in the Florida waterways—were gone, of course, replaced by similar family shots reflecting Teresa's life. He saw one shot of himself with Teresa, standing at the rail the night they took one of the Circle Line cruises around Manhattan. They were smiling and he had his arm around her with the skyline lit up in the background.

She led him on into yet another, even smaller, room with black leather furniture and a television set and refrigerator and wet bar. She made them each a vodka and tonic. Gin had always given her a headache.

"I found his body."

She flinched, looked up.

"You? I thought it was the chopper pilot or the houseman—"

"No, I was there first."

"When?"

"Middle of the night."

"Why?" She couldn't seem to believe her ears. A second question broke to the surface: "Does the President know?"

"I called him when I found the body. He told me to get the hell out of there and not tell a soul. He wanted me here. So I came."

Her face was registering bewilderment, sorrow, shock, and he told her the whole story. She asked all the same questions, suggested the connections, excoriated Ballard Niles and the campaign of rumors that dogged the President. She leaned back in the leather chair, crossed her legs, unbuttoned the navy jacket. It had big crested gold buttons, braid on the sleeves, a stiff navy collar. She'd been around long enough now, had seen enough, that she could submerge her grief over Summerhays's death. She'd already moved on, past her private emotions.

"I wish I'd had the chance to talk again with Drew," she said. "I've been hearing from various quarters that the Republicans are thinking about asking for some kind of investigation into these blind rumors, investigations of the White House and Drew, regarding some vague improprieties. There have also been people who want an investigation of Bascomb, Lufkin, and Summerhays—no, I'm not kidding—all about undue influence on policy, favors for clients. Surely 'for the good of the country.' House Minority Leader Arch Leyden, for one, is supposed to be planning a visit with me, a little chat—you've heard him, that high brittle voice, *Is there some factual cause for all these rumors? Are we sitting on a powder keg?* He's going to ask me for a special prosecutor out of the Justice Department. Anyway, I did talk to Drew about ten days ago concerning the condition of the campaign, and he said we'd have to start planning a series of defenses to build around the administration—but first he stressed that we need to find out what we're defending against. The President's a target in a shooting gallery, a silhouette against the painted moon, that's how he described it. We were going to talk again soon." She swallowed against the sudden urge to cry.

"Then I talked to him again," she continued, "about a week later, three or four days ago. I was prepared to have a substantive talk about our worries. But he wasn't as specific as I'd expected him to be, he'd been so insistent that we talk, and now it was all general and vague. I thought at the time that it was as if possibly he'd spoken to someone else, someone he trusted more in some way, and decided to cut back what he was prepared to say to me. Anyway, he said the whole campaign against Bonner was . . . sleight of hand, he called it. Now you see it, now you don't. I remember his exact words: 'We're all at risk, every single one of us. We are all sitting on a potential meltdown. I've never seen anything like it.' He actually said that, and he'd seen everything for a million years. Never seen anything like it."

"Like what? Never seen anything like what?"

"He wouldn't go further," she said. "But he did say, just before he hung up, 'Don't think you're immune, don't think you're safe, Tessa, because you're not. You're hanging by the same thread we all are—these are serious problems.' Ben, he was right on top of things, but it was like he couldn't get to the point, or the point was too big or nebulous or awful for him to get to. Then when I heard the news this afternoon, somebody from CBS called me for a reaction. I gave the standard couple of sentences but my first thought was, whatever he'd been warning me about had made him a victim. And you discovered the body and got the hell out."

"He wanted to talk to me, too—about the President—he said Charlie was in the soup but he, Drew, thought we could help him out. I wish I knew what he was talking about."

"You're on tricky ground if anyone finds out—"

"Landesmann's already been after me on it."

"He's never forgiven you for being Charlie's friend."

"I had to keep the President out of it."

"I'd have done the same thing. But, still, you have begun a cover-up. There's danger in it. But it means nothing if nobody finds out you were there. Who knows?"

"The President, Larkspur, Ollie Landesmann, and I think Charlie told McDermott and Ellen Thorn later."

"And me. That's six. A lot of people if you want a secret kept." She noticed he hadn't touched his drink. She plopped another ice cube into it.

"I've had enough iced tea and gin and tonic to float a battleship," he pleaded. His head was beginning to throb.

"If it makes you feel any better, I'm just as guilty of a cover-up. I'm the chief law enforcement officer in the country and I'm bending the rules for you. I sometimes wonder how long a person can go on in this job and keep looking in the mirror in the morning. Dammit. It's a cover-up, Ben. The top people in this government now know you found Drew's body and skipped out because of politics." Suddenly she grinned. "And so it goes, senior partner. Politics."

"The President and Larkspur told me to leave the scene—"

"Prove it, big boy."

"That's what Landesmann said."

"Not exactly a surprise."

"Look, the last thing Drew read was a fax of a Ballard Niles column that's very critical of him . . . that won't run until Monday. Nobody sent you a copy, by any chance?"

She shook her head. "Who would send it to him?"

"Nobody knows. But here's what the President thinks—he thinks that Drew was murdered. He's serious."

"All right, Ben," she said after a long, ruminative pause,

"here's what I think. I think the President may be right. The Drew I spoke with may have been scared . . . but he was up for the game. He was excited. He was ready. He wouldn't kill himself."

"Well, that's my feeling but . . . I'm out of it. Charlie told me to go back to New York and take over the office—deal with all the Drew stuff. Keep my ear to the ground." He shrugged.

Finally she put her hand on his knee, stared into his eyes. "You're always your own man, Ben. But Charlie's playing you like an expert fisherman. Don't get too comfortable in New York, that's all I can say. When he needs you, hell won't have it until you're on board. You think you're out of it and free—and you're an old friend of Charlie Bonner's—so it's going to be hard for you to accept what I'm about to tell you. But he's still got you right by the balls, my friend. All he has to say is, *I tried to keep you out of it, Ben, you know I sent you back to New York . . . but now I need you, pal.* Your commitment to him is deeper than mine. It's older. But you'd better believe what I'm about to tell you. You can't trust anybody, Ben. Remember that. What was it about Prince Hal and Falstaff? You and Charlie Bonner have heard the chimes at midnight. You've been friends and drunk of the night. But . . . but he's the President of the United States. He'll do what he has to do to survive and stay President. That's all that matters. He's *already* got you covering up a murder and we've just begun to try to find out the truth. You remember what Drew told us that no president ever realizes or understands? He told Charlie Bonner on the eve of his inauguration, *Don't get too comfortable, son. Before you know it, it'll be time to go. We're all just passing through.* Presidents begin to think they belong where they are, that the job will last forever—and they'll do anything to hold on to it."

"This evening one of America's great men lies dead on Big Ram Island at the end of Long Island in New York. Drew Summerhays, ninety-two years old, a political powerhouse throughout most of the twentieth century, was found dead today in the greenhouse of his magnificent estate. He apparently died by his own hand. Our Geoffrey Dickason reports from Big Ram. Geoffrey, there seems to be a good deal of mystery surrounding Drew Summerhays's passing. What's going on out there?" John Hunter was anchoring and began a two-way split screen with Dickason, who was a young comer at WCBS in New York.

"It's *all* mystery, John. Mr. Summerhays's body was found by the man who takes care of this big house, along with his wife. His name is Burt Molder." The shot expanded, taking in the front gate of the estate now guarded by highway cops with several patrol cars drawn up, blocking the road. "Mr. Molder, tell us what you found when you arrived here this morning."

Burt Molder kept rubbing his snuffling nose. "I couldn't find Mr. Summerhays when I got here so the wife and I had a look around. The door to the greenhouse was banging—we went out and found him. He was dead." Molder was a sixtyish man in a Big Yank work shirt. He needed a shave. "Shot himself, I guess. Don't make sense to me, I gotta tell you."

"The weapon was beside his hand?"

"Well, there was a gun there, course. I don't know. I suppose it was the gun. . . ." Suddenly tears were streaming down his face. "He was a fine man. Drew Summerhays. I've never known a better one."

"Thank you, Mr. Molder. Now, John—it may or may not be an open-and-shut case of suicide. The police are not saying much of anything. They've been in the house since about ten o'clock this morning. Doing *what* we just can't say. What we do know is that Mr. Summerhays intended to take a helicopter back into the city early Monday for breakfast at the Harvard Club with one of his law partners. Summerhays was, of course, a close political adviser to President Bonner. That's about all we know at present. Back to you, John."

Hunter wouldn't let him go yet. "Is anybody saying anything about Summerhays being *so* close to President Bonner?"

"There isn't much to say. And there is no official spokesman for Summerhays, though my guess is that his law firm, Bascomb, Lufkin, and Summerhays, one of the most prestigious firms in New York City, will have a spokesman out here by this evening."

"And finally, Geoffrey—are there any theories as to why Drew Summerhays might have taken his own life?"

"Not yet, John." Rain was drizzling across the camera lens.

"All right, thanks, Geoffrey. We'll obviously be tracking this story very carefully. Again, Drew Summerhays is dead this evening, the result of a gunshot wound to the head. Within the hour, in Washington, White House Press Secretary Alexandra Davidson has met with the media." Cut to Alexandra in a somber blue blazer, standing at the lectern in the press briefing room downstairs. Alexandra's voice began:

"The President is deeply saddened at the passing of his old friend and longtime adviser. President Bonner, upon receiving the news, said, and I quote, 'Drew Summerhays was a giant during times when giants stood all around us and also at times when his was the only great shadow cast by a man in this country of ours. We have all been blessed by the great length of his life, almost seventy years of which was spent serving his country. His legacy is all around us— America at peace, economically powerful, setting a moral standard that is the world's standard. The world will miss him as a leader. I shall miss him almost the way I miss my own father.' "

Ben Driskill sighed. "I miss him a helluva lot more than I miss my own father. . . ."

Britt Yamamoto, the network's polling expert, was reporting. She was striking and poised, but to Ben she looked like she should have been in grad school someplace. She was speaking to the unseen anchor.

"Things are looking increasingly grim for the President, John," Miss Yamamoto said. "On the basis of our overnight polling, the President's lead in New York and Pennsylvania—roughly ten percent a little over a month ago—is now at about one percent, which as you know is well within the boundaries of statistical error. Which means that, basically, President Bonner and challenger Bob Hazlitt are in a dead heat in these two huge states where primaries were fought so recently, and it's Hazlitt who is on the uptick. I spoke earlier today to Clark Beckerman, chairman of the Democratic National Committee, and he said he's not worried, the new guy on the block always gets the attention. But, he added to me, it's his belief that when the delegates at the Chicago convention cast their ballots, they'll remember all that President Bonner has done for them and for this country and do the right thing." Miss Yamamoto looked doubtful, though no less beautiful than she had a few seconds before. "I also checked with Arch Leyden, the Republican minority leader in the House, who was speaking here in New York today, and he would say only that it looked real good for Hazlitt, and his Republicans would just have to keep hammering away. He didn't make clear whether he meant on behalf of Price Quarles or by following the swing to Bob Hazlitt among the Democrats. Clearly a Hazlitt nomination would drain votes from the Republicans. John?"

"One thing, Britt. Did anyone say what effect they thought the news about Drew Summerhays might have on the convention?"

"No, John, that news hadn't broken yet. But we should have something for you tomorrow."

It was still raining when Ben's car let him off before the Willard, which had been restored and refurbished to its original splendor, maybe more so. The marble and the potted palms and the gleaming brass made the lobby one of the most beautiful in the world. In its glory days the Willard had been the presidential hotel, the center of an enormous amount of Washington's political life. It was less so now. Time had moved on, other key spots had come into being. But the look of the place was a showstopper. Driskill crossed the lobby with a glance down a long hallway lined with perfect palms, receding like an exercise in perspective, and took a right, hooked around a corner, and entered the small Round Robin Bar that had long been presided over by Jimmy, the man Gore Vidal had called the greatest bartender in the world. Jimmy was at his post, seen through the groups of people converged around the bar. He was polishing something or other, breaking off to build a drink or decant one of the wines he so loved. The tables were full beneath the caricatures of the Republic's great men.

Driskill pushed through the crowd and found a stool at the bar. There were two senators five or six seats away, and the chairman of the House Appropriations Committee was holding court in one of the corners.

"Good evening, Mr. Driskill. Good to see you back in Washington." He might have been a regular. Jimmy's memory was phenomenal. "I'm terribly sorry about Mr. Summerhays. We saw a lot of him here at one time."

"Thank you, Jim."

"What can I get for you?"

"Vodka and tonic, weak as a cat, if you please."

Jimmy was clinking ice cubes into a tall glass. It was a relief to hear his calm, measured voice. With a little prodding, he began telling Driskill about a journey he had made not long ago to his favorite California vineyards. It was mesmerizing. He knew which grapes grew on which sides of the roads in which vineyards, how much sun each field got, everything.

"Well, what do you hear these days, Jim?"

Jimmy, having put the drink before Driskill, kept his eyes on the perfect Manhattan he was making. "Things are getting a little tense in this town, Mr. Driskill. I've had people tell me something big is coming down. I can't help hearing, you know. Don't know what it is—but I've been hearing this one for several days."

"Maybe it was Mr. Summerhays's death?"

"No, that's shocked everyone. No, this is something political."

"Good?"

"For whom?"

"The President."

"Well, that's not the way I hear it, Mr. Driskill."

"Guess we'll just have to wait and see."

"Ah, here's Mr. McDermott—I'll leave you two alone."

"Not until you get me a vodka collins, Jimmy." McDermott moored himself at the bar. "Ben, you know Jimmy—Gore Vidal's favorite!" Driskill nodded. "Jesus, Ben, what a rotten day." McDermott's face was flushed and he was perspiring across his forehead. "Rotten, fucking . . ." He didn't sound right. Then it occurred to Ben that Mac was drunk. The chief of staff was loaded.

"You sound like a man who's had a little liquid consolation. You're right, though. It was a pretty bad day." Less than twenty-four hours ago he'd found Drew in the greenhouse.

"Oh, it's bad enough about Drew, sure, sure . . ." Mac was speaking slowly, carefully. "But what frosts me, personally, I mean, y'know, *personally,* is that I'm practically the last man in Washington to hear about Drew! Honest to Christ, it was on goddam television before the President tells his chief of staff—how the hell d'ya think that makes me feel? Shit. I don't know about Charlie these days. Sometimes I think he's freezing me out." He lit a cigarette, cupped it in his shaking hands, blew smoke into the air over his head. He was having a little trouble focusing his eyes. He waved the cigarette, shrugged heavily. He took a deep drink. "You knew all about Drew, right? He told you, got you down from New York—it was important that Ben Driskill know, and to hell with his chief of staff."

"I knew."

"Well, fuck yourself." He was squinting through the smoke. His hair was hanging down in his eyes. He looked a lot older than his years. His hair had gone gray during the campaign four years ago. His hand holding the cigarette was trembling.

"You asked me to come here to tell me to fuck myself?" Driskill was sliding off the stool, ready to leave.

"Come on, Ben—Jesus, don't be so sensitive." Mac was caving in as if someone had pulled a string inside him, as if he were a hollow man. "I'm sorry . . . you're right, I've had a couple of drinks . . . gimme a break, Ben. I need to talk to you, I'm not kidding." He was tugging on Driskill's lapel.

"Well, get a grip, for God's sake. Your getting drunk at the Willard isn't going to be much of a help to the President."

"May I say, without offending your tender sensitivities"—he was stumbling over the words—"that today I don't really give a damn about helping the President?" He took another long swallow of his drink. He slid a handkerchief from his back pocket, dropped it, laboriously leaned over to pluck it from the floor, and patted his forehead. "Just fuck him, that's what I say. I need your help, Ben . . . or he's gonna make a terrible fucking mistake." He was whispering. Jimmy glanced over, caught Driskill's eye, shook his head. "Somebody's got to tell him that he can't leave me out in the cold and take hold of this campaign himself. He'll fuck it up." His mouth was nearly touching Driskill's ear. "Over the last few weeks I'm always the last one to know." He belched softly into his fist.

"I don't know what I can do about it, Mac. He hasn't told me about it either." So this was it. McDermott—drunk or sober—wanted someone, a special pleader. It would be like walking into quicksand. Driskill knew if he did it, he'd be swallowed alive by the process, he'd be in the campaign for good. "I'm just passing through. I've gotta catch the train back to New York tonight."

"Come on, Ben, you're his oldest friend. You can't just walk out on me, on us. I'm not suggesting you do anything drastic . . . just a word at the right moment." He mopped his face again.

"I don't know, Mac—"

"Listen to me, Ben . . . he's gonna lose. Big-time. Everything is going against him. Hazlitt's squeezing him and the juice is running out. He's turning on his closest allies. Me . . . and Ellen, for instance. He's gonna fire her ass because he can't take all the bad news. He's gonna kill the messenger." He grabbed a handful of cheese fish from the bowl and chewed. "If he fires Ellen, I might as well tell you, I'll probably go, too."

His affair with Ellen had begun in the early days of the first campaign. His wife had a bookstore in Maryland and didn't much concern herself with Mac's comings and goings. She was an heiress. Maybe it just didn't matter anymore. There was no doubt in anyone's mind that Mac and Ellen loved one another. He was a Catholic and, for him, that was a problem when it came to the idea of a divorce.

"Mac, I'd think twice before I did that. Maybe she gets on his nerves a little—she can be pretty abrasive when she puts her mind to it."

"He said something to you! Well, if he wants a cheerleader—and somebody he can fuck—he can always find somebody, he's the President for God's sake."

Driskill had never seen McDermott so bitter, so combative.

Driskill shook his head. "I'm just heading out of town. I'm not going to be seeing him again. I really don't think—"

The talk was burbling all around them, Saturday night on the town.

"You're out of it—that's the story?"

"That's the truth, Mac."

"Bullshit! You're such a smooth bullshitter, Mr. Fucking Sincerity—no, wait, I'm sorry, Ben . . . just wait . . . but you *are* a smooth New York lawyer, your type always thinks they know every goddam thing, all you big-time insiders—"

"You're mixed up, Mac. I'm as far from being an insider as it gets—"

"You're the insider, hotshot insider, but you can't trust Charlie anymore. Hell, I'll bet you don't know about Hayes Tarlow—hunh? Right? He didn't tell you about old Hayes, did he?"

"What are you talking about?"

"See, Ben—he's got secrets from everybody! He's playing everybody against everybody else . . . and he's screwing himself up. Just himself."

"What about Tarlow? He's a friend of mine—he worked for us. . . ."

"He was a friend of yours, old chum. *Was*." He was whispering again, mopping his face. "He's dead as a fucking doornail. The old warrior has cashed 'em in. Coupla days ago. Dead. Old Hayes is dead!"

McDermott's elbow slipped off the bar and the ice in his glass spilled across the polished surface. He began to lurch off the stool, would have fallen if Driskill hadn't stood up and taken his arm. A few people nearby noticed, whispered to one another without taking their eyes off Bob McDermott, one of the President's men.

Hayes Tarlow . . . Could Hayes be dead? Hayes and Drew dying at the same time?

"Mac, you need some sleep. You're all worked up, everything looks terrible to you. Time to go." He gave some bills to Jimmy, who had materialized like the spirit of hospitality.

"You'd better get him to bed, Mr. Driskill. He's a time bomb tonight. He could wind up in the papers."

"You're right, Jim. Mum's the word."

Jimmy nodded solemnly. He was possibly the most discreet man in Washington.

Mac sighed, slumped on the stool, finished his drink. He looked at his watch. "I gotta get back to the office. The great man may shummon me at any moment."

"Let me come with you. We'll grab a cab."

"Ben, old chum, I gotta make a call from the lobby. You get the cab."

Driskill waited in the lobby, watching the people in the lights of the marquee waiting for cabs on the glistening rain-slick street, watching McDermott. He had his back to the lobby and was hunched over the phone. Driskill knew he was calling Ellen Thorn.

His shoulders were shaking as if he might be crying.

Jesus, it just got worse and worse. And now Hayes Tarlow?

Chapter 5

Driskill guided Bob McDermott out of the lobby of the Willard and into a cab. "Where the hell we going? Help, Officer, I'm being kidnapped." He laughed softly, worked his tie loose, pulled the handkerchief out of his pocket again, and slowly mopped his forehead, then the rest of his face. He fumbled for a cigarette, gave up. "I don't feel all that great, Ben, if the truth be known. Where we going?"

"I know a place. You're gonna love it."

"Not that place, Chief Ike's Mambo Bar . . . Room, whatever . . . not that place, is that the name? Ben? Hello? You there, old buddy?"

"I got another place."

McDermott fell asleep about thirty seconds later.

They got to Dupont Circle and stopped in front of an elderly four-story town house that still looked like the home of a doddering multimillionaire. Driskill emerged from his dark, dire thoughts about Hayes Tarlow, his growing anger that the fact had been kept from him, paid the driver, and spent several minutes trying to shake McDermott back to life. "Goddammit, Mac, let's get with the program here."

It was pouring rain. He didn't want to be in Washington. And he certainly didn't want to be shepherding a drunk through the night. Most particularly not the White House chief of staff. And yet, he was. He truly had hoped to get back to New York. He hadn't wanted to go to the apartment Elizabeth kept in Washington. She was there a good deal of the time, and he used it on those occasions when he had to be in the capital. It occupied the second floor of the town house. He'd never felt at home there; when he was alone he found it particularly troubling. It reminded him of Elizabeth, reminded him that he hated being away from her, and away from her was where he usually was.

He helped Mac up the stairs and into the blindingly overheated apartment.

"Jeez, hot in here," Mac mumbled.

Driskill stood him in the corner. "Stay, boy. Stay."

He turned on the Friedrich in the living room window, then the matching unit in the bedroom. While they whirred and blew out cold air and began dehumidifying the place, he went back into the hallway and found Mac still standing in the corner, snoring softly, sound asleep. He walked him across the room to the couch in front of the fireplace and then folded him at the knees and stretched him out on the couch. Did Mac do this often? He hoped not. It had to be the stress of the day, his concern about Ellen and being left out of the loop by Charlie. It just had to be.

"Thatta boy, Mac. Sleep the sleep of the just. It has been a long and trying day."

Mac snored, belched in a gentlemanly way.

Driskill sat down behind the desk by the window at the far end of the room, looking out on the garden and the sycamores rising up past his sight line. He punched the buttons on the answering machine, listened.

There were two calls for Elizabeth, not counting his own, just in case she showed up in Washington, which made it clear that she was in Los Angeles for another day or two covering the "Women in Politics" who were convening and wondering if Charles Bonner had done enough for them. Theirs was the number one cause, the only cause that mattered, and God help you if you didn't pass their litmus tests. It was always the same, no matter what the group. Good luck, Elizabeth. . . . Then, another voice came on the line, friendly, with a midwestern inflection. "Mr.

Driskill. This is Nick Wardell in Saints Rest, Iowa. I don't know if you remember, we shook hands four years ago at the convention. You might want to give me a call, as soon as you can."

Driskill immediately dialed his home number in New York and picked up essentially the same message. Then he got up and went to the kitchen and found the instant iced tea. He stirred the mixture in the glass, lots of ice, and went back to the desk.

Quickly his mind refocused on Hayes Tarlow. He'd known Hayes for years. He'd done a lot of investigative work for Bascomb, Lufkin, and Summerhays. Summerhays had introduced them, calling Hayes "a shamus, Ben, a footpad." And Hayes had laughed: "He means private eye, Mr. Driskill." Together Driskill and Summerhays had recommended him for Democratic National Committee and White House jobs. And, unless Mac had it all screwed up in his stupor, Hayes was dead. Hayes and Drew . . .

Mac snored peacefully, muttering something every so often, then seeming to forget it. Driskill sat at the desk thinking about Elizabeth now, damning Washington for taking her away from him so much of the time. She was always hinting that he might want to involve himself again in politics, in Washington, the way Drew had. She never badgered him, just left the hints in his path like perfumed, frilly undergarments leading up a staircase to the treasures beyond. Elizabeth . . . Well, today should strike her as pretty wonderful on the deeper-into-Washington scale. But in the end she'd be disappointed.

He leaned across the desk and flicked on the little TV in the corner. Sipped his tea. Right, there it was . . .

Arnaldo LaSalle's *On Deadline* was just coming on. Ben Driskill lit a cigar from the stash in the refrigerator.

You had to understand about Arnaldo LaSalle. He was the latest thing. He was a hate merchant. He posed as your friend, the friend of the people . . . indeed, the *voice* of the people. The *mind* of the people. But he thrived on hate,

drew life from it, like a spider needs heat. When he hated
the people you hated, he was a hero—if you could live with
yourself in the morning. Otherwise, he sent lawyers scurrying to their books and precedents, looking for a way to sue
the sonuvabitch off the edge of the planet. Nobody had
managed to stop him yet, but every time you saw him, you
couldn't help but wonder. The public loved him. His ratings were great. Hate, hate, hate. The new aphrodisiac.

Arnaldo LaSalle had bent the meaning of the First
Amendment so far out of shape that it looked like a Mob-
ius strip, a license to kill. LaSalle made his show work by
saying or implying anything he pleased about anyone he
noticed, anyone darting across the day's news, anyone who
might draw viewers, although with his show based in
Washington, politicians tended to be his main prey. Some
people Ben knew watched the show because they thought
it was funny, Arnaldo was basically an entertainer. It was
entertaining, he supposed, in the sense that a public drawing and quartering might be entertaining.

Thus far Arnaldo had gotten maximum usage out of the
flood of rumors that had been trying to drown Charlie
Bonner for the past six months, but he'd come up short on
facts, results, blood. But tonight's show held the promise
of red meat on a hook, dripping on the floor.

Within a couple of hours of his staff in New York getting
the news of Drew Summerhays's death, chartered helicopters in stormy weather began circling the estate on Big Ram
and shot plenty of video of the goings-on within the gates.
LaSalle himself had flown up and gone to the estate and
been turned away by security guards and cops while he
shouted out questions about what they might be hiding behind those gates—what were they afraid to let the American people see? It was all on the videotape and it was
classic LaSalle. Now, on television, the first words out of
his mouth immediately put the Arnaldo spin on the ball:
Somebody with power and money was hiding something
juicy from the American people. Arnaldo didn't know
what it was but somebody was trying to screw the peo-

ple—the real people—and he for one was pissed. Somebody was going to pay.

From the Arnaldo LaSalle obituary file came a Summerhays film history dating back to the first term of Franklin Roosevelt, moving along with him through World War II and helping put Europe back together via the Marshall Plan and on through JFK and LBJ and Jimmy Carter and negotiating with the Ayatollah's terrorists and then on to Bill and Hillary Clinton and his final post as a presidential adviser with Charles Bonner. When that was done the camera turned again to LaSalle in the wind and rain outside the gates on Big Ram where he stood solemnly.

"Inside these walls, out of sight of your eyes and mine, the death of Drew Summerhays is being cleaned up and sanitized and made ready for public view. He'll lie in state and flags from one end of this nation to the other will all fly at half-mast and notice will be paid to the life of this man. But the secrets of his death will be kept dark and deep, smothered in one of the usual cover-ups. What are they afraid of? Where might these secrets lead us? Already there are rumors that the police are not satisfied with suicide . . . my informants tell me there is no back-blow on his sleeves, meaning that he didn't pull the trigger—is that true? And an *On Deadline* exclusive report! We know who Drew Summerhays planned to meet with first thing on Monday at the Harvard Club—none other than his law partner and President Bonner's oldest friend, Ben Driskill, who is slated to assume Summerhays's position as godfather at Bascomb, Lufkin, and Summerhays. What is going on between the lines here? Was Drew Summerhays murdered? You may recall that I predicted several days ago that disasters awaited the Bonner campaign this weekend—obviously I could have known nothing about this terrible tragedy . . . but what else awaits the Bonner campaign? Together, you and I are going to find out . . . and let me tell you right now the question that's on the lips of political insiders tonight is simple. Does the mysterious death of Drew Summerhays lead all the way back to the White

House? To the troubled administration of President Charles Bonner?

"Tomorrow night we'll have more . . . right here . . . *On Deadline* with Arnaldo LaSalle." Music up and out, a roll of drums, martial music for LaSalle's army of viewers, as LaSalle turned to stare past the gates toward the fogbound mansion beyond.

Driskill was sound asleep when the telephone rang. His eyes snapped open, registering the view of the rain streaming down the window, and he remembered McDermott sleeping in the living room and knew he didn't want to deal with waking him up from a binge. He grabbed the phone in the middle of the second ring. Maybe it was Elizabeth. The bedside clock said it was eleven o'clock, only eight in Los Angeles.

He answered the phone almost eagerly.

"Is that you, Ben? This is Charlie." He sounded like he wanted a good long talk.

"Yeah, it's me, Charlie."

"You weren't asleep, were you?"

"No, of course not. I never sleep when my nation needs me."

"You're lacking in reverence, sonny—"

"I'm lacking in sleep, Charlie. Now since we're such old pals and all"—he took a deep breath—"let's cut the bullshit. Why the hell didn't you tell me about Hayes Tarlow? He was a friend of mine—he worked for the Bascomb office—"

"What about Hayes Tarlow?" The voice of the President had grown suddenly cool and remote.

"That he's fucking dead, that's what about Hayes Tarlow! What are you trying to pull here? Am I the enemy? Why shouldn't I know? Am I getting the big chill here?" His mouth was dry. He was trying not to wake Mac but he was pumped. He wanted to throw something through a window.

"You're not the enemy—don't be childish. I need to be able to count on you at all times."

"What's to count on if I don't know anything? How good is the advice of the uninformed, dammit?"

"You've got to be patient, Ben. Can I level with you?"

"It's your only hope, I promise you."

"Okay." The President was having another drink. Driskill could hear him sipping, could hear the ice. He never showed its effects. Never. "You're not going to like this—"

"I don't like any of this already. Get to it."

"The fact is, odds are you're about to become the big Numero Uno at Bascomb, Lufkin, and Summerhays. And I have to tell you—that's going to be a full-time job and I'll tell you why. Because two men have died mysteriously in the last few days . . . Drew and Hayes Tarlow. Everybody knows Hayes worked for Drew and was a troubleshooter for the administration. There are ties to the White House if they dig deep enough . . . and they will. The problem you've got is this . . . a real pall is about to be cast over the Bascomb office. The firm is going to look bad, there's going to be intense media attention—"

"Where did you get such a silly-ass idea? Oh, wait . . . oh, Jesus, it's Ollie! Ollie's been bad-mouthing the firm, and you just swallowed it whole! Charlie, maybe you *are* losing it—"

"You've got to get over this thing you've got with Ollie. The White House counsel simply pointed out to me some simple facts. What's so terrible about being worried for your firm's reputation? He's right, Ben, plain and simple."

"He's full of crap, plain and simple, and he hates our being friends. He thinks he plays second fiddle to you and me—it drives him nuts. This little job of sabotage should put his mind at rest."

"Look, you didn't want to get involved in this Washington stuff, anyway—so what the hell are you bellyaching about? And who told you about Tarlow?"

"It's beside the point."

"Was it Larkie?"

"No, it wasn't Larkie—"

"God damn that Mac! It was Mac, wasn't it?"

"I heard it at the bar at the Willard. It's common knowledge in Washington, everybody but me knows about it."

"Don't con me—"

"Charlie, you're gonna have to send the Secret Service to sweat it out of me—"

"Oh, Ben, for chrissakes!"

"Now tell me the story. What happened to Hayes?"

"Take my word for it, I can't tell you now. Be patient."

"Not a chance. Either you tell me what happened, Charlie, or you kiss my ass good-bye. I'm not kidding. I'll never take a call from you again, I won't lift a finger for you . . . I'll be the ex-presidential chum. Believe me. You know me."

"You are one son of a bitch," the President said softly. "You think I *need* you. . . ."

"Tell me what happened to Hayes or say good night, Charlie. And good-bye."

"All right . . . I'm not one to forget the old times. And I hope for better times ahead. So, I'll tell you what happened. You'll be in the picture, if it's so goddam important to you." He took another sip of his drink. "We got word this morning that Hayes Tarlow was stabbed to death two days ago."

"Murder . . . Where did this happen? What was he doing?"

"He was murdered in a town called Saints Rest—"

"Iowa."

"That's right. Iowa."

"Not exactly Tarlow country. What was he doing out there?"

"Meeting a man named Herb Varringer. He wasn't on any mission for us or for the DNC. He was killed, they think, maybe Thursday night. Then Drew died Friday night. I know what you're thinking—was he working on something for Drew? We have no idea. What do you think? Have you seen Hayes lately?"

"No, and I haven't heard Drew mention him in ages. I

think Hayes visited the office last fall sometime. But who's Herb Varringer?"

"Far as I know, he's a friend of Bob Hazlitt's. And a member of the Heartland board."

"Well, what does Varringer know about all this?"

"We don't know because right now we can't seem to find him."

"Tarlow was going to see a friend of Hazlitt's? What's the story on that?"

"I don't know, Ben. All words of one syllable. I . . . don't . . . know."

"How did you find out about the murder?"

"The chairman of the Democratic Party out in Saints Rest called. He'd heard something from the cops who found the body, I think. Anyway, he called Clark Beckerman at the DNC—they know each other pretty well. And Clark called Mac about six o'clock Saturday morning . . . my God, that was this morning. Man, when it rains it pours."

"Any leads on who killed him?"

"None."

"That's why you think Drew was murdered."

"Ben . . . I figure that if they can kill Hayes, they can kill Drew. I say coincidences are bullshit."

"What are you going to do about it?"

"We can't go poaching on a murder case out there in Iowa."

"But Drew—he's my business, real personal business—"

"The hell he is! Now you listen to me, Ben—I can't go into all that with you. You get back to New York and keep everything on an even keel at the firm." He paused, then said, "So, now the slate's clean between us."

"I suggest you keep an eye on Ollie Landesmann, my friend. If you need to use the cattle prod, don't hesitate. If you've got an enemy on the inside, look first at Ollie."

"Good night, Ben."

Driskill heard the click. He was relieved that the friendship had been pulled back from the abyss. Charlie had known he wasn't kidding.

He was too wide-awake to go back to sleep. He went to the kitchen for a glass of ice water, passed Mac sleeping, snoring peacefully. He went back to the bedroom. He had to figure out what he was going to do. Landesmann had trashed the firm, his "family," to the President. Would it now be under a kind of shroud of suspicion? Maybe. If Ollie had anything to do with it. Ollie might leak it to the press. But the Bascomb office could take care of itself. No firm in America could be more imperious and frostily self-righteous than the Bascomb office. The problem was with Hayes Tarlow's murder. What had he been doing in Iowa, Bob Hazlitt's state? Who thought he had to die?

He flicked on the small TV by the bed. Maybe there'd be something from the West Coast. It was eleven-thirty. He found a special edition of *Nightline* and Ted Koppel was speaking, looking very serious.

"Coming directly on the heels of the death of Drew Summerhays, the President's longtime adviser, a death which is tonight being looked upon as 'mysterious' by the Long Island police, we have what may be even bigger, and worse, news for President Charles Bonner. In a speech before the Veterans of Foreign Wars in St. Louis this evening, former President Sherman Taylor has come out fighting, but not for the Republican candidacy of his former vice-president Price Quarles. Less than an hour ago Sherman Taylor threw the biggest bombshell of the campaign—he has switched parties. Sherman Taylor as of tonight is a Democrat, and he has thrown all of his considerable support behind Iowa billionaire Bob Hazlitt, who is challenging President Bonner for the Democratic nomination. Let's take a look."

The screen suddenly filled with a long shot of the stage in St. Louis, then a close-up of the lean, determined, somewhat imperious face of the onetime Marine general, then Republican president, Sherman Taylor: the level gaze, the clear eyes that shone with an implication of leadership, the close-cropped hair with gray at the temples. He was smiling and nodding as the crowd cheered. Then a cut to Taylor in mid-speech, teeth supernaturally white, muscles flexing along his jaw. "You . . . and I . . . know what it means to be Americans in the face of incoming fire. We know that the times are full of peril. And we must find the best man for the job of leading this great nation. Let me say, I hold the honorable Price Quarles, the certain nominee of the Republican Party, in the highest personal regard, and I have a great deal of respect and, yes, even affection for the man who defeated my candidacy four years ago, Charles Bonner. But I must make known, as a matter of conscience, my clear choice for president . . . and that man is Bob Hazlitt, of the great neighboring state to the north, Iowa!" Prolonged applause drowned him out.

Koppel was back on the screen. "We have Parker Dennis standing by in St. Louis and after these messages we'll have a report . . ."

Driskill's head had started to ache. So, yet another shoe had dropped. This had to be LaSalle's rumored disaster. Sherm Taylor, the heroic general who had become president, now supporting a Democrat just to nail Bonner—but how was it going to play? Would the Democrats take heed of the former Republican president? Would he bring any Republicans with him?

Parker Dennis came back on from St. Louis and Koppel asked him what he felt all this meant.

"Well, Ted, I spoke with General Taylor, and he indicated that he expected to fly to Minneapolis tomorrow for a Hazlitt rally at the Hubert H. Humphrey Metrodome. He said he will be onstage with Hazlitt and will, indeed, speak to what is expected to be a crowd approaching fifty thousand. He will then stay with Hazlitt right on through the convention. I think the strategy is for the addition of this bipartisan team member to deny Bonner the nomination by staking out the absolute center of the party's ideology, which is moving to the right all the time. If they successfully move Bonner to the left or make him appear to be playing me-too politics, then they figure his delegates will fall away in great numbers in Chicago. We'll just have to wait and see how it plays, Ted."

Parker and Ted kept talking, but that was all they had to say.

Driskill turned off the bedside light and the TV and lay awake listening to the rain, wondering just how big a fool he was. Teresa Rowan had warned him, the President knew that all that mattered was getting reelected. Anyone could be sacrificed for the good of the candidate.

She sure as hell had that right.

He was having a tough time going back to sleep. Drew dead, Tarlow dead out in Iowa, Taylor suddenly a Democrat backing Hazlitt . . . *Somebody had called him from Iowa. Was it Saints Rest?*

It was thundering above Dupont Circle and lightning lit up the window as the rain streamed down and he was finally just on the edge of sleep.

What the hell was going on?

Chapter 6

The insides of the windows were sweating, condensation running down the glass, the Sunday travelers looking bedraggled even as they started the day—that was all Ben Driskill noticed as he sat back and felt the air shuttle lift off, Washington growing ever smaller far below.

Crammed against a window he went to work on the *New York Times*. It was disorienting, reading their version of events that he had been involved in.

Driskill folded the paper and faced up to considering events that had swallowed him since arriving in Washington the day before—less than twenty-four hours before. The President had asked him to go back to New York and take over the reins at the Bascomb office. To go back to New York and exercise damage control regarding Summerhays's and Hayes Tarlow's relationship with the law firm and, implicitly, the Democratic Party and the White House. So far so good—from the President's point of view. Driskill's out of the way and performing a kind of tertiary function that really wouldn't amount to much. *We can always run old Ben into the game if we need him.*

But the problem was, the President had held out on him. He had called Driskill to Washington because of Drew's death, yet before you could turn around everybody within shouting distance was telling him that *he* was beginning a cover-up. The more he thought about it, the more irritated he became. He knew you had to watch your back in Washington. He didn't need Teresa Rowan to warn him. But Charlie . . . he'd never really entertained the idea that Charlie might set him up just in case they needed a fall guy.

And then Charlie had held out on him about Hayes Tarlow.

And Hayes Tarlow was a man Driskill had grown fond of over the years. A kind of scavenger at the groaning board of politics. An old freebooter ready for anything, up for any adventure, willing to cut some corners in a good cause. Hayes had been a rounder, one of the old school, a man who risked the consequences for his sovereign. The British Empire had at one time produced such men by the lorry load. You owed such men your loyalty and you visited the distant battlegrounds where they fell, you paid your respects to men who had been mentioned in dispatches from the front lines, and goddam it, you remembered men like Hayes Tarlow when the flag went by.

By the time he was back at La Guardia Ben Driskill had reached some conclusions. If the President didn't like the consequences, all he had to do was look back on cutting Ben Driskill out of the loop.

He picked up the Buick at the Penn Station lot where he'd left it, went to the town house, which echoed with its emptiness, threw some clothes into a bag, and headed north on the West Side Highway, then up along the Hudson, through all those pretty little towns like Dobbs Ferry and Tarrytown. He felt better already.

His mind was wandering down other corridors, darting in and out of other rooms and other cities, remembering Hayes Tarlow, who had been quite a character, no matter how you cut it.

Hayes Tarlow was his own creation, definitely as good as fiction, maybe better. It was as if he'd sculpted himself out of smoke and shadows, something of a conjurer's trick. He had a genius for self-dramatization, which made him good company, made you think you were spending time with the real thing, and then later on you found out you truly were. His version of the past was never quite the same from year to year, and there was no checking up on him because everything he'd ever done had been under the table, behind somebody's back, off the books. None of the stories he told you matched up with anything else. But they rang of the truth.

He'd done a lot of strange jobs in his day, most of them in the service of his country, one way or another. "Not exactly the sort of thing they'd ever admit, Ben," he'd said one night at Tommy Makem's bar on East Fifty-seventh. "Deniability's always the watchword when they turn to the last of the Tarlows. I've lived in a twilight world, I promise you. The land called Deniability where you're always on your own, just this side of the Bottomless Pit. Don't worry about me, Ben. That's the way I like it. If I can't handle it, well, that's my problem, and the boys can all drink to the memory of Hayes Tarlow."

That conversation at Tommy Makem's had taken place three years ago. As usual Hayes had just dropped in out of the blue and called the law office and required Driskill's presence at Makem's. He'd wanted Driskill's company to celebrate their own connection with the newly elected President.

They had retired to a dark booth and over several pints of the best had traded war stories of the campaign. Hayes Tarlow had been point man on digging up dirt on the other side when the news came out that Bonner had once upon a time, in some misty past, nearly been charged with beating his first wife. *Nearly* was the key word, since the woman in question had merely been trying to blacken his reputation. Bonner, the young congressman from Vermont some years before he'd become governor, had fought it off at the time and he was going to fight it off again nearly thirty years later as he doggedly battled his way toward the White House. This time Hayes Tarlow came up with a child molestation charge against the incumbent president's chief of staff and blew the phony old wife-beating story out of the water. It turned out that nobody had actually molested anybody, but by the time the *Times* and the *Post* and *Hard*

Copy and *A Current Affair* and *On Deadline* got done with the poor bastard he was on his way back to California and Bonner had been elected. And the opposition had learned that fucking around with Hayes Tarlow's master was a bad idea, indeed. It was the hardest kind of hardball, Hayes Tarlow's favorite game.

"Let's face it, Ben, sometimes it's not so pretty," he had said. "Take our friend Charlie Bonner, nicest guy in the world, but he gets his ass elected president and suddenly he's got magical powers. He can make people . . . *disappear.* So, in case I suddenly disappear, I want you to know a couple of things. If I ever go west, beyond the horizon in search of Amelia Earhart or Howard Hughes, say, figure that I was on a mission for my masters and cashed out trying to do my job." He had smiled, a rich and plummy expression. "We don't want the last of the Tarlows to go forgotten and unmourned, do we?"

And now he'd finally disappeared.

"You're a private eye," Driskill had mused. "The President's private eye. Public payroll. You're in a peculiar position. No medals likely."

"You have it in one, my old dear. *Exactement.* A little job here, a little job there, cleansing the pavement after the hit-and-run. I'm his eyes and ears abroad in the land. I'm invisible. I walk by night." He pulled at his lower lip, then decorated it with the last Lucky Strike in the pack. He hummed, *While I've a Lucifer to light my fag, I'll smile, damn you, smile,* and lit it. "We expect no medals, we who labor in the fields of Deniability." He had seen the look of concern cross Driskill's face and patted his hand. "Don't worry, bucko. I'm at home in the fields of Deniability. When finally I croak, put a smile on my face. I've had a good run. Bury me near a river. I'd like that. Every river is the river of life when you think about it."

Three years ago.

Hayes Tarlow had a secret hideaway. Driskill knew about it only by chance. Did anyone else know, or was he the only one? Most of the time Tarlow had lived out of hotels or at friends' country homes or government safe houses; he was always on the move and trying not to leave a trail. It had been that way for years. But sometimes he came to rest, thought problems through, made plans, gathered his thoughts, listened to some music. One weekend, just by chance, he'd had the impulse to invite Driskill to his hideaway up the Hudson, and Driskill had had the uncharacteristic impulse to go.

So that was where he'd start looking for answers to all the questions Hayes Tarlow had left behind. Why had he gone to Saints Rest? Who was he working for? Why did he have to die? Why did Hayes Tarlow and Drew Summerhays both have to die?

Ben Driskill was going to find out.

And the chips could fall wherever.

Driskill finally reached the turnoff with the bar and restaurant on the other side of the road and began the ascent, winding up through the narrow streets doubling back above the Hudson River, which the painters had been immortalizing ever since they came upon it and were overcome by its warmth and majesty. The sun was still high and the river lay like a leisurely golden, shimmering ribbon. The narrow road left the crumbling outskirts of town behind and kept turning, curving, constantly changing directions as it snaked up the hillside. The afternoon light dimmed once he was deep in the trees, firs and pines.

He turned off the two-lane road onto a dirt road, then onto a pine-needled single lane, hoping very hard that he was remembering it all properly. Trees were brushing and scratching at the fenders and doors where the big car barely squeaked through, like a curious, snuffling snout burrowing ever deeper and deeper into the hill. Then, like a cork pushed through a narrow-necked bottle, the Roadmaster popped into a roughly circular clearing with, yes, the rickety barn on the right, weathered with once-red siding, the door padlocked, and at the far side of the clearing, toward the river, there was the hideaway. Overgrown with weeds and shrubs, deep with wet leaves decomposing in the shade with shoots of yellowish-green grass poking through, some shingles on the lawn where the winds of the previous winter had deposited them.

The house was low and dark brown and rambled here and there, shooting off at odd angles. Summer screens were peeling down to the raw wood, beaten up by the weather through the past winters, but they were still on the windows. Leaves bulged up out of the gutters and drainpipes. Driskill walked up the stone pathway to the screen door, which hung slightly askew. It was the most deserted-looking place he'd ever seen.

Driskill tried the door, which was unlocked, of course: Why lock up a house so totally hidden? He went in, switched on the hall light. The kitchen was on the right, and down a few steps was the wood-floored main room with its big throw rugs and Adirondack chairs and Stickley mission-style pieces, which were very old and were probably worth a small but tidy fortune. Hayes had known it, too: He'd said some of the furniture was part of his retirement fund. He also said he had a fortune worth millions tucked away in the house and the barn and hidden in the woods around the house—not money, not gold, but information he hoped he'd never have to use. But if times got tough in his old age, and some of his old employers and friends forgot about him and were letting him wither away penniless and unloved—"Well, I'll fix their wagons," he'd said. "I'll offer some of my information for sale. No, not to those old employers, but to a publisher who'll set me up with a writer—after all, think of *The Pentagon Papers*, that was legit. Offering to sell it to the old employers, well, hell, that's blackmail, Ben, and Hayes Tarlow is no blackmailer."

Standing in the living room, looking out the huge, multipaned window with a view all the way down to the Hudson far below, Driskill wondered what exactly Hayes had hidden away up here, where it was, what would happen to it now that old Hayes had gone paws up. In this kind of business, you could never just mourn: You had to think of all the angles, all the ways everything could blow up like a pipe bomb under your car. All the information—

somewhere in the house, the barn, buried out in the woods. Just rotting away as the years passed . . . It was crazy. What had he known? Who knew he knew it? But that was another whole trail. Nothing to do with this campaign, this mess that got him killed. What was he doing this time? That was the question.

Driskill clicked on the lights in the living room and kitchen, made a drink from Hayes's stash of gin and tonic. The kitchen was clean. Newspapers were neatly stacked on the counter, May third, fourth, fifth . . . It was hard to believe Hayes wouldn't be coming back.

Driskill remembered Drew saying something one day, casually remarking, *I hear he's been away for a few weeks* . . . Now he wondered: Why would Drew Summerhays have known anything about the travel schedule of Hayes Tarlow? Unless he'd had a part in it. Where and when had Driskill heard Drew make the passing remark? At the office, very casually; someone might have needed Tarlow for a job. Drew had called him *Brother* Tarlow . . . fondly.

He took his drink and settled down on the floor with his back to the couch, in the middle of one of the big rugs, surrounded by the contents of the top of Hayes's desk and the drawers. There were lots of papers to go through, files secured by rubber bands, address books, clippings, all the detritus you might expect.

And slowly he drank to the memory of Hayes Tarlow.

An hour later he looked at what he'd found. And tried to make it mean something.

A sheet of cheap yellow paper with the scribble "*R>DNC*," which sounded like a rap group and meant nothing other than a reference to the Democratic National Committee. A telephone number was scratched in below the note. Driskill checked it against his own address book: It was Clark Beckerman's number in Arlington, Virginia. He was chairman of the DNC. Maybe he'd know what the *R>* meant. The note did raise the question: What exactly was Tarlow doing with the DNC? Working for them? Spying on them, checking somebody out? Had he been in Iowa on a DNC job?

On another sheet of paper, traced and retraced, were three more initials.

ISO.

The satellite agency.

Suddenly, in the total silence, he heard a motor, the scraping of branches. Fear kicked him in the belly and he got to his feet. He went to the hallway, stood out of sight, peering out the screen door.

The nose of an old Pontiac poked out of the tangle of trees and bushes and turned toward the house. Apparently someone else knew about the hideaway. Driskill tried to calm his breathing. The motor was still running but someone was getting out of the car, tall, coming toward the house, up the stone walk.

A voice came: "Hello in there? Anybody home? Hayes, are you in there?"

Driskill stepped into the doorway, holding his breath. "Hayes isn't here," he said. "He let me use the place for the weekend—"

"And who might you be?"

"Bob Janowitz," he said, thinking of a teammate at Notre Dame. "I'm from Ohio. Canton. Visiting the city and Hayes told me I should see some of the countryside so here I am." Driskill knew he was making it too complicated but he couldn't stop. "Helluva hard place to find, I'll give him that."

"That's true enough. You're Mr. Janowitz, then."

"And who are you?"

"Cyrus. I run the post office down in town. A special delivery came in late yesterday—hell, a two-day sticker on it—cost a fortune so I thought I'd bring it out on my day off. Best I can tell, Hayes musta sent it to himself . . . but I guess you might as well take it and just leave it on his kitchen counter." Cyrus looked like he was right on top of seventy, reedy and tough as an old bird. He might have been a refugee from *The Andy Griffith Show* or *Psycho*. Impossible to tell.

"Be glad to. I'm leaving tomorrow. He'll get it as soon as he walks in the door."

"You'd better sign this receipt for me. Right there." He handed Driskill a small clipboard and a Bic. "You must know Hayes pretty well, Mr. Janowitz. First time I've ever known him to have a guest."

"Really? Well, I am flattered. He brought me up here the first time in the fall. Relaxing spot. But you have to enjoy your solitude." He handed the clipboard back. Cyrus gave him the envelope, which was practically covered over with stickers. Plain business size, what felt like a single sheet of paper within.

Cyrus looked at him appraisingly. "Well, I guess this is all in order, then. Really supposed to deliver a special to the person it's sent to but . . . well, heck, you signed for it. You look like an honest fella."

"Well, I do my best."

"G'night, then. The wife's gonna kill me for making a delivery on my day off. You enjoy yourself here in all this . . . what was it? Solitude?"

"That's it." Driskill stood in the doorway, smiling, then waved as the old car turned around and headed back into the tunnel of trees and shrubs. Then he took a deep breath. He hoped Cyrus hadn't noted down the Buick's license plate number. It was all goddam Washington. Once you stuck your little toe in to test the water a big fucking monster grabbed your leg and pulled you in and you never knew why or how but you knew it was happening to you. Less than forty-eight hours ago he hadn't yet found Drew Summerhays's body. Now he was worried about his license plate number.

When the car was gone, Driskill opened the envelope. Whatever he'd been expecting, the single sheet that fluttered into his hand wasn't it.

There were no words, no message of any kind.

Just a lone hand-drawn line snaking its way across the page. Looking like the path of a river, maybe. Or a country road. Just an erratic line about eight inches long, slanted from the upper left to the lower right corner. Unless it was upside down.

Driskill inspected both sides of the paper, then put it

aside and peered at every inch of the envelope. It had been
sent from Saints Rest, Iowa. It was something that Hayes
had found or been given in Saints Rest. It was important
enough to send to the hideaway; conversely, too important
to keep on his person. The return address was merely a
quick flick of the pen that amounted to the initials *HT* if
you looked closely enough. "Special Delivery" was printed
in block letters, as was the address. There was just nothing
else to see. The stamps, the postmark. Nothing else.

And a sheet of plain white paper, folded in three.

One lone line.

Yet it was important. Important to Hayes Tarlow.
Maybe important enough to die for.

But it didn't mean a damn thing to Ben Driskill.

He went to have a look at the bedroom. He flicked on the
light and was taken by surprise by what was hanging on
the opposite wall, at the foot of the bed. It was tacked up
to the log walls of the bedroom, which had apparently
been added to the house after the original structure was
built.

It was the huge poster Sherman Taylor had used in his
run for a second term, when he'd been beaten by Charlie
Bonner. It was one of the best political posters anybody
had ever created, a triumph of Madison Avenue's most ex-
pensive creative minds.

Two very heroic almost-profiles of Taylor. One was a
Marine hero in dress uniform, obviously taken during his
days as a commanding officer in the Persian Gulf—the ultimate recruiting poster, the face like something etched and
chiseled in granite, turned just enough so that you caught
the steely glint in his squinting eye as he stared down the
enemy. The other Taylor, similarly angled toward the middle of the poster, was the strong-willed yet sensitive world
leader, handsome and lean as Clint Eastwood, the lines
deep in his face denoting the kind of character that reflected a man's heroic soul, yet a vague and rather miracu-

lous aura of warmth mixed with the steel in those unflinching eyes.

Driskill knew the poster like he knew his own face. It had been everywhere. Billboards, television, campaign buttons that featured whichever of the two Sherman Taylor faces was your personal favorite, newspapers including the famous double-page color spread in *USA Today*. Beneath the two faces was a sleek, gleaming Marine sword that looked like a samurai weapon made of mirror glass. Engraved in crimson across the blade, *In Peace and War*. And beneath that, in bold type, VOTE FOR A GREATER AMERICA. There was not a single mention of the candidate's name nor his party, presumably a first in American political campaigning.

The best the Bonner campaign could do in combating that poster was a line that the vice-presidential candidate David Manders got off early in October. He looked at the crowd, asked them what they thought of the poster, they all booed like good Democrats, and Manders said: "It perfectly represents the man . . . two-faced . . . and leaves no identifying clues behind him." The Democrats got unlimited mileage out of the line for the rest of the campaign.

There was however something quite wrong with Tarlow's copy of the poster, and when he realized what it was he laughed out loud. Tarlow had turned the whole thing into a dartboard. And, curiously, a black-and-white newspaper shot of Bob Hazlitt's head had been Scotch-taped above and between the two faces of Sherman Taylor. There were a couple of ancient, ratty old darts stuck in the poster. Tarlow's last joke.

Driskill was stripping the plaid blanket off the bed when he saw the pad of dog-eared Post-it notes beside the extension phone. On the ninth sheet he saw something that rang a bell, however faint.

A phone number with a Boston area code, 617.

It was a number Driskill knew. He reached into his memory and began feeling for it, muttering the number, and then it came to him. It dated from the campaign three years ago. It was the number for Brad Hokansen, New England fund-raising chairman for the Bonner campaign. Hayes Tarlow had been dealing with Hokansen. At least it looked that way.

Driskill was suddenly wide-awake. It was something specific. Something that had a meaning for Driskill. A name to go with Beckerman, the DNC chairman.

It was just past four-thirty. He dialed the number and spoke briefly with Brad Hokansen. In fact he scared him half to death. He was smiling when he hung up.

He rinsed out his glass and dried it, made sure he had the envelope with the paper bearing the odd scrawled line, started up the Buick, and headed slowly out of the dark woods.

Finally he reached the road and found his way back down to the highway, where he took the first turn east that looked promising, headed for the Saw Mill River Parkway, and turned north toward Boston.

Chapter 7

Driskill blew into Boston with a wind spitting rain at his back and a smidgen of hope in his heart. The stoplights were reflecting brightly on the slick streets. He wound around the convoluted traffic pattern, up Mass Avenue, got sidetracked and funneled in the general direction of Radcliffe, then back into Harvard Square. He parked on a big ramp connected to a motel, walked back to the Square, and called from a pay phone. Hokansen picked up on the first ring.

"Here I am, Brad. Tear yourself away from the Sunday-night Red Sox game and get down to that muffin joint on the corner of the Square."

"Driskill, you incredible asshole!" He was whispering, sounding as if his vacuum-sealed lid had just been punctured. "What the hell do you think you're doing?"

"Just being my playful self. Relax."

"You mean that place we went to that time?"

"None other, pal. And make haste. I have to get back to New York tonight."

Brad Hokansen was president of an ancient Boston financial institution, North Shore Fiduciary & Trust Company. He ministered to the tidy fortunes left in the hands of overbred, undereducated, and only mildly motivated descendants of Beacon Hill aristocrats. The money had all been made some time ago when the family gene pools had been well and fully stocked; as the sharks in the pools had died out, minnows and goldfish had eventually taken their places, which was where Brad Hokansen came in. The bankers to the original moneymakers had been receivers of orders; Brad Hokansen now held the upper hand: He gave the orders to those with the money, he did what was best for them and tried to explain it to them. He was good at it. He was connected by marriage to a Brahmin family; he himself was descended from a man who had started his business career running booze for old Joe Kennedy. His wife had grown up living among the cobblestones and gaslights of Louisburg Square. Her family had placed him among the pillars of the Myopia Hunt Club. No doubt of it, Brad was up there with the best. He had a jaw like Dick Tracy's and long brown hair combed back from a high flat forehead, hair as thick as Citation's mane. He was just about the only Democrat in his circle.

When Hokansen had coordinated New England fundraising for the Bonner campaign, Driskill had come to know him fairly well: He was much more of a machine kind of Democrat than Driskill, who was a Bonner man but otherwise kept his distance from politics. Hokansen would have performed the money-raising functions for just about any party nominee. In fact Hokansen's favorite candidate had been Governor Claude Dalrymple of Georgia.

Once Ben had connected the telephone number with Hokansen, Hayes Tarlow's having the number made at least *some* kind of sense. Hokansen and Driskill had both worked through Clark Beckerman, who was chairman of the Democratic National Committee, and Hayes had occasionally done jobs for the DNC.

Tarlow was the guy Clark Beckerman and his predecessors at the DNC hired to counteract Republican dirty tricks with dirty tricks of their own. That left the White House out of the loop and preserved blessed deniability. Not that it mattered all that much in the end. The Democrats never really got the hang of it but Hayes was the best at creating standoffs. You don't do your dirty trick, we won't do ours: that sort of thing. The RNC was pretty wary of Hayes. They didn't like seeing him on the case.

And now Hayes Tarlow gets killed and he's got Brad Hokansen's number beside his nightlight. You had to be curious.

Hokansen entered the muffin place and Driskill beckoned. He checked his irritating, computer-wonk's black plastic watch and sidled through the tables. Hokansen shook the watch, gave it a dirty look, and stuck out his hand. "Benjamin, how are you? I'm not at all sure I'm glad to see you." He also thrust out his jaw, the parody of every aggressive Choate-type Bostonian. Absolutely Protestant and built for determined self-righteousness.

"Sit down, Brad. Just stay calm." Driskill motioned to a waitress. "Blueberry for my friend—"

"And decaf," he added.

"It's okay with me," she said and went away.

Hokansen leaned forward: "So what do you make of Taylor's switching parties and backing Hazlitt? Christ, ever hear of anything like it? I mean, what's going on—what do you know about it?"

"I don't know anything about it, Brad. I saw it on TV just like everybody else—"

"But you must have talked to the President and Larkspur and Mac—"

"I haven't talked to anyone, Brad . . . now just calm down."

"I'm calm, I'm calm."

"Hayes Tarlow's been murdered, Brad. Better just to get it out there. Out in Saints Rest, Iowa. You were working with him—"

"For God's sake, gimme a minute here—Hayes Tarlow. You're telling me he's . . . oh, Jesus . . . is Tarlow *really* dead?"

"You were working with him—you could be next, my friend. I suggest you confide in old Ben. Maybe we can get you out of this alive."

"*Please* don't talk like that," Hokansen implored him.

His face had lost its normally high color. "Jesus. Are you working for the President on this one, Ben?"

"You know I can't answer that. What I need to know is this—why did Hayes have your number beside his bed? What were you guys up to? Why is he dead? Are you next on somebody's list?"

Hokansen looked as if his blueberry muffin had been transformed into a plaintive, dying haddock. "What the hell . . . Ben, you gotta be straight with me. What do you know? You're on thin ice here—" For once it was working for Driskill, the idea people had that he was an insider because of his friendship with the President.

"Brad, Brad, come on . . ." Driskill was trying to sound as insufferable as possible. Brad liked knowing important, insufferable people. "This is strictly need-to-know. You understand. Just plug me in on this Tarlow thing. As usual, those inside the Beltway don't know a damned thing." Brad loved Beltway-type talk.

Hokansen's face was recovering its pinkness with excitement. His thick brown hair was positively alive and straining. "Jesus, it's Washington. Oh, man, is it because of Summerhays? Ben, are you tying Hayes Tarlow's murder to Summerhays's . . . suicide? *Murder?* You're not telling me Drew was murdered, are you?"

"You haven't heard me say anything of the kind. Just ease off on the gas, Brad. Don't try to set a new land-speed record, okay? You'll get all confused. I just need to know your piece of information—it's like a piece of a puzzle. Give me your piece and you can forget we had this conversation. Just tell me about Hayes, what's been going on."

Once Hokansen got to talking he didn't want to stop. Driskill felt himself becoming the therapist and Brad was downloading everything, getting it off his chest. It was a three-muffin and six-cups-of-coffee story, and that was just Brad's consumption.

"Ben, you must promise me—this goes only to the highest level, okay? We're dealing with pretty fringe kind of stuff here . . . and with Tarlow and Summerhays dead, who knows what kind of a mess we're getting into? I've got a family, I've got the bank—that might make me vulnerable. I wouldn't want anybody to find out I knew a damn thing about any of it—"

"Don't worry, Brad. Just ease back, kick up your feet, and tell me the story."

"It starts with Bob Hazlitt, actually. Not him personally but with his brainchild, his baby, Heartland Industries. Biggest communications techno-group in the world as of a couple of years ago. All those satellites flying around up there, all the TV stations, the newspapers, the radio stations, all the computer programs and interactive videos and virtual reality—hell, Bob Hazlitt got a great many of the laws of this land bent and transformed and changed just so he could get into empiring this way. We at North Shore have looked at Heartland Industries strictly as an investment phenomenon.

"Then, last fall, we got a tip about funny business going on at Heartland—some shady practices, payoffs, big-time bribes, blackmail, the works, to get laws passed in their favor, to secure some contracts. Well, hell, every big-time business player has done that—everybody knows it, it's the way things work. And then along comes Hazlitt riding this little boom for president—last fall, who'd have thought he could challenge Bonner? Then the President makes that speech and it's a brand-new ball game. Folks began taking Hazlitt seriously and we began thinking about that tip we'd gotten. And then we got another one. Some kind of skullduggery out there in the middle of Iowa and weren't we just a little worried about pumping so much investment into Heartland? I'm talking about North Shore Fiduciary now. We'd gotten in pretty heavily, see, and it started looking like a pretty relevant question to me—"

"Brad—let's get back to Tarlow. . . ."

"I'm getting there, trust me. The DNC has a portfolio, too, and I'm the guy who manages it. And they're very heavily into Heartland—well, hell, it's been a great investment for a long time." He set his mouth firmly, defensively, as if expecting a mighty challenge.

"I understand," Driskill said. "Nobody's trying to hang

you, Brad. I'm just collecting information. The DNC—now there's a way to bring the tale back to Tarlow."

"Just hang with me, Ben. I'm getting there—I just want you to see the big picture. Now . . . who does just about all of the DNC's legal representation? Well, obviously, it's Bascomb, Lufkin, and Summerhays . . . and specifically Drew Summerhays himself. We've also got the Harvard portfolio, a lot of it, and there's Harvard money in Heartland all the way up the kazoo. If something nasty happens and Heartland stands revealed as soiled goods, we'll be out there up to our ass in alligators." He finished off blueberry muffin number one and signaled the waitress for more.

"Where does Hayes come into this, Brad? And who was giving you these tips about Heartland? Who came up with the first one?"

"Well, that's another somewhat sticky point—I don't want people knowing this, any of this." He was pleading, and Driskill tried to look reassuring.

"Who?"

"Tony Sarrabian . . ."

Driskill stared at him over the rim of his coffee cup. The photographs of Summerhays with Sarrabian . . . "You're telling me that the one and only Tony Sarrabian's a client of North Shore?"

"Well, why the hell not? He's a citizen, he's got a lot of money, and he represents lots of people who, believe me, are right up there with the Church and Harvard when it comes to investments."

"He ought to be doing life plus a thousand years."

Hokansen and Sarrabian. More strange bedfellows. Summerhays knowing Tarlow had been out of town. Sarrabian chatting up both Brad Hokansen and Drew Summerhays. Driskill said, "But I don't quite get it. Sarrabian is supposed to be backing the Republicans—Price Quarles—in a big way. That's the story that's been going around for the last couple months. Are you saying that he's out to get Hazlitt in order to resurrect poor Quarles?" Driskill shook his head doubtfully. "No, I don't get it."

Hokansen shrugged dramatically. "You know the way

these guys think, how their minds work—they're not like us. They've got a million angles and nothing is ever what it seems. Quarles isn't going to be president, but that doesn't mean he can't help Sarrabian in payment for services rendered that'll do him some good in the private sector. Look, I don't know what you've run into in your career but I'd bet you've seen just about everything. Me, in the world of money? You wouldn't believe the stuff I've seen, sometimes I've just had to shut my eyes, Ben, pretend I *didn't* see. But I'm cleaner than most. It's the world we live in. Corruption is like technology, it's growing exponentially. You just have to work around it. Anyway, Sarrabian gave me that tip months before the Hazlitt thing began to cook, y'know?"

"Did he have you out to his house?"

"Are you kidding? That's an invitation for his *clients*, not his banker. I was down in Washington on business and he found out I was there, called me, asked me to meet him for drinks at the Four Seasons one evening. Nothing out of the ordinary about it, just drinks. We're sitting there, it's all hushed and comfy, you know the place, and he drops it in my ear. A word to the wise, that was the tone. You've scratched my back, I'm returning the favor—you know how it is. Do as you wish, he was saying, but you might want to look into Heartland. . . . This was back in January, I remember because it was a hellish night, snowing. Not long after the President's speech. Hazlitt was just about to announce and start suing to get on primary ballots, a few people already thought he was looking real serious and the President was still trying to pretend he didn't exist. Shall we say Sarrabian got my attention? Tips from Tony are worth noting, I'm sure you agree." The second muffin was gone and Brad was wiping a fleeing blueberry from the corner of his mouth. This time Driskill waved to the waitress.

"Having been tipped off, what did you do?"

"Well, I thought it over and figured this was a good time to hold tight, keep my eyes and ears open. Then Hazlitt was suddenly off and running for the Democratic nomination. Hell, look at it this way—better that *we* find out about any dirty linen at Heartland than the Republicans and that idiot Price Quarles. I was about to give Tony a call when I got one myself."

"All right. Who followed up with the second tip?"

"Well, here's where it gets a little spooky—particularly when you tell me about Hayes's murder and where it happened." He stoked himself up with a sip of steaming coffee. "The second tip came from a guy out in Saints Rest . . . oh, two weeks ago. A man named Herb Varringer. He's on the board of Heartland, that's the board of the parent company, the big board. Old-timer, been with Hazlitt from the beginning—I think he may have folded his own company into Heartland years and years ago. He called me and he was worried about something at Heartland . . . real worried, Ben—"

"But why you? Why didn't he call somebody else?"

"Simple. I've been out there, I've talked to their top financial people, I've gotten to know that company—of course, a lot of it's secret with defense contracts and the real high-techie satellite and communications stuff. It's not just a healthy company, it's the healthiest company, it's the Future, Ben, with a capital *F*. Cutting-edge research and development, right on the money with current product . . . it's all in place. I got a handshake with Hazlitt himself, but one of the men I talked with most was Herb Varringer. I picked him out because he went back so far with Hazlitt. This was a few years ago and everything was different then. Hazlitt wasn't dabbling in politics, for one thing . . . and Herb Varringer spoke well of both Hazlitt and Heartland. Oh, Herb didn't love Bob, but he respected his genius and, frankly, Herb was rich beyond his wildest dreams because of Bob Hazlitt.

"After that first meeting, I'd occasionally give him a call just to check in on funding stuff for the Democrats. It was no big deal. I'd call him, I'd call Nick Wardell, I'd call various people in lots of states. Anyway, a couple of weeks ago, I get this call from Herb Varringer and it's not the Herb I'd known before. He's very somber, no chitchat. He told me he'd learned of some Heartland activities that were bothering him a lot, he didn't know quite what to do about it, and he wondered if I did. Well, all my alarms were going off but I didn't want to know too much myself—I just wanted to pick up what I could. If Herb was bothered I was going to start looking real hard at Heartland investments—I had quite a lot of faith in Herb's attitudes and morality, if you see what I mean. So he wanted a name, a highly placed guy with access to the President, someone who might be able to understand this stuff that was bothering him and use it to put a crimp in Hazlitt's campaign. If—if, I repeat—they thought that was the way to go. I'm telling you, Ben, it was a helluva conversation." He bit off a large portion of muffin and stared at Driskill.

"All right, who did you tell him to talk to?"

"Well, it didn't take a rocket scientist. . . . I told him to talk to Drew Summerhays."

Driskill felt a creeping unease. "Did Varringer know Drew?"

"No. I said I'd arrange for the call, I'd prepare Drew for a call from Herb—that's all. I didn't mention content. I just told Drew it sounded like it might be very important."

"And . . . what next?"

"Well, it all happened over two or three days. I didn't talk to Varringer again, though he left a message with my secretary to thank me for the help I'd given him. But I did talk to Drew—just a follow-up call to see if they'd gotten together all right and, frankly, to sound Drew out on what he thought about it. Not the content, but the seriousness of Varringer's concern. Drew kept that cool reticence, you know how he is, *was*—he just said there might be something in it, he wasn't sure, but it was a job for Brother Tarlow. That's the last I heard about any of it until I heard about Drew's death, and then you arrive out of the blue and tell me Tarlow's dead out in Saints Rest. I'm telling you, Ben, this has scared the shit out of me." And then he remembered. "Where's Herb Varringer? He's the guy you should be talking to—"

"Brad, we don't know where he is. Tarlow's dead and we can't find Varringer. There's just one more thing, though—take a look at this." Driskill took the folded paper from the pocket of his jacket and handed it across the table.

Hokansen unfolded the paper and looked at it, turning it as if there were a top and a bottom that made all the difference. "What is this? I don't get it."

"You're absolutely sure—it means nothing to you?"

"Ben, this doesn't mean anything to *anybody*. It's just a line . . . a funny line, like somebody was drunk." He handed it back.

"Just what I thought, Brad."

They walked outside together, shook hands, and Driskill watched him set off toward the MTA entrance in the middle of Harvard Square. He walked with his feet pointed out slightly and he was a little flat-footed. He looked like a regular guy, but he knew a lot more than most guys. And he was scared.

Chapter 8

Driskill left his car at Logan. He could send somebody from the firm up to Boston to drive it back: He wanted to get back to New York before evening had turned to morning.

Now he knew why Hayes Tarlow had gone to Saints Rest.

Now he knew that Drew Summerhays had sent him.

He knew that a man by the name of Herb Varringer, long-time friend and ally of Hazlitt, was at the bottom of it. Varringer believed Heartland was up to something but nobody left alive knew what . . . nobody but Herb Varringer. Had Varringer talked to Tarlow? Was that why Tarlow had been killed? What did the strange crooked line have to do with any of it? And where was Herb Varringer now?

What was Heartland up to? The corporation was so huge, how could anyone ever pin it down? And why did the first tip have to come from Tony Sarrabian? Driskill hated it every time Sarrabian surfaced, and it was beginning to look like he'd left his fingerprints all over this thing.

And why was Sarrabian sandbagging Hazlitt? Like the scorpion in the story, was it just his nature? Or was there a current sweeping along beneath the surface, a riptide that took anyone it could find?

Driskill grabbed a cab at La Guardia and sat back with the window open and the damp breeze blowing in his face on the drive into town. The skyline was lit up like a distant shining, shimmering lacework, infinitely tempting yet so crass and cruel up close. The smell of rain was everywhere. An occasional raindrop made a big soft splat on the windshield. The storm system coming up the East Coast was stalled off Long Island, and the people out strolling on the upper East Side were looking wilted and disconsolate.

Brad Hokansen had never been to Tony Sarrabian's New York apartment but he was able to tell Ben the address. Sarrabian's New York base was a duplex penthouse looking down on Central Park and the Metropolitan Museum of Art and across to the Art Deco towers of Central Park West. Ben spoke with the doorman, who gestured him in toward the elevators. So far so good. It was past eleven o'clock, but late visitors seemed not in the least uncommon.

The butler turned out to be a Korean gentleman who gave the general impression that giving him any lip might result in having your head twisted all the way off and pitched through a wall. He ushered Driskill from the mirrored foyer past two large Picasso drawings, a lovely springlike Monet, a Pissarro, and a routinely troubling Bacon, down two steps into the living room, which was appointed with understated Japanese *objets d'art* and screens as well as low cream-colored couches and chairs and a severe fireplace framed with polished black marble. Very faintly he could make out the strains of *The Mikado,* almost subliminal. Clearly Sarrabian was decorating against type.

The faint glowing light entered the room from the open French doors above Fifth Avenue. Virtually no sounds of the bothersome outside world intruded. Driskill was admiring the set of three small, discreet paintings of Portuguese fishing villages by Wayne Norman when he heard behind him a voice speaking his name.

"Mr. Driskill, it's a pleasure to meet you, sir. I'm Raymond, Mr. Sarrabian's secretary and aide. I don't believe you have an appointment. Is it possible I'm mistaken?"

Driskill turned and took in the whole picture. Late on a Sunday night. Raymond was actually wearing an olive-green Armani suit, lots of shoulder. His blond hair was cut in a standup flattop. Maybe he was planning a little club hopping.

"I came by on a whim, Raymond. Thought I might catch him in."

"I'm terribly sorry, sir. He's dining with some United Nations people tonight. A charitable function. The plight of children, as I recall. Mr. Sarrabian has so many causes he supports. Perhaps I could—"

"No, nothing. You might just tell him I stopped by. I'd like to see him." Ben pulled out a business card and jotted down his cellular number. "He can reach me here."

Raymond took it with a gesture of deference. "Let me say how terribly sorry I am about Mr. Summerhays, sir. A great leader. A man among men." He paused for a paragraph break before moving on. "Mr. Sarrabian was very saddened by the news."

"I hadn't realized they knew one another."

"Mr. Sarrabian knows everyone, doesn't he?"

Driskill was standing in the doorway to the terrace, feeling the breeze high up, looking out at the New York of power and great wealth, the Plaza Hotel far down to the left, the Met's sculpture garden below, the Delacorte Theatre, all the rest of it. The Empire State Building and the twin towers of the World Trade Center, still standing after the second terrorist bombing three months ago, were ghosts lingering behind the foggy mist.

"A lovely view, isn't it?" Raymond was enthused in a languid sort of way. "Mr. Sarrabian often sits out here of an evening and thinks. He says he communes with his spirit family. His is a very ancient family, you know."

"I'm sure it is," Driskill said. "Well, I'll leave you to your own pursuits, Raymond."

"Very well, sir. I'll see you out."

Raymond bowed slightly in the foyer, his reflection

flickering in the hundreds of mirrored strips. Thousands of Raymonds, it seemed. A regiment.

"Good night, Raymond."

"Good night, sir."

Going down in the elevator, it seemed to have been a brief journey through the rabbit hole, up to the Mad Hatter's private aerie. But Tony Sarrabian was famous for surprising you, messing with your assumptions.

Still, the communing-with-his-spirit-family routine had been a little much.

When he got home he checked the answering machine in the kitchen while drawing off a glass of cold water from the Brita in the refrigerator. The first message was from Elizabeth. She sounded strained, as if she'd been crying. "Oh, Ben, I've been going crazy trying to catch you. I'm just devastated about Drew. I'm stuck out here in LA. I feel like I'm on another planet—the wrong planet. Having a good cry. He was such a grand old man. Oh, dammit! How are you holding up? Oh, darling, tell me what's been going on—where have you been? I'll be in Washington tomorrow night. But please call me at the Hilton here in LA. I'll be waiting."

He was listening for the emotional distance that had developed between them. He thought he heard it, in and around the words. The endless struggle, Ben's wanting her to get settled and stay closer to New York, Elizabeth's wanting him to get more involved in the political life she found so compelling, so that they could spend more time together on the road. Every so often it flared up, a bonfire in the night of their relationship. Now this campaign with its attendant demands on her had made it worse than ever. Their dispute lay between them whenever they were together. They couldn't seem to avoid it, couldn't just look away.

He called the Hilton in LA. She was out. Not waiting by the phone. Of course not. She'd be having dinner with colleagues. He left his name with the operator and hung up.

He took his glass of ice water out into the courtyard and sat at the table beneath the trees. The breeze rustled the leaves overhead. Several of the windows overlooking the common garden area were still lit, and somebody was playing a Stan Getz recording. He recognized the piece. "Her." One of Getz's signature works. He mopped his face with a towel, sipping the water, replacing the fluids the heat had drained from him during one very long Sunday. Washington, Tarlow's hideaway, the talk with Hokansen, the flight back to New York, the peculiar interlude at Sarrabian's. And now he couldn't wind down. He went back inside, flicked on the small TV, and turned to CNN and their nightly "Race for the Presidency" broadcast repeated from earlier in the evening.

The President was landing for an airport reception and a luncheon speech in Miami, then a dinner-hour speech at Disney World and a televised town meeting at nine o'clock that would be carried throughout the South.

Charlie looked good, smiling, waving, Linda right behind him, her sleek honey-streaked hair catching just enough of the breeze, the Chanel suit minimizing her hips, which always bugged the hell out of her. Perfect, he'd heard her say, appraising herself, well, okay, not perfect but pretty good all things considered, "but the biggest caboose in Christendom!" Her willingness to make light of herself made her an immensely likable woman. Her intelligence spoke for itself. In the end, she was probably brighter than Charlie. But he was a politician and he was a more accomplished bullshitter and he was President.

The crowd at the airport was fine. They'd been outfitted with "Bonner's Our Boy" and "Don't Fix It If It Ain't Broke" banners, but nothing was ever perfect. One reporter asked the President if he knew why the police on Long Island were being so secretive about the death of Summerhays. A look of irritation flickered across the President's face, and then he said he had no idea. He said a few words about how much he missed Drew, and that was the only part of the airport appearance that made it into the show.

Driskill was fully hypnotized by the glowing box, a caveman around his own little campfire hearing the stories of the day, how Og had fared in the search for seismosaurus and whether the village of Bog had survived the pterodactyl attack. On the screen the interviews were beginning.

The first guest was none other than Flying Bob Hazlitt himself. Driskill had never really taken the time to kick back and watch the man closely, without trying to do something else at the same time. This was the perfect opportunity. Hazlitt was speaking from the campus of Yale University, from some college master's immaculately booklined study. He was a man of middle height, solidly built, naturally somewhat pink-faced with a thatch of silvery hair that was always slightly mussed. He had a short, wide nose, summer-sky-blue eyes, and a wide smile. On occasion he wore an in-the-ear hearing aid, the result of flying extremely loud jet planes during a couple of wars. He was known to be a pipe smoker but never did so in public because, as he often said, "It makes me look like a horse's ass." Tonight he was sitting in a muted green-and-red-plaid wingback chair, wearing a faded blue denim shirt open at the collar and gray slacks, a perfect picture of the candidate taking his ease after a hard day of rattling the enemy's cage.

Bernard Shaw opened up with a genial softball question. "Mr. Hazlitt, I'm sure we all are concerned about raising the level of campaign discourse. So I ask you, as someone who is in a position to benefit from them, what are we to make of these almost daily rumors and revelations about the Bonner campaign? Is there any substance here? Or are we drowning in a flood tide of innuendo and backstabbing and tommyrot?"

"Well, Bernie," Hazlitt said, "that's about a fifteen-dollar question—"

"Sir, since *Forbes* magazine has suggested that you are the second richest individual in America, you can probably spare the fifteen dollars."

"I'm just wondering if you could make the question a little simpler for a plain-speaking country businessman?"

"If I could find a plain-speaking country businessman, I'd certainly try. But I'm asking you, Mr. Hazlitt, and frankly it seems unlikely that you're going to convince anyone in this nation that you're the hayseed you seem to enjoy playing—"

"Now, Bernie . . ." Hayseed chuckle. The straw to chew on was the only missing prop.

"—but I'll make it a simple question. What do you make of this Hayes Tarlow business? As you know, though some of our viewers may not, there's a breaking story out of Saints Rest, Iowa, that Mr. Tarlow has been murdered there sometime within the last few days—Mr. Tarlow being a sometime investigator for the Democratic National Committee as well as the law offices of Bascomb, Lufkin, and Summerhays . . . and a man reputedly known to the President. What do you think this may mean for the campaign?"

"Well, the thing about it that bothers me is just this—I don't say it's so awful, we don't know to what extent the White House or the Democrats are involved with the man—but it seems like it's always *something* when it comes to Charlie, that is *President,* Bonner. There's always something hidden that comes out and there's a hullabaloo and we all have to worry about it and waste time scratching our heads and wondering what it all means. When you come right down to it, I suppose it's character. It's the chickens coming home to roost. And it's a question of the people he's surrounded himself with. We've got a murder and the death of Drew Summerhays in the space of a couple of days and you begin to ask yourself, what's going on here? We get this crazy wife-beating charge cropping up again—I'm not saying I put any stock in that whatsoever, Bernie—but you've heard all the rumors, there's just this constant buzz of unsavory news coming out of this administration. I don't know what to make of it, Bernie, and that's a fact."

"Well, wait a minute, Mr. Hazlitt. Are you suggesting

there is some connection between the deaths of Summerhays and Tarlow—?"

Driskill's interest quickened. Had the media discovered
the Varringer factor?

"You're the man with his finger on the pulse, Mr. Shaw.
You tell *us,* is there some connection? I'm just a guy running around the country trying to set the record straight
and offering people a way out of the mess we're in. A way
to deal with this Mexican thing . . . a way to deal with
national security and our borders in general. Charlie
Bonner is way off the mark. Is there a connection between
Summerhays's death and Tarlow's? You tell me." Hazlitt
was vainly trying to look concerned. He had a good-
natured face, not a grave one.

"Not that I know of, Mr. Hazlitt. But you seem to be
saying that the deaths of these two men are somehow connected to the White House—your press secretary implied
as much yesterday and again earlier today. I want to know
if you have any information that specifically leads you to
that conclusion . . . and if so, do you intend to make it
public and turn it over to the attorney general?"

"Well, I'm not so sure that turning it over to this particular attorney general would make much sense—"

"Excuse me, Mr. Hazlitt, but what is that supposed to
mean?"

"Good lord, Bernie . . . wake up and smell the coffee!
She's not exactly my idea of a heavy hitter. Fine lawyer, no
doubt, but attorney general? And she herself is right out of
the Bascomb law office, a protégée of Summerhays, and
now she's suddenly in charge of this intelligence-CIA thing.
Come on, my friend . . . I don't think she's an objective
player here. Seems a little fishy to me but, then, I'm just a
plain-speaking American citizen. I grew up worshiping
Harry Truman, a plain speaker if ever there was one. And
I'm trying to be as plain as I can with you—I don't have
any information that you don't have. I'm in possession of
no information that isn't available to any American who
pays attention and reads the papers and watches programs
like yours—"

"With the planet ringed with all those Heartland satellites, my question was not merely whimsical, sir. I'm sure you do have access to information the rest of us don't. And I'm asking you if you have any knowledge that directly ties the White House to these two tragedies?"

"You think I have information that you don't have? I reckon that's pretty unlikely, Bernie. Talk about satellites, what about CNN's satellites?"

"But even *they* are Heartland satellites, Mr. Hazlitt—"

"Look, here's what I know—get your pencil ready and take it down. I know that two men are dead. I know that the detective who worked for the Democratic National Committee and the White House was murdered. I know he was a licensed private detective because that's what TV has told me and nobody is out there denying that he has done jobs for the DNC and for the President—or for this White House, in any case. At least, I haven't heard any denials." He leaned forward in his plaid chair.

"Let me tell you something about Bob Hazlitt. I've always found in my life out in Iowa—it's a small state and we're simple people out there, our heritage is in the soil that sustains us. I've always found—and my dear mother, Lady Jane we call her, she's celebrating her one hundredth birthday right about convention time, Bernie—she always tells me that sometimes you just have to judge folks by the company they keep. I learned that at her knee and, darn it, it seems to me it just stands to reason. And lately the President's friends, the company he keeps, have a way of getting into trouble, don't they?"

He took a breath and Shaw jumped back in. "Just to make things clear for our audience who might start thinking of you as the simple son of the soil you proclaim yourself, I'd like to point out that you, after all, were educated at MIT, took an advanced degree at Oxford, if I'm not mistaken . . . and were in fact a Rhodes scholar. But, please, do go on."

"Well, I plead guilty to the Rhodes scholar thing but I was young and didn't know better—but just let me finish my thought about the President and his problems. We all know how down on defense and intelligence he is." He counted off his ideas on his fingers. "Well, we need the latest weaponry and the best army and navy and air force on earth. We need the CIA, there can be no doubt about that. We need the best intelligence we can get in an unpredictable and often hostile world. We need the cornerstones of national security. Enough said. But, sure, we must beef up the CIA and its agencies, we must make it stronger, we can't make it captive of oversight committees pledged to keep it from doing its job—and I promise that in a Hazlitt administration, you can be sure that the CIA and its agencies will have their hands untied. The CIA would be given the latitude to operate effectively and do the job the American people rely on it to do. What it all comes down to, Bernie, is that I'm just sick and tired of worrying about the President and his cronies and what new kind of mess they're going to find themselves in. Every week, darn near every day."

Shaw looked stern, an imposing sight. "You imply that something else may come out. Sir, I want you to put your money where your mouth is, so to speak. Is that what you're saying?"

"Well, why should the surprises stop now? I stand by what I've said here and I'm not going to say any more about any of it right now. But I do wonder why the devil the police can't just come out with it. Is Drew Summerhays's death a case of murder, as people are saying?"

"Well, time's up and I want to thank you for joining us tonight, Mr. Hazlitt, as the Democratic convention looms ahead of us. Then, and only then, will we learn the outcome of this all but incredible fight for the Democratic nomination. We'll be back in just a moment with a spokesman for the other side. And now, this word."

When he came back with a guest in the Washington studio it was none other than Ellery Dunstan Larkspur. He looked large and stoop-shouldered in his three-piece blue pinstripe with the bright red bow tie. He was very comfortable in the role of the interviewee and had obviously just watched Hazlitt's performance. He was massaging his chin with a wrinkled, papery hand. Shaw was introducing him as "possibly the closest adviser to President Bonner, a man utterly at home with the powerful and mighty from around the world, the founder and chairman of what is known in Washington as 'The Larkspur Office,' the preeminent public relations firm in the city. He is a man at home in the world of politics. Good evening, Mr. Larkspur."

Ellery Larkspur had what was once called "bottom." It was the best thing to have. He was one of the Wise Men. In fact, he was just about the only Wise Man left. Drew Summerhays had epitomized the type.

Shaw said, "Now, Mr. Larkspur, you've heard what Mr. Hazlitt just said. What can you say regarding his description of the President's week in light of the deaths of these two men?"

"To begin with, the only connection between the two tragedies is the time frame in which they occurred. Drew Summerhays was, in my view, the greatest living American. He was my mentor for much of my life and then quite possibly my closest friend, my most intimate confidant—I held no man in higher regard. I don't fancy letting an unproven upstart like Bob Hazlitt pass judgment on him in public or private, and I really have no more to say about Mr. Hazlitt's unsubstantiated opinions, one way or the other. At the end of the day, historians will have to decide which of these two men, Drew Summerhays or Bob Hazlitt, made a greater contribution to his country, and I for one am not in doubt as to what judgment will be rendered."

"And Hayes Tarlow—not exactly in Drew Summerhays's league—where does he fit into the puzzle of this Bonner administration?"

"Mr. Shaw, you've really got me there. I believe I might have known Mr. Tarlow by sight but I rather doubt that I ever had a meaningful conversation with him. As I recall he was occasionally employed to do field research for the Democratic National Committee. I must say I don't really connect him with the White House or the Oval Office."

"Are you saying that President Bonner did not know him?"

"Please don't put words in my mouth, Mr. Shaw. I do not speak for the President. How in the world would I know that? The President of the United States knows a great many people I do not know."

"So you're not worried about political damage control in the wake of these two deaths?"

"Good lord, I fail to see how they are involved in any way with the President's political reactions, his ability to govern, or the programs he's running on. Perhaps you can enlighten me, Mr. Shaw, as to any connection—I am always willing to learn, and I pride myself on keeping an open mind."

"Well, with all due respect, Mr. Larkspur, if you don't see any connection, then you must be the only person in Washington tonight who doesn't. The President is in trouble, Mr. Hazlitt is coming on fast—"

"First, Mr. Shaw, I have never been particularly bothered by standing alone if I am right. I am sorry, but I can't say I accept your contention that the President is in trouble. The President seems very much in control, enjoying the campaign—he's enthused, he's excited about meeting this challenge, he's delighted to be involved in an energetic race which will allow him to say a few things he wouldn't be saying if he were coasting to an easy renomination. He is able to sharpen his positions in the eyes of the electorate—to get himself ready for the campaign against the Republican nominee, should it be Price Quarles or some other worthy." Larkspur had done hundreds if not thousands of these interviews. His command of the geometry involved was impressive. Always calm, always aware of the perimeters of the discussion, always knowing how far afield he might go, how to disagree without offending, always setting up the next question so he knew he had the perfect answer, like a pool shark always leaving himself the shot he wants. What he was trying to do with Shaw was make a lobster salad with canned tuna. He had damn little to work with. He knew it. Shaw knew it. But that didn't stop either of them.

"That's all very well, Mr. Larkspur, but when I say the

President is in trouble you know perfectly well what I'm talking about. This town has been deluged with rumors of disaster for months, rumors that there was a cancer growing on the presidency, rumors that it would prove fatal—"

"Now, now, Mr. Shaw, I cannot believe that you asked me to come in here tonight to comment on . . . rumors. Rumors are just that, and as such they are nonsense and unworthy of our time."

"Nonsense to you, perhaps, but not apparently to the American public. The existence of rumors is a fact." Shaw consulted a folder of clippings, then looked up and spoke carefully. "For instance, Ballard Niles's column in the *World Financial Outlook* that will appear tomorrow morning—it's all over Washington tonight. Much has been made of it here within the Beltway—Niles contending that Summerhays was involved in some kind of secret machination with Mr. Tony Sarrabian. Niles contends that it represents a level of corruption to which Mr. Summerhays had fallen at the end of his life. What do you make of that?"

"The dogs will bark but the caravan moves on, Mr. Shaw. You have made my point exactly—consider the source, in the first place. Ballard Niles has so far as I can tell not even a passing relationship with truth. He prefers to invent, to embroider, to misinterpret. In the second place, it might have been me deep in conversation with Tony Sarrabian. Indeed, I saw *you* deep in conversation with this same Tony Sarrabian at the Jockey Club—let me see, was it two weeks ago?"

Shaw smiled suddenly. "Three."

"Am I to conclude that you are suddenly a social pariah? Shaping stories as Sarrabian wants them? I think not. Ballard Niles is a rumormonger of the most deplorable sort, as I have told him to his face on many occasions, as recently as dinner ten days ago at Citronelle in Georgetown. These rumors you speak of are entirely new in my experience of public life . . . now *this* is a subject worth discussing. This phenomenon—the use of rumor itself as a political bludgeon. *They are rumors about rumors,* you see. No substance to them, not even an imaginary substance. Well, it will take a lot more than tactics like these to cause Charles Bonner to miss a night's sleep . . . or to fool the American people. Rumors about rumors," Larkspur snorted dismissively. "The very idea!"

"Well, the polls are not rumors, and last night the CNN poll showed a continuing disturbing trend, accelerating since last January. President Bonner—"

"Oh, come, come, Mr. Shaw. Polls. *Really.*"

"And you tell me tonight that the President isn't losing any sleep over all this? Maybe he doesn't quite grasp the seriousness of the situation. What can he do to avert the apparent disaster that's bearing down on him?"

"I said he wasn't losing any sleep over the rumors," Larkspur said, chuckling. "The fight for the nomination is a hard fight."

Shaw couldn't resist interjecting: "And he stands by his State of the Union message? No matter what it costs him?"

"He stands by it. He believes in it. He is willing to take an unpopular stand." He was taking the tension out of the moment, and the feeling was one of relief; he wasn't stonewalling. "But these polls, they're just the polls, aren't they? They're really very volatile at this point, aren't they?" Pause. "Or at least they'd better be." He smiled again dryly. "They bounce, they fluctuate. You must realize that the President is a known quantity, that he had virtually a hundred percent lead over 'Anonymous' until Bob Hazlitt got into the race. Bob is an engaging son of a gun. He's a genius, in fact—he has created his own technological revolution, nothing less." The bullshit level was just astonishing but old Ellery was selling it, closing the deal. "Bob has tremendous appeal and, quite frankly, I wouldn't be surprised if the President asked him to assume the directorship of one of several very important commissions in the second term—but our sampling of Democrats shows that most of them feel that the President will be renominated. In the meantime, they find Bob Hazlitt an interesting fellow—"

"But if too many of them find him so interesting, he could grab this nomination before the game begins. Is there a chance that the President, if he takes a sounding and finds

the delegates turning strongly against him, might just fold
his tent and drop out?"

"Oh, I really don't think so, Bernie. Of course, he's never
lost an election. But it looks like we're going to the convention undecided. And in that circumstance, I feel sure the
President is content with his chances. You might even find
the party pulling together, the way we Democrats do after
a good fight—Bob Hazlitt might even wind up giving the
President's nominating speech. I don't need to tell you
what a funny business politics is, Bernie."

Shaw said, "Truer words were never spoken," and
turned to the camera. "Bob Hazlitt and Ellery Dunstan
Larkspur, two men with a great deal at stake as the Democrats seek a presidential nominee. A few months ago it was
no contest. Tonight we've got a horse race. This is Bernard
Shaw, in Atlanta for CNN. Good night."

It was thundering over the city, lightning was flashing. At
nearly one o'clock Monday morning Ben was watching the
electricity on display when the phone began ringing. It was
Elizabeth, back from dinner on the West Coast, she was
returning his call. . . .

It was Ellery Larkspur.

"I just watched you with Shaw. Are you ever *not* on television? You were having a pretty good night. Where are
you?"

"Back in Virginia. We did the interview at seven. Look,
Ben—"

"Larkie, what the hell is Taylor doing in this thing?
What's the point?" He hadn't spoken to Larkspur since
Taylor's announcement Saturday night that he was not
only bringing all his support to Hazlitt's campaign but
going all the way, becoming a Democrat, as well.

Larkspur sighed impatiently on the other end of the line.
"Ben, it would be helpful if you paid closer attention to
politics. Really."

"So? You sound like Elizabeth—"

"Okay, I'll run through this once, Benjamin—it's not

why I called. Sherm Taylor's loss to Bonner was one of the closest in history. Less than a point. To some extent, Sherm blamed himself—he believed he'd taken his own popularity too seriously, he'd waited too long to get in gear, he'd have won if the campaign had lasted another few days. Well, he wouldn't have won, of course, he'd peaked and was going down by then, but it was true, Taylor might have won if he'd been quicker off the mark. So Taylor believes he should have been elected to a second term. He believes in a real sense that Charlie Bonner stole the election when he, Taylor, wasn't watching. But that's not all. . . .

"Sherman Taylor believes he'd earned a second run against Bonner. And viewed dispassionately, I suppose he's got a point. But the Grand Old Party strategists said no— they said that Taylor was a used-up button, that the electorate were afraid to push it, that they wanted a technician this time around, not a star. And they had, in their infinite ability to miscalculate a situation, settled on Price Quarles, Taylor's own veep, which pissed Sherm off all the more— getting left behind for a moron like Quarles. Quarles was calming, he was your favorite accountant, down to the plastic protector in his shirt pocket with all the pens sticking up like tiny missiles. Those were the closest thing to missiles Price Quarles was ever going to use. There was no excitement, no thrill of leadership, no capacity for danger, and none for greatness in Price Quarles—or so Sherm Taylor sees it. This is not exactly a secret, Ben. Read George Will. And every poll shows Sherm to be right. In a race against Quarles, Charlie's up about sixty-five–thirty-five. So . . . Benjamin, the GOP fucked our friend General Taylor and now he's fucking them back—and fucking Charlie at the same time."

Driskill smiled to himself. "He's probably a pretty happy man, then."

"If he's *capable* of being happy, I daresay he is. Now, Benjamin, the reason I called—"

"Yes, master."

"I just talked with Brad Hokansen—he's got the wind up and it looks like your doing. His whole life is passing before his eyes. Worse, after speaking with him, his life is passing before *my* eyes. He's afraid if the murders of Tarlow and Summerhays turn into a major political investigation he's going to be sucked in and destroyed—"

"You don't say?"

"He says it will eventually come out that he allowed some money laundering through the good offices of North Shore Fiduciary and Trust. During the Bonner campaign."

"Bonner money?"

"Maybe. How the devil should I know? I'm telling you what he told me."

"Silly bastard! If he'd just shut up—that's not what an investigation is going to be about."

"How do you know what it will be about? No, you can't blame him entirely, Ben. Frankly, what were you doing talking to him at all? You were supposed to be going back to New York—"

"Last time I looked I could go anywhere I damn well wanted. You can tell that to Charlie, too." Driskill took a deep breath: no point in taking it out on Larkie. "I thought it might be a good idea to find out what Tarlow was doing when he got killed. And I'm working on it. Turns out he wasn't working for the White House or the DNC. He was working for Drew. . . . Drew asked him to go out to Saints Rest—"

"Doing what, for heaven's sake?"

"Investigating some problems with Heartland. Brad had a tip from a Heartland board member—Heartland was supposed to be up to some shady business and North Shore has some big clients up to their necks in Heartland—"

"Like the DNC," Larkspur growled. "And Harvard—I keep track of these things." He sighed. "So . . . did he find out anything?"

"Who is asking, Larkie?"

"The President, wise guy." Larkspur chuckled wearily.

"Well, how the hell should I know? He's dead and there's no report." There was no point in telling Larkspur about the paper with the indecipherable line drawn across it. It was crazy enough without that.

"Ben . . . a tender point. If you think you're going to keep poking around in this mess, I'd say you'd be well advised to remember what's happened to Drew and Tarlow. Seems like a dangerous undertaking—though I'm sure you'll just go on doing whatever you want to do. Stubborn damned Irishman!"

"The thought has crossed my mind, to be frank. I'm not an idiot."

"Being an Irishman is bad enough!"

"Why do you say Drew was murdered—"

"Of course he was murdered, Ben. I don't give a damn what the cops say publicly—it's obvious to me. And we've got sources up there telling us that yes, it's murder. Anyway, he wouldn't let anything a creep like Niles wrote about him drive him to commit suicide—the very idea is preposterous. I've thought about it and slept on it—the President is absolutely right. Murder it is."

"Why did you call me, Larkie?"

"Look, Ben, the President wants to talk to you. He's not enchanted by your running off to Boston and digging around in this—"

"Oh, gee, and my plan was to enchant him, too. Bullshit."

"You know how he is during a campaign. He can't bring himself to trust anybody completely. He thinks everybody is sabotaging him. You and me and Ellen and Mac and everybody else near him. He doesn't like the news about Tarlow getting all this publicity—the papers are going to be full of it tomorrow. He keeps seeing those headlines, *White House Private Eye Murdered*, and more and more speculation about Summerhays. You know—"

"Well, poor Charlie! Why not just suspend freedom of the press and close down the newspapers—works wonders in the Third World! Just who the hell does he think he is, Larkie?" Driskill remembered Teresa Rowan telling him about presidents, how they would do anything to preserve themselves, no matter who got hurt. Warning him not to trust anyone, to watch his back.

"Calm yourself, Benjamin. It's just his fear talking. It'll

pass, he'll move on. Let me take care of the President. He's going up to Boston tomorrow—rally at Harvard and a big interview with Koppel. He wants you to come to Boston."

"A command performance? Wants to send me off to the guillotine himself?"

"He'd like to talk with you. If *you've* got a problem that gives *him* a problem—well, talk it out, get on the same page. And, Ben?"

"What?"

"I would not recommend flying off the handle with the President of these United States. It's a nonstarter, I guarantee you."

"In other words, come to Boston or go into hiding."

"Benjamin, you're in desperate need of an attitude adjustment." Larkspur sounded amused. "Believe me, I've been in your shoes and I've wanted to go into the Oval and start screaming bloody murder . . . but that's not what is called for at the moment. Agreed?"

"Sure, sure. But Charlie ought to realize he needs every damn friend he can get these days. He really ought to be careful who he turns against—"

"Why not bring Elizabeth to Boston? In all truth—and don't go crazy on me again—he'd like to speak with her, too, since she's a journalist and she has access to you. He doesn't want her to start leaking—"

"Not another word, Larkie. Not one more word! When he starts picking on Elizabeth I'm outta here. I'm a memory. Put that one in his ear and push hard. You got that?"

"Of course, Ben. I'm just trying to put you in the picture so you won't be taken by surprise—"

"Just tell him what I said, that's all. He's not the only one who can surprise people."

"Indeed. I'll be at the Ritz. See you tomorrow, Ben."

"What a treat it's going to be."

He left Larkie laughing softly as he hung up.

Chapter 9

Ben was in his office early, wanting to beat the crowd. He was going to be laying down some laws today and he wanted to be in the proper mood to dictate rather than discuss.

The atmosphere in the office was palpably somber, unlike anything he'd experienced before. Work was going on beneath a shroud of sorrow, yes, but even more, within a kind of fishbowl of curiosity: Everyone seemed to be moving in fits and starts, glancing about for a clue to what they might expect. He could see the questions implicit in their eyes: What's going on? We know you can tell us, Mr. Driskill. They wanted to hear from him that everything was going to be all right.

He nodded and smiled sadly, reassuringly as he passed among them, left his office, and made himself visible to the clerks and associates and secretarial staff, spoke with several of the long-termers and saluted Summerhays with little blowing pennants of memory. It felt like Drew had been gone a long time, not just two days. After commiserating and sharing a hug of regret and loss with his secretary Helen Faber, he told her to call the two reporters who'd left messages on his machine and get them on the line at once. "They're not going to make your day any easier," she cautioned. She was only in her early thirties, but she'd somehow sensed that with Mrs. Driskill gone so much of the time, he needed a bit of looking after.

"You always tell me to get the irritating stuff taken care of first," he said. "Anyway, I'm just warming up." He grinned and went into his office. He summoned his old friend Bert Rawlegh to let the partners know there was a meeting in exactly one hour. He was assuming the role of the firm's leader now that Drew was gone, sidestepping committees, as Drew had done, exerting his will on them all. It was always best to strike first, clear out the barbed wire, and head for high ground—then look around for trouble.

Rawlegh stroked his jowls. "That's how you got so popular—fear and intimidation." He had a small nose, beady eyes, a dour smile, and a slight wheeze. He was a better, more formidable friend than he appeared, which was one reason he was so valuable to Driskill.

"Their hearts and minds," Driskill said, "will follow."

"You all set for Percival? He's not going to like you being the one to call the meeting."

"Good lord, I hope he doesn't think *he* should be calling a partners' meeting. Nobody would come."

"Nevertheless, you know Dade Percival. Thinks you're an uppity bugger."

"A challenger from the mists, our Percival on his charger?"

"More or less. Course, all the partners do the voting."

"Well, whatever it is, I vote for me. Now call the meeting, will you, Bert?"

"It's a privilege, managing senior partner."

As Rawlegh was leaving, Helen gave him the high sign. The two reporters were on the line gabbling questions when he picked up the phone. "Whoa," Driskill said. "I count three and hang up if you guys don't behave." They grew quiet. "Okay, now I don't like to reward reporters who call me at home. But yours were the names I picked up from the answering machine. So, here's my piece of the story. I was scheduled to breakfast with Drew Summerhays this morning at the Harvard Club. Subject—normal office business. Nothing bearing on his state of mind or what may have happened out there on Big Ram. That's my story and I'm sticking to it. Thank you, gentlemen."

"One thing, Mr. Driskill. We hear that it's going to be chaos at the Bascomb office. Everybody's worried about the President's campaign, now Summerhays's death, and the word leaking from the cops is that he was murdered. What can you tell us about all that?"

"Everybody's just fine at the Bascomb office. Always has been, always will be. Thanks to people like Drew Summerhays. The mills of the law grind on, gentlemen." He paused a moment. "And I haven't heard this leak of yours, but if he met with foul play, I'm sure the authorities will do everything in their power to apprehend the guilty parties."

"Can you give us a comment on Mr. Summerhays's passing?"

"Yes and get this right. Are you ready?"

"Fire away."

"He was the greatest man I've ever known. Period."

"Would you care to elaborate for us—"

He hung up because the questions would keep coming until he did.

He sifted through papers Helen had put on his desk, checked off and initialed various items, scribbled a few notes, then took three Advil with the ice water on the side table and headed out to the partners' meeting.

Though the tower was one of the grandiose lower Manhattan creations of the eighties, the partners room was something else entirely. Unless you were a student of law firms throughout the Northeast, it wasn't a particularly prepossessing room: long mahogany table, matching captain's chairs with hunter-green cushions, windows at one end looking out over Battery Park and further on to the Statue of Liberty and Staten Island. Antique English hunting prints on the walls, an even older Persian rug almost filling the floor space. Nowhere was there a touch intended to impress anyone. This was the partners room. The first example of received wisdom at the firm was simply this: There was *nothing* in the practice of law more impressive than the partners of Bascomb, Lufkin, and Summerhays.

The partners were seated around the table when he entered. Two cigars were lit and smelled good, like the way the law had once been practiced, or the way Ben Driskill remembered from his youth. They looked up.

"Good morning," Driskill said. "It's a sad morning on Olympus."

Dade Percival, looking like an anchorman, an effective cover of misdirection for his razorlike mind, said, "Very amusing, Ben. We all appreciate your bits of humor. But—"

"Good. They are just bits, as you say, and sometimes I'm afraid they're not fully appreciated. I'm going to make this short and sweet. Nothing leaves this room, as you all know. This is the first time we have met since the death of our leader. I have a very brief agenda. First, the partners room. It is a hallowed place for those of us, the partners, who have pledged our lives to this firm and love it and what it stands for. I propose it be given a name. A real name. The Drew Summerhays Room. I don't want to vote on it right now; I put it forth for your consideration and I would be pleased if you all agreed, to a person, with me. Second, when the police on Long Island release his remains, I'm sure the Church will hope for a very big deal at Saint Pat's and I think Drew would have gotten a kick out of that. The Church has every right to a big do—he was a distinguished son of Rome. He'll no doubt be watching from on high and chiding Nixon about something or other. Again, no voting now, just consider it. There is no family— no, I lie. We in this room are his sons and daughters, we are the core of his family. He dies one of us . . . and I will brook no argument on that point. It falls to us to teach those who come after us what sort of man he was. Champion of the poor and oppressed and downtrodden, adviser to the mightiest of the mighty. He was their conscience and he saw they paid the piper."

"Amen," said Joe Cochrane. "Said and done."

"All right. Obviously Drew's death creates a kind of vacuum at the heart of this office. We should all think long and hard about how we want to fill it. To think of *replacing* him is preposterous. We must think in terms of the work Drew was doing, our relationship with the Democratic Party, and the relationship this firm maintains with the Church. There doesn't need to be any rush . . . let's all do some thinking."

Percival was nodding. His chances to take on Drew's role weren't dead yet. He had time to sound out allies and build bridges to hold the weight of his ambition.

"There are those who think that the . . . uncertainty . . . surrounding Drew's death casts a certain pall over this firm as the party moves toward the convention. As a firm we are associated closely with the President. He may not be President much longer and, indeed, he may not even be the candidate of the Democratic Party. We must face this very real possibility and consider how we maintain our ties to the party. It is possible we may choose to go into a kind of eclipse for a while. As far as the party and politics are concerned, I assure you that if we do, that eclipse will be temporary. These are all issues which need deep thought and the most serious consideration. Agreed?"

Ted Flanagan ran his slender hand through his thinning red hair, caught Ben Driskill's eye. "Of course we agree. But I for one don't see how the hell we can work with Hazlitt . . . not after what he's done to the President. Am I being shortsighted?" Bert Rawlegh nodded sagely, in agreement.

Dade Percival said, "Our relationship with the party is more important than our distaste for Mr. Hazlitt." He fingered his batwing bow tie, peered over his half-glasses. "We might consider that, partners. We may find ourselves well advised to work with Mr. Hazlitt and I for one could see myself doing just that. Let's not burn our bridges nor cut off our noses, if you see my point."

Driskill said, "This is why we each need a chance to think, to discuss the issues with one another. I suggest that we say nothing to the press and say it in the most helpful way. We don't want them after us. But we don't want our guts all over the floor either. Now, a personal note. Hayes Tarlow. If any of you has had anything to do with Hayes over the last few months, please let me know. I'll be in my office the next few hours."

"Are you going to be in touch with the President?" Percival being nosy.

"I may run into him. Maybe not. But I will be very busy." He looked around at the faces. "Everything's been covered for the moment, I think. This office should obviously carry on as usual. And cut out the long faces—the Bascomb office is officially celebrating the life and career of a great man. If Drew had anything pending it can either wait or you should inform me of it. But I don't anticipate anything urgent."

Driskill went around the table and shook hands with each partner. When he got to Patricia Adair and Bert Rawlegh, he said softly as the others gathered their papers in preparation to leave: "Pat, Bert, I've talked to Helen and told her she should take anything that can't wait and give it to either of you. I may be out of touch for a few days—but I'll stay in touch with one of you or the other. You can baby-sit any clients who've truly got the wind up for some reason. I know you'll do exactly the right thing."

"Thanks, Ben. I appreciate that." Adair smiled. Rawlegh nodded through the smoke from his cigar. "Of course," he said.

"It's only the truth, partners." And then Ben Driskill left the partners room and headed back down the hall to his corner office. From a distance he saw Helen motioning him to hurry up.

"It's Elizabeth," she said, as he swept past. She looked hopeful. Whatever she could do to help them hold it together, she'd do.

"Oh, Ben," his wife gasped with relief. "Thank God you're there."

"I called you back in LA last night. Nobody there."

"I decided to catch a flight back to Washington. Got in late last night—Ben, I can't believe Drew's dead."

He hesitated. There were things he didn't want to say until he saw her.

"Ben, are you all right?"

"I'm okay."

"The word I'm hearing since I got back to Washington is murder—"

He gave her the outlines of the last few days.

"So you went down to see the President?" She'd caught the salient fact: He knew it as she breathed the words. *Are you getting back into the game?* That was the question she was asking. "Well, how was he? How's he handling it? And there's Tarlow and, I don't know, what next?"

"Charlie's all right," he said. "I'm not that crazy about doing this over the phone, Elizabeth. It looks like two men have been murdered—I'm damned if I think tapping phone lines is beyond whoever did it—"

"Ben, are *you* all right?"

"No. Not really. There's going to be some infighting here at the firm . . . and I'm afraid all this is going to be very bad for the campaign." Did he really care? He wasn't sure he knew anymore.

"Charlie *is* taking it hard, isn't he?"

"Who the hell can tell with Charlie? He's not just Charlie—he's the President. I don't know if he even knows how he feels—he has to react as two men, not just one. Everybody is saying his campaign is dead in the water." He took another long sip of water, wondering just how to put it. "And there are some problems in the campaign that are just coming to a head." He had to give her something, let her know he wasn't withholding because he was angry with her and her job. It wasn't her fault. Well, yes it was, actually. But he loved her. "Charlie's getting really tired of Ellen and the endless flow of bad news—"

"It's not *her* fault!"

"Be that as it may, the truth is she needs advice in diplomacy and tact when dealing with the most powerful man in the world, that's my take on it. Mac thinks the President is going to give her the push . . . and if Ellen goes then Mac says he's gone and . . . you know."

Elizabeth sighed and he heard her tapping a pen against her coffee mug, imagined her at her desk in the Washington flat. "It's bad when it starts tearing the team apart. The team is just about all Charlie's got left. Ben—now don't get mad at me, I'm not pushing you—but they *need* you. *He* needs you—"

"Well, I've got some problems there, too."

"What in the world are you talking about?"

"Landesmann seems to be in one of his let's-kick-the-shit-out-of-Driskill periods. He hates me, he can't stop rubbing it in, and I can't help telling him what he can do about it. Not a nice atmosphere . . . and, as I recall, Charlie was not amused by either one of us."

"It's not a school yard, Ben."

"Tell that son of a bitch Landesmann." He laughed softly, let it go. "And anyway, I'm not required down there—"

"What's that supposed to mean? Who says so?"

"I was all ready for it, I knew Charlie was going to try to drag me into the campaign, bring me down to Washington to be his faithful old sounding board. I probably would have said yes. So he calls me at the apartment in the middle of the night, I've got Mac blotto on the couch in the living room—don't ask, it's a long story—and you won't believe what old Charlie said. *He tells me to butt out.*"

"He did not!"

"He told me that Drew's death would put this firm on the spot. He said the Bascomb office was now officially under a cloud—the mystery concerning Drew's death, then Tarlow's death—which he tried to keep me from finding out, for God's sake . . . their association with the White House and the party—"

"Somebody in this equation has lost his mind." She was moving around the kitchen now, banging things, turning the water on and off, making another cup of coffee.

"And he said he wanted me to be here running the firm and fielding the problems."

"What problems? A question or two? That's utter nonsense."

"I noticed."

"What's gotten into him?"

"Our friend Landesmann. Ollie put the idea about the pall over the firm in his head and Charlie took the bait." He sighed. "Though I'm not really complaining, mind you. I didn't want to be shanghaied into this campaign. But to learn he didn't *want* me—that's a bit much, dammit."

"Oh, Ben . . ."

"It's not just the butt-out routine. Charlie gave me a pretty good working over while I was down there. He actually tried to keep me from finding out that Hayes Tarlow had been killed! Can you believe that? It's in the papers today, for God's sake! But no, Mac told me—while he was tight at the Willard, trying to convince me what a bastard Charlie is, trying to enlist me in the pro-Ellen forces. So when Charlie called me in the middle of the night I hit him with it right away—what's the point in pulling a fast one on old Ben? He did a song and dance but there's something our President doesn't know. The sky's going to fall on him if we don't find out what's going on pretty damn quick—so I'm conducting my own investigation into what Hayes was doing out in Iowa."

He heard her lighting one of her three daily cigarettes, expelling the first cloud of smoke. He thought of Larkie, using the nicotine patch, determined to quit smoking. Larkie had, beneath the surface, a will of tempered steel; he'd quit if he said he was going to quit.

"Ben, there's something odd going on down here. I got a call this morning—a young woman named Rachel Patton. Very insistent, very upset, says she must talk to *you*. She's going through me to get to you—I guess she thought you wouldn't take her call . . . I don't know."

Driskill felt a little ringing in his alarm system. "Who is she? What does she want to talk to me about? Can you check her out? Make her talk to you—"

"All she'll say is it's about Hayes Tarlow. She says the President's involved, too . . . *but her instructions are to contact you.* And it can't wait."

"That's it? What instructions? What the hell is she talking about?"

"She wouldn't say. But she's scared to death—I'm not kidding. I heard it in her voice. She says she's being followed."

"Is she crazy?"

"No, I don't think she's crazy. She . . . look, I don't get this either but she says she's afraid to come to you directly—she wants me in on it, too—but you're the one she has to talk to—"

"Elizabeth, listen to me. Stay out of this—do you hear me?"

"She says she's afraid that maybe they'll kill her, too. That's a quote. So you listen to me, Ben—I'm not going to walk away from her. I'm going to meet her, talk to her—"

"She's either a head case or somebody really is following her and might kill her—either way, stay the hell out of it."

"With all due respect, counselor, I'm the journalist here. This just doesn't sound like you. Can you just let me evaluate my own business?"

All the frustration, the built-up discord between them—he heard it flaring in her voice.

"Wrong. It sounds *exactly* like me."

"Ben, she's frightened and she came to me and I think she knows something—"

"When are you going to see her?" He was resigned: There was no point in arguing with her.

"I don't know—"

"You don't know?"

"Ben, you're jumping all over me for no reason. Now cut it out. I'm a big girl and I even know what I'm doing. She said she'd get back to me when she made sure she wasn't being followed. I'm going to wait for her to call, that's how it's done."

"Take care of yourself. We've got two people dead, let's keep the number down."

"Ben, you didn't hear her. I did. And why must she see you? I intend to find out that at least." She was draining the heat out of her voice, trying to paper over the little row, making believe it didn't happen. "I've got it, why don't you come down to Washington and meet Rachel Patton with me?"

"I've got to go up to Boston and see Charlie. Larkie called and said Charlie wants to talk to me. He's doing a big interview up there."

"Ben," she said softly. "Ben, are you back on the team?"

He smiled to himself. "We're the only team I'm on—"

"But you're trying," she teased him.

"You get high marks for determination, Elizabeth. But when it comes to this mess, all I want to do is find out who killed Hayes and Drew. Poor Hayes was a friend of mine, but more importantly now, he worked for the firm and for the President and he doesn't have quite the heavy hitters looking out for him that Drew does. I figure Hayes died in the line of duty—and I'd like to know why. That's all."

"I'm glad you're not on the sidelines, Ben."

He sighed. "For God's sake, be careful with this Rachel Patton. We don't know where she's coming from."

Chapter 10

The traffic tie-up all around the Boston Public Garden looked bad enough to last a lifetime, but it was just presidential business as usual. The entire area had been cordoned off, sawhorses, ropes, cops in good moods chatting up the passersby. The presence of most of the world's known reserves of Secret Service men with the electrical spaghetti dripping out of their ears was sufficiently daunting to avoid rebellion in the streets. It was cloudy, the air thick with humidity. The trees were luxuriously green, shining in the artificial lights set up along Arlington Street. The expanse of grass surrounding Frog Pond was giving off the aroma of hot, humid summer. The unique smell of tons of electronic equipment hovered like exhaust. There were six television trucks along Arlington and up Commonwealth with microwave dishes hanging on the sides, antennae sticking out like big white bugs feeling their way. Everywhere you looked there were antennae buggy-whipping in the wind, cables like bloated boa constrictors were soft underfoot, winding their way into the serenity of the garden where Ted Koppel was preparing to interview the President, live at seven o'clock sharp. Koppel, his once reddish hair now fully white, had become the senior states-man of the news corps as Dan Rather and David Brinkley had moved off into the mists of history.

Driskill found one of the checkpoints and presented the official tag Mac had left for him at the Ritz. Boston's finest were doing the grunt work while Secret Service men were attending to the more glorious activities, like scanning the sky with an eager eye for rocket attacks or beating the bushes for potential assassins. The cop checked his name; a Secret Service guy checked it against his list on a computerized clipboard.

For all the security, it seemed like much of Boston had crowded into the nearby streets. Driskill elbowed his way through the tightly packed supernumeraries and then saw the President and Koppel standing in front of the great equestrian statue of George Washington. It was so massive, so real, that it seemed to move slowly, a hoof slapping the earth, the giant sitting easily on the broad back. You could almost hear the snorting of the huge horse.

Driskill crossed Arlington and buzzed the door on the huge trailer marked PresCom #1, and the guy at the door ducked out, recognized him, checked his credentials anyway, and waved him in. There were twenty TV monitors lining the walls, twenty pictures flickering on the Sonys. Six of the screens were devoted to the goings-on in the shadow of Washington and his horse.

Bob McDermott turned and nodded Driskill over toward the editing console. A team of technicians were preparing to produce instant commercials. Mac looked like absolute hell.

"What's wrong, pal?"

Mac said softly, "Everything—and then some. Charlie just keeps dropping in all of our polls, Hazlitt keeps coming on. It's a point a day—damn near a free fall. I wish he'd never given that goddam speech!"

Driskill nodded. Mac had been pretty well indoctrinated by Ellen Thorn. He didn't often give in to such despair.

"I've begged him to do a dozen different things, but he just smiles like the damn sphinx and says no, not to worry. I'm getting real tired of that smile while the campaign goes in the dumper. He doesn't seem to realize how lucky we were to come out with that draw in the New England primaries." Mac ran his hands back through his hair, left it in disarray. He was talking compulsively, airing it out, and realized it, stopped.

It had begun to sprinkle, as if the atmosphere just couldn't hold any more humidity. Men with umbrellas were suddenly at hand, doing a kind of dance, circling the President and Koppel and the aide carrying Koppel's notes. Then Linda came out of the knot of ABC-TV reps and Charlie put his arm around her; she shook hands with Koppel, who made a gesture somehow conveying his hope that she'd join them for the interview, and she was smiling and backing away—no way, not a chance. Charlie kissed her and she went back to the group of TV execs and Ellen Thorn joined her, whispered something in her ear. Everything was fine. Everything was normal. Of course, it was all an illusion.

Then the show was under way.

McDermott lit a cigarette, ordered a couple of cheeseburgers and beers from an assistant, and they strained to hear what was being said on the monitors as Koppel and the President began their stroll down to Frog Pond beneath the weeping willows, with the swan boats at rest on the gentle water. Somebody turned up the volume.

It was all foreign policy stuff, mainly about Mexico. The answers were as predictable as the questions, and Koppel moved on as quickly as he could to the subject of the rumors and how effectively they'd been used against the Bonner campaign, trying to get the President to speculate as to the precise sources.

"What do you want me to say, Ted? That Bob Hazlitt sanctions the lies? How do I know?"

"Well, Mr. President, tonight in a speech Mr. Hazlitt will for the first time denounce the rumors and innuendos, disassociating himself from them, condemning them in the strongest possible terms."

"I'm glad to hear that, Ted. What it's worth, we'll have to wait and see."

"What do you have to say about Sherman Taylor coming out of the Republican pack to lend his support to Hazlitt?"

The President flashed that smile, those teeth. "It's a free

country, Ted. I've got my hands full with the coming convention. I really can't worry about what General Taylor and Mr. Hazlitt do or don't do. We can win this thing. It's up to us, the Democratic team."

"Well, let's talk about your Democratic team. It seems to many observers that it's in rather extensive disarray at the moment. Over the past few days the nation has learned of the death—now called murder by the local Long Island authorities—of the legendary figure Drew Summerhays . . . and now, in a story that has kept developing yesterday and today, the murder half a continent away of a longtime Democratic Party investigator, Hayes Tarlow. The 'team' has lost two players, Mr. President, and now there's another related story that broke today in the *World Financial Outlook* linking Drew Summerhays with the financier and lobbyist Tony Sarrabian—and I have to ask you now, what was Drew Summerhays doing with a man who would seem to be such a natural enemy, Tony Sarrabian?"

"Ted, I have no idea. But Tony Sarrabian is a fact of life in Washington. He knows everyone, everyone knows him, he throws big parties, and as you know parties are pretty crucial to the work of Washington. What he and Drew were doing seems irrelevant to me. What Ballard Niles wrote about Drew in today's *Outlook* is, in my view, ill advised and unforgivable. Beyond that," the President shrugged, "I really have nothing else to say."

"And I must also raise the question of Hayes Tarlow, killed last week in Iowa, the day before Drew Summerhays died. Did you know Hayes Tarlow, Mr. President?"

"I seem to recall that I may have been introduced to Mr. Tarlow after the election almost three and a half years ago. In a general sort of way, you know. Tarlow was someone who'd helped the DNC—it's just a general, vague memory, nothing specific. It wasn't the sort of thing you make a point of remembering."

A couple more questions elicited nothing more concrete about Hayes Tarlow, and they broke for a commercial. Mac swallowed the last of his cheeseburger and turned to Driskill.

"There are wheels within wheels here, Ben, and I for one am going around in circles. Jesus, I feel like I'm so far out of the loop . . . and the fact is everybody on the staff, all of us, feel the same damn way." He ground the cigarette out in a pristine ashtray.

Koppel and the President were back for the windup and Koppel closed it out by asking, "Are you going to win it? Will you be the nominee of the Democratic Party in the general election? That's the heart of it, isn't it, Mr. President?"

"I want to say something, Ted, in answer to some questions I've been hearing and reading lately. People seem to wonder if I regret what I had to say in the State of the Union message six months ago—in light of the attacks that have come my way since then. Let me assure anyone who doubts me, what I said needed saying. What I said still stands. And what I said will be the one thing that without question makes my service in the White House a part of American history. I can't make it much clearer than that. The secret government needed to know that their days of having things their own way in our great land are coming to an end. And we're all going to be happier and freer and better off in every way as a result. A nation cannot realize its greatest potential if there is rot at the core . . . and we have begun to remove the sickness and make America healthy again. That I guarantee." The President took a deep breath and Koppel almost spoke, then realized with his perfect sense of timing that they were finished.

"Thank you, Mr. President."

"A pleasure, as always, Ted."

Mac swallowed some beer and gave voice to the mantra of the day. "Charlie's trying to hit a six-run homer in the bottom of the ninth." He shook his head skeptically. "That fucking speech . . ."

Ellen Thorn was sitting at the far end of the couch in the hotel, grim-faced, going through folders of computer printouts. More research. All she was good for now—you could see it in her face—was gathering data. All the strategy making had been taken from her hands; she was no longer giving advice based on the data. She had no more angles to play, no more ways to affect the outcome. She looked like she believed her polling data, that Bob Hazlitt might be the best man to lead the party into the future, a man for the people. She looked like she thought Charles Bonner was over.

Bob McDermott was staring at a television set, smoking a cigarette, squinting at the screen where CNN was already analyzing the President's interview with Koppel.

Surprisingly Ellen Thorn defended Bonner. "He's playing his cards as well as he can. Make the speech a plus, be proud of it—you're trying to save the country. Who knows? We'll take what we can get. It's the hard patriotism. Hazlitt's cornered the market on the easy patriotism." That was her strength. She had a way of seeing the truth.

Larkspur sighed. "I've been looking at your numbers and the delegate roundup—we've lost a lot of ground. It's not what Hazlitt is doing, it's what keeps happening to us. How many more disasters await our gallant band? I feel so helpless." Such an admission cost him something. He was a proud man, yet here he was, a man without the answers.

The President and First Lady were having dinner with the president of Harvard and his wife at the official residence before heading to the stadium for a rally. They were, Driskill reflected, bound to be having a better time than their staff in the hotel room. Maybe Charlie and Linda were offering their credentials, lining up cushy university jobs for after the day of reckoning. They were probably laughing about something at this precise moment. Charlie was so damn good at turning his back on the unpleasant realities. Ellen would have said he was in denial.

Driskill finished his drink and poured another, went back to the window, staring out into the misty night. Oliver Landesmann was standing beside him, peering up at Driskill over his thick-lensed half-glasses.

"Ben, here you are in Boston—I must say you do get

around. I understand you're up here to report to the President, and I find myself wondering, about what?"

"You hear a helluva lot. Who's your source?"

"I have many sources. Have you reported to the President yet?"

"Ask your sources."

"I'm asking you, Ben. Try not to be hostile or defensive or otherwise irksome. I'm getting a cold. I can feel the sore throat starting. Nothing worse than a summer cold."

Dinner arrived and they all looked at it listlessly, except for Landesmann, who had worked up quite an appetite. The waiter set up the table like a buffet and fussed over it until Driskill thought seriously about rushing him and pitching him out the window. Larkspur signed the tab. Ellen checked her watch and said it was time for Arnaldo LaSalle's show. Mac groaned but turned the TV back on.

You could tell right away there was something wrong; it was all screwed up, from the minute you saw LaSalle's heavy-featured face, the brows beetling together in a mask of extreme, theatrical concern. He was on the air live and Ellen was shushing everybody.

"We had intended this evening to present a roundtable discussion with political reporters and columnists from across the nation analyzing where the candidates stand with so little time remaining before the Democratic convention in Chicago. In fact we taped that roundtable in Washington this afternoon.

"But in the covering of the news we must remain flexible at all times—nothing must come before our responsibility to you, the people, and tonight we're in the middle of a fast-breaking story that we're sure you will agree must take precedence over our original plans. It's a story that once again spells big trouble for the Bonner administration, and for this campaign in particular. We'll be back after these messages—don't go away."

"What the fuck is this?" Ellen whispered, licking mayonnaise from her lower lip. Larkspur was looking on with a deep frown. Mac said, "Honest to God, somebody ought to do something about this prick!" He grabbed his drink, sloshed it over the rim, and polished off half of it. Larkspur murmured, "What's he onto now?" Landesmann passed a hand over the tight little curls on his head, blinked like a sleepy frog. He was shaking his head slowly to and fro.

LaSalle returned, a tight shot of his face, then the camera pulled back to reveal a huge photograph behind him of Drew Summerhays's Big Ram estate. "You will remember the death of Drew Summerhays Friday night at his Long Island estate. You may have heard reports that now the authorities have officially declared that Mr. Summerhays was the victim of foul play." Drew's face filled the screen, slowly morphed into Hayes Tarlow. "And you know by now that a small-time private eye named Hayes Tarlow was murdered out in Iowa, in a Mississippi River town called Saints Rest. You may have heard that Mr. Tarlow is known to have worked for the Democratic National Committee as well as for the White House during the Bonner administration . . . and to complete the picture it is also known that Mr. Tarlow was frequently employed by the famous law firm of Bascomb, Lufkin, and Summerhays . . . yes, the same Drew Summerhays. So, there is now a connection between the two murdered men—they both were deeply involved with the DNC, the White House, and the Bascomb law firm, and we have talked with people who will acknowledge that Summerhays and Tarlow knew one another, that Summerhays may well have engaged Mr. Tarlow's services for the law firm. . . ." He waited while the photograph of Saints Rest that had replaced Tarlow's face slowly dissolved and began to reshape in the blurred outline of a man's face, which a computer was slowly, dramatically bringing into focus.

"We now have a private source who must remain anonymous for his own safety who has told our *On Deadline* reporters that . . ." He looked at the face taking clearer focus behind him. ". . . this man . . . attorney Benjamin Driskill, one of the senior partners at the Bascomb law office . . ." He cast a look at Driskill's photograph on the screen behind him, and Driskill felt suddenly like throwing up. Landesmann had choked on a bite of sandwich. He was wiping his mouth and peering at Driskill, wide-awake, and wearing an expression of general condemnation. ". . . and a valued adviser of President Bonner, as well as an old friend going back to their football-playing days at Notre Dame . . . has been named as the man who met with Drew Summerhays at Big Ram Island on the night of his death!"

The camera returned to LaSalle's face. "We have spoken with a witness who saw Mr. Driskill on the ferry to Shelter Island that stormy night, saw him enter the estate's gates. Now let me caution you—our witness wants it made clear that he did not actually see Mr. Driskill kill Mr. Summerhays. And we do not suggest that Mr. Driskill is necessarily the murderer! But we do want to know what Mr. Driskill was doing at Big Ram, at Drew Summerhays's estate that night! We do want to know why Mr. Driskill has not come forward with what is surely crucial, vital testimony. We demand that Mr. Driskill come forward with his story, we demand it on behalf of the American people . . . the public has the right to get to the bottom of Murdergate!"

Driskill's picture hung there, slowly growing in size until it filled the screen with his name printed at the bottom, like a mug shot in a rogue's gallery.

He heard himself uttering a short expletive, but for a moment he didn't quite feel as if he were actually in the room. LaSalle had launched his face out there into cyberspace for a quick trip around the moon.

Landesmann's voice came from behind him. "Dammit, Ben, I told you you were on thin ice. Jesus, where was your judgment?"

"Ollie, I'll tell you just once. No more bullshit or your trip back to Washington will begin by going through one of these windows. I'm not kidding. There won't be a second warning."

Larkspur spoke with the full weight of his authority. "Gentlemen, I don't like this one damn bit. Now can it, both of you."

Ellen Thorn looked up, bemused, measuring the situation. "Listen to Ben, Ollie. Once a man's killed his first victim, the second's a lot easier."

She grinned broadly, but Ollie just stared back at Driskill, chewing on his chicken-breast sandwich. He wasn't afraid of Driskill. He wouldn't be afraid as he hurtled through the broken glass. But he was probably calculating how much he could sue for if he survived the impact.

Ellen had gone to stand by Driskill, touching his arm protectively. She was always the first to come to another's aid.

Mac said, "I don't buy his goddam witness for one minute. He'll never produce him 'cause he doesn't exist. Somebody tipped him off . . . believe me, ladies and gentlemen, million-to-one shots simply don't come through. Forget that. There was a leak."

Driskill wondered who had told Ellen and Mac, who had been excluded from that part of the meeting with the President. But that was Washington. People just found out. It was as if secrets were whispered, were planted and nourished in the atmosphere of the White House, and flowered, became public knowledge. It was scary.

"But who?" Larkspur asked, leaning back, forcing himself into his mask of urbanity. "The circle is too small. Just us and . . ." He looked at Ben inquiringly.

"The attorney general . . ."

"Elizabeth?"

"No, Larkie. She's been on the West Coast. I haven't seen her—"

"The telephone, then?"

"Absolutely not. Not a word."

Larkspur shrugged. "Maybe there *is* a witness—"

Mac said, "Don't believe it for a minute. Trust me."

"But it's got to be somebody from the Hazlitt camp," Driskill said. "Is there a mole in the White House? Somebody in this room? Ridiculous!"

He had never seen Larkspur's face so white, try as he might to disguise his concern. For a moment Driskill wondered if he were having a heart attack. Wiping his face with a white linen napkin, Larkspur said, "The leak . . . we've got to come up with a name . . . or a way it could have happened. And we need to come up with a way to handle this. Let's just think calmly for a moment, let's not go off half-cocked."

Driskill said, "There's only one thing I can do. Stonewall 'em. Deny everything. Did their fucking witness take pictures of me in the middle of the night? Make him prove it. Treat it like a figment of some overheated imagination. There's nothing else I can do—"

Ellen said, "The problem is the public has heard it. Once the toothpaste is out of the tube you can't get it back in. It makes it look like the President is somehow involved in murder—people who believe that, there's no way to change their minds—it's done."

Larkspur had recovered himself. He stretched out his long legs, rested them on the coffee table, buried his chin on his chest. "The attorney general . . . she knew you were out there, Ben. I'd like to ask her if she felt justified in telling anyone else."

Ellen said, "All right, we'll check it out with Teresa, but right now, let's all try to remember—has any of us shared the information with anyone? Talked about it in anyone's hearing? Anybody?" She paused. "I'm sure I haven't. Seems like Mac is the only person I ever talk to. You, Larkie?"

Larkspur shook his head. "Not after that meeting in the White House. I can't imagine any one of us would have blabbed. Ollie?"

"Of course not. I'm the one who thought—"

"We know what you thought, Ollie," Driskill said. "But telling me I'm an asshole isn't really productive at this point. Somebody leaked—and there aren't a helluva lot of suspects. Of course, we've left out one person—"

Mac said, "What are you talking about?"

"We've left out the President . . . did he tell Linda? Did he tell anyone else in the administration? Did he leak it himself?" He heard Teresa Rowan's voice: *Watch your back, Ben.* Could he be taking the heat off himself? Was there a hidden agenda? *Don't trust anyone . . .*

"Well," Larkspur said softly, "we can't pursue that at the moment, however clever an idea it is, Ben. We do, however, have to come up with a plan of action for Ben that we all agree on. For instance, we've got to believe the cops are hearing what LaSalle's saying—if they haven't developed this information themselves. They'll probably want to talk with you, Ben—"

Ellen interrupted: "The cops are nothing compared to what the press is going to do to you, Ben. You're going to have to have a press conference, Ben—"

"I'm not going to have a press conference. The only response I can possibly have is total denial. Anything else is begging for crucifixion in the media."

Landesmann had lowered his lids. He might have been sleeping. "And did you introduce Hayes Tarlow to the President, Benjamin?"

"This should make your day, Ollie. Yes, I did. I brought him to the attention of the DNC and the President. Through the good offices of Drew Summerhays. Yes, I'm the master criminal behind the whole nasty business. Guilty, Ollie, guilty as sin!"

"I say, Benjamin, get a grip—"

"Good God, do I sound just a bit pissed off? I can't imagine what's gotten into me—hypersensitive, I guess. It's just that you're such a major-league shit, Ollie. You bring out the worst in me—what can I say?"

"Stonewall, that's the answer. Ben is exactly right." That was Larkspur. "I go back to the Nixon days. And that was something they understood—it wasn't always a bad idea. If he'd burned the blasted tapes and they'd kept stonewalling, he might have survived it. His presidency might have survived."

Landesmann looked at him with raised eyebrows. "Now we're down to using Nixon as our model? May I remind you of one of the few times Bob Dole had it right? You remember what he called Carter, Ford, and Nixon? Hear No Evil, See No Evil, and Evil."

"He was deeply moved at R.N.'s funeral," Larkspur said neutrally. "So was I, if it comes to that. He had a lot of swine in him, R.N. did, but he was a surprisingly courageous man in his own way. Standing up to all those Bohemian Grove boys—oh, he did, y'know. He ran the risk of assassination when he wound down the war in Vietnam—frankly, I'd have bet good money they'd have had him killed. If they'd had their way, that war would have been a permanent feature of our lives. Of course, it had its good points, I suppose. In any case . . . stonewall, Benjamin. You weren't there, Mr. LaSalle has been had by someone to whom he'd doubtless paid a good deal of money—we'll never know who, I expect." He sighed. "It's a little disturbing, this mystery man being so right, but in the absence of photographic evidence, I say he can't prove it."

"You suggest we lie?" Landesmann said. "Lie to the press? To the people? I can't believe my ears." It was impossible to tell if he was making a joke or was in fact offended.

Larkspur smiled softly. "Lying in a good cause . . . That's politics. The Republic's built on it. You heard it here."

"Damn good idea," Mac said.

Chapter 11

It was a quarter past nine when Driskill returned to his room at the Ritz, 9:17 when the telephone rang. It was Elizabeth. She'd just seen the LaSalle report.

"It's not true, is it, Ben? He's such a bloody liar."

He took a deep breath. "Yes, I'm afraid it is true. But very different than he implied. I wanted to wait until I saw you in person. Larkie called me that night, worried about Drew—said he hadn't seemed himself lately. I decided I ought to go out to the island and keep him company that weekend. Big storm coming. Seemed a good idea. So I did, but I didn't get there in time. He was dead."

"My God, Ben . . . then you went down to Washington?"

"The next morning. I couldn't get off the island that night. Look, I'll give you the whole story when I see you. Now, backtrack—I want to see your Rachel Patton as soon as possible. Have you made contact again?"

"Not only made contact, I've got her with me."

"I'll come down to Washington—"

"No, no, just listen to me, listen carefully. Ben, there's a back channel in the White House—"

"What? What in the name of God are you talking about?"

"It's Rachel Patton, that's what she told me."

"Elizabeth, I'm not quite getting this—"

"Rachel Patton was being used to help set up a private

channel involving Drew and Hayes Tarlow and someone else—someone in the White House."

"What kind of back channel? What was in the pipeline?" He was thinking back to the Reagan years, the Nixon years. There were always back channels. . . .

"I don't know, Ben. She won't tell me."

"Okay, okay. Look, I'll come down to Washington, next flight. I have got to talk with this woman now. Right now."

"She was afraid to stay in Washington. She's terrified. And she has damn well convinced me. Ben . . . we're up in Middlebury—"

"Vermont? You're in *Vermont*?"

"I had to come up to cover the President's campaign. He'll be at Sugar Bush. I couldn't leave her behind. She's terrified. Ben, look, there's a complication—now she's afraid of you—"

"You're kidding!"

"No, I'm not kidding. We watched the LaSalle show together, and now she's afraid you're somehow involved in the killings—no, don't say it, I know it's crazy, but she's living in a world of fear—"

"That bastard LaSalle!"

"Rachel is just torn. She trusts me, but she doesn't know if she can trust you."

"You have got to convince her, sweetheart. I've got to talk to her."

"I'll do my best."

He paused, waiting for the pieces to drop into place. Something was eating at him. "And if she tells you everything she knows, are you going to tell me you have to report it? Or investigate it? Or some damn thing. The reporter's creed? A back channel in the White House, what a story! And then Charlie may be royally screwed out of his job."

"Don't worry about the reporter's creed, my darling. It requires me to know the facts of what I'm talking about—which we don't. But I wonder, do you think Charlie could be part of it? Or is the point of the back channel to circumvent the President?"

"She's the one with the answers, not us."

"Ben, she hasn't given me a hint of what it's about. I don't know how much she knows." Her voice trailed off helplessly. "All I'm sure of is how terror-stricken she is—I'm trying to calm her down, make her realize that Tarlow wouldn't have sent her to the wrong man."

"We don't even know that's true. All we know is what she's told you. She drops Tarlow's name . . . well, maybe she's the real thing. Maybe she's not. Remember, it's politics."

"You'll understand when you see her, Ben."

"Okay, hold the fort. I'm coming up. Now."

"Well, hurry. It's nine-thirty, darling. The Middlebury Inn. Step on it." She gave him the room number.

Half an hour later he had a pilot with a Lear jet waiting for him on a Lexington airstrip. By ten minutes past ten o'clock he was in the air.

The lobby at the Middlebury Inn was a genial madhouse, full of reporters, staffers, the whole lot that were particularly crucial to the presentation of the President to the public. Favored treatment for certain TV people. Some columnists for the national magazines. Cronies of the President. It was a kind of party, driven by the Koppel interview and the subsequent LaSalle show putting Driskill at the scene of the murder. That was plenty to get the evening into high gear.

Driskill, watching from a hallway, felt like a man of a certain age stumbling into an elaborate frat party. He went up the back way, missing the crowds. When he knocked on the door he heard Elizabeth call out, "Who is it?"

"Don Mattingly of the Yankees." That was their password, had been for years.

She opened the door.

He wasn't entirely prepared for the flood of emotion he felt when he saw Elizabeth with her wide smile and the glossy dark brown hair and the level gaze. His heart leaped in his chest like a kid's and she stretched out her arms and he was holding her tight, forgetting all the frustrations her career brought and remembering what had brought them together, the warmth of her love and passion. He felt her breathing against him, felt her cling to him, his arms enfolding her. He smelled her hair, her scent, and kissed her until she pulled away gasping and said, "And this is Rachel Patton. Rachel, this is my husband, lest you get the wrong idea. Ben, Rachel." She took Rachel's hand and gently pulled her toward them. "Try to trust me, Rachel. He's not going to hurt you."

The surprise on Rachel Patton's face was obvious. She cast a sideways glance at Elizabeth, reproaching her. "You didn't tell me—"

"I had to do it," Elizabeth said.

"You should have told me he was coming."

"It's too important to worry about hurt feelings," Driskill said. "She and I know damn well I'm not one of the bad guys—you're going to have to show me that you have good information. The real thing, do you understand?"

"Don't try to get tough with me," she said, staring him down. "I'm the one who's come forward." Her small fists were clenched at her sides.

Driskill looked into her gleaming dark eyes. Slowly he felt himself smiling. "Miss Patton, if I sound too tough—well, you're not the only one with problems. You heard LaSalle tonight—every reporter in America would like to find me at the moment, to say nothing of cops investigating Drew Summerhays's death. I'm on the hot seat, you're on the hot seat, and people are getting killed. You're afraid. Okay. But try not to be afraid of me. All I want is to do my best for the President. He's your candidate, isn't he, Rachel?"

She nodded.

"We don't want to wreck his chances, do we? We can't have Bob Hazlitt in the White House . . . can we?"

"No, I don't want that."

"That's why I need to hear your story. It's that simple."
He held out his hand.

Rachel Patton shook hands with him. She smiled tenta-
tively, her dark eyes still wary, suspicious. She was small
and solid, one of those very cleverly put-together girls, her
hair black and shining and pulled back tight, not a strand
out of place. She said in a small voice, "Mr. Driskill, Mrs.
Driskill—Elizabeth—has been more help than I can tell
you and . . . I'm going to have to trust you, aren't I? And I
have to trust what Mr. Tarlow told me—that if anything
happened to him you were the one I should turn to."

"That's good, Rachel. Hayes wouldn't lead you astray.
Now let's get down to it." Ben slipped out of his jacket and
threw it over the back of a couch. "My God, it's gonna be
a long hot summer," he muttered, and Elizabeth nodded,
smiling. He settled down in an armchair. "Let's see. Were
you followed leaving Washington?"

"I pray he's not here," the young woman said. "But I
think . . . maybe he is." She made an anxious gesture with
her hands. Elizabeth was arranging two ice buckets and the
tray of soft drinks on the table between the couches flanking the fireplace in the suite.

Elizabeth slipped out of the tobacco-colored linen jacket
and placed it next to Ben's. "Diet Coke," she said, pointing
at the coffee table.

"Dream wife," Driskill said. "And two buckets of ice.
I've never been so hot—it's ghastly in Boston." He was
emptying the can over ice cubes. "Rachel? Elizabeth?"

He poured them Cokes. "Okay, Rachel. We might as
well get started. What about this stalker?"

"He *changes* . . . changes what he looks like. . . . I only
recognize him when I've had a chance to watch him for a
while. . . . I don't know how he does it, but he's always
different. Sometimes he's middle-aged. Sometimes he's like
a grad student in Georgetown."

"All right—so begin at the beginning. I want to hear
some of it and then we'll decide where to go from here.
Okay?"

Elizabeth leaned toward him from her end of the couch.

She took his hand and squeezed it, as if by reflex. He squeezed back, wondering for a moment why he got so bent out of shape with her schedule. But it was easy—he simply missed her presence whenever she was gone. Unequivocally, Elizabeth was the best thing that had ever happened to him. In a way, she had civilized him, drawn the anger out of him and continued to do so.

Rachel Patton's voice was still reluctant, soft and husky. She sounded hesitant, as if she might clam up and bolt the room if he spooked her. "I can't quite get it through my thick head that I'm here, talking with both of you—so many horrible things have had to happen to put me here . . . and you make me feel like a kid . . . but I am serious, I swear to you, there's nothing more serious than this. You just have to believe me." She was scared. She was very careful. She didn't know what the outcome would be but she was willing to take a chance. Just barely willing. It was in her voice and in the pauses.

"Look—Hayes told me to call you if anything ever happened to him. If he *went west,* that's the way he put it. He said you were at the Bascomb office in New York. But when I heard he was dead I couldn't find you, you weren't at the office, and finally I found a friend at DNC who got me Mrs. Driskill's number in Washington. I got hold of her and decided to tell her things and see if she thought I was crazy—well, I didn't know what else I could do." She looked at Elizabeth. "And she didn't think I was crazy . . . so here I am." She was twisting her hands together. The bright red nails on two forefingers had been chewed and were ragged, the only flaw in the picture. She was wearing a navy-blue blouse, well-pressed chino slacks with double pleats and a watch pocket. A light gray blazer with navy buttons lay over the back of a chair. She looked like a girl from a family with money.

"I used to be at Justice. But this doesn't have anything to do with Justice. It was something else entirely. Hayes didn't leave you any hints?"

"I'm completely in the dark on this, Rachel. I'm trying to find out what he was up to—it's the only way to find out who killed him. I'm assuming the authorities don't know about your connection to Hayes."

"No one knows."

"You've got to help me out here, Rachel."

"There was a back channel," she whispered. It was hard to hear her, but he didn't want to scare her by asking her to speak up. "I'm so afraid of my apartment being bugged . . . or this room. I'm very vulnerable on this, Mr. Driskill— there's almost no defense if they know where you are and you're not in an electronically shielded room. I learned that at Justice, I promise you." She breathed deeply, trying to calm her heart's racing.

"Go on. A back channel." There was a throbbing behind his eyes. There were no more frightening words in Washington than *back channel.* Kissinger running his, the back channel around Reagan during Iran-contra . . . all the back channels that had spelled disaster for somebody.

"Between the President's office and Mr. Summerhays and . . . somebody else."

"Between the President and Drew Summerhays?"

"Please, listen to what I say. I didn't say *that.*"

"All right," he said patiently. "How did you get involved?"

"I was investigating Sarrabian and Associates and ran into something about a company called LVCO that involved the DNC, so I called my superior at Justice. He put me in touch with Mr. Summerhays. He called me because he was the chairman emeritus of the DNC and we got on well and he wound up asking me to work with him." She sighed, remembering.

"And you're a *secretary?*"

"I'm a *lawyer.*" She drew herself up in the chair, curled her feet under herself. "Not a secretary."

"I'm sorry," he said. "You look so young."

"Well," she smiled quickly, "I am so low on the totem pole I do a lot of secretarial work. Paralegal work on occasion. Mr. Summerhays liked my appearing to be young. He said nobody would suspect that I was part of such a thing as a back channel . . . and he knew I was ambitious. He knew I liked being on the inside of something. And then they killed him."

"Why do you say that? *They* . . ."

"Look, Mr. Driskill, get real—they killed him."

"Who killed him?"

"I don't know. I hope to God they don't think I know who did it. If they'd kill Mr. Summerhays and Mr. Tarlow, they certainly wouldn't hesitate to kill me. Nobody would miss me, no front page of the papers for Rachel Patton."

"When did you get involved?"

"About six weeks ago."

"This back channel—Summerhays, somebody in the White House . . . and who was the fourth person? How did it work?"

"I don't know who the fourth person was. I don't know who it was in the White House either. I only know about Mr. Summerhays and Tarlow. All I did was, I moved information that came to me through both Justice and the DNC. Stuff would arrive marked to my attention, I was the only one who'd see it, nobody was jealous of anything I got from the White House. I was just one of those kids at Justice. Everybody got stuff from the White House now and then, nothing important. I would get mail and I'd send it to Mr. Summerhays." She took another deep breath, as if she were nearing the end of a marathon. "Yes, I would move it on to Mr. Summerhays. Or Mr. Tarlow. Or between them. No reason anybody would know. It was out in the open in that regard, nothing suspicious. If it had been marked to either of them, somebody would have paid attention."

"It never went through the AG?"

"No. I had my instructions from Mr. Summerhays. We used accommodation post drops in Washington and New York. And one in Georgetown."

"And you have no idea who the man—"

"Or woman," Elizabeth interjected.

"—in the White House was? Or who the other man was?"

"Mr. Tarlow sometimes called the fourth person 'the

man of mirrors,' but I never knew what that meant. But Mr. Summerhays had told me often how important this all was to the White House. Critical, that was the word he used . . . critical."

"Well, where did Tarlow come into this?"

"He'd send me stuff, sometimes Mr. Summerhays would give me stuff to send to Mr. Tarlow. I know they were in it together. Sometimes Mr. Tarlow and I would meet for coffee and talk, I'd pick up bits and pieces. Sometimes he just needed to talk for a minute or two. He'd talk about the man of mirrors. He didn't *explain* things to me. I was just a courier, or a mailman for the back channel. Sometimes I had to open packets and sort and route messages—they trusted me. And I didn't try to read stuff. There was a lot of coded material, I guess. It meant nothing to me—the little I couldn't help but see. It was pretty cool, too, the way it worked. It was foolproof, if you stop and think of it."

"Well," Driskill murmured, ". . . Summerhays and Tarlow are dead. That part wasn't so foolproof, Rachel."

Tears glistened in her eyes. She sounded a little shaky. "I know, I know."

"Are you absolutely sure the President knew nothing about this back channel?" It was the first big question. There couldn't be any doubt. "Think hard, Rachel."

"I don't think so. No, no, I don't think so. But it was somebody in the President's circle, somebody with access to him, somebody who could report on him to Mr. Summerhays and the man of mirrors." She mused for a moment, gnawing the forefinger. "I mean, the President *could* have known it was going on, I guess, but I never got the feeling that he was part of the process. No, I always had the feeling that it was *about* the President. There was a *plot* of some kind, what else could it have been? Then two weeks ago, it must have been two weeks ago, something sort of odd happened. Hayes Tarlow said something to me, one of those offhand things that you get the feeling isn't offhand, y'know? Like he was trying to tell me something. He said the back channel was 'all legerdemain' . . . and I asked him what he meant and he said, 'You know, it's like a trick, sleight of hand, it's all a trick, we're getting back at them, little girl, trust old Hayes.' That was all, I don't know what he meant. He'd had a couple of martinis, he was giving me something, an envelope, at a bar in George-town somewhere, and he just sort of thought out loud. . . .'"

"And that's all, no elaboration? 'It's legerdemain . . . we're getting back at them'—but he didn't say who? Getting back at the President maybe?"

"I have no idea, believe me."

"All right, by then you'd moved on to the DNC?"

"Yes, but it didn't matter to them where I was. *I* was the post office, not the place I was working. As long as I was just a worker bee, somebody nobody ever heard of, they trusted me. That's what it came to—Mr. Summerhays had trusted me first."

"And now half of the back channel is dead—"

Elizabeth broke in. "Well, not really. I mean, I know there was the man—or woman—in the White House, the man of mirrors, Mr. Summerhays, Mr. Tarlow . . . and Rachel. That's all I know of. And two of five are dead."

There was a catch in Rachel Patton's voice. "The back channel is . . . finished."

"You must have known what it concerned—"

"But I didn't! Now I'm afraid someone will think I did. I don't know what to do."

A sudden knock at the door rocketed through the room like gunfire. Rachel Patton flinched, the fear running wild across her face. Elizabeth leaped to her feet, calming everyone. "It's our bags. They were so busy downstairs when we got here." She opened the door and the bellman, smiling and ready to help, stood there with two bags. He put them inside the door and took the tip, said they should ask for Jack if they needed anything else. Driskill looked closely at him. Rachel Patton's eyes followed his inspection, terrified again. Elizabeth closed the door, leaned on it.

Watching Rachel Patton, he said, "You looked bad there for a minute."

"Look, you think I'm a lightweight, a dumb little flake who got caught in something serious—like a girl in a Hitchcock movie. You don't understand—I'm afraid I *was* followed here. I'm afraid he's waiting for me to come out of my room, out of the hotel—he could come to the door and we'd open it and we'd all be dead! If you can kill Drew Summerhays, we're all pretty small potatoes, even you, Mr. Driskill."

"Are you *afraid* he followed you? Or do you *think* he did? There's a hell of a difference. I don't see how he could have got here, how he could have known where you were going—"

"He knew where Drew Summerhays was, he knew where Hayes Tarlow was . . . and they were a long ways apart. Think about it. There's no reason in the world he might not be here. Look, Mr. Driskill, I'm not some kid who's scared of the dark and the bogeyman. I know I've been watched at home, and now I think he's here or will be by morning. This man has been following me for days now . . . people have been murdered, people I've been working with, and then he's reappeared over the weekend—you've got to believe me, he's got this face—"

"What do you mean? Slow down."

"Ben," Elizabeth said soothingly. "Give her a minute, don't yell at her."

"I'm not yelling at her, dammit!"

"My God, I don't know," Rachel said, "his face changes each time I see him."

"Then how do you know it's the same guy? How can his face keep changing?"

"Well, it does—what can I say? But not his eyes, his eyes, they don't always change. His eyes are funny. One time I saw him and his eyes were light blue or maybe more like very light gray, very strange, like those dogs with light blue eyes—and the next time I saw him watching me his eyes were dark brown. The first time he was wearing a suit at the main-floor bar at the Willard . . . then he was at a place called Sir Nemo's Underground in Georgetown and he looked like one of those perpetual grad students you see hanging around Dumbarton Oaks . . . but it was the same guy. Don't ask me how I know, I just know, there's something magnetic in him, like he's tapping into your brain from across the room."

Rachel was wiping her eyes. She excused herself and went to the bathroom. Elizabeth turned quickly to Ben, whispering.

"Ben, take it easy on her—"

"She's got to realize how important this all is."

"She's doing her best."

"She hasn't said that Charlie's *not* involved."

"Ben, what do you want from her? Ease up. And she's right, you know. Somebody is killing people, both in Saints Rest and on Big Ram, what, a day apart? And how do you think LaSalle found out you were out at Drew's place?"

"Either a tip or a crazy shot in the dark. The truth has never been exactly sacred to these people—"

"If you hadn't gone out there, you wouldn't be involved."

"Look, I did what I thought was right. Now we get hit with this back-channel business—"

"You've got to take this to Charlie, somebody's got to tell him as soon as possible."

"What if Charlie's involved, what if *he* set up a back channel to keep himself out of it, preserving deniability? What if Charlie's in on it?"

Rachel was coming back, face washed, eyes brighter.

Ben turned quickly back to Rachel Patton. "This post office box in Georgetown . . . was there an address on the envelope beyond the number?"

"Yes, they usually said some kind of acronym. FCAT."

Driskill blinked at that, looked at Elizabeth.

Elizabeth said, "FCAT. F-CAT. Fat Cat? Ben, what does it mean?"

He sighed, shaking his head, as if denying the answer. Then: "Fishercat."

"So?" Elizabeth said. "What's that supposed to mean?"

"It's Charlie's code name. . . ."

Rachel Patton looked from face to face: "Charlie?"

"The President."

"Oh, no, he can't be involved!"

"Rachel, we don't know what it means, do we? It's all a mystery. Answers are very scarce. . . ."

Driskill slid an envelope from the pocket of his jacket and handed it to Rachel Patton. "Go ahead, open it. Take a look at it . . . it's just the one sheet."

She removed the paper, looked at it, turned it around as if she might have had it upside down. "I don't get it . . . it's just a scribbled line. Does it mean something?"

"Give it to Elizabeth."

Elizabeth handled it in much the same manner, trying to get some kind of fix on it. "It's nothing. Just a meandering line. What does it have to do with anything?"

"Well, it does mean something. Hayes Tarlow sent it to himself from Saints Rest, special delivery, the day he died. I was at his place when it arrived. It *is* important. But it's impossible to decipher. Just another unexplained element in this mess." He refolded the sheet and put it back in the envelope. "All right, Rachel, let's get back to you." Driskill was fighting physical tiredness, but he couldn't just turn her loose for the night. He had to push it through to the end. Break the mood now and she might chicken out, leaving him with only part of the story. Elizabeth was paying close attention. "What was it all about, Rachel?"

She wrinkled her brow, intent. "Well . . . I think it had to do with money. I saw bank deposit slips once or twice marked with FCAT as the account. I think there was money—a lot of it, being moved around."

"That's good, Rachel," he said, ". . . but what do you think it *means*? Just in case you're right."

She pursed her lips. "It seems to me there's one obvious explanation, like it or not—I think maybe they were stockpiling unaccounted-for money for use in the reelection campaign."

"Well, let's grant that for the sake of argument, let's say that the President knew all about it. What's the quid pro quo? Nobody's coughing up that kind of money out of concern for Charlie Bonner's old age. What did they get in return from FCAT?"

She pointed her forefinger at him and said, "You see, that's the point, Mr. Driskill. This was a back channel—set up to *circumvent* the President . . . not to take care of his retirement! It's not for his personal use! I don't think he knew about the FCAT accounts. Mr. Summerhays knew, the man of mirrors knew, Mr. Tarlow knew. . . . I concluded that the money was being collected by Mr. Summerhays and the man of mirrors, funneled through them to various bank accounts in Europe, off our own shores, and in banks all over the United States. All the FCAT accounts. Mr. Tarlow was the bagman and I was the insulation which separated the three of them. Tarlow may also have been the man who went to the banks to make deposits and open accounts . . . and since they wanted virtually no paper trail, they did it using Tarlow in person, no doubt with many personae and all the necessary documents to match each identity. . . ."

There was no doubt in Driskill's mind: This woman was a lawyer, through and through. "So . . . *what's the point?*" he said.

"They knew the President wouldn't stand for their building up this fund, so they set it up for him on their own?" She frowned, wrinkling her nose.

"Well, at least you hope that's the case. This is your show, Rachel. You've seen all this money floating around. You've got FCAT. You've got your back channel. You're a lawyer and you have a lot of pretty strange information . . . there may be a crime of some sort . . . it sure as hell sounds like there is . . . taxes, for one thing, and maybe illegal campaign financing."

Elizabeth said, "And two murders."

Rachel Patton was shaking her head, worried. "You're the President's friend and lawyer. How do I know you're not involved? Maybe you're the man with White House access . . . how can I really, truly know?" Rachel Patton looked suddenly lost, began gnawing a forefinger. Elizabeth turned to Driskill.

"Ben, it seems to me that you've got to go to the President with this."

"I'm not arguing—"

"He's the only one who can do anything about it—"

"He's already told me to stay the hell out of it—"

"I know," Elizabeth said. "And now he's angry that La-Salle's story is out. But he's got to look inside the White House now and clean this up . . . before this is spread all over the media, before LaSalle mysteriously finds out about the back channel and the secret fund stashed away."

He stared back at her.

"I'd just like to hide," Rachel said softly.

"Well, I don't think you're going to be able to. The odd thing," Driskill said, "is this. The back-channel people are getting killed . . . *not doing the killing.* Is the mystery person inside the White House running scared now? Is he going to be killed next? Does he know who the hell is killing people . . . or who is stalking you? Elizabeth, you're always at pains to remind me that things are never quite what they seem once you start poking around inside the political machinery. Well, Elizabeth, you're right, it's more complicated than any sane person could imagine." He looked at his watch. "Rachel, can you go through it again, one more time?"

She nodded.

It was going to be a long night.

Chapter 12

At two-thirty with Rachel Patton sleeping on the couch in the suite's living room, Elizabeth having crashed into bed, Driskill sat by the window with a dim lamp glowing and the telephone at hand. He called through to the Sugar Bush Inn where the official presidential party would have arrived by now and spoke to Bob McDermott.

The chief of staff was found in the bar and answered the phone in the lobby. Driskill could hear the usual merry-making in the background, all the journalists and staffers who covered the President on a daily basis hanging out with the staffers and PR people essential to the care and feeding of the President himself.

"Ben, where are you? There's a hell of a racket going on up here. And Larkie just told me the President wants to see me before he hits the hay. What's going on?"

"I'm in Middlebury. Now listen very carefully, Mac . . . you with me?"

"Sober as a judge. Fire away."

"I've got to see Charlie—"

"Ben, look at your watch—it's going on three o'clock in the morning. He can't—"

"I don't want to hear can't. Can't doesn't exist. This is top priority. There's nothing more important than this. Are you getting this? We're talking about his personal welfare."

Mac's antennae sprung up. "Personal safety? What are you saying to me?"

"No, not safety. His welfare. I've got information he has to have as soon as possible. Trust me."

"Okay," Mac drawled, very slowly. He was thinking. "I'll be up there by three, have a word with him. Course, he wants to chew your ass about this LaSalle thing anyway. He usually gets three hours of sleep in this kind of situation, adrenaline running like a sumbitch." He was thinking aloud. "Ah, Ben, lemme call you when I get this straightened out with him. I'll get back to you when it's time to come visiting. Figure six, seven o'clock. 'Kay?"

"That's great, Mac."

"I sure as hell better not regret it."

Driskill was stretching out on the bed in his underwear, trying to stay quiet and as cool as possible. He heard rain slowly begin drumming on the metal box protruding from the window. He couldn't remember when it hadn't been hot and rainy.

"What was that all about?" Elizabeth spoke from the edges of sleep.

"Mac. He's gonna call me when Charlie can see me. Don't worry about it. It'll be breakfast. I'll tell him about Rachel." He kissed her as she fell back asleep.

He was sitting in a rental car, wearing headphones, listening to a late-night jazz station out of Boston. He munched a Big Mac with extra cheese. The Middlebury Inn glowed like a movie set, a warm summer night with maybe a little rain coming and lots of summer students in the streets. There were plenty of out-of-towners at the inn, mostly journalists who chose it over the quarters up at Sugar Bush. They were all sucking off the administration's dwindling energy, retooling press releases, doing what they were told—that was how he looked at it. It was all a load of liberal bullshit; that was what was wrong with newspapers and television.

He'd known where they were going because of an intercepted satellite transmission. There was no such thing as privacy anymore, not if you had coordinates and filters and access to technology. Or just a telephone number. His people had locks on most of the relevant numbers. They'd been watching the Patton woman once they discovered how things had begun to go wrong a week or so ago. They'd locked on to almost everybody involved, and once she'd contacted Elizabeth Driskill things began to look lousy for her. And here he was, staking her out in Middlebury, living on starch and carbohydrates and fat.

The question was, How was he going to separate her from the Driskills? The sooner he took care of everything, the better. He could see the light on in their room, then he saw it go out, but there was still the blue glow of television from one window. Somebody was staying up. He shook his head. Television was disgusting. How could people watch most of that crap? The question answered itself: Civilization as he'd known it in his lifetime was sending forth its death rattle and television was one of the places you could hear it. His country was being mongrelized by inferior beings who didn't care, who lived without brains or values, who just kept multiplying like cancer cells, killing everything that had once made sense and mattered. . . .

Just for the hell of it, he got out of the car, went into the bar which was closing down, got the last beer, went downstairs to pee, stood awhile afterward on the front porch. There were still some reporters in the lobby telling each other lies and laughing cynically, like they'd all gone to school to learn to act like reporters. Leeches, bleeding the electorate of whatever ability to judge the truth might still be alive in the public conscience.

He lit a cigar and stepped down off the porch and slowly began walking, circling the inn, meandering here and there, checking front and back and side exits, trying to nail down how he might keep the Patton kid in his sights. It wasn't going to be easy. She was telling them her sob story, how scared she was of the stalker. He knew she'd made him in a Georgetown bar, he'd caught her staring at him and he knew the penny had dropped, she'd seen him before . . .

and then Summerhays had been killed. And Tarlow, of course. She was no dummy. The killings had activated her as if he'd pulled a switch, and now he had to clean up the mess she was making. It was like the old days.

Miraculously his people hadn't forgotten about him. He'd done their bidding and they had been loyal to him, had come to him when he was needed. They knew where he stood, what he believed in, and they needed the skills he could provide. They remembered how he'd survived the tiger cages during the insurrection in Nigeria, they remembered how he'd escaped and killed his captors with nothing but a belt buckle, they remembered how he'd struck a certain kind of fear into the junta generals by not only murdering his captors and interrogators but by ripping and cutting the heart from the chest of the secret police chief and tearing it to shreds with his teeth and leaving it at the center of the carnage. In his world, he had become a whispered legend, spoken of with both fear and reverence. Secrecy was all. His name was little known and never mentioned. Few people on the planet had seen his face in its business mode and lived to tell the story. It all counted with his masters. They had known and they had remembered how he'd stayed on and tirelessly aided the good generals . . . and then disappeared on schedule.

Warrior One, they'd said.

America's secret weapon.

And he'd been rewarded with the villa in Morocco and the home in the South of France and he was protected by the kind of security only Arabs could normally afford. Sometimes he thought they'd kill him for knowing too much, but it had never come to that. They trusted him. They told him he was the only one. They told him there was no Warrior Two. They could never be sure when they might need him. Sometimes more than a year had passed without a call, but the checks never stopped going into his bank in Zurich. They had never failed him. When his mind wandered down these corridors he smiled at the way they thought of him. Like a comic book hero.

He was only of medium height. Weighed about 170

pounds. Wasn't a kid anymore. Nobody remembered him when they'd seen him. Except maybe for the eyes. His late wife had called them his Paul Newman eyes. But only one was blue, the other something else. That was back when he'd come out of the Point and they had fallen in love. Lifetimes ago. And, in any case, he had lots of lenses in his bag of tricks. He was always somebody different.

Maybe that made him a comic book hero. Mr. Nondescript. Mr. Anybody. Mr. Nobody.

They had brought him back from Morocco to save his country. They had set him up on a nameless island off the coast of Maine. He'd been there for two weeks before they'd activated him.

He was a killing machine. He'd been trained. He had excelled at his job. Sometimes in the middle of the night he momentarily doubted his own sanity. But, of course, he was perfectly sane. As sane as any priest or monk. He had his calling, his vocation. He had his weapons. Guns. Explosive materials. The scalpels . . .

He was happy in his work. It was important work, worth doing well. He was trusted by his masters. He worked alone, both by training and nature. He was always ready. They knew that. When the call came, Tom Bohannon was ready to kill and die for his country.

It would be so easy to go to Sugar Bush, infiltrate the surrounding mountainside, kill the President whose hands were soaked with the blood of Americans . . . the President of the weak, the helpless America. But that wasn't the plan. He had his orders, and orders were something he understood and took very, very seriously.

He remembered the Special Forces executive, the man who'd trained him in much of the hand-to-hand arts. He'd had a favorite saying.

The night is always your best friend.

He savored the cigar smoke, walking the quiet streets near the Middlebury Inn. All around him families slept safe in their beds because he was on guard for America. He didn't want credit. But it made him feel good, knowing that he would always do his best for America, a strong America that would protect and defend its citizens. . . .

When he got back to the car he looked up.

The television glow still came from the window.

The call from Sugar Bush came through to the Middlebury Inn at seven o'clock in the morning. Driskill jerked out of a half-sleep, felt Elizabeth's body leaning against him, relaxed and exhausted. She murmured softly, turned onto her stomach, and sighed without opening her eyes. "Yes," he said softly into the telephone. Through the closed door to the suite's other room he heard the distant voices of the TV. Rachel Patton was apparently up and watching television. "Driskill here."

"It's Mac, Ben. He wants to see you. Brace yourself, he's wired and ready to detonate. Can't have had more than two hours of sleep. He's ready to go off on this little campaign tour today and he said why don't you call Ben, get him on the bus and then we'll bring him up here later. Linda's still asleep, God love her. So, are you ready?"

He got dressed and when he went through the other room he saw that Rachel Patton was sound asleep on the couch, *The Magus* by John Fowles open on the floor where it fell, the Three Stooges on the tube, the lights all on, the window open, and rain spattering on the sill.

The inevitable was waiting for Driskill when he headed for the presidential bus. Sam Buckman of the *San Diego Union* caught sight of him first and began hastening his three hundred pounds toward him. Felicia Lang of the *Miami Herald* saw him half-jogging and followed, and Bill Murge of the *Des Moines Register* was already on the way. By the time they reached him a couple more print reporters, one from *Time* and one from *Rolling Stone,* had gathered around him.

"Hey, Ben," Murge began, "what have you got to say about LaSalle's report?"

Felicia Lang joined in: "Mr. Driskill, what were you doing out on Shelter Island the night Drew Summerhays was murdered?"

Buckman added with a wheeze: "You might as well speak up now, Mr. Driskill. Clear the air or . . ." He shrugged his massive, rounded shoulders, leaving the alternative hanging out before them.

Driskill waited for them to run out of questions.

Several other reporters had noticed the mini-commotion and were coming toward them. How the hell was he going to defuse them? He didn't have any options, of course. It was Nixon time.

"We all know perfectly well how Mr. LaSalle conducts his programs. I see a group of idea men gathering around him in some dark room proposing unsavory story angles to him. Who can we hurt the most? Where's the pain? Somebody obviously came up with this crazy story and La-Salle liked it, figured how to play it, and went on the air. No wonder his source is anonymous—it's probably somebody who works for him, the guy who came up with the idea. Let me make it clear—I was nowhere near Shelter Island that night, and LaSalle is way off base, which is where he permanently stands."

"You're calling him a liar, then?" Murge said.

"Is that too far out on the limb?" The reporters smiled, but there was no laughter. It was apparently too early in the morning for irony. "Of *course* I'm calling him a liar. Now let's get on with the rest of the day."

He good-naturedly pushed his way past them, heading for the bus. It was going to get worse. It was going to distract people from the President, which was both good and bad, he supposed, but it was bad for Ben Driskill. He wanted to get out of sight and stay there. The face of a delighted Dade Percival flickered across his mind. Goddam LaSalle! And if he actually did have a witness . . . well, there was no point in worrying about that. It wasn't La-Salle's style to have a real live witness.

They were sitting in the back of the President's campaign bus. The President and Linda were up toward the front, gabbing at the center of a group of working press.

Linda Bonner caught Driskill's eye through the crowd, held up her hand, fingers crossed, a huge grin on her face. Things couldn't have been rosier. You could see it in her face. Maybe she was in denial, as Ellen Thorn put it.

The first stop was in the tiny town of Lincoln, Vermont, where the President had been born and where he still maintained a small law office with some cousins. The bus made a big turn and pulled up in front of a general store straight out of the old days at MGM, when Mickey and Judy were looking for a barn so they could put on a show. Three busloads of journalists followed the same path as well as two vans full of television equipment, all pulling up close to the bright red-and-yellow flower beds. Time had stood still in Lincoln. Twenty or thirty townspeople were standing in front of the store, and they broke into applause when Charlie and Linda appeared. They'd known him all their lives. They liked him, but it wasn't as if Clint Eastwood had come to town to make a movie or anything.

"How's it goin', Charlie?" somebody called, and somebody else held up a baby in a sunsuit and a bonnet and called, "Mr. President, I got a new voter for you to kiss!" And sure enough, Charlie—looking like he was going for a golf outing—came on over and kissed not only the baby but the mother and shook hands with the father and must have said something graceful and amusing because right away everybody was laughing.

Somebody took the President's arm and he quickly moved his body between the man and the Secret Service agent who was moving in for the kill. In a place like Lincoln, back among the hometown folks, the Secret Service went nuts at the hopelessness of their job. Charlie knew these people and by God nobody was going to protect him from them. It was a huge photo op. Reporters, photographers, TV crews all filled the street, crowding into the local citizens and pushing them out of the way. The President got everybody's attention and then quieted them down.

"Just a word for you reporters, get your day off to a good start. I am today sending a personal letter—call that an appeal—to that great American Sherman Taylor asking him to join in our vital Mexican peace initiative. I'm asking him to join Admiral Sam Lord as cochairman of our mission to Mexico. I hope he responds at once and in the affirmative. Nothing would make me happier than to see General Taylor, such a hero in war, accepting a Nobel Prize for peace as a result of his efforts in Mexico. Admiral Lord will be leaving with the delegation in just a few days.

"Now, Alexandra will have copies of the letter for distribution to you all when you're back on the buses."

The baby started crying, but what looked to be the grandmother had snapped a picture of the President bestowing the kiss, so all was well and the President was past them, going on into the general store. Driskill and Mac were close enough to him to be sucked inside in the aftertow. The scene was, if anything, even more movie-set perfect than it had been outside, a Norman Rockwell painting come to life. There was a potbellied stove and an ice machine encased in wood and a Coke machine that must have dated from the late forties, a couple of old guys smoking pipes full of cherry blend tobacco and honest to God one of them was sucking on a Popsicle. Five or six regulars were standing around with cups of coffee, grinning quietly at the President as he came through the door.

He didn't disappoint. "Arthur, how are you? Haven't seen you since last summer—how's that leg of yours? Sam, how's it going? How's school, young man?" The cameras were clicking, the handicams whirring. "Betty," stepping closer to an older woman standing beside a pickle barrel, lowering his voice so only a few could hear, "sorry as hell to hear about Owen." The woman looked up, lower lip trembling. "It was his time, Mr. President. He'd be so pleased you remembered."

"He knows, Betty, he knows. You gotta be strong, sweetheart," and he put his arms around her, shielding her tears from the cameras, her hand patting his broad back again and again. When he turned to the counter he let out a whoop of pleasure. "Maggie, you dickens!" he said, lean-ing across the stacks of key rings and candy bars and jugs of Vermont maple syrup to kiss her cheek. She was a large woman with long light brown hair and a red-and-black cotton-flannel shirt with the sleeves rolled up and a vest. Fiftyish, with one of those breezy faces meant to run a store or a truck stop or drive a bus and know every customer inside out.

"You back again?" she said so everybody could hear her, and everybody laughed. "Seems like I seen you just four years ago. You look more like one of them carpetbaggers every time you show up." She was secure enough to kid him and he ate it up. The cameras moved in, devouring the scene.

The President bought his fishing license for the year from Maggie, then tried to trade his old pocketknife for her an-tique tin Necco candy box. "Are you kidding me?" she ex-claimed. "I traded a guy four pairs of thick hunting socks and a pair of long johns for that box fifteen years ago. Now here's what you need." She led him toward a clothing room behind her and handed him a fishing cap with a green plastic bill. He modeled it, pronounced it a good fit, and bought it. "Shall I keep the change?" she asked.

"Are *you* kidding *me*?" he called after her, and the room broke into laughter.

And then he looked up and saw a big political poster hanging beside the archway. Bob Hazlitt, white scarf flying dramatically in the breeze, stared confidently down at him. Everyone in the room watched the President do a well-calculated, very funny double take, looking on in mock horror. "Why, Maggie, who could have put up such a sign? While your back was turned, no doubt?"

Maggie gritted her teeth and held her ground. "Well, Charlie—I mean, Mr. President, I admit it. I did it."

He advanced on her, holding the fishing cap in one hand, reaching out to put his other arm around her shoulder. "Would you like to confide in me, Maggie? Feeling dis-gruntled, are you?" He was smiling. The cameras were going, everybody half-tense, half-smiling.

"Well, I think it's time for a down-to-earth man in the White House, somebody who'll go in with guns blazing . . . you know, crime in the streets, everybody's a crook, all these foreign problems that just won't go away, America's got to be strong."

Charlie turned to the crowd. "Do you folks hear what I hear? This is a Vermont woman, owns her own business here, she's far from the things she fears—she's not speaking out of short-term self-interest. She's a thinking woman and I've known her all her life. She voted for me as governor and as president, isn't that right, Maggie?"

"Sure did, Charlie."

"And now she's thought it over and she's heard my friend Bob Hazlitt and he makes sense to her—can you blame her? Can I blame her? No, not for a minute. But Bob Hazlitt believes in taking the most dangerous path, the path that leads to a mountain of smoking bodies, no matter whose. He's a brilliant communicator and I give him credit. He'll be a benevolent tyrant—follow me, he'll say, we'll kick some behinds . . . but the fact is he's a dictator himself, a dictator of the old sort, the kind of man who'll front the secret government, as I said in my State of the Union speech.

"Bob Hazlitt the man, he's all right, I suppose. He can tell a joke as well as the next man . . . but I'm trying to communicate my ideas—about him and about me, our ways of getting things done. He believes in doing things the old way. He believes the United States can act out of a power principle without regard to moral leadership, without regard to consequences. And I believe there are always consequences. And our old way of doing things, all of our secret wars and secret payoffs and secret deals and assassination attempts and throwing governments out to suit our fancy—they're behind the fate of lots of people dying of disease and poverty and hunger, dying of economic powerlessness and terrorists' bombs, and we have aided such terrible practices. Hell, the secret government has *paid* for such practices.

"Well, that's all over, everybody. I'm not kidding. It's a

new day and it's already under way. Do you think Attorney General Rowan is hanging about with me today, doing a photo op? Hell, no, she's back in Washington undertaking the biggest shake-up in the history of our intelligence forces—making them accountable. It takes time, it won't happen overnight—you folks are well informed enough to know that. And you know you won't see Bob Hazlitt changing any of these secret deals our people are always bungling and screwing up, making us the laughingstock of the world. You won't see him undertaking a worldwide peace initiative—too much of his wealth and support comes from the people who profit from all of these old approaches. War is good for them—do you get it? It's not good for the rest of us. We're not just nations anymore—we're all in it together, all interdependent, we all want our families safe and healthy in the future. Life is not simple, as old Bob says, no matter how much we want to believe it. I wish it were." He looked around at the crowd. "But it ain't. Now that's enough of a sermon for today, folks. Maggie, you vote for anybody you damn please, but go to bed tonight knowing that I'm your President and I'm working for a world you'll like better. Now give me a couple of minutes, honey, and you'll be mine forever."

Maggie reached out to him and kissed him on the cheek and hugged him and he engulfed her in his arms and it was the most powerful image of the campaign, Charlie Bonner reaching out in all his flawed humanity and drawing a Norman Rockwell American to him, smiling as if to pass his strength on to her.

And in a moment of pure theater she reached up and tore down the Hazlitt sign and with tears on her cheeks let the President of the United States pin a Bonner button to the lapel of her vest. Bonner . . . A President for All Mankind.

The moment was so overpowering that when the folks who habitually gathered in the general store began applauding, many of the reporters sheepishly found themselves clapping their hands, as well. It was irresistible. You had to see it happen, and thanks to all the cameras the nation would be seeing it, starting on the evening news.

From the corner of his eye Driskill saw Ellen Thorn brush away a tear. "Honest to God, Ben, he gets me sometimes. There's nobody like him. He reaches right into your heart. I'm a cynic, but I'm so bloody glad that every so often I realize I'm not so cynical I'm beyond reach."

They were leaving the store, trying to drift out of the crowd, when Driskill said, "Was that a setup? It was great TV but was it real?"

"You don't seriously think it was a setup?" Ellen said.

"No, I guess not. His instincts are just so damn good."

Alexandra Davidson, the press secretary, fell into step beside them. "As God is my witness, Ben Driskill, what we just saw was the rarest thing in America today. Unrehearsed, pure reality."

They all followed along while Charlie and Linda returned to the bus and headed out of Lincoln. For the thousandth time Driskill was struck by the President's vitality. He couldn't quite understand how a man could be under so much pressure and somehow shake off the depression and fatigue and the prospect of a humiliating defeat and turn on such a Niagara of charm. It was like watching a great actor drawing on all the reserves of character and training to come up with one more brilliant performance. It no longer mattered if it was real or not. Was anything in politics real?

Driskill still needed to talk to him about Rachel Patton and the back channel, and there wasn't any time that was better than another. He asked Bob McDermott what Charlie was doing during the rest of the afternoon and could he see him. Mac just looked at him and chuckled.

"Come on back to the house, pal. We'll squeeze you in."

Driskill stood at the curving window watching the rain glistening in the lights illuminating the ski slope. Down below the house the communications trucks huddled together, and more or less out of sight in the blowing rain. The guards moved in and out of the shadows, in and out of a prefab HQ building that would disappear when Charlie Bonner was no longer President. There was a lot of fire-power in the vicinity.

In the enormous stone fireplace, which described a circle fifteen feet in diameter, huge logs with thick bark were carefully stacked to draw properly and make a perfect fire. Presidents always had perfect fires; it came with the job. But it was hot and muggy and there wouldn't be a fire until autumn. The main floor was divided into pie-shaped pieces by furniture and bookcases and countertops and screens. The bedrooms were up above. The house had warranted a six-page spread in *Architectural Digest* when Charlie was governor of Vermont. When Driskill turned back from the rainy vista, the President was speaking.

"Well, Ben, it seems like a month of Sundays since I've laid eyes on you."

The President was standing with a glass of what looked like iced tea in his hand. He wore a bottle-green cotton sweater with no shirt, chinos, penny loafers with no socks. He was smiling.

"It's been what, three days?"

"Whatever. I've been busy as hell but you've been pretty busy yourself. Doing everything but what I asked you to do—go back and mind the store in New York." He made a sweeping gesture with his hand as if to say, Okay, there's nothing I can do about it now. "Mac says you want to talk to me, so I'll hold off on my thoughts re LaSalle and his story last night. Let's go for it."

Driskill told him all of it. The President was zeroing in, going into a zone where he heard everything as if it were in Big Print, as if it were being laser-printed on his mind.

Tarlow's hideaway.

Brad Hokansen.

Tony Sarrabian.

Nick Wardell.

Driskill was playing his cards right. He had to build up to Rachel Patton. He couldn't hit the President in the face with it before he'd built a context.

"Now, let *me* go through the highlights." Bonner had remained utterly impassive during Driskill's recital. Now he began to speak. "Tarlow. You knew he'd been murdered in Saints Rest. We all knew. At the hideaway you basically learned a couple of things and they're what got you going. You got a special delivery from Hayes himself, sent from Saints Rest, but all it is is a goddam line—we'll have it analyzed. It must be something important, but we sure as hell have no idea what. And you discovered that Hayes was having some dealings with Brad Hokansen in Boston. So off you went to Boston.

"Hokansen was a font of information, right? He had a lot of clients' money tied up in Heartland, including the DNC's . . . and Drew Summerhays was the chairman of the DNC . . . and Tony Sarrabian tells Hokansen that there are problems with Heartland but he's supposed to be a Quarles supporter—so we don't know what's going on there, right, Ben?"

Driskill nodded. "So far."

"Then Hokansen hears some more about Heartland— this time from the guy in Saints Rest, Herb Varringer, who's on Heartland's board and is an old pal of Hazlitt's. And Hokansen knew Varringer from a few years ago when he went out there to vet Heartland. Now Herb says he's got some real problems with Heartland activities and he wants a name high up in the administration to go to with what he knows. And Hokansen passes him on to Drew Summerhays. And they talked, right? And Drew didn't tell Brad the content of his talk with Varringer but he did say it was a job for Tarlow . . . so Drew sent Tarlow out to Saints Rest . . . and the next thing we know, both Drew and Tarlow are dead within about twenty-four hours of each other."

"That's it."

"Y'know, Ben, it's like one of those questions on an IQ test. You can almost figure out the question, but just when you think you've got it, it kind of wiggles away—it's hard to keep all the properties together. But we know we've got Sarrabian, Summerhays, Varringer, and Tarlow all tied together with something funny going on at Heartland." He had taken a notepad from a coffee table and made check marks beside the notes he'd now taken as he'd recounted Driskill's tale.

"So then you tried bearding the lion Sarrabian in his New York den—dammit, Ben, sometimes you just astonish me. But you played football the same way, I guess, kept throwing guys away until you got to the guy with the ball. . . . And Sarrabian, no doubt luckily for him, wasn't there."

"The important thing," Driskill said, "it seems to me, is that so many folks are tied in to it. Sarrabian to Hokansen to Varringer to Summerhays to Tarlow—all of them are mixed up in the tips that something bad is going on at Heartland . . . they all lead to Hazlitt, you see?"

"Sure, sure," the President said. "They all seem to be connected to Heartland and Hazlitt. I got that."

"Now there's something else . . . it's the most pressing reason why I needed to talk to you right now, why I couldn't just wait until you had the spare time. There's a young woman named Rachel Patton . . ."

Fifteen minutes later the President murmured: "Now let me see if I've got this back channel straight." His face, even his eyes, seemed to darken and his voice grew very quiet. He was rolling a cigar between his fingertips, making sure it wasn't too dry. He leaned back on the couch and lit the cigar with the flame from a big, clunky glass lighter. The self-control was taxing him. Smoke swirled away from him. The wind was blowing harder outside and the rain was tapping on the glass.

"There was some kind of betrayal going on in *my* White House. And the man I trusted most apparently set it up . . . Drew Summerhays. And he enlisted Tarlow and this Rachel Patton."

Driskill nodded. "Drew had set it up, apparently. With an acronym of your code name. It went from Drew to somebody in the White House to somebody Rachel Patton calls the man of mirrors—"

"What kind of shit is this?" the President exploded. "My White House? Man of mirrors? What is this, *The Phantom of the fucking Opera?*" He stopped, then said, *"Drew Summerhays?"*

"I told you you wouldn't like it. But I don't know how to interpret it any other way . . . at the moment. Rachel Patton was the courier when she was at Justice. And then at the DNC."

The President was off the couch, giving Driskill a hard stare. "You're a genius—I *don't* like this one goddam bit. What kind of back channel was it? What couldn't I know about? Why did they have to go around me? What the hell were they doing? And why? Setting up my retirement fund? Shit!" He turned and with a wicked sidearm flicked his glass at the fireplace. It hit the stonework and exploded like a gunshot, bits flying everywhere. Driskill flicked a shard off his cheek. The President glared at the fireplace, the mess on the floor, ignoring Driskill.

"Well," Driskill said, "at least you didn't throw it at me."

The President sighed. "Do you think this Patton woman is the real thing?"

"I believe her. Charlie—she's terribly afraid. You're going to have to put some security around her until this is over . . . whenever that is. She needs protection. She's very important to you at this point."

"Ben, I'll put somebody on her right away, you're right. But it's tricky—I'm only gonna say this once. The President never knows whose side these people are on. It's hard to trust anybody. FBI, Secret Service, the goddam CIA . . . where the hell is she?"

"I can have her here tonight."

"Bring her. We're gonna fly back tomorrow. I'll take her along. When did you find out about this? You should have told me right away."

"I found out around midnight last night, Charlie. So don't start on me—there's nobody working harder for you than I am. I am the only one trying to find out what's going on."

He looked away, kicked at some of the broken glass. "I know, I know." He went to the window and stared out into the blowing rain. The sky was growing lighter. "Where the hell's my iced tea?"

"You're walking on it."

"Ah, so I am." He went to the table and poured himself another glass and turned back to Driskill. "I'm gonna put some heads on pikes when I find out what's been going on. Bank on it. Ben—thanks, pal." He grabbed Driskill's hand and held it for a moment. "I don't know where I'd be without you. Everything you've done—"

"Don't forget how mad you are about LaSalle. Believe me, I have no idea what's going on there."

"Fuck LaSalle. We'll deal with all that later."

Driskill was on his way out when the President grabbed him by the shoulders, spun him around.

"Bring me Rachel Patton, goddammit, Ben. Understand? I'm gonna put this babe through the wringer. That's a promise."

As he left Driskill heard the President's voice following him. "Bring me Rachel Patton!"

Driskill opened the door of the Middlebury Inn suite and saw his wife standing with her fists clenched, then turning, startled, as he entered.

"What's the matter?" he said reflexively.

"Ben . . . she's gone."

"Rachel? What do you mean?"

"What part of it don't you understand?" She flared at him, dangerous with anger and frustration. "She's gone. I lost her. Just like that. It never occurred to me she'd pull something like this. She was so scared—"

"How did it happen?"

"We went downstairs for something to eat. I didn't believe the stalker could possibly have found her, I thought I had her completely calmed down. Then, when we finished eating, she excused herself to go to the ladies' room and Anne Furlong from Reuters came over, we were chatting about the convention, all the President's problems—and I realized about fifteen minutes had passed and Rachel hadn't returned. I went to find her . . . she was gone. Nobody at the desk had noticed her in the lobby. I ran upstairs like a maniac and she wasn't in the room . . . that was half an hour ago, her overnight backpack is gone. Ben, I'm not kidding, she is gone!" She slammed her hand down on the desk to make the point and an ashtray fell off. "How could I do this? She just walked away, nothing to it. Ben, I just trusted her and didn't pay attention—I never thought she'd do this."

"Did she leave a note?"

"Oh, yes, I'm sorry for being so crazy—the note." She read from a piece of hotel stationery. *"He's here. I've got to go. Please don't start them looking for me. Thanks. R."* She sank down on the bed, handing him the sheet of paper. The word *Please* was underlined three times. "She must have seen the man stalking her—"

"Or thought she did."

"Or maybe she just thought she'd be safer on her own. There's no hint of where. *I've got to go.* I don't know what to think, Ben, but it's my fault."

"Look, nobody would have figured she'd light out. Don't crucify yourself."

"I'm so worried. What if he was here, what if she did see him . . . what if she tried to flee and he was waiting? My God, Ben, she could be dead."

"There's no way to find out. We don't want everybody in Vermont looking for her. The sooner somebody finds her, the sooner the stalker will know where she is. She's going to be safest—unless he's already got her—on her own. Elizabeth, she's a smart cookie. Very impressive—I think he's going to have his hands full trying to find her." He had to hold out hope to Elizabeth. She was too close to the edge. But she suddenly surprised him.

"Then I got to wondering," she said, "what if she was using us? Think about the rumors, the way they've been everywhere for weeks. Who's to say she wasn't planting this one on us, hoping I'd put it in print, or you'd go to the President and it would all leak out. You can see the head-lines about the President betrayed by a secret back channel in the White House. Maybe she was just a spook, Ben. Maybe it was a dirty trick . . . to implicate Summerhays and Tarlow, who can't defend themselves, in some kind of plot against the President. It would just be added to every-thing people are saying about the administration. . . ."

"We have no idea if she is who she said she was," he mused. "She just convinced us. With her fear, with her comments about Drew and Hayes. She may just be one hell of an actress. And now, when we get to crunch time, when she was about to see the President, she made herself disap-pear. . . . Maybe the whole thing *was* a trick."

Driskill felt the ground shifting beneath him. And he didn't like the idea of failing to bring Rachel Patton to the President. Charlie was, he felt, awfully near the end of his rope.

Where had she gone? Why?

Had she merely set them up with a phony story?

Chapter 13

The road stretched out before them like a landing strip in the bright moonlight. Traffic was lighter than he'd expected but it was late and there were no cities anywhere near, not many night people. It was a long way to Washington, but they were safe: Nobody could find Ben now that they were in the car, there would be no questions, no exclusive interviews with Ben Driskill that could be used to embarrass the President, and no grueling conversations with Charlie. They had lost Rachel Patton. Or she had lost them.

Past the open windows there was the sense of the grass pulsing and growing, the warm damp air rising in thick clouds. An occasional cloud crossed the moon. They were listening to an all-night, all-news station. As a prelude to the remarks of callers, the host ran through some comments he was drawing off the wires from journalists about the primaries and Charlie's new bid to have Sherm Taylor go down and help out in Mexico. It seemed unlikely, the host concluded, that Sherm Taylor would respond.

Once they'd exhausted the dregs of their curiosity about what Rachel Patton was or wasn't up to, they stopped for hamburgers and Cokes at a rest stop.

Sitting in the weirdly unreal light with the velvety darkness beyond the parking lot, waiting for the burgers, sipping their drinks, Elizabeth emerged from the silence.

"Ben, she may be dead. It was sort of amorphous before.

I was scared but it wasn't completely real, it didn't have a face. Now it's got a beating heart."

"I don't know what to do."

"Larkie told you to be careful. The attorney general told you. Drew told you how concerned he was with the President's situation, and then he got killed and Hayes went out to Iowa for him and got killed. If Rachel was real, if they were watching her—we could be killed, too."

"No, we can't get paranoid. But we've still got a lot more questions than answers. We don't know who and what Rachel Patton was and is . . . and we don't know what Charlie is really up to." He was halfway through the burger when he couldn't wait any longer: "Hell, I've got to call Mac. There's a phone booth."

"Don't pull a Rachel Patton on me, okay?"

"I'll be back."

Ben called Mac at Sugar Bush, woke him up. He sounded groggy. It was past two o'clock. "Ben, where are you? What's going on?"

"Are you sober, Mac?"

"Very funny. What the hell do you want, Ben? And where are you? Charlie said you were supposed to get back to us—"

"It doesn't matter where I am. The point is, I was supposed to deliver something to the President tonight and I can't do it. The item has disappeared."

"Oh, no . . . Why is it always bad news with you, Ben? Can't you—Look, he's not gonna like this, right?"

"Good guess, pal."

"Ben, you're playing with fire so far as Charlie goes. He's already pissed off about LaSalle's story about you. Where are you? He's gonna want to get hold of you."

"I'm on the road."

"Thanks for leaving me with the fun job. Jesus, Ben!"

Driskill hung up. A load of tourists had arrived on a huge superbus, yawning, rubbing their eyes, for a pit stop and some chow. The bathroom filled up just behind him. He left the phone booth and went back to Elizabeth.

Back on the highway, she spoke out of the darkness. "Ben, I'm scared for you. I think you'd better seriously think about getting a lawyer."

"I am a lawyer."

"So, more than most, you should know when you need one."

"What do you think is about to happen?"

"Ben, LaSalle has put you at the scene of Drew's murder. We don't know how he did it but it means you need a lawyer to represent you, to operate as a first line of defense when the police or a special prosecutor come calling—"

"It'll just make me look guilty," he said, smiling to himself. "Hiring lawyers always makes you look guilty. Everybody knows that."

"Ben, I'm serious. And now with this Rachel Patton thing—we have no idea what's going on, we don't know where she came from or where she's leading us or what she's led us into. I repeat, you need a lawyer." She paused, but he knew she wasn't done. "I won't have you running around the countryside with someone trying to kill you. And don't tell me I'm being paranoid. You're following in the footsteps of dead men." The lines at the corners of her mouth were hardening and she wasn't kidding. She looked scared. Storm warnings. "Now that Charlie is bound to be even angrier with you . . . now's the time to get out of this altogether. Do you hear what I'm saying to you?"

He said, "You want me in . . . you want me out. It's confusing."

"Ben . . . ," she said. He'd made enough jokes.

He nodded, watching the road. She was right, of course. It was all connected in some crazy way, a pattern he couldn't see, and somehow he was too close to the center of it. As if he were deep within one of those English mazes, hedges reaching far above his head, he knew he had to be careful and think carefully. All of which was hard to do when you were angry. And he was angry.

And he was alone.

Elizabeth would stand with him and fight for him and fight with him, but he couldn't drag her into the maze. He had to keep her out. There was too much danger around, too many smart missiles. They were finding his friends. He didn't want them finding his wife.

They were nearing Washington at dawn when the voice on the radio caught their attention again. They had a statement from Bob Hazlitt, made while he was arriving for an interview with *Good Morning, America* at a television station in Miami where he was courting delegates. He was trying to sound calm but his fury seemed genuine.

"Let it be understood . . . I would never call the President of the United States a traitor . . . but, if he were a traitor . . . he could not betray the values and strengths of his country any more effectively than he is doing now, trying to get a man such as Sherman Taylor to go down to Mexico in a lost cause. It's heresy, and I might say not very smart. In January in his Declaration of Surrender, he set America on a course which will leave this nation easy prey, virtually undefended! Fortress America has become an old lady in a darkened parking lot late at night, waiting to be mugged. Good men and women have fought and died for the security of this country and they did not die to see us sink into a bottomless sea of helplessness! The President has railed on about some mythical, invisible secret government, he cries from the rooftops that there's a bogeyman we can't see . . . and now he's called out to sacrifice Sherm Taylor on a fool's errand! Well, it's a cheap trick and it won't work, because anyone can see what he's doing to this country. We are all at risk, my friends, with that man in the White House. He's right—there's no greater enemy than the enemy within—and his name is Charles Bonner!"

It was Wednesday.

He awoke at noon, still groggy, remembering that they'd checked into a small Georgetown hotel to avoid being run to ground by the press or anyone else at their Dupont Circle flat. As he came awake he looked for Elizabeth. She wasn't there. He leaned up on his elbows and forced everything into focus. He picked up the telephone and hit the zero. He asked for room service, ordered coffee and juice. He was awake. Or damn close to it. He shook his head like a big dog blowing the cobwebs away and dialed his office in New York. Helen answered, crisp as ever.

"Helen. It's me—does it sound like me?"

"More or less."

"Okay."

"Where are you?"

"You don't want to know."

"Ah, but Dade Percival wants to know. As well as your loyalists."

"Tell Percival he can—" You always had to worry about men like Dade Percival. He wished he hadn't sent Percival to Washington to work with the White House staff on the legal side of certain legislation during the past winter. He'd come away thinking he understood Washington and knew how to fix it. Dade Percival. Well, the hell with him . . .

"You'll have to tell him that yourself."

"Is everything under control up there?"

"The press keeps calling, looking for you. They're a lot of fun."

"I'm sorry to put you through this, Helen. But it's not going to last forever. Anybody else call?"

"A client or two. Nothing important, and I told them you were with the President. That always stops them. And Mr. Larkspur has called this morning—wanting to know if you were all right."

"What did you tell him?"

"I told him you're a Notre Dame man and as such you're bound to be just fine."

"You *are* bucking for a raise."

"And you must not have answered Mr. Wardell's call on Monday—"

"Damn, I forgot. I haven't had the time."

"He called back this morning, a little insistent. From

Saints Rest. He wanted to know if you'd gotten his message. I told him how busy you'd been and I was sure he was on your list and he said I'd better get a move on and put him at the top of your list—"

"Okay."

"He said it's about Mr. Summerhays and Mr. Tarlow—"

"I wish he'd said that before. Well, I'll call him. My mistake, Helen. Is that it?"

"Yes. Is Mrs. Driskill in New York or Washington?"

"She's with me. Look, I'll be in touch in a day or two. Just hold the fort. And Helen, I need Bert Rawlegh."

"Right away."

"Ben." Rawlegh's voice came over the line, sly, ironic, friendly. "How goes the President this morning?"

"You're asking the wrong man, Bert. I am not in overly good standing with him at present. But I assume he's probably in good spirits this morning. I'm sure all the President's countless men are out twisting delegates' arms today."

"To say nothing of Hazlitt's men," Rawlegh said. "It's like a whorehouse fight on a Saturday night."

"How are things at the office? Morale holding up?"

"Ben, let me be serious for a moment. Dade Percival is hard at work. He's been speaking to partners in little private meetings in his office. He's wondering if we can afford the controversy you're bringing to the firm . . . he's talking about the firm's reputation for discretion. He's talking this morning about some 'reservations' he has about the President's 'imprudent' behavior, whatever that means. We've got people who are hearing him out."

"Well, you could just hint that I'm a terrible hardass when it comes to the infighting."

"Hinting might not be enough, Ben. He may need a demonstration."

"I'll come back if I have to. But try to hold the son of a bitch at bay, all right? And organize the good guys."

"Of course, Ben. Look—don't worry about this stuff. It sounds like you've got enough on your plate. I'll let you know if things get really out of hand here."

Elizabeth appeared at the door, fully dressed, carrying an armful of newspapers. Behind her was the bellhop with a tray. "I caught him before he set out," she said. "Croissants and brioche have been added to go with the coffee." She signed the check and tipped him and dropped the newspapers on the bed. By the time she had poured coffee for Ben, he had started working the newspapers.

Elizabeth flicked on the television. "LaSalle's first show is just coming on at one. I can't resist."

He saw the head shot of the President on the screen behind a close-up of LaSalle. It was the first of two daily broadcasts LaSalle made; frequently, however, this, the earlier show, was actually hosted by one of his assistants. Today it was the man himself, which usually meant something big was happening. The Hazlitt campaign was firing back fast following the President's comment about Taylor in Lincoln. And maybe this was more. It was all in the timing these days, there were no weeklong lags as the punches flew back and forth. Now it was measured in hours. Driskill felt his stomach lurching. Superimposed across Bonner's face were the block letters LVCO. It had to be something. Rachel Patton had said it was something to do with LVCO that had brought her together with Drew Summerhays in the first place. He turned up the volume.

"The story begins years ago with a small company which was founded by two men in Delaware." LaSalle was wearing his most solemn face. "It was a metal fabricator. They made things out of various kinds of metal which other industrial firms needed either to make their machines run or to make their products work. In that sense, LVCO was a machine shop. It was successful. They acquired numerous contracts and eventually expanded with small factories in Massachusetts and Florida as well as in Delaware. Later on they opened another in northern California. And they entered into another area—geological surveys. It was a unique little company. Highly profitable but with no desire to expand too fast for its own good. Well managed. Conservatively run. LVCO."

On the screen, with LaSalle's voice-over, viewers saw

footage of the machine shops at work, the two founders meeting with new clients—some wearing military uniforms—and signing contracts. The new operations needed new buildings, new employees, and the viewer saw graphics of the company's stock history, the rising price of shares, the beautiful forested mountainsides of northern California rising behind a strikingly beautiful Wrightian building. It had grown considerably from the little machine shop. Ben Driskill wanted to know where the story was going, what the hell it had to do with the President. LaSalle was going on.

"All this in a quarter of a century. A real American success story.

"In recent years the metal-fabricating division of the company has gone heavily into government contracts manufacturing arming devices for rocketry and sophisticated piecework for armaments firms. The other division has gone particularly high-tech in its computer-programming division with highly sophisticated three-dimensional model building dealing with the effects of undersea explosions, including both man-made and volcanic, as well as analyses of tectonic plates and their movement. Earthquakes to you and me. This division also has attracted huge contracts from both the government and private sectors.

"So," LaSalle said, his most concerned ombudsman-like expression set in his heavy features, "why am I telling you this? What does this highly successful American company have to do with the President of the United States? We'll be back in just a moment with the answers to that and many other troublesome questions."

When LaSalle came back he was sitting by a roaring fire in a studio somewhere looking as presidential as he could. He was holding a folder crammed with papers. A prop of some kind. A symbol of research, no doubt.

"What has all this to do with the President of the United States?

"Twenty-five years ago Charles Bonner invested some twenty thousand dollars in the stock of a fledgling metal-fabricating firm. Then over a period of several years he increased his investments annually until he had purchased stock worth well over three million dollars. He didn't pay that for it—don't misunderstand me. *By the time he became President the stock was worth in excess of three million dollars.*

"He never divested himself of the stock, though the company was directly and indirectly involved in many government contracts. On the contrary, we have developed information that reveals that the Bonner investments have continued to grow during his presidency. Obviously the value of the stock grew—*but what I am saying is that the President of the United States has continued to buy more and more stock in LVCO.* Surely, it is not a flight of fancy to suggest that this creates an enormous conflict of interest, unrivaled in the long history of chicanery in Washington, D.C."

He waited as if gathering strength to go on in the face of such malfeasance in office.

"These are facts," he said finally, the camera moving in close. "There has been no response from LVCO, but that won't stop us. We're digging into the SEC records, brokerage house records, we are sending investigators to the United International Bank of Paraguay in Asunción, a private investment bank in Belize City, Keystone Financial of Jamestown, New Hampshire, and various financial organizations in Europe. We are following a trail of criminal transgressions generated by the man in the White House, and before we're through we'll have all the answers. . . ."

The rest of the show passed in a blur of recapitulation and rehash, but the bell, as Ballard Niles would write the next day, had been rung, and there was no unringing it.

Elizabeth was already standing up. "Good Lord, Ben, it just keeps going on and on, it's becoming a mushroom cloud. Now it turns out Charlie has huge investments in a company Rachel was investigating. Drew was in on it, too." She took a deep breath. "Another huge piece of the puzzle has just been revealed, and we don't know where it fits. We have no idea . . . but this is another reason why Drew and Hayes died, why Rachel Patton may be dead, and why it's worth killing them. . . . National security, the battle for control of this government . . . maybe the country . . ."

"I'm at a loss, sweetheart."

He stood up, went to the phone, and dialed the number in Iowa and heard a voice.

"Nick Wardell," Driskill said, "what can I do for you?"

Wardell wasn't shy about telling him.

Chapter 14

I t was nearly five o'clock in the afternoon of what was promising to become a very long day when the commuter plane clawed its way up out of the shimmering, boiling fury of O'Hare and headed west toward the Mississippi, banked over the detritus of Chicago's urban sprawl, and straightened out over the neatly tended farmland below. Driskill leaned back in the tiny, child-sized seat and tried not to think about his knees jammed into the back of the seat ahead. The old twin engines rumbled loudly a few feet away. He closed his eyes. Forty-eight hours ago he'd been heading for Boston from New York. He felt like he'd been in a frantic sprint ever since.

He jerked out of his reverie as the plane turned upriver and crossed the great, wide, brown Mississippi, the banks on either side thick with dark green vegetation. The high arched bridge crossing to Saints Rest gleamed in the slanting rays of the afternoon sun. Suddenly a fist of turbulence socked the plane sideways, knocking it backward off the broad river. They were rushing over the bluffs, steadily descending. The plane shivered and suddenly dropped ten very abrupt feet and hit the runway a solid right to the chops and then itself wobbled away like a punch-drunk heavyweight and finally slowed and pulled itself together and rolled sedately toward the small but spiffy reception building. The pilot stuck his head out from behind the little sliding door and smiled back at the passengers. "Like a sparrow on a limb, folks," and everybody laughed too loudly with relief and he ducked back into the cockpit. Iowa. A folksy, friendly place.

The sun was melting the tarmac, making it soft and clinging, and the heat waves rose, taunting you, as if the airport were about to fade like a mirage. The heat was dripping wet. He figured the corn must be growing like there was no tomorrow.

Nick Wardell was waiting beside the baggage claim. Driskill remembered him now from the campaign four years ago. Rotarian, law degree from the University of Iowa at Iowa City, Peace Corps after law school, married, two kids in their teens. Nick was a regular at the Saints Rest Golf and Country Club. He had come to the Democratic Party as a high school kid working for Eugene McCarthy in 1968, worked for Hubert Humphrey after the nightmarish convention in Chicago that year, got into grassroots organizing for George McGovern in 1972, and continued as a dependable county and state worker from then on. Now he was the county chairman. He owned the Wardell Agency—real estate and insurance, depending on what you needed. He filled the perfect delegate profile.

"Oughta have a band to welcome a high mucky-muck like you." Wardell's voice was deep, resonant.

"You and I must not be reading the same papers." They were shaking hands. Wardell shook hands gently, like a man who'd been told to ease up on people, for God's sake. "This mucky-muck is on that great big shitlist, if you'll pardon the expression. And more important—this old mucky-muck is definitely not in Saints Rest. So . . . how are you, Nick?"

"Full of it. I'm glad you're prompt." They had left the terminal and were heading across the parking lot. "They found Varringer. He's pretty well chewed over, being in the river a week. Some of the stuff that lives in the Mississippi, stuff you've never dreamed of, my friend—well, it gets hungry and it made a meal out of Herb. But my friend the chief of police got him IDed all right."

"Any idea who might have done it?" It was a shot in the dark but worth taking.

"In a way, I guess they do. Surprising. Real detective work." Wardell's voice was deep and gravelly, oddly comforting. "And this is a little spooky, Ben. The cops have discovered that a guest at one of the bed-and-breakfasts in Saints Rest the day Tarlow was killed, a guy who identified himself as a professor at the U of Missouri and used a credit card in the same name to check in, this guy *does not exist*. They ran a check through the university and there's no such guy, no such guy in Columbia, Missouri. So we got a ghost in town and maybe he was a ghost because he was killing Tarlow and Varringer."

It was the first clue of any kind. Could this have been the same man who so soon afterward had been at Big Ram killing Drew Summerhays? Could he be the chameleon following Rachel Patton?

Wardell was driving one of those four-wheel-drive vehicles with leather buckets, a five-grand stereo system, and a ten-room house in the back. He was wearing a Saints Rest Golf and Country Club shirt in navy blue, cotton chinos, and black-and-white saddle shoes.

"I'm going to show you where our friend Tarlow met his maker. We'll talk. I'd like to know what's going on, too, Ben. Like what's this I hear about the President and some crooked stock deal? I heard a report on the news driving out here."

Driskill nodded: "I don't know anything about LVCO except what was on TV." He was watching the town of Saints Rest appear as they crested a rise of highway. It lay sparkling in the sunshine, the golden dome of the courthouse gleaming, the high bridge arching like a silvery streak across the Mississippi to East Saints in Illinois. Suddenly they had passed through an industrial park, the glittering gambling boat at rest in its harbor. One turn and they were heading toward the river, toward the tower of brick rising up from flatland. A huge billboard dominated the landscape, a portrait of a smiling Bob Hazlitt with the airplane in the background and the white silk scarf furling out behind his head.

"These are Heartland warehouses," Wardell said, "thus the billboard of Brother Hazlitt. He's got a lot of support in Saints Rest, sad to say. Favorite Son. Over there, that's the shot tower. Civil War." He'd stopped the truck at the floodwall and they were walking across the gravel lot. "That's where they found Tarlow. Sitting at the foot of the tower. Knifed through the heart. Last thing he saw musta been that big grinning Hazlitt."

"Did Hayes come calling on you?"

"I picked him up at the airport, dropped him off downtown. Way he wanted it. He picked my brain about Heartland and Herb Varringer. . . ." He was looking at the shot tower, shielding his eyes from the sun, which had not yet dropped below the great limestone bluffs bordering the downtown area of the town. "I told him what I could—didn't have a lot of time. I told him how Varringer and Hazlitt were old, old pals, how Herb was a key man on the Heartland board, how things seemed to have soured lately."

"What do you mean?"

"Hell, I've known Herb Varringer all my life. I handled his insurance." He pronounced the word *inn*-surance. "Life, hospitalization, disability, cars and trucks, house, household goods, the works. Herb wasn't a particularly outgoing kind of guy—friendly enough, old-school kind of guy, but he had a whole lot of money and that kinda sets you apart, owned the newspaper, moved in his own very small circle . . . and I'm not sure he even did much of that anymore. But I knew he was worried about Heartland."

They had turned and walked back toward the underpass with the railroad tracks running above. The railroad bridge extended across the river over into Wisconsin and Illinois. The heat was oppressive. Driskill was carrying his seersucker jacket over his shoulder, and sweat had soaked through his shirt. Stepping into the shade of the underpass felt like a moment in a refrigerator by comparison. He took a deep breath, heard the intense hum of the insects in the scrub grass.

"There are witnesses who saw the two of them walking down this way, all the way from the Fourth Street elevator to a couple of guys who saw them at the brew pub right over there."

"Talk to me about Varringer. Why did he tell you he was so worried about Heartland? What did you have to do with it?"

"Herb Varringer and I went hunting with a group of guys this past winter, and you know how it goes on a hunting trip. We're up in northern Minnesota, it's colder 'n a witch's tit and Herb and I are sitting by the fire at this lodge one day, everybody else out hunting but we figure it's just too damn cold, and we're having a drink or two and Herb begins to talk. Little firewater loosened him up, I guess. And he had something on his mind, all right. He had given his life to Heartland, to Bob Hazlitt, and what he mainly was, was disenchanted big-time. He didn't get too specific but he told me I wouldn't believe some of the shit that Heartland was into. He said it all came from having too much money, money to throw at this, money to acquire that, money to build something nobody else had ever dreamed of, just vaults of money and more credit than you could count. He said he'd made a helluva lot of it for Heartland himself, so that made him to blame and he didn't like it a damn bit. You with me so far?"

"Sure." Driskill was thinking about Brad Hokansen and the money that worried him, about Sarrabian apparently tipping Hokansen to skulduggery at Heartland.

"So Varringer was going on about how Heartland had become power mad and corrupt, operating as if it owned the world and the space around it, and he was unhappy. He felt he'd been taken advantage of, all his years working with Hazlitt and how they were just as greedy and crooked as everybody else."

"Got any examples?"

"Nope."

"Sure?"

Nick Wardell was staring into the swirling water of the Mississippi, watching it lap up near his feet, smelling the pungent river in the midst of a heat wave. He flexed the muscles in one arm, making a fist, thinking.

"What else, Nick?"

"Varringer had come to distrust and dislike Bob Hazlitt and everything he stood for. Not just personally, it was on a larger scale than that. He said to me, 'Y'know, Nick, Bob's not as big an asshole as he sounds when he's yakking at the poor wahoos who really do believe he's got a solution for every problem. Bob wants to convince folks that America is all that matters, that everybody else can go to hell.' But Herb told me that Bob believes in one thing . . . absolute national security. You have that, you can tell all them furriners to go fuck themselves. Well, Herb says that Bob's a liar, that there is a foreign policy that works and it's not the US of A's foreign policy . . . it's Bob's, it's Heartland's. Now Ben, don't look at me that way. I can't elaborate because there's nothing to elaborate about—that's what Herb said and he never spoke to me about any of it again. Which leads me to my question for you—if old Herb was right, if Bob's got all this power, are we looking at a Hazlitt presidency? With that bloodsucking Sherm Taylor hangin' on to his coattails?"

"You tell me—how's the Iowa delegation stacking up?"

"Sorry to say about three to one for Hazlitt. Iowa boy." Wardell shrugged his massive shoulders. "We're arguing over how long we're committed to Hazlitt. But his people worked hard, took over the Democratic organization like a swarm of bees, elected a slate of delegates. But we've got a few Bonner loyalists. I'm working on some folks, I'm letting them know that if they support Hazlitt and he doesn't get the nomination, they'll be going under the collective name of Shit for the rest of their natural lives because they deserted a sitting Democratic president."

They were sitting in the corner brew pub soaking up the cool beery atmosphere, drinking Wild Boar. Ben stared at the shot tower where Hayes Tarlow had died. Wardell fell silent, excused himself: "Gotta make a call, Ben. Be right back."

Two guys sitting at the bar asked the barman to turn on the television; it was time for the news. Driskill watched it almost listlessly, the lack of sleep catching up with him, when he suddenly focused in on a commercial. . . .

A week ago the President had enlisted the aid of Alec Fairweather, a Minneapolis advertising enfant terrible, who believed that the underpinning of trying to sell anything was to gain an unfair advantage. Fairweather claimed he could get a serial child killer elected head of the school board if given half a chance. Now, on the network news shows, the first fruits of his labor were appearing.

It was a single black-and-white still photograph with the camera slowly showing the full picture, then slowly moving in to the face. . . .

A young girl of perhaps ten stood by herself in a bombed-out street, flames forming the background. She was wearing a torn sweater and a pair of jeans and her face was almost ethereally beautiful—the bone structure, the huge eyes, bangs pasted across her forehead with blood. Rivulets of blood streamed down her face as she stared into the camera. Her sweater was spattered with blood, and her arms were held out and slightly forward in a kind of beseeching gesture, beautiful, slender fingers streaked with blood and dirt.

When the screen was entirely filled with her face, her shining eyes beseeching you at the center, several lines of print appeared, bright red, the only touch of color.

> **Mexico City today.**
> **Bob Hazlitt doesn't care.**
> **The secret government wants it this way.**
> **Charles Bonner is the answer.**

When the final words were wiped away the shot had morphed without your realizing it into Hazlitt on a stage, shot from below, making him look like a strutting fascist thug, circa 1938. The counterpoint of the fire cannonading between the Bonner and Hazlitt camps was mesmerizing. The President's offer to ship Taylor off to Mexico, Hazlitt's traitor remarks, now the LVCO charges and the emotionally powerful attack ad by way of return fire.

You had to pay attention.

Driskill was still staring at the TV screen, shaken by the power of the words and images Fairweather had strung together, when Nick Wardell returned, stood with his fingers rapping on the table. "Come on, Ben. We got us an appointment."

Ten minutes later he turned off a tree-lined avenue and pulled into a big circular parking lot nestled among the poplars and sycamores and oaks and tennis courts. The white sign with the black lettering hanging from the white post told the visitor it was the Saints Rest Golf and Country Club. The building was low and white and rambling with trees and flowers all around it and a long screened-in porch and a terrace that overlooked the big swimming pool. The pool was full of screaming, laughing kids watched over by their mothers and nannies and the lifeguard. There were dark green shutters and little gables rising out of the shingled roof. It was the midwestern country club of Hollywood's dreams, perfectly realized, and you could smell the damp grass that stretched away like a field of velvet, hilly and wooded, dotted with members in pursuit of whitey.

Wardell led the way around the fieldstone walkway circling the main porch and curving back toward the Grill Room. The pro shop was next door, and a gravel path led to the first tee where several golfers were waiting to have at it. He headed upstairs into a quieter venue.

The "new" bar was dark wood polished to a high sheen, and nearby a huge brick fireplace in a fancy pattern. Most of the room was in deep shadows even though the louvered shutters were open to the sunlight. The room was almost empty. In the corner across from the cold fireplace, out of the way, sat a tall, hawkish-looking man with close-cropped gray hair, a blue linen blazer, a striped polo shirt with the collar open, and a glass of beer before him.

Nick Wardell introduced him as Lad Benbow.

Benbow leaned forward in the booth, looking at Wardell as if to ask what the hell this was all about. He shook Driskill's hand. "Driskill," he said. "I've been reading about you lately." He gave the line a dry reading, and Driskill knew he'd noticed all the trouble Ben was having with the President and the press. "I see you're still in one piece," he added as Driskill and Wardell settled themselves across the table.

"Too dumb to know how serious the situation is," Driskill said.

"Ben, Lad was Herb Varringer's lawyer. When the chief downtown needed an identification of Herb's body, they went to Lad and he identified a ring, a pocket watch . . . well, Laddie's hinted to me that there's some problem with the beneficiary of the will, but that's all outta my league."

Ben looked surprised at the mention of a third party. "Wouldn't his wife be his beneficiary?"

"Herb never married," Benbow said. "But he had a special friend."

"Mind if I ask you a few questions?"

"You can ask to your heart's content, Mr. Driskill. It's getting the answers that's hard." He sipped his beer and cast another long look at Nick Wardell. "Nick here has blindsided me on this one. I had no idea he was dragging you into this situation, which really has nothing to do with you—"

"Well, you never know what's of interest to anyone, do you? Now, this business of Varringer's beneficiary . . ."

Benbow waited silently.

"I need to know everything I can find out about Varringer's state of mind, what he was thinking about these past few weeks, which culminated in his meeting with Hayes Tarlow." Benbow was smiling faintly at him, not making anything easier. "Maybe this woman, this 'special friend' knows something that bears on what prompted Varringer to ask Drew Summerhays for help."

Benbow took another sip of his beer and leaned back in the booth. Beneath his short gray hair he was tanned and his eyes were arresting, a light gray that seemed to be coming from a very great distance, as if from a star that had died millions of years ago.

"What would you say, Mr. Driskill, if our positions were reversed at this moment? Say some Important Suit from the Washington/New York big leagues shows up in your nice little town sniffing around the murder of one of your most prominent citizens. You know this Suit's got an ax to grind but damned if you know what it is . . . is he a good guy or a bad guy? But there's murder going around, and the White House is mixed up in it to one degree or another and the President's mired in a mess . . . and this new fellow wants to dig around in your clients' personal lives. What would you say to such a person?"

"Depends. If I were a jerk I might be a real hardass about it. If I were a caring and sensitive late-twentieth-century male, I'd look into his honest face and tell him everything he wanted to know. Which are you, Mr. Benbow?" Driskill stared into icy gray eyes.

"That's just too easy. I am without a doubt the hardest-ass lawyer you've ever met."

"I've met some real honeys—and I know who you are, Mr. Benbow. I know your reputation. I know you can play hardball. I'm just asking for some help."

"Let me put it this way . . . this violent, crazy country is going straight to hell. Every day that something awful doesn't happen to you is a cause for thanksgiving. I protect my clients, do you understand? Just the way you may be doing now, protecting the President and the administration. You're his new personal lawyer, right? You've made your choice . . . but three people are dead already and I will be goddamned if I'll give up an innocent human being to the carnage." He was smiling still. Driskill couldn't read the smile. Was it intended to take the sting out of his words? Or, more likely, not? "No deal, Mr. Driskill. Herb's dead and my client is grieving. My client wants to stay anonymous. That's the way it's going to be."

"Take a look at this for me," Driskill said. Benbow was trying to get him to blow, trying to make him play the bad guy. It was taking a little effort to ignore the provocation. He took the envelope from his jacket pocket and pushed it across the table.

Benbow opened it slowly, slid the paper out. "Do I want to see this, Mr. Driskill?"

"No harm in it. It's nothing anybody can hold against you."

Benbow unfolded the sheet of paper. Driskill watched him closely as he stared at it, turned it to another angle, then let it flutter back to the tabletop.

"All right, I've looked at it."

"Does it mean anything to you? Have you ever seen it before?"

Benbow watched him with that little smile playing across his mouth. He shook his head. "No and no."

"If it comes to mean anything to you, I'd appreciate your letting me know."

"Indeed, I'll bet you would. But why ask me?"

"Hayes Tarlow. Maybe the last thing he did before he died was put this piece of paper in the mail. He spent that afternoon with your client, Herb Varringer. And then he was murdered. And so was Herb. And, so far as I know, this piece of paper is the only souvenir we've got. I'm curious. He mailed it to himself rather than keep it on him. I wonder why, that's all."

Benbow shrugged. "Beats me." He slid out of the booth and stood up, shrugged out of his blazer. "Gentlemen, I have a tee time in fifteen minutes. Between now and then, I've got to cure a lifelong slice. Beware, Nick, next time I get the chance you can be sure I'll piss in *your* boots. You are a scoundrel, leading Mr. Driskill to think I might be useful to him. Mr. Driskill, I can't help you. But I'm sure you understand. Who knows, maybe we'll run into each other again . . . but for the moment I think the President should stop sticking his nose into our business out here and clean up his own act in Washington. He's got dead advisers, he's got this stock thing that looks like it could be the tip of the iceberg, and he's got a short job expectancy. How do we know he's not just trying to cover his own tracks?"

Driskill had been in Saints Rest four hours and twenty-nine minutes when Nick Wardell approached the airport for the second time that day. A commuter flight was leaving in fifteen minutes for Chicago and Ben could connect back to Washington.

"Quick visit, Ben," Wardell said. "I'm sorry as hell Benbow backfired."

"Get in, get out, nobody gets hurt." Driskill thanked him for the information and the crack at Lad Benbow. "You were right, it was a shot worth taking."

"Y'know, Ben, there was one more thing. Just popped into my head. Might mean something to you."

They were standing at the ticket counter while the woman in uniform ran Driskill's credit card. "Try it out," he said to Wardell.

"Well, it was something Tarlow said. He called me a second time that day. I was out playing golf, rained off and on, and Julie, my secretary, was off somewhere. So the machine took his call. He said that if anything funny happened while he was in Saints Rest—which made me wonder what the hell he could be talking about—there was somebody I was supposed to call. He was just leaving me the phone number and the damn message tape was full, cut him off. But I remember the name—it just came back to me. Meant nothing to me—Rachel Patton, that was her name."

"I'll check it out, Nick. And thanks for everything." Driskill had gooseflesh on his arms. He watched Nick head back to the car, then headed down to the boarding area.

Ben Driskill had just found out that Rachel Patton was the real thing. She was one of the good guys. . . .

Wherever she was.

Chapter 15

The crowds at O'Hare had thinned substantially when Driskill climbed the stairs from the commuter gate and headed through the terminal for the Washington flight. There was something disconcerting about the sound of his own footsteps in the nearly deserted corridors. Twenty-four hours ago he and Elizabeth had been driving back to Washington from Fort Ticonderoga. He was beginning to wonder how long he could handle the pace. Elizabeth was right: He wasn't a kid anymore.

When he got to the gate there was a fifteen-minute wait before boarding. He found a telephone station and dialed a Washington number.

Teresa Rowan sounded raw and tired, waking up to take the call. "Ben, for God's sake, what time is it?" She muttered something and answered her own question. "Oh, God—it's only ten. Ben, I fell asleep in a pile of papers and files and—oh, what a mess."

"What's the matter?"

"I'm exhausted, that's all. Where are you?"

"What difference does it make?"

"Ben, I just woke up and I want to know where you are, that's all. No need to be so cagey with me. Good lord!"

"Chicago."

"Advance work on the convention?"

"No, no—"

"It's Iowa!" she said triumphantly. "You've been poking around out in Iowa, haven't you? Tell me!"

"I'm not telling you a damn thing," he said good-naturedly.

"Are you sure going out there is a good idea? Did you clear it with the White House?"

"Oddly enough, I'm still just an American citizen, free to travel wherever I want—not just where Saint Charlie lets me go. First you tell me not to trust anybody, including Charlie, you tell me to watch my back—and now you're telling me to clear my schedule with him—"

"I didn't say he's a saint and I didn't say he's Satan, either. I want you to get out of this in one piece."

"What's the story on these stock market charges LaSalle is making about the President? I didn't catch the whole story—is it another disaster?"

"Ben, it's all made up. That damn LaSalle!"

"How do you know? Or is it your heart talking?"

"The President's issuing a denial tomorrow morning. He told me if Drew were here he'd have all the answers. He said that Drew was the man who put things in a blind trust or sold them outright." She heaved a mighty sigh. "If only Drew *were* here . . ." She trailed off.

"Is he just giving a performance? Or is he clean?"

"Ben, how should I know? At least," she said softly, "I don't see a way he can blame this on you. By the way, Landesmann says he wants your hide on the barn wall—something about a delivery that didn't get made to the President. An item? I don't know what he's talking about but I'll bet you do."

"Nobody in that town can just shut the hell up!"

"And, Ben, I'd better tell you, the FBI guys have been onto me, they want to talk to you—"

"Well, I don't want to talk to them—"

"Just a word of warning. They probably want to discuss LaSalle's report that you were out at Summerhays's the night he was killed."

"I still don't want to talk to them."

"Then lay low, that would be my advice."

He suddenly heard a muffled beep he couldn't recognize for a moment. Then he remembered: the cellular telephone, a tiny thing, that Elizabeth had pressed him to take. She knew how he disliked the encroachment of technology but she'd been worried about losing contact with him.

He fumbled in his jacket pocket for it.

"Hold on a second, Teresa. Elizabeth's buzzing my cellular." He turned away from the pay phone, answered the toylike receiver, listened for a moment, then went back to the attorney general. "Listen, I gotta take this."

He hung up the one phone and picked the other up from the shelf. Technology. He felt like a comedian.

It was Elizabeth's voice. "Are you all right?"

"I've been much better."

"I'll pick you up at National."

"I can get a cab." He felt silly saying it. He wanted to see her more than anything.

"I want to, honey. I need to see you. Something's happened."

"What?"

"Don't worry. I just need to tell you in person."

"I'll be there in two hours."

A cloudburst exploded without warning from the humidity-laden atmosphere as Driskill landed back in Washington. He finished the last of a Scotch and water. It seemed he'd just gotten aboard the plane.

Elizabeth met him at the gate wearing a Georgetown sweatshirt and jeans. She could have passed for a college kid. She kissed him: "May I welcome you to Washington, sir. And let me say I'm glad you're back."

She was bursting with nervous energy. On the way to the lot, she said, "Ballard Niles is going to carry a story confirming LaSalle's allegations in the *Financial Outlook* tomorrow. He says it's true."

"How did you find out?"

"It's all over town." They reached the parking lot. "So what happened in Saints Rest?"

He ran through it for her as she drove. "And then right at the end Nick Wardell remembered something important Hayes had told him. Hayes had said, if anything happened to him out there, meaning Saints Rest, he wanted Nick to contact a certain person . . . Rachel Patton. But her phone number got cut off Nick's answering-machine tape. How's that for interior proof that our phantom lady is the real thing? We've got Tarlow's word for it now. Which means the back channel is for absolute real. She might have been good enough to fool us but she'd never have fooled Hayes."

"Thank heavens! So the whole thing holds together. And what did happen to Varringer?"

"Knifed. They found him downriver."

"Oh, my God," she shivered. "This is awful . . . everywhere we turn, somebody's been murdered."

"There's more. Wardell told me that Varringer was worried about Heartland and Hazlitt . . . I mean, *afraid* of Heartland. Afraid of their power, afraid of their role in government."

"It seems he had every reason to be afraid—"

"But we still don't know that Heartland had anything to do with killing him."

"Oh, we know, we just can't prove it."

She pulled off the expressway and headed for the little hotel they were temporarily calling home.

"It's a mess, Ben. I want you to get out of it."

"It's not as easy to get out once you're in. I'm involved. The firm is involved. And one of my oldest friends is involved. I can't run out on everyone, Elizabeth."

"Ben, think of it this way: It's just like the Jesuits. You left the Society. Sure, you can go out and try to clean up the mess Charlie's in—and for all we know it's a mess he made. And you're out there on the point and he's angry at you because of LaSalle's story—but loyal old Ben goes marching into the jaws of death, following all the other victims!" She pulled into the small parking lot behind the hotel. Her face was flushed with anger. "I'm scared for you. It's not worth your life. You *can* get out of it, get a lawyer to represent you . . . and retire to the safety of Wall Street and the halls of the Bascomb office."

"You want me to turn against Charlie?"

"Give it to the FBI! Tell Teresa everything you know and tell her you're getting out, you're not part of the administration—"

"How can I? For all I know the FBI could be involved."

"Ben . . . the *FBI*?"

"Look, you've always wanted me involved, Elizabeth. Don't run out on me now that I'm in up to my neck. This just isn't something you can walk away from. For one thing, we're the only ones who know about Rachel Patton—"

"Charlie does now! And what about the stalker? *They* know about her!"

"But now I've got more information about Varringer and Tarlow than anybody in Washington. We've got a responsibility here, Elizabeth. We've got to help the truth come out."

"Are you sure?" She was watching him intently. She leaned against the door to their suite. "Think about what the truth might be. Are you sure . . . really sure, Ben?" She watched him intently. "Think about what the truth might be and then tell me we're sure we want it to come out. I'm not so sure we do. I'm not so sure we want to be a part of this. Not anymore. It's crazy, it's so complex."

"I can't believe what I'm hearing." He got up out of the couch and stood in front of the air conditioner, drying himself with a towel. "You of all people, the intrepid journalist, the searcher for the truth—"

"You've begun acting like a true believer, Ben. That scares me."

"You're missing the point. There's something god-awful going on here, somebody is trying to control this election, and we don't know what else. Are they trying to destroy Charlie? Or is he part of it? I can't just say the hell with it and walk away—"

"No, you're the one missing the point, Ben. Charlie's making you his latest soldier, like Drew was his soldier and

Hayes was his soldier, and *they're* both dead. He can't turn you into poor Hayes Tarlow *unless you let him.*" She took a deep breath. "Let somebody else save the country, Ben. I want you out of this. *I want you alive.*" She paused but never took her eyes from his. "And that's just about the last thing I have to say on the subject."

"Elizabeth . . . Drew's the reason more than Charlie. I keep asking myself, what was Drew doing in this mess? I just can't make it out yet. But Drew and Hayes, it's like they're at my shoulder, somehow pointing the way. . . ."

"And that's exactly what someone isn't going to want. You've earned some time at peace, time to sit in your Wall Street tower and be a gentleman lawyer and take over *that* role of Drew's . . . and eventually become a grand old man. Leave it at that, Ben. For my sake. I don't want anything to happen to you. It's not worth your life."

"I've spent a lifetime, Elizabeth—a lifetime refusing to be dictated to. If my father were alive he'd tell you. It's too late to start giving in now. I'm sorry, Elizabeth. I can't become someone else."

She sat down. "You've spent your whole life getting out of scrapes of one kind or another. You think you can wiggle out of anything. You think you're Bugs Bunny! But you're not a kid anymore and Bugs is a cartoon, for God's sake, he *never* gets any older. Wise up, Ben. I'm not saying you *can't* handle it—but I am saying it's possible you might not. The odds are more against you with every passing day."

Driskill didn't know what to say.

Elizabeth curled up on the couch, staring into space, and then she closed her eyes.

He slept less than an hour, restless, just beneath the surface of consciousness, driven by adrenaline, and woke up. She was sleeping next to him. He smiled and put his arm around her, went back to sleep.

When he awoke again she wasn't there. He got up and stared at the television set she'd left on with the sound turned down. He blearily watched CNN's newsreader and shook his head to get rid of the cobwebs.

Sitting on the edge of the bed, he called Mac at the White House.

The chief of staff came on with an edge in his voice. "Ben, where the hell have you been? You've got everybody going nuts around here, wondering what you're gonna do next! You're here and there and nowhere, like a loose fucking cannon."

"Pull yourself together, Mac. Remember, I'm the guy who was told to butt out—"

"But you didn't butt out, you got in the ring and started throwing punches and didn't seem to give a good goddam who you hit. Well, Himself is sitting in the Oval using your face to line the cat box. Where the hell is this woman Charlie says you were supposed to bring in? Did you find her after you lost her?"

"Just shut up, Mac, or I'll hang up on you and that won't help you even a little bit. I don't work for you, and I don't work for the White House."

"All right, all right, fine. What are you calling me for?"

"I need to talk to the President. I want to get his story on LVCO and I want to talk to him about Iowa. He needs to hear it from me . . . stuff he doesn't know yet."

"Oh, but stuff you know! Right?"

"Right."

"Not again, Ben."

"You'd better talk to him. He needs to hear from me."

"Have you ever noticed I always wind up with my ass in a sling every time I take him a message from you? I oughta get combat pay—"

"You oughta tell him he should see me damn quick."

"Ben, this is going to come as a hellish shock to you, but he's got enough problems of his own at the moment. He's getting ready for a press conference on the LVCO stock thing right now . . . so I'll give him your message but I can't guarantee when. Get it? He's so deep in alligators right now, I can't make any promises, Ben. I'll get back to you."

"Okay, Mac. You'd better convince him."

"Where can I reach you? It would make more sense if I could reach you—"

"To you, maybe. But let's just say I'm at no fixed address these days. I'll be in touch."

He hung up.

He wandered into the kitchen, mad at Mac. Elizabeth had left a note. There was a name on it. *Ben,* she had written, *Give him a call. He's the man to get you out of this.* The name and number belonged to Christian Bracken, a Washington insider and attorney to be reckoned with. At least, he thought, she knows nothing but the best will do for Ben Driskill.

He was hungry and didn't want to sit there with the note and thoughts of Elizabeth and how everything between them had gotten out of control. He took a shower and left.

He parked near the Willard, the White House gleaming and perfect in the sunshine. The Round Robin Bar wouldn't be open yet, but Jimmy would be there, straightening, polishing, taking control of his domain. He passed through the lobby, not giving a damn if anybody spotted him, and lifted the velvet rope across the entrance to the bar. Jimmy was checking a case of wine. He looked up at the intruder and smiled.

"Mr. Driskill," he said.

"I'm running on empty," Driskill said. "Could we smuggle some scrambled eggs and lox in here and wash it down with a gin and tonic?"

"For you I think we can manage that." He was away for a moment during which he must have ordered the food. He came back with a tall glass of fresh orange juice. "Why don't you start on this, sir?"

"You think of everything."

"If only that were true," he said softly.

The small television behind the bar was always tuned to CNN. He saw the television screen, the familiar look of a presidential press conference—as promised by Mac—and there was Charlie entering the room from the main-floor hallway in the West Wing, headed for the podium with Mac. There was no sound from the site yet. The anchorman was setting it up.

Charlie had had no real choice but to call a press conference, which he chose to handle by coming to the informal press room. Reporters often joked that it contained the world's largest reserves of aluminum ladders, which were used for seeing over the heads of all the people in front of you who were standing on the folding chairs. The press secretary usually held daily briefings there, but the President seldom appeared for a press conference in less than the austere, formal surroundings of the ballroom upstairs, where they covered the paintings with plywood panels to keep the TV cameras from swinging around and puncturing the canvases. That was the room where the cameras would pick up the President coming forward down a long red carpet, smiling, sometimes holding a bundle of note cards, looking like a man on a movie set. Today was different. Ben assumed the setting this morning was Larkspur's inspiration.

At 9:36 A.M., with as little warning as possible, the President was standing at the podium bearing the presidential seal and looking out at the familiar faces. Outside on the lawn sun streamed down. Tourists lined Pennsylvania Avenue, peering in through the fence, hoping for a glimpse of someone. The President nodded and smiled briefly to somebody who caught his eye.

McDermott was beside him. "The President has a few words he'd like to say. He'll make a statement and I don't think we're going to have time for questions. Very tight morning." He looked at his watch. The director cued him and Mac looked into the camera. "The President of the United States."

The President took his place behind the podium. It was hot in the room and he was in shirtsleeves, the cuffs rolled up on his forearms. He was the first president ever to address the people in casual dress. More people liked it than didn't. He figured it let the folks out there know he was just like them, working his ass off.

"Arnaldo LaSalle's recent accusations made during a television report, and Ballard Niles's column today in the *Financial Outlook,* came as an unpleasant surprise, and there's no point in saying they didn't. While I'm disappointed that the rest of the media covered the accusations as if they were actual news, rather than checking them out independently, I've grown used to that sort of behavior. The fact is that I haven't even had time to follow the paper trail of stock transfers and blind trusts, but it seems to me the American people deserve a quick, forthright response from their president, and my main financial adviser is dead." He was ad-libbing. Nobody did it better. "So, here I am and this is what I know about the LVCO stock business.

"Many years ago when I was a lawyer practicing up in Vermont, I had a modest stock portfolio which included some stock in the company that preceded this octopus called LVCO. I wasn't a stockbroker, I didn't spend time following the market, I relied on a broker who suggested purchases. I have a memory of this little Delaware company, this metal fabricator. My broker—and this is merely human memory, fallible as it is, at work—mentioned to me over a hot dog lunch one day that this outfit had picked up a couple of small government contracts and looked like a good buy. It was, as I recall, very cheap. A dollar or two a share, something along those lines." Close observers of his daily performances noted that he was considerably paler than normal, but his voice was strong and candid.

"I never gave that stock another thought. Not from the time I bought it until it was brought to my attention on television." He couldn't bring himself to say LaSalle's name again. His shirt was sticking to him in the humidity. "I became a congressman, then governor of Vermont, my stocks went into a blind trust, and since the governor of Vermont doesn't play much of a part in the metal-fabricating business, that was that. My accountant handled the portfolio, did my tax returns, the works. In terms of my awareness of it, that little company ceased to exist. When I became president my lawyers and people over at Justice went through my stock portfolio which, let me add, hadn't grown much in the intervening years, and I was assured that they had divested me of anything that could possibly be affected by anything I might do as president. Since the president can affect a great deal, most of what I owned—I was told—had been sold and the money put into an interest-earning savings account in a New York bank.

"I have no interest in buying stocks, selling stocks, or in any way having anything to do with stocks. Consequently, I'm at a loss to make any further comment, except to make it clear that the television report and what's appeared in the newspapers today is nothing more nor less than a continuation of the attacks on me that have characterized this campaign from the very beginning. These reports are baseless and I dignify them with this comment today only because the media coverage makes it necessary that every lie be faced and denied, for whatever good it does me. Once the lie reaches television and the print media there is, of course, nothing that will remove it from people's consciousness. I can only do the best I can to set matters straight. Thank you for hearing me out. When I have any further pertinent information you may be sure I will report to the people on it."

He leaned back from the podium for a moment, indicating that that was all he had to say by way of an announcement. He was mad and it showed. Mac leaned into the mike: "That's all, folks."

Bernard Shaw came on from Atlanta. "So, because the President will answer no questions, we must now wonder where his new legal adviser is. And that seems to be Drew Summerhays's colleague, Benjamin Driskill. But Mr. Driskill is not returning calls these days." Ben looked up, appalled, at a clip of himself caught unaware outside the Ritz-Carlton in Boston after being "involved" in the matter of Drew Summerhays's death. Elizabeth was right. He was getting drawn deeper and deeper into it.

Jimmy slid the plate of eggs and lox before Ben, toast on the side, and the gin and tonic. "Tired of seeing yourself on TV? It's your fifteen minutes of fame."

"Give me a lifetime of anonymity, Jim."

"It's a truism that politics is a rough game, rougher in Washington than anyplace else in this country."

"That's more or less what my wife said to me this morning. She wants me out of it. Out of town. Out of the political mud wrestling. All the way out of it."

Jimmy nodded. "I'd say she just might be onto something. Hard, you and the President being such old friends . . . but if it were me, I'd listen to her."

"She says she wants me to get out alive."

Jimmy watched Driskill's face. "You know, that column made me wonder about Mr. Sarrabian. What did Drew Summerhays have to do with him, anyway?"

Ben stared at him. "What did you just say, Jim?"

"I was just thinking about Mr. Summerhays and Mr. Sarrabian and how all this stock business is coming out of nowhere, catching the President pretty much by surprise. Looks to me like somebody's got it in for this old country. Big-time."

"It sure as hell does." Summerhays. Rachel Patton. Charlie. LVCO.

After his breakfast, he called the office in New York and connected with Helen.

"Look, Helen, can you go personally and find Bert Rawlegh and have him do a check for me . . . ? That's right, LVCO."

He went back and ordered a Virgin Mary. The call came back in about an hour. It was what he wanted to hear.

Ben Driskill had no trouble finding Tony Sarrabian's home. It had been the subject of stories in everything from the *Washington Post*'s Style section to *Architectural Digest* during the past eighteen months. Sarrabian had purchased two vast parkland mansions overlooking the Potomac. He had then built a long connecting wing joining the two houses, which was said to be a ballroom unlike any other in America, three hundred feet long, the length of a football field. He and his family lived in one of the mansions, the other being completely renovated as a huge guest house. He found it fitting and indeed deductible for Sarrabian Associates, since the firm operated much in the manner of a small country when it came to state dinners, visiting royalty, parties of the year.

Driskill was driving a rented Chrysler convertible with the top down. The hot breezes rustled in the trees. A haze of humidity hung like cobwebs in the branches. He approached the estate by way of a five-mile drive from the two-lane highway, winding among poplars and sycamores, perfect white wooden fencing on either side. In the meadows beyond, perfect chestnut and black-and-gray horses loped among what were doubtless four-leaf clovers. This, Driskill mused, all this, all these exquisite surroundings were quite literally the wages of sin. Perfect. It was perfect.

When he got out of the car a pair of dalmatians came running up, beautiful creatures who had no problem with his arrival. They were just curious. Not part of the security system, though Driskill knew he'd been on television ever since turning off onto the five-mile private road. He knelt and spoke to the dogs, petting them, rumpling their ears. Tony Sarrabian was standing in the front doorway, smiling. He looked as if Driskill was one of his best friends.

"Ben Driskill," Ben said.

"I know who you are. Come in. It's humble but we call it home." That was his idea of making a joke at his own expense.

"You may actually have too much money." The dogs were prancing, showing off.

"You're not the first man to make that point. But it keeps Fred and Ginger here"—he nodded at the dalmatians—"in Kibbles and Bits. Come, have a look around."

Sarrabian led him through the main floor—parlors, holding rooms, a dining room, a library, a media room, a billiard room, a kitchen, and finally into his study with a wall of windows looking out across the lawn, which swept down toward the Potomac. There was a white gingerbread gazebo about fifty yards away. Two women seemed to be riding herd on a party of fifteen or twenty children with several nannies helping out, carrying trays, tending hot dogs on a gas grill, comforting the crying kids before they charged back into the fray.

Sarrabian stood watching the scene. "My daughter is having a birthday party. The clown is downstairs in the changing room. My wife tends to maximize this sort of situation. I tell her the children will never remember any of it, and she gives me such a look, tells me I don't know what I'm talking about. She could well be right. I didn't have a privileged childhood. Now, Mr. Driskill, what can I do for you?"

"It's about Drew Summerhays." He said no more, letting it sink in.

Finally Sarrabian said, "I'm terribly sorry about his death. But I didn't know him all that well. I'd have thought you were an expert on Drew Summerhays."

"He was a good friend."

"We appreciate friendship and loyalty in my country," Sarrabian observed. Driskill wondered what country that was. The exact lineage seemed murky and Sarrabian kept it that way. There were lots of stories floating around. Some of them may have been true. "I can't say I'm truly surprised to see you here, but it does seem that you have many problems of your own these days."

"My problems are mine. You've got plenty of your own."

"Forgive me, but I fail to see them."

"*Niles to Go.*"

"*Niles to Go.*" Sarrabian murmured the column's name scornfully. "He's queer, you know. I have people who've told me he's tested HIV positive. I certainly hope so."

"What have you got against him?"

"You read the column, Driskill. It's drivel. Lies. Freedom of speech is for the birds, and you can quote me. There are a lot of good things about this country but freedom of speech isn't one of them." He didn't raise his voice. He was all matter-of-fact calm. He sat down in the high-backed chair behind the desk, leaned back so his peripheral vision included his daughter's party. "The problem with Niles is that people believe the son of a bitch. The world would be better off without him." His dark eyes shone brightly beneath thick black eyebrows.

"He was unkind regarding you but it was just a column. I've read *books* about you that took pretty much the same view of your life and times. How can you have a thin skin at this point? You must be used to a rather bad press."

"Fixer. Facilitator. Mediator. I bring people together, I arrange for people with mutual interests to meet, to discuss what they have in common. It's not hard to understand. I make people comfortable. I make them feel at home. I put them in a mood to deal with one another. Every great institution in this country and every other country has such people—how do you think the huge defense contracts get made, Mr. Driskill? You've been around Washington for a long time. You know how it works. People who are comfortable with each other, they do business. You want to make missiles for the government? You want to build the new bottom-feeding subs? You want to build a moon rocket? I have lots of people overseas who want to do business here. It's more than a bid on a piece of paper—it's not what you know . . . it's who you know and where the money goes. Every big outfit has battalions of these guys. I work for myself, that's the only difference. Am I right? Then why should I be abused in the press or anywhere else?"

"I don't really know. I think most of what you do is probably outside the law—don't take it personally."

Sarrabian threw his head back and laughed. "Ben, Ben, Ben, by the letter of the law, we should all be headed for a federal prison. But it's the way things have got to be done . . . it's the law that's wrong. It forgot to consider human nature. By the letter of the law we're all crooks. It's politics. Being an independent working man I can make myself safe—and I am safe, believe me—by ensuring that I do business with the best, the biggest, the most powerful companies and people and their governments. Don't waste time worrying about me."

"An association with you, a photograph, that was

enough for Niles to try to smear Summerhays. And then there's Brad Hokansen up in Boston . . . you dropped a word in his ear about Heartland and he practically went into cardiac arrest—"

"Lawyers should have more concern for the truth, sir. If I had any idea of what you were talking about, I'd tell you that Brad Hokansen is not easily scared . . . particularly not when you give him a solid tip."

"Your name is coming up everywhere, Tony. Now I've learned that it's surfacing right next to the President's. My, my, what is one to think?"

"What the hell are you talking about? I'm not involved with the President."

With a silent thank-you to Bert Rawlegh, Driskill said, "You, my friend, are the largest shareholder in a company called LVCO which we've all been hearing rather too much about lately. Doesn't that make you just a wee bit nervous?"

"I don't understand . . . the President and I invested in the same company." He shrugged massively, dismissively.

"You weren't in it until a few months ago. And the stock you acquired was bought under eleven different corporate names, all of which are owned by you or companies you control. The President has been in it for years and years. Now why, I wonder, did you suddenly start picking up stock and then, all of a sudden, LaSalle comes up with his story about the President's money being invested and reinvested and making more and more money? You and Charlie Bonner—"

"Mr. Driskill, I must say—"

"No, just let me finish. You're going to love the big finish here. I'm not sure how it all fits together, mind you . . . but we've got Drew Summerhays—the President's closest adviser, the man who handled his holdings when he entered public life—and the President in LVCO. We've got you tipping Brad Hokansen about some problems at Heartland, which means Hazlitt . . . and Hazlitt is trying to take the nomination away from the President. I'm playing connect the dots and you're everywhere. Which I'm thinking makes you a major player—"

"This is gibberish, my friend."

"—between Heartland and LVCO. I'd bet on it."

Sarrabian went to the windows and stood with his back to Driskill, hands on hips, staring out at the clown bouncing around and mugging for his little daughter and her birthday guests. "Such innocence," he mused. "The last three presidents have come here for dinner. I do favors for people. I do favors for their brothers and sisters and kids and nieces and nephews. Now you tell me an interesting tale, Ben—"

"I thought it was gibberish."

"But you're a lawyer, I must assume that you don't deal in wild supposition—flights of fancy. I can't imagine where your story is going."

"Oh, I'll prove it all before I'm done. I know you're involved with Heartland and LVCO. I don't know how the President's involved—"

"The President and I are involved *together* because we own stock in the same company? My God, that's mad." He was smiling broadly as he turned from the view of the birthday party. "It has all the legitimacy of a witch-hunt."

"Well, they burned a lot of witches. Remember, we live in an age of appearances—not facts. I don't think Charlie Bonner will think this is an unsubstantiated witch-hunt. Not when he learns *when* you started buying up LVCO and *when* you were talking to Brad Hokansen. Then he'll put that together with your talking to Summerhays out here and having your picture taken. You, Mr. Sarrabian, are the link between Heartland and LVCO, and when I know more the President's going to be interested in that, too."

"What are you really talking about? You're playing games with me. What am I to think?"

"I'm talking about appearances. The papers and television will run with this story. The Sarrabian angle, they'll call it. They'll love it. Then I'm going to talk to the President and maybe I'll have a talk with the people at Justice.

In fact, I've heard that Justice is already starting to poke around in your investments—"

"You're wasting your time, Mr. Driskill. Ballard Niles said I'm connected to the biggest dogs in the pack, and therein lies my safety. He's right about that much, I promise you. You've come to my house, you've insulted me as if I'm a common thief or stock fixer. Now that's just about enough—"

"I thought your view of life has us all being thieves and fixers, that's just human nature—isn't that what you believe? Well, there are people who are now saying that the President is just that . . . and he's a friend of mine. And Drew Summerhays, the best man I ever knew, is dead because of all this . . . and the path has led me back to you. I thought I'd just come and let you know. Maybe there's still time for you to save yourself from taking one hellish fall. Just think of your legal fees alone. And the loss of face." Driskill shrugged. "You're a man who understands self-interest. If you're involved in this, my interest is going to be to make you suffer."

"We're not on the same wavelength at all. You might as well accept that."

Driskill hadn't heard the door open. He saw Sarrabian's head tilt slightly.

"Mr. Driskill, I really have to make an appearance at the birthday party. Jeffers here will help you navigate your way out of this maze. I'm sorry I couldn't help you out, but I'm glad we had a chance to talk. I have the feeling that you had a very inaccurate picture of me." He grinned in a pleasantly predatory way.

"It's been a blast," Driskill said, standing up. "Jeffers, lead on."

"Good-bye, Ben. Don't be a stranger," added Sarrabian sarcastically. He stepped out through French doors and was heading across the lawn. A little girl had detached herself from the group and was running toward him, arms waving.

Driskill followed Jeffers out to the foyer, glimpsed a view of the ballroom. Something made him stop, turn to the butler. "Tell me, Jeffers—could I take a look at the ballroom? Mr. Sarrabian intended me to see it and we got side-tracked."

"Of course, sir. It's a beautiful room. It was featured in *Architectural Digest*, sir."

"You bet it was."

The room was done in white and gold with a touch of royal blue, and a goalpost at each end would have fit in pretty well. The polished inlaid parquet shone in the after-noon sunlight. The tall windows marched down the Poto-mac side of the room. The birthday party was in full swing. The clown with a red fright wig and great floppy feet was making the kids scream with laughter. Sarrabian's wife, a petite, dark-haired woman, was helping direct a game of some sort.

"And over here," Jeffers was saying, "is the reason why it was in *Architectural Digest*. It's modeled after a room in a French palace. I'm sorry I can't say where, but great pains were taken."

Driskill turned. The long wall was fitted with huge mir-rors in gilt frames that matched the windows. Looking into the mirrors, you could see the party going on outside. The mirrors were huge, disorienting.

"A splendid hall of mirrors," he said.

Chapter 16

The Rock Creek Croquet Club was something of a dinosaur, a carryover from a tradition begun in the thirties, but it was still a major power center one day each year. In those early days a group of writers, lobbyists, money men, and politicians used to gather and play croquet at the home of one of their number, a mansion above Rock Creek Park. Mainly they got drunk and fell down and chased the ball down the hill and ate too much and excoriated "that man in the White House," Franklin Delano Roosevelt. FDR had outlasted them, taken the fun out of their revels, and the Croquet Club had perished, another victim of the war, inevitably replaced by other people with other excuses for getting loaded among powerful friends.

Then, during Nixon's days in the White House, it had been reborn, though the all-too-common Nixon was never actually invited. A few members of his administration did make it into the club until the wages of Watergate began claiming them for appearances elsewhere. Still, the club clung to life during the less-than-uproarious Ford and Carter years, fully recovering its former luster with the arrival of Ronald Reagan on the Washington scene. He had occasionally appeared at the annual gatherings, presumably when the First Lady's astrologer gave the okay. And it was during the Reagan years that the frolic moved to its present venue and, oddly enough, grew more inclusive.

Then the Bergstroms bought it—Walther and Invicta

Bergstrom from Stockholm. The Bergstrom media empire included the syndicate that employed Elizabeth Driskill. Both she and Ben were standing invitees to the big bash. Although he had never attended before, and had come without his wife, and found the very idea of the party emblematic of everything he detested about the insiderish aspect of Washington, on his way back from Sarrabian's Driskill decided to attend that evening's shindig. There were some people he wanted to speak with and they were almost certain to be in attendance.

The house and grounds were infested with Secret Service people. The lights softly flooded the scene as Driskill passed muster and followed the flagstone walkway around the house toward the back lawn. Before him a large greenhouse glowed, his mind flashing on Drew's greenhouse, the door swinging in the wind and rain, the feel of gravel beneath his feet as he was drawn toward the old man's death. Lush shrubbery rimmed and punctuated the expanse of lawn with trees towering overhead, catching whatever little breeze came their way. Red and green and blue Japanese lanterns hung on poles surrounding the pool and cabana area and were strung through the trees.

There must have been two hundred people in clusters and moving waves, standing by the heavily laden food tables manned by caterers and drifting toward the back of the lawn. A huge Italianate fountain flushed punch down its elegant twists and curves. There was an infinite supply of Perrier-Jouet champagne, and several full bars were scattered about the lawn. It had the tone of a truly fabulous wedding.

Perched on a promontory at the back limit of the property was a gazebo bathed in a soft blue light, high above the creek. And in the middle distance, centered on the lawn, was a large tent. That's where the crowd seemed to be heading. Driskill followed, noting many of the well-known faces on all sides. Much of the media had turned out, but it was an off-the-record night; you were supposed to be having a good time.

Inside the tent the Bergstroms had arrayed a lot of trees

and fans to blow the leaves to create the idea that it might not be as hot as it actually was. Some of their more or less museum-quality pieces of sculpture included three Henry Moores, two Giacomettis, and a stunning battle shield by the great Iowa sculptor Tom Gibbs hanging on a standard and weighing what appeared to be at least two tons.

Bob Hazlitt was standing in the center of the crowd with the Bergstroms flanking him, and everyone was applauding. Hazlitt was smaller than television would lead you to believe, about five foot eight and stocky like a good middleweight thirty years after winning his championship. Spread out before him on a table maybe fifteen feet square was a scale model of the Boston Harbor and the Back Bay as it had been in the latter part of the eighteenth century. On the topographical model were arrayed figures of soldiers in red coats, rebels, townspeople and children and cannon and boats and houses and whatnot, all doing their thing as the battle was joined.

Bergstrom was speaking. "And we want to thank our dear friend Bob Hazlitt for this incredible gift for our museum—a scale model down to every historical detail of the Battle of Bunker Hill." He lifted his glass of champagne to Hazlitt. Applause rolled through the tent again.

Hazlitt nodded, smiling, and began speaking. His voice was deep and masculine, described by one writer as "having hair on it."

"This is just a small gift, Walther, Invicta, and you are very kind to accept it. It represents one of my little obsessions, a lifelike reproduction of the Battle of Bunker Hill . . . or, I should say, Breed's Hill. I can walk around it for hours on end, putting myself in the minds of the actual participants. I've spent thousands of hours working on it. So, with my deepest thanks for giving us this wonderful evening, Walther and Invicta, it's your problem now." Polite laughter. "I've just finished up Guadalcanal in our Dallas offices and I'm working on the first couple of hours on Omaha Beach at our Miami offices . . . but there's no reason you should find my little indulgence as interesting as I do. But whenever you're in Dallas, come on by and take a look. Now I've spoken as much as you can stand. Thanks for humoring me."

From Hazlitt's side former president Sherman Taylor stepped forward: "I keep telling him to commemorate some of my finer moments . . . but so far, no luck." That brought down the house, and then people were all milling around, chatting, leaving the tent. Driskill blended in, looking around to see if Elizabeth was in the crowd. He didn't see her, but the array of Republicans was stunning. Price Quarles, the presidential-candidate-to-be, was surrounded by a raft of supporters and several men and women who would have sold their spouses and children to be tapped for the second spot on his ticket, no matter how hopeless it was. Ballard Niles was talking with a couple of network White House correspondents. Arnaldo LaSalle was deep in conversation with a woman said to be the capital's premier investment banker and a major candidate for the Fed in a Hazlitt administration. Oliver Landesmann had arrived with a statuesque model six inches taller than he. The height disparity did not seem to bother him in the least. Bob McDermott was at the champagne fountain with Ellen Thorn. The Chairman of the Joint Chiefs was talking baseball with a Supreme Court justice. But no Elizabeth.

When he saw an opportunity he closed in on Hazlitt and Taylor. Hazlitt saw him approaching first, made an instantaneous calculation, and turned on his high-powered smile. The whites of his eyes behind aviator glasses were preternaturally clear.

"Look what we have here . . . Come on over, Mr. Driskill, here's my friend Sherman Taylor. I believe you two know each other. Sherm, Ben Driskill's venturing into enemy territory."

"No need to keep our public postures in place," Driskill said.

Hazlitt smiled, full of humility. "You'd be surprised how hard it's been for me to learn this dichotomy in politicians' behavior. At each other's throats in public, laughing at each other's jokes in private. It's different in my world. Part of the game, I guess." Still, his pugnacious face bore an aggressive, campaign-ready look.

Sherman Taylor always came on like a chilly breeze, bearing something of the Arctic with him, though he tried not to let you know. His face was made of what seemed like perfectly flat planes, his eyes close to the surface and very direct, the tan perfect and aristocratic like JFK's in the long ago. He carried himself with stern Marine precision, and the navy-blue double-breasted suit on the stifling night might just as well have been a uniform. He still looked like a president, or maybe a man who couldn't quite believe that he hadn't been crowned emperor for life. He gave Ben's hand a firm shake.

"Good to see you," he said with that calm manner, full of military sincerity that was no sincerity at all, just good form. "You're looking well."

"As you are, Mr. President—"

"Come on, it's been a long time since I sat in the Oval. Four years since we kept running into each other during the debates—where does the time go? Here we are at it again—seeing if we can separate Charles Bonner from his rabbit's foot."

"He's in pretty good shape considering what you guys are doing to him."

"Whatever is happening, he's doing it to himself."

"You throw enough mud at somebody, some of it's bound to stick."

Whatever slight friendliness had informed his manner was gone. That was all over now. It had taken about five seconds. Sherm Taylor said, "As you know, I'm not a politician, Ben. I was never any good at the dichotomy Bob was just mentioning. I wear my feelings on my sleeve—no pretending."

Bob Hazlitt threw up his hands: "Well, I'm as shocked by this whispering campaign he's having to endure as you are."

"Whispering? Is that what you call it? Feeding all the garbage to LaSalle and Ballard Niles and God only knows who else? Forgive me, but I don't think whispering quite

covers it. I've been to see Tony Sarrabian." Driskill was
trying to keep his temper controlled. So far they were
fighting words, but the delivery was more ironic than
angry. There were too many people around.

Hazlitt tried the folksy approach. "No point in arguing
over this 'cause nobody ain't gonna convince nobody." His
smile wasn't really working. "But we're not responsible for
Drew's meeting with Sarrabian, and we're not responsible
for Niles's article. Now I'm wondering, what can I do for
you tonight? Do you have something for me?"

Driskill said, "What are you talking about?"

"I thought perhaps the President had seen the handwrit-
ing on the wall . . . and for the good of party unity you
might be bringing me his withdrawal—"

Driskill said, "I think we ought to take a walk. I've got
something to say, all right, but I think a little privacy is
called for." He pointed toward the gazebo fifty yards away,
shaded by huge oaks, back at the end of the property above
the ravine and the creek itself. They strolled past people
dancing dreamily by the pool. The Japanese lanterns created an atmosphere straight out of *The Great Gatsby*.

When they were far from the party, barely able to hear
the music, as if they were watching from across a no-
man's-land, Hazlitt said, "What's really on your mind?"
Taylor walked beside them, saying nothing, in his role as a
faithful supporter of his new political friend.

"Oh, I've spent some time out in Iowa. Picking up bits
of this and that."

"You don't say," Hazlitt said. "Every day I'm on the
trail I miss Iowa."

"I can understand that." The music wafted faintly
toward them. Empty Adirondack chairs sat facing the
creek, overlooking the trees on the hillside opposite, lights
of other houses, other people living other lives. Bats flitted
in the trees as darkness grew complete.

They mounted the few steps into the gazebo. Taylor
leaned against the railing, waiting, saying nothing. There
were a few colored lights screwed into the roofline of the
gingerbread structure. Soft blue light bathed their faces.

Bugs swarmed at each lightbulb. "All right, Ben," Hazlitt said, "here we are. No witnesses. Now to what do we owe all this privacy?"

"Herb Varringer. I'd say we owe it to Herb Varringer."

"Well, that's a surprise. He was a friend of mine."

"He was more than a friend, wasn't he, Bob? He was your partner for a long time and then he served on your executive board. He was closer to you than anyone else for a long time, wasn't he? And now he's dead. Bodies are littering the landscape. *Your* landscape, in fact."

"What the hell is that supposed to mean? *My* landscape?"

"You've lost an old friend," Driskill said softly. "And I've lost Drew Summerhays and Hayes Tarlow . . . and the funny thing is, they're all three connected."

"I can't imagine how," Hazlitt said. He couldn't quite keep his voice down.

Driskill said, "Well, lucky for you I'm here. I can tell you. It's so simple. Drew Summerhays and Hayes Tarlow were killed because Herb Varringer spoke to both of them—problem is, they weren't killed quite soon enough. Which is your tough luck, I'm afraid."

"You are beginning to get my goat, Ben, as my mother says. I didn't come down here to be insulted."

"That's what you think, Bob. As Groucho Marx used to say. Hayes Tarlow and Herb Varringer got killed in your backyard, too. Saints Rest, Iowa. And why was Hayes in Saints Rest? Because your friend Varringer called Drew and Drew sent Hayes to meet with Varringer . . . to hear everything Varringer had to tell him."

"I have no idea what you're talking about. For all I know Varringer wanted to contribute to the President's campaign fund—"

"Well, he sure as hell wouldn't have been contributing to yours. No, he was making a contribution all right, but not the kind you're talking about. Varringer was pretty unhappy with you and the role of Heartland in the way this country works. He didn't much care for so much power concentrated in the hands of one . . . man. You."

Hazlitt nodded in the blue light. "It's true that Herb had turned away from me, from Heartland. That was one of his weaknesses—he wasn't cut out for big business. He was a genius, he built his own company in the old days, he made it work . . . but he knew he could go only so far on his own. George Bush used to call it the vision thing. Herb didn't have it. He knew I had it. And he let my vision turn him into a very rich man. He bought a controlling interest in the newspaper there in Saints Rest . . . and then he couldn't face the responsibility that goes with the kind of bigness he saw in Heartland." Hazlitt shrugged. "It's all true. He turned against me and I couldn't make him see what he was missing. Which was the point of American business. Doing the best job you can and expanding on it. In the end, old Herb had lived on into a world he wasn't prepared for . . . and then he died."

"You are an expert bullshitter, Bob. He didn't *die*. Somebody stuck a knife in him and dumped him in the Mississippi—and then that same somebody stuck the same knife in Hayes Tarlow. They didn't *die*, for chrissakes. They were *murdered*. There's a difference."

"Semantics," Hazlitt said. "It's a very sad story, whatever you call it."

"Sad isn't the half of it," Driskill said. "He wasn't disenchanted with big business. He was sickened by what he saw going on in *your* big business. He felt it had to be stopped. So he went to Drew Summerhays wanting to know what he should do—and people started dying. Now, ask yourself, who had a motive for killing them?"

Suddenly Hazlitt's eyes narrowed, his jaw clenched in a rictus of fury. "You are a fucking liar," he said, the anger exploding. He lunged forward at Driskill, who was more than six inches taller. Driskill put out the flat of his hand to ward him off, but Sherman Taylor had coolly stepped forward, interposing himself between the two men.

"Now a joke's a joke," Taylor said. "Always leave 'em laughing, Mr. Driskill," he added under his breath. "No point in turning into the evening's unscheduled entertainment, is there?"

"Nobody near us," Driskill said, "to see us or hear us. No witnesses, just like Bob here said."

"Son of a bitch," Hazlitt said. "You're a son of a bitch, Driskill."

"Now, Bob," Taylor said. "It's politics. Forget it." He turned to Driskill: "Where are you getting all this off-the-wall information, Ben?"

"A lot of it's coming out of Iowa."

"That's pretty general, isn't it? Even for a New York lawyer?"

"As I said, Hayes Tarlow got the whole story from Varringer, but he shipped a critical piece of information back east. I've got it now. It's not very flattering, Bob." Birds were squeaking again in the trees. An owl made a noise. There was a scuffle among the leaves. Something small was dying.

Hazlitt yanked his arm from Taylor's grip. "Don't bullshit me, dammit. While you're running around trying to make a bunch of trouble over just plain nothing, I'm trying to save this country of ours. You piss around about people like Tarlow and Varringer who just don't make a damn bit of difference in the great scheme of things, you turn the whole process into a joke. Well, it's no joke. You may try to make America's honor and sense of responsibility a joke, you may think it's just fine to let the Mexicans run around killing each other and taking possession of American holdings—when the reality of the situation is that we ought to goddam *annex* Mexico and stick some real American values in there and keep the pedal to the metal. But sooner or later our citizens will see the truth and they will rise up, they will realize that Charles Bonner is letting our greatness atrophy and grow weak and die—*that's* what this Democratic convention is going to be about. Everything turns on this—can America be strong when there is no longer a single great enemy to defend against? That's why Charles Bonner must be defeated. If you don't see the truth of that I feel sorry for you. We're not just one nation among a great many equals. We're not simply *equal*—we are America, we have almost unlimited power at our disposal, we have a value system that respects decency and integrity—and there are a helluva lot of nations who absolutely don't. We are the hope of the world. We are sanctified by God to guide this planet in the course of what is right!"

"Sanctified?" Driskill said softly. "Jesus . . . Can we just get back to you and your part in the murders of Drew and Hayes and Herb Varringer? For one thing, after Hayes met Varringer, he sent us this curious diagram. . . ."

"Spellbinding," Hazlitt said. He was dripping with sweat, trying to mop it up, his face red with anger and heat.

"Might be. Hayes seemed to think it was pretty important. I'm going to take it to the President and the attorney general."

Taylor said, "Why tell us? What's your point?"

"That's not all," Driskill said.

"What else?" Hazlitt was recovering his composure. He was wiping his face with a handkerchief.

"Drew went down to Tony Sarrabian's place on the Potomac. Now the President is being tarred with a connection to a company that Sarrabian has just bought a controlling interest in."

"So?"

"Way too many coincidences. You get enough coincidences, they turn into connections. With a logic of their own."

"Well, however you may see it," Hazlitt said, "it looks to me like the President is in trouble. And in Chicago next week, on nominating night, I'm going to kick his ass out of politics altogether—so brace yourself for that, my friend."

Taylor broke back into the conversation. "Time to lower the temperature here, gentlemen. The President's a resilient man, he'll bounce back—and in the end we'll all support the nominee of the party." The words fell oddly from his lips, as if he were repeating something he thought was the right thing to say.

"Watch yourself, Ben Driskill," Hazlitt said. "Consider yourself warned."

"Lay off the leaks to LaSalle and Niles and all your other

tame flacks. Cut out the lies. Think about everything I've said hitting the front pages of the papers. You could be Arnaldo LaSalle's hot new lead."

"You threatening me again, Ben?"

"You bet your ass, Flying Bob."

"You're speaking for the President?"

"He's too much of a gentleman. I'm speaking for me. I'm not running for a damn thing. I can't lose the nomination. But you can be sure I'm not gonna win Miss Congeniality. I can make a helluva run at making sure you lose it. So, *you* watch it, Bob Hazlitt . . . and my advice, should you be interested in taking it, is just this. . . ." He dropped his voice to a sibilant whisper. "Stop killing people . . . okay?"

"Get away from me, you miserable shit!" Hazlitt looked like he was ready to go another round or two.

"Bob, what are you trying to do? Is all this worth it?" Ben persisted.

Sherman Taylor said, "He's trying to save the nation from the weak, Ben, from the abdication of our destiny . . . save the nation from a man who refuses to let our nation be strong—"

"General, tell your bug-eyed little friend here to get a grip. We kicked *your* ass last time. You should have learned a lesson. We're gonna kick his this time. So hard his grandparents are gonna feel it. This jingoism and saber rattling just doesn't cut it. The people have wised up."

"Now, Ben," Hazlitt began, jabbing his finger into Driskill's chest, but Taylor, at his imperial best, cut him off with a wave of his hand. "That's not what America said when I took on the Islamic terrorists based in Iraq and Iran."

"I remember it well."

"Well, lots of Americans got down on their knees and thanked God for Sherman Taylor not backing off from what he had to do." Taylor was speaking softly, as if chatting among friends.

"General, you vaporized roughly two hundred thousand people that day, counting both raids—"

"And Iraq and Iran have behaved themselves ever since, and the Middle East has calmed down because they now know that America is not afraid of its own power. You know what they call Sherman Taylor over there now? I'll tell you; they call him Death Bringer . . . and we can all sleep easier because he saw his duty and he did it." Taylor looked at him. "It's about hope, Ben. America is the hope of the world. We can bring peace—just like Charlie wants to do—which is what all men hope for if their heads are on straight. But Bob Hazlitt knows that we must *impose* it— Pax Americana, if you like. Hope and peace come through strength and the willingness to use your strength—"

"You act as if our strength is infinite, our manpower and weaponry without limit. You'd have us in Mexico in two minutes and you'd make sure that Africa only existed to be colonized and brought to heel right now and all because the poor old Russians no longer give a shit about any of it—"

"That sounds okay to me," Taylor murmured, smiling as if it were an Oxford Union debate.

Hazlitt, calmed down, was at it again. "We must keep some semblance of moral order in the world, Ben. Surely you can't dispute that—we're suffering from a debilitating lack of confidence. It may be terminal unless we can pull ourselves out of this nosedive. We need to recall our past greatness, draw on it for strength. We need to bring order to the Western Hemisphere—"

"Whoops," Driskill said, "there goes Mexico."

"—and we need to regain our belief in ourselves, we need to square things with our moral compass. History tells us that the quickest, most profound road to wellness is war in a great cause." Flying Bob wasn't just whistling Dixie. "Order must be restored in Mexico and in other parts of the world and Charles Bonner just doesn't have the guts to see his duty and goddam do it. Why not just make it stop, that's my question?" Hazlitt was dripping with sweat again, pounding his fist on the gazebo railing.

Sherman Taylor smiled that cool smile that came from somewhere out there in the vicinity of Neptune.

"Well, Ben, be that as it may," Taylor, the peacemaker, said, "let's just turn down the heat. In fact, why don't you and I just take a walk. I'm almost ready to call it a night. Let's just leave Bob to calm down a little. Politics is new to him. He gets riled. It's the campaign, the pressure. Big goddamned executive, not used to having to defend himself, not used to being attacked . . . well, hell, you know how it is. Just forget what he said . . . but Ben, you're a lawyer, you know better than to go around accusing people of murder unless you're pretty damned sure. Now you can't be sure because, let's face it, Bob Hazlitt isn't killing people. I'll try to get him calmed down. No hard feelings. We've been to the political wars, you and I, we know it's a dogfight. But I'd think twice before I went to the TV and newspaper people and the Justice Department and opened up a can of worms that just might have been out in the sun too long."

The three of them—Hazlitt had refused to be left behind—were slowly walking back across the lawn. When they'd reached the edges of the party Taylor said, "Ah, late arrivals."

The band had broken into "Hail to the Chief" and the President and First Lady were standing at the top of the stairs leading down toward the bubbling fountain of champagne.

"Well," Driskill said, seeing Ellery Larkspur and Elizabeth behind them, "the gang's all here."

"I must go say hello to the President," Sherman Taylor said. "Haven't seen him in ages."

"You go ahead," Driskill said. He lingered in the shadows, watching his wife and the others being greeted by the Bergstroms and, subsequently, by Bob Hazlitt and Sherman Taylor, the two presidents shaking hands, smiling formally as was expected of them.

Before he left he caught Larkspur standing momentarily by himself, watching the crowd with an appraising eye. Tony Sarrabian and his wife had just arrived.

"Larkie, it's too damn hot."

"Well, *there* you are. Elizabeth couldn't find you. She

called me and asked me if I knew where you were." He shrugged. "I didn't. Where have you been?"

"Elizabeth and I need a little time off, Larkie. But I've got to ask you a favor. Charlie . . . I have got to talk to him. It's important. It's very important—and Mac is pissed off at me, just blew me off today. Then I heard that LVCO press conference—I can tell him things he needs to know. He can't head for the convention without seeing me."

"What have you found out now, Benjamin?" Larkspur's bow tie seemed to have somehow caught a breeze in the utter stillness of the night. "It had better be very hard product 'cause he's in a foul mood. He's very upset about the lost lady you promised him, the whole story of the back channel. What have you found out, Ben?"

Driskill hesitated, shook his head.

"Good God, Benjamin. Come on—it's me, Larkie."

"I'm sorry—but I wouldn't trust Mother Teresa on this one, I wouldn't trust anybody. I've got to talk to Charlie."

Larkie sighed. "You don't make it easy, Ben. But I'll do what I can. I'll try to get him later tonight. Give me a ring in the morning. Now, I insist on getting you together with your wife. This is ridiculous, being at the same party and not—"

"Let it go, Larkie. It's just a case of frayed tempers. I feel like I haven't slept in a week. I'm gonna crash and it'll take all the king's horses and all the king's men—"

"Okay, Ben. You know best." He looked around at the crowd. "My God, it's so *hot*." He patted his face with a pocket square by Hermès and slowly moved away into the crowd.

On one hand, there was the mess involving Sarrabian and LVCO and stock manipulation charges. But that was just the half of it. On the other hand, there was Rachel Patton and the back channel and Drew's participation and somebody in the White House. . . .

Ben Driskill left without looking back.

What next? That was the question.

Chapter 17

He came out of a deep sleep to discover that the air conditioner had kicked off at some point and the sheets and pillow were damp with perspiration. Sunshine was falling in a blurry stream across the bed. He realized he'd slept alone. A car alarm had gone off outside the little hotel and the scream was drilling a hole in the upper-left quadrant of his forehead.

He lay there getting his bearings, then crawled out of the sunlight and took a drink of water from the glass on the bedside table. He looked at his wristwatch. It was past one o'clock in the afternoon, and he knew he still wasn't back to even with his biological needs. He was so goddam hot he couldn't face taking a whiff of himself. For half an hour he stood under a lukewarm and then cold shower as a sense of what he was doing seeped back into his consciousness. Elizabeth . . . She must have gone back to the Dupont Circle flat. That was okay. The press wasn't after *her.*

He called Ellery Larkspur at his office.

"Benjamin, I've been waiting for your call."

"Well, this is it. Have you gotten hold of the President?"

"Before we get into that I've got to ask you, what in the name of all that's holy happened at the party last night? Mac's been on the horn to me this morning raising absolute hell, said you got into a shouting match with Hazlitt and Sherman Taylor."

"Gee, that's certainly bad news . . . somebody from the

President's camp getting into an argument with the guys who are trying to put him in the ground. Talk about poor form!" He scratched his head to make sure this conversation was real, that he was alive and waking up. "Anyway, whatever did happen was well out of earshot of anybody at the party—"

"Well, the Hazlitt people certainly took exception to your behavior. I get the impression that Flying Bob himself called his campaign man Herbie Rich and laid into you. And then Herbie called Mac . . . and thereby hangs the tale."

"Good. Do you think the fact that I called him a murderer could have had anything to do with Flying Bob being irked? Probably, right? And Sherm Taylor wants him to invade Mexico and annex it. These guys are nuts, Larkie . . . that's what Mac ought to be worried about, not my keeping the crazy dipshit wriggling on the hook for a few minutes."

"Well, it's not just Mac. The President is apparently having a fit, too."

"Larkie, he ought to just shut the hell up and meet with me."

"So you're the only guy who knows how to behave?" Larkie was smiling across the telephone lines. Nothing riled him.

"I'm beginning to think so. Somebody ought to tell me it was good to see somebody raising hell with these guys—"

"You're a dreamer, I'm afraid. Remember, in Washington no good deed goes unpunished. However, I did talk to the President—he wants to know if you've found the item he's waiting for?"

"No. But he'd better see me or he's going to wind up reading about it in the *Post* tomorrow morning—"

"No point in threatening the President, Ben."

"I'm not threatening. I'm promising. There's a difference. I've got enough stuff here to blow everything else off the front pages. You know they'll print any goddam thing they're given and this stuff is just too damn juicy to ignore. LaSalle's had all his secret sources. Well, I'm prepared to be a source on our side and let God decide who was right when the smoke clears. I want to see him. Yes or no?"

"I'm just not sure, Ben—"

"Bullshit! If this is as fast as he can act, you'd better tell him to read his paper tomorrow."

"I have a suggestion, Ben. Why don't you stop by my office in about an hour. Be just about time for a hair of the hound. How about a Pimm's cup? We've got the weather for it." He was being good-natured in the face of Driskill's short fuse. Larkspur had a record of getting things done. This was just another unpleasantness to be papered over.

"See you in an hour," Driskill said.

Larkspur's Georgetown office overlooking the Potomac was always a surprise to Driskill. Larkspur himself was such a clubby type you'd expect plenty of dark paneling and bookcases with lots of morocco-bound volumes and Persian carpets and heavy draperies and leather furniture. What you got was a glaring minimalist room, all white with floating islands of furniture and tables, indirect lighting, transparent curtains, marble and glass tables, a few stacks of papers, all looking like a movie director's idea of the anteroom to heaven. You felt you should be wearing something classical, a snow-white toga, and carrying a lyre and making sure you didn't irritate Saint Peter.

But his usual surprise was nothing compared to what hit him as he walked across the off-white industrial carpet and saw the three people waiting for him.

Larkspur was sitting behind his desk, his long legs crossed and the mirrorlike caps of his black shoes protruding into the room.

Elizabeth was sitting on one white chair, wearing a faded brick-and-white cotton dress that recalled the Southwest.

On the chair next to her was a young woman wearing jeans and a tank top, sandals on her feet, her hands clasped in her lap.

Rachel Patton.

Larkspur said, "Welcome, Benjamin!" He pointed to the

pitcher on the chrome-and-glass drinks cart. "Pimm's cup as advertised . . . you could probably use a drink along about now. Please, build your own."

"What the hell is this? Somebody's idea of a cute surprise? A party?" He scowled at all of them and poured the Pimm's mixture into a glass tankard containing a slice of cucumber and plenty of ice. "I'm so glad I was invited."

"Ben," Elizabeth said. Then, placatingly, "*Please* . . ."

"Miss Patton . . . Rachel . . . how are you? You left so suddenly—"

"I'm sorry, Mr. Driskill. Really . . ." Her lower lip quivered.

"Are you? Well, so am I, so am I. If anybody starts crying, maybe it should be me."

"I was so afraid. I panicked when I saw him watching me. Are you disappointed I'm not dead?" She tried to smile. He wished he could raise a little plain old-fashioned hell with her.

"Larkie, what kind of crap is this? You ask me an hour ago if I've found her and I say no and now you're sitting here with her? I hate games!" He shook his head. "Aw, the hell with it." He drank deeply. "Elizabeth, aren't you carrying this all a little far? Am I the enemy now? Wasn't I a part of this whole Rachel thing? Don't I warrant a call?"

Elizabeth spoke up: "I went back to the flat last night . . . and there she was, waiting for me."

"Look, Ben," Larkie said, "we've settled her down. We've assured her that you're not the bad guy—"

"Oh, well, that's a helluva relief—I feel ever so much better. Christ. We dealt with that issue up in Vermont," Driskill snapped. "Or so I thought."

Elizabeth said, "There isn't time for you to be angry. There's work to be done—"

"But there's plenty of time to jerk my chain all over Georgetown. Elizabeth, I thought your big number one concern was to get me out of this business—"

"Larkie seems to think I'm a little late with that."

"No kidding? Who the hell died and put Larkie in

charge? Well, Larkie, I don't know how to thank you. This is my lucky day, I guess."

"Ben," Larkspur said, "do you have anything more to say about your run-in with Hazlitt and Taylor last night?"

"Yeah. It was the best time I've had since this whole thing began."

"Why did you take 'em on, Ben?"

"My original intention was to show them a drawing of a strange line, find out if they knew what it meant—"

"And what does it mean?"

"*I don't know.*" Driskill took another long swallow of Pimm's just to calm himself down. "Hayes Tarlow sent it to himself the day he was murdered and I happened to get it. It was important to him, I have to assume he got it from Herb Varringer, and then they were both murdered. What the hell does it mean? I'm trying to find out. I say Bob Hazlitt knows. Maybe it's a real estate deal, maybe it's a property line and Hazlitt is pulling a fast one . . . maybe it's some river somewhere . . . maybe it's a country road—I just have no idea. But it's important."

"Would you like to try it out on me?" Larkspur held out his hand. He was smiling reassuringly. "I know, I won't have any idea, either. But try me."

"All right." He took the paper from his wallet and unfolded it, laid it on the severe, empty slab of glass, making Larkspur reach for it.

Larkspur gave it a quick look. "It doesn't mean anything. What *could* it mean?" Driskill shrugged. "What did Hazlitt say?"

"Nothing. I didn't show him. He was too busy screaming at me." His eyes kept shifting to Rachel Patton.

"Well, you spent an extraordinary evening," Larkspur said. "I somehow think Drew would have been proud of you—"

"He knew there was a time to take action. Whether he'd have thought that was the right time . . . I don't know. I'm less patient than Drew was. But he had balls and he knew when to probe."

"We could use his wisdom now," Larkspur agreed.

"The President, Larkie. What's the deal? And doesn't he want Rachel as soon as he can get her? He did the last time I heard him yelling at me!"

Larkspur sat doodling on a white sheet of paper.

Finally Rachel Patton spoke softly into the silence. "Mr. Driskill . . . I've been hiding with an old college friend in Pennsylvania. I was afraid, but I knew I had to do something. I couldn't hide forever. I came to see Elizabeth. I didn't see how that man could have followed me. Just wasn't possible. I came in late last night. . . . There's something more I have to tell you, something I remember Hayes Tarlow telling me. He said the secret was deep inside intelligence 'but they don't even know it.' I don't know what he meant but I remembered it in the middle of the night, after I left Middlebury. He said that what he and Drew and I were doing was . . . *showing it to them.* Making them see it. . . . Somehow *that* scared me. But I was scared all the time by then . . . and then they were both dead and I didn't know what I was supposed to do, what could I do to help them find . . ."

"Maybe," Larkspur said soothingly, "it will come to you."

"Mr. Tarlow asked me if I knew what was going on at ISO . . . the satellite agency. I didn't. I don't. But maybe it was there."

Driskill rolled his eyes heavenward.

"Ben," Larkspur said, "Miss Patton has told me the story of the back channel. And I'd already heard Charlie's version, of course. I think we need to arrange a chance for her to speak to him. Make sense to you?"

"Jesus, what have I been saying? Of course! But I assure you that none of this makes any sense to me yet. That's why I want to speak to Charlie first. Then we can set him up to hear Rachel. You can baby-sit their meeting. But I want a go at him first. He'll thank you." The sunshine was bouncing along the Potomac, reflecting in the window, glinting off the desktop. It hurt his eyes.

"He's going to call me back. He's trying to clear time for you. In the meantime, are you all right?" Larkspur was looking at Rachel and Elizabeth. "Shall I call Justice and lay on some security for you now?"

Elizabeth looked at Ben.

He shook his head. "No FBI."

"There can't be any danger—I know I'm clean, Mr. Driskill. The man who was following me before—he couldn't know where I am now."

"My God, you've got a lot to learn," Driskill said. He turned back to Larkspur. "Call me at this number. It's my cellular phone. I want to see him as soon as possible. Like tonight."

"I'll do whatever I can, Benjamin. I can't make a miracle."

"You'd better this time, Larkie."

Tom Bohannon was having a drink in the promenade café at Washington Harbor, which was crowded in the late afternoon. A steady breeze blew off the water; the fringe on the umbrella over the table fluttered, and pretty girls in very short skirts wiggled their behinds on stools around the bar. Everybody was tan. It was all like something out of a chummy yacht club, but it was just a bar trying hard to keep the image going. He was drinking a Cuba Libre, sipping it, tasting just a hint of the rum, lots of Coca-Cola. It was the easy life he had given up—or never been allowed to have. He wore a fine patina of sweat. He'd sweated a lot in his day.

In Africa he'd sweated, in Beirut he'd dripped with it. Seemed like it was always hot wherever they sent him. Why wasn't there ever a problem in Norway or Finland? Let him wear a sheepskin coat. In hot weather he remembered too much, remembered the blood dripping out of the pulp where his fingernails had been only seconds before . . . remembered the hot wire pulling tighter and tighter around his testicles and the effort of will that drained the blood from his brain and erased the pain and fear. He smiled up at the pretty waitress and said no, he was fine, he didn't need another drink. He peeled off a five and two ones and pushed them under the saucer so the breeze wouldn't blow them away. He'd been taking up the table for quite a while. He took the two ones back, replaced them with another five.

When the three of them came out of the office building they stopped at the top of the arc of stairs leading down to the plaza where he sat watching them. Then they conferred and followed the man, Ben Driskill, down the steps in his direction. Bohannon meant nothing to them. They'd never seen him before. Today he was a businessman, long dark hair swept back on the sides and hanging well down over his collar. His eyes were dark brown. He was wearing a Nicole Miller necktie, the bright one all about baseball, a striped shirt, a cream-colored linen suit, and Gucci loafers. Mr. Asshole. The ad game, a media buyer maybe, some nonproductive shitbrain having a drink and checking out the chicks who were half his age, his dark glasses in their thick black frames hanging on a chain around his neck since his back was to the sun. Fuck 'em, let 'em sit right next to him. It was okay with him. All the better.

It was already a lucky day. Lucky the girl finally showed up at Elizabeth Driskill's apartment. That was the trouble with a one-man tail. Once you lost the object of your concern it could be merry hell finding them again. You had to go watch the spot where you thought they'd eventually turn up. They usually did if you were patient.

They sat two tables away. He picked up his copy of *Ad Age,* watched them over the top of it. He'd been trained to listen hard.

He had been monitoring them for hours. He'd wired Elizabeth Driskill's car.

"Keep driving," he said. "Just like sightseers. Take in the Kennedy Center, have a look at the Smithsonian, just keep it going. Make a long night of it, stay out late, then I'll meet you at Gepetto's for pizza. Don't come to rest before that. I'll only be an hour or so with the President."

"We'll have to come to rest somewhere," Elizabeth said.

"Pretend you're the Flying Dutchman, doomed forever to—"

"I get it, I get it."

"Am I making myself absolutely clear?"

"Ben, she said she couldn't have been followed."

"Maybe not. But the flat might have been staked out. You just don't know. She's sure he saw us in Vermont. If he lost Rachel there, that didn't mean he couldn't pick her up at the other end. I know damn little about this sort of thing, but I know that much. So don't go anywhere near the flat. Okay? Sooner or later, Rachel is going to need some security . . . but she's got to see the President first. Once she sees him, it's too late, she's not a danger to them anymore."

Elizabeth was driving her car. "Anybody for a Big Mac?"

"I'd kill for one," Rachel Patton said.

While they were sitting in the McDonald's his cellular phone rang.

"Larkie?"

"It wasn't easy, Benjamin. But you're on." He sighed as if he'd done more than any man could be expected to do. Ever. "It's got to be quieter than quiet, you understand? It can't come out or the President will look like a liar and a hypocrite and a conspirator. Not a good look at this particular juncture."

"Never really a good look, Larkie."

"It's the National Cathedral. Take a cab from in front of the Willard at midnight. Have him drop you at Massachusetts Avenue and Cathedral Avenue Northwest. Go to the cathedral. The new high-security gates will be open. Walk through them, all the way up to the cathedral itself. There'll be a light on at only one door—I don't know which one, just trust me. Go through the lighted doorway. He'll be waiting for you inside."

"Is that where I find the surprise corpse?"

"Benjamin, I can't recall anything in recent memory that is a less fit subject for humor. So spare me."

"I love you when you're pompous. Lighten up, Larkie. Think of your blood pressure."

"That's what I am thinking of, thank you. I'd kill somebody, anybody, for a cigarette. But I believe in the patch and the patch will set me free. I'm giving it a stiff test. Remember, you'll be under close surveillance from the moment you step through the security gate. Don't wander about or pick the wrong door. These are nervous men. The President is definitely not supposed to be out and about in secret. I hope you appreciate that, Benjamin."

"Hope springs eternal, I guess." He waited for Larkspur to reprimand him for inappropriate lightheartedness, but the other end of the line was silent. "Thanks, Larkie. I do appreciate your going out on a limb for me."

"Mmm. Don't be late, Benjamin."

At eleven-thirty Driskill got out of the car in front of the Willard.

"Ben, hurry up." Elizabeth was grinning at him. The pressure had gone off. Somehow they were back on the same side. Maybe because she was included and not bouncing around inside a vacuum. They were doing it together.

"Okay, it won't be a long meeting. I'll have somebody drop me when it's over—a Secret Service guy can run me down to Gepetto's, okay? Just wait for me."

"Sounds perfect."

He leaned down and kissed her mouth.

"I love you," she whispered.

"You say that to all the guys. Rachel," he said, "don't let Elizabeth out of your sight. Stay together."

"Whatever you say, Mr. Driskill."

Everything went as Larkspur had promised. The night was muggy with occasional gusts of wind and rain. The headlamps caught the rain in their light beams on Wisconsin Avenue passing before the cathedral. The tires hissed in the wet street. The huge shape of the cathedral, its Gothic limestone towers catching the glow of the city, loomed across the street, splendid in its parkland behind the high-security fence that was intended to discourage the ever increasing number of vandals. He peeled off bills for the driver and got out of the cab.

He crossed during a lull in the traffic and saw the doorway in the fence standing open. It wasn't one of the big gates as Larkspur had implied. He guessed he wouldn't mention it to the great man, who had no doubt just repeated what he'd been told. The Secret Service was watching him now through their night sights. When he went through the doorway Driskill felt their gaze almost like a physical presence, a finger pressing steadily into his ribs to remind him he was not alone.

The light over the door into the cathedral itself presented no problem—as promised there was only one. The wind rushed in the trees, brushing the branches and shaking water from the leaves. The night smelled like rich, freshly turned earth. He opened the door and stepped inside.

It was dim inside but he could make out his surroundings. He waited, leaned against a cold stone pillar. After a few minutes he said in an unnaturally loud voice: "Oh, for Christ's sake, what the hell did you get me out in the middle of the night for? Speak up, Charlie, or I'm gone and you'll regret it, I promise you. I'll take my chances with the bushes full of sharpshooters outside."

A voice came from the shadows very close by.

"I thought of having you follow a trail of bread crumbs way downstairs to those vaults."

"Mr. President, I've been following a trail of bread crumbs for a week."

"So I've been told. Let's go for a walk." They fell into step, the President leading the way. "I love this place. You probably didn't know about the ninety-six angels circling the central tower—the Gloria in Excelsis tower, by the way. Each angel has a different face. I like that. Over there, the Space Window commemorating *Apollo Eleven,* they have a piece of moon rock sunk right into the glass. Don't tell me you knew that—but everybody should know it. I don't like to be a cornball, but this is quite a country we've got here."

"We're going to need all ninety-six of the angels."

"Okay, you'd better get to it. What do you mean? Why are we here?"

"That's the question: Why do I have to get you out in the middle of the night? What the hell is going on with you and the campaign? All this LVCO stuff—I have got to know . . . because I'd just as soon not dump you out with the trash—"

"Ben, I don't know a damned thing about that stock, you've just got to believe me. Even if you think I'm a greedy, crooked bastard, do you think I'd be dumb enough to pull a stunt like this? Dumb enough to think that in this age of Arnaldo LaSalle and Ballard Niles nobody would find out? Jesus, Ben, get real. I'm the kinda guy—I'm afraid somebody'll dig up old Howard Carruthers, the janitor in high school, who caught me jacking off in the boys' john when I was fourteen."

"All right. You're innocent as a newborn babe. But La-Salle is pretty damn sure of himself. Or he's bluffing. Let's call his bluff and make him come up with the proof. If it's not true he's going to have a helluva lot of trouble showing some stock certificates, photocopies of some records . . . *if* he wants to pursue the issue. You say you're clean . . . so he can't prove it—"

"Oh, hell, guys like LaSalle can prove anything, go around waving forged records and whatnot, just like old Joe McCarthy and all those Communists in the State Department. Look, I've already had your New York office start checking through Drew's files, the blind trust, and the initial report says there's no LVCO stock."

Ben shook his head sadly. "Charlie, Charlie—you've been in this dirty business long enough to know there's going to be *something* on paper, something that says Drew arranged for the shares to be sold or put in a blind trust. And a blind trust won't do us any good since LVCO was picking off government contracts all along, getting bigger and bigger, fatter and fatter, and who the hell was the head of state? You, Charlie. Blind trust my ass, you'd still know LVCO was cleaning up on contracts. Believe me, if the documents don't support you, you know where they're gonna show up—"

"On LaSalle's show," the President said with a dying fall.

"That's right. He doesn't like going out on limbs and falling on his ass." In the low, sepulchral light of the deserted church, with the cool dampness of the stones all around them, Driskill felt bolder than usual with the President. In the darkness Charles Bonner was robbed of some of the trappings of great power, became more just a man in deep trouble. "Charlie, during the course of a long career in the law, dealing with families fighting over massive inheritances, dealing with owners plundering their companies, dealing with unions annexing pension funds for illegal activities, I've seen a setup or two. Now, let's agree that you knew nothing about this. Somebody's playing for high—incredibly high—stakes here, and they're sure they can make you look guilty as hell. LaSalle's too smart to go with the story and then hope the proof turns up. He doesn't give a damn who's president, you're just the poor unlucky bastard in office—he's after the story. Somebody has set you up, Charlie. We've got to find out who's doing it." Driskill took a deep breath, forged on.

"Another thing. Why did Nick Wardell call me from Iowa? You already knew about Hayes Tarlow's death when I came down to the White House from Big Ram— you didn't tell me but you knew. Nick must have called you—so why did he call me?"

"He called Clark Beckerman at the DNC. It was Clark who called me. I had Clark call him back, speaking for me, asking him to call you—"

"*What?* What the hell are you talking about? You're the guy who was cutting me out of the loop on Hayes, on everything—"

"Ben, I *needed* somebody! I needed someone out on the point. Don't you see, *there's nobody else I can trust* . . . really, truly trust. But if I'd asked you to take it on, I was afraid you'd have said no, Charlie old pal, I don't want any part of your goddam sleazy political intrigues, I want no part of the Washington bullshit. You'd have said Drew sent Hayes out to get killed and you'd be goddamned if you were gonna follow in his shoes—I couldn't let you say no. But you're so fucking predictable—if I cut you out of the loop and you found out I had, you'd be so pissed off you'd take matters into your own hands. You've been the same way all your life. So . . . I did what I had to do." The President was standing with his hands in his pockets, leaning against one of the huge columns, regarding him with what seemed to be a concerned smile. "It's a true story, pal."

"Jesus H. Christ. You are one scary piece of work—"

"Ben, who was the real leader of the team at Notre Dame? The hotshot quarterback? Me? You always acted like you thought so. But the leader of the team, the guy they'd have run through the brick wall for, was you . . . because they knew you'd sink your teeth into the enemy, you'd hang on, and only one of you would walk away. Either you'd win or you'd be dead. We knew that, we saw you hit a ball carrier, we heard the pads crack like a gunshot, we saw him go down and we saw you climb up out of the mud like some Darwinian madman and leave him to meet his maker. I needed that Ben Driskill, somebody who'd dig for the truth, somebody who'd find the truth and save my ass. Sure, Ben, it's the truth that will save my ass, but the truth seems to be doing a disappearing act, it's blowing away right before our eyes. And you're not doing it for me, I'm not asking you to do that just for me. . . ." He'd drawn close and was looking up into Ben's face, his hand on Ben's sleeve. Sweat glistened on his face in the dim, flickering candlelight. "I'm asking you to do it for the best man either of us has ever known . . . Drew Summerhays. And even more than that, I'm asking you . . . to do it for your country. That's what Drew would have wanted. You and I know that. You gotta hang in there on my side. The team needs you, pal. Biggest game of all . . ."

"Bastard. You've just played all your cards, Charlie. The

Notre Dame card. The Drew Summerhays card. The patriotism card . . . Your hand is empty."

"That's right. You got me where you want me, Ben."

"What am I supposed to do? Tell you to go fuck yourself because you held out on me? Because you played me like Fritz Kreisler played his fiddle?"

"I sincerely hope not. I want you on my team, Ben. It's time for one last goal-line stand—"

"All right, all right, you're murdering the metaphor. I'm on the team, I'm on the team . . . but you'd better be working on cleaning up the mess, too. You gotta go to Chicago in a few days . . . and Bob Hazlitt's eating your lunch."

The President turned, paced away, stood with his hands on his hips looking up at the angels. "I can't stop thinking about that goddam back channel operating right under my nose. Drew . . . what did he think he was doing? Tarlow. Who else was in on it? Man of mirrors! Jesus. If someone was setting me up with LVCO, Ben, I hate to say this, God, I *hate* to say this, but Drew was in charge of my portfolio. Drew was in the back channel . . . all that FCAT money. Tarlow was working for Drew, the Patton girl was just a messenger and she thinks somebody is going to kill her. Larkie tells me she's shown up on Elizabeth's doorstep. And this cornball man of mirrors—is he for real or just somebody's idea of window dressing? Ben, I keep thinking the unthinkable, I can't help it. . . . Did Drew set me up? He *could* do it, he'd know how, he had the access—he could do it better than anybody I know—"

"Look, Sarrabian is the man of mirrors. Trust me." Charlie looked surprised. "But . . . aside from the fact that your theory is absolute bullshit, what are you saying? Drew was out to get you? That he'd put everything in play, got the whole thing under way and then someone, whoever's behind all this, killed Drew and took over the plot? That's your theory?"

"Well, it fits what we know—"

"But there's no motive for Drew to undertake any of this. *Why would he do it?*"

"Ben, have you ever thought of this? Maybe he thought

I was a bad fucking president! Maybe he thought his last act of statesmanship would be to destroy me!"

"Oh, for God's sake! That's paranoid nonsense. Next you'll be telling me he had a secret brain tumor and it was making him do weird things—well, no, that shot's not on the table. Drew was Drew. Whatever the back channel was, it wasn't Drew trying to nail you. If that's a possibility, then I'm not your man." He wished he were as sure as he sounded.

The President shrugged his broad shoulders, frustrated, at an end. "I'm just saying it fits the facts. I think it bears the earmarks of Drew's work. It's complicated, it's ingenious, it's well conceived—well, maybe Drew believed it in his heart. Either he believed it or they blackmailed him into doing it. . . . I guess that's possible. And then they killed him." He reached out and put his hand on Ben Driskill's arm. "You gotta find out the truth, pal."

"What if you don't like it, Mr. President?"

The President laughed softly. "But you forget, Ben . . . the truth will set us free. One way or another. Won't it? Are you on board?"

"If you let me do it my way. Carte blanche . . ."

"Whatever you say, Ben."

"Then I'm on board."

The President turned to face the shadowed pews. "Did you hear that, Larkie?"

Driskill spun, saw Larkie approaching from the darkness.

"Of course I did, Mr. President. I told you all you needed to do was appeal to his better instincts. Fact is," he said, approaching them, "Drew Summerhays is dead. But this fella here is the closest thing to him we're ever going to find."

"You guys play rough," Driskill said. "You spring Rachel Patton on me, he springs you on me—I'm going to be scared to go through the door next time."

"Not you," the President said, "never you, Ben." He stretched his arms out in front of him, a momentary exercise to get the blood flowing. "And Rachel Patton—when do I see her?" He looked from Larkspur to Driskill. "When?"

"Why not right now? She's eating pizza with Elizabeth at Gepetto's in Georgetown. Have a couple of Secret Service guys run me down there, I'll turn her over to them."

"Perfect. She'll sleep tonight in the White House! It's all going to work out, Ben. Everything's going to be fine . . . and you'll discover that I'm no crook."

Larkspur chuckled as they headed out of the cathedral.

Chapter 18

As she drove the capital's streets, wipers on intermittent to handle the mist, he was behind her, listening to everything on the bug. She knew nothing about tails. She and the target were blissfully sure they were safe. The target hadn't seen her stalker; he'd given up while she'd dropped out of sight, she was sure of it. Their conversation was remarkably empty, girlish, stupid. They were a couple of silly bimbos. The world would be a better place without them. Without the one, anyway. His commission included only the one. He had to remember that. Actually, the other one, Driskill's wife, impressed him in several ways. He was just disappointed that she babbled on in the car. Then he began to pick up on it. She was trying to keep her nerves under control. She was worried, whether the girl was or not. . . .

He watched them checking out the Lincoln Memorial. Deserted in the mist, regal, impressive. He admired Lincoln. He'd once owned ten different miniature Lincolns. Long time ago.

They didn't leave the car. He waited behind them, his mind roaming.

He followed them to the Jefferson Memorial, sat watching through the mist. They were doing the historical tour. Killing time. He kept them in view, waited for his chance. He watched them driving past the Vietnam Memorial. This one had special meaning for him. His father had fought there.

He followed them as they wandered back through Georgetown, down by the canal, up on to M Street, which had begun to calm down for the night. It was past midnight. They took a right up past a bookstore with one light on, then another right into the tight little tangle of old and narrow streets running more or less parallel to M. It was dark and it was quiet and the mist just speckled his windshield. The cobblestones were slippery. . . .

"I'd rather not park right on M," Elizabeth said. "Sometimes people come out of the bars late. And drunk. Somebody broke into this car a few months ago—cracked the windshield, stole the CD player—"

"I hate when that happens," Rachel Patton said.

A car behind her had flicked on its brights, was weaving in the narrow street. The lights flickered on and off as the car fishtailed, slowed.

"See what I mean? Some guy totally loaded, trying to drive home."

Suddenly the car behind her speeded up, made to pass her where there wasn't enough width to the street, swerved erratically, and she felt the sickening metallic thump as he nosed in and hit her door, scraped along the fender. It was like hearing a cash register running up the repair bills or her insurance premiums, take your pick.

"Shit," she yelled. Leaning out the window: "You idiot!"

She tried to slow down, pulled back, and the other driver, realizing what he'd done, miscalculated and yanked the steering wheel in the wrong direction and cut sharply in front of her. She slammed on the brakes, they skidded on the wet stones, and she saw Rachel Patton slam forward toward the windshield, felt herself thrown against the steering wheel, no air bags to soften the impact.

Her car had stopped but she had smashed into the other car's door. Rachel moaned and slumped backward. Her head had popped the windshield into a million strands of a spiderweb.

Elizabeth struggled to get her own breath back. She felt like vomiting.

The idiot drunk was coming back around his own car, heading for the passenger door.

"Jeez, I'm really sorry, ladies . . ." He sounded drunk all right. Big surprise. "Accelerator stuck . . . fuck it . . ." He was weaving. She remembered the self-defense course she'd taken while in her training for the Order. Nuns could be targets in big cities and she'd learned a move or two.

"You blinded me with your brights—you're drunk!" Words failed her. She leaned across toward Rachel. "Are you okay?"

"Yeah, I guess." She was running fingertips experimentally along her forehead. "My head hurts."

"Listen," the guy said, standing a few feet from Rachel's door. "Let me make good on this, okay . . . no need to get our insurance companies, like, involved, y'know. . . ."

Elizabeth pushed hard, felt her own crumpled door finally give and swing outward. She got out and glared at him across the hood.

"We're calling the cops," she yelled again. "We're reporting this—you're drunk and you're a danger on the road!"

"I'll give you five hundred bucks, cash money, you can take it to this friend of mine, he's got a body shop in Virginia, y'know. . . ." He turned to Rachel Patton. "Say, miss, you don't look so good—you gonna barf?" He opened the door. She staggered out, held up by him. "Man, I am so sorry, ladies." He looked at Elizabeth. "Your friend's gonna be sick here. . . ."

Rachel Patton slipped from his grasp, made a gurgling sound, and fell to her knees. Thank God, the bastard caught her. Elizabeth heard her gasp.

"Steady there, miss," he cautioned her. He looked at Elizabeth again. "I think she needs to lie down."

Elizabeth was still trying to catch her breath. She was coming around the back of her own car. She heard another choking sound from Rachel, got to her, and knelt where she lay. In the light of the headlamps she saw bright red blood bubbling out of her mouth, heard the wet gurgle, saw blood smearing across her chest, pooling beneath her.

And she knew.

The man above her had taken a step back. "She looks real sick—I'll go call nine-one-one. . . ."

Elizabeth lunged up off the cobblestones, driving her fist into his crotch, catching him, knocking him backward, but she slipped on the wet stones, slipped in the blood, and fell. Her head slammed down against a bulging cobblestone and she felt something crack and everything began to spin and when she struggled up to her knees he was looking down at her again, bent forward slightly, holding himself, fighting off the pain of the blow.

"Stay down," he whispered. "Just stay down. This isn't about you."

She tried to grab his leg and he batted her hand away and she fell forward, her head slamming into a fender, then a bumper, then the stones again. She knew she was losing consciousness, everything was spinning and she knew he was backing away, she heard him starting the car on the lonely street, she heard him pulling away and then she was fading, fading. . . .

Ben couldn't find them at Gepetto's.

It took an hour for the Secret Service to locate them through the District of Columbia Police Department. Driskill, heart pounding, sick to his stomach, got to Saint Peter's shortly after Bob McDermott had arrived. Mac was getting things under control. Secret Service agents had been dispatched by Teresa Rowan just in case there was some kind of further attack on the powerful people converging on the hospital as dawn first flickered to life on the eastern horizon. McDermott saw Driskill in the emergency admitting lobby. He went to him and instinctively threw his arms around him. "Don't give up hope, Ben. She's a fighter and she's still alive. We've already found a bug in her car. Somebody was listening to them. I don't know what to say, Ben."

"Rachel Patton?"

"Shit . . . she's dead. Never had a chance."

"Stabbed in the heart, right?"

McDermott stared at him. "Who told you that?"

"Nobody. I knew."

"Yeah, that's how it happened. Just like Hayes Tarlow—"

"And Herb Varringer . . . it's the way he does it."

Ben felt like he was going to vomit. "I gotta sit down."

Mac sat next to him. The hospital was starting to bustle, coming out of the particular emergencies of the night, getting ready for those of the day. The call buttons were bonging. "Where is she, Mac? I want to see her. What do the doctors say?"

"She's in surgery, there's some kind of cranial hematoma. Jeez, Ben, I'm just reporting what I got from a doctor when I got here. The President's on his way, Ben. Somebody's gonna pay."

Driskill smiled wearily. "They won't find the guy. Nobody's gonna pay until we find the guy. Mac, he's one scary son of a bitch, I'll tell you . . . a bug in the car, my God, he knew everything they were planning." He felt tears welling up in the corners of his eyes. She was still alive. He had to cling to that. If she died, he knew he'd flame out, be consumed by hatred and the need for revenge, and that would be the end of Ben Driskill. "Have the papers and TV got hold of it yet?"

McDermott looked at his watch. "It'll be on the news at six. Hell, maybe noon. Late editions of the papers. It was all on the police frequency. Come on, Ben—she's a well-known person. Crime-ridden Washington strikes again and it's a celebrity this time. There was no way to keep it hushed up."

"I understand. It's okay." He leaned back, closed his eyes. "They didn't give you any prognosis?"

"Nobody would give me any information. I don't think they know. She's alive now and I figure that's good news."

The President arrived accompanied by Ellery Larkspur. Bonner threw his arms around Driskill, hugged him tightly. "Listen, Ben, if she were going to die, she'd have died when she was attacked. It's God. He wouldn't have saved her, he wouldn't have brought those cops to find her only to let her slip away from us. She's gonna be okay, I can feel it."

"Thanks, Charlie. I pray you're right." He bit his lip, unable to say anything more at just that moment. There were Secret Service men everywhere now, the corridor had filled and an ambulance had arrived outside, the driver screaming at the official cars—he had a man with three bullet wounds in his back. The President's caravan was screwing everything up. Nurses and interns were running by, gurneys at high speed.

Time was blurring. A few minutes later they were down an empty hallway talking to a doctor who had been watching the surgery.

"Mr. Driskill, I can't say anything definitive about your wife's condition. We've drilled her skull, reduced the subdural hematoma—relieved the pressure on her brain, and her neck is immobilized. Her head took a beating, several blows—the cobblestones. We're doing what we can. She had some movement though she never regained consciousness, which is not entirely unexpected." He raised his hands and his eyebrows. "That's about it. She'll probably be out of surgery in an hour or so, then she'll be in the ICU."

"Is she going to make it?"

The doctor shook his head. "No way to tell. My guess, she'll live. But in what condition, who knows? Let's just take this one step at a time. I'd be crazy to predict. But I think she'll live. Coma? Very likely but you never know how long . . . could be a matter of days, could be—well, hell, I had a fellow who got shot and was in a coma for a little over five years and woke up one day and was more or less normal, just five years behind the times. You just never know."

"When can I see her?"

"Once she's in ICU. She ain't gonna be pretty but all that

will go away and you can be sure she'll be as beautiful as ever."

Driskill smiled at the doctor. "She'll be beautiful for me as long as she's alive."

"I understand. I just didn't want you to be shocked by swelling and discoloration." He looked at his watch. "Give us an hour or two, okay?"

Charlie Bonner said, "Thanks, Doc. That was a very good rundown. She's mighty important to us."

"Mr. President, I'm used to that. Pretty much everybody is important to someone."

The President watched him go, then turned back to Driskill. "Ben, I need to talk to you. From what I hear"—he nodded to Larkspur—"it sounds like Rachel Patton died the way Hayes died—that square with you?"

"Exactly. It sure as hell wasn't just a mugger out for an easy strike that went wrong. This man's a pro. This is just one more killing among the members of the back channel—"

"If it isn't the goddam back channel," Bonner said, "it's that goddam Hazlitt! I'm beginning to think you should have clipped him one at the Croquet bash—oh, hell, I'm just blowing off steam. Larkie told me you accused him of murdering Varringer and Tarlow. Did you really do that, Ben? I meant to ask you last night but it slipped my mind."

"Yeah, I did. It was too good an opportunity to pass up. I was just trying to shake him up, force him to make a mistake or an admission—but Taylor kept papering it over, kept bringing it back to politics and how you were destroying America and they had to save the country from you. The standard crap."

"God, they must regret your ever seeing the light of day."

"I'd like to put a helluva lot more pressure on Hazlitt. I think these murders were somehow connected, Charlie—"

"But Varringer had nothing to do with the back channel."

"I know . . . I know. I'm trying to figure it the hell out, okay?"

Larkspur tugged at his bow tie, folded his arms across his chest. "Ben, what are you thinking about doing now?"

"Charlie told me to find out the truth last night. You heard him."

"I'm trying to convince you," the President said, "that I'm clean in all this mess. I don't have to fear the truth. But now we've got Rachel Patton dead and Elizabeth upstairs in surgery." The President looked into Driskill's eyes for several seconds, searching for something. "Ben, you can opt out of this now. Last night I had no idea it was going to blow up in our faces like this. I wouldn't blame you—I'd get out myself."

Driskill nodded. "Not now. Now," he said with a heavy sigh, "I want to see my wife."

When he presented himself at the floor station near the ICU they were prepared.

"Of course, Mr. Driskill," the nurse said, consulting the watch hanging by a chain on the front of her uniform. "We've been expecting you. Dr. Lucas has given his okay, so we'll be taking you in. We've got a chair at her bedside. It's not very comfortable in there, lots of bustle going on all day and all night." She smiled apologetically, a middle-aged black woman with a lilt of Jamaica in her voice. "But you may stay as long as you like." She smiled again.

"How is she?"

"She needs a long sleep. Her body and brain have had a terrible shock. I always say when there's a coma, there's a good chance she'll rest until her body and her brain decide they've rested enough and then it'll be time to get up." She pushed through the swinging door into the strange, other-worldly atmosphere of the intensive care unit. Lots of beds and millions of dollars' worth of diagnostic and life-sustaining and monitoring devices, a kind of off-blue light that somehow allowed the wounded and broken inhabitants to sleep while the bustle around them never stopped. "Over here, Mr. Driskill. Here she is."

She lay on the bed, almost like an effigy until you saw

the slight rise and fall of her breathing. There was a bandage on her head and she was hooked up to a variety of electronic monitoring gear. The nurse had left them alone. He leaned over the bed, his fingertips barely touching her bare arm, and kissed her cheek. She felt warm, soft, even smelled good. Her eyelids fluttered and he thought she was about to open them, but it was an illusion. Just a tremor. He sat down beside her. He couldn't take his eyes off her. There was some bruising around her eyes. She looked better than he'd expected.

Nurses moved constantly, rubber soles making them almost soundless as they checked all the readings, noted their findings, peering closely at the LEDs. ICU was a place where there was always that eerie light and the chugging of pumps and the clicking of machines making sure nobody just up and died when it wasn't their turn.

Elizabeth.

The white bandage was neat and clean and precise, blending in with the pristine whiteness of the pillow. Suddenly he had a kind of flashback, remembered photographs of her when she'd been so young, a new member of the Order . . . a young nun on one of the rare occasions when she'd worn the traditional long black habit with her beautiful face, huge-eyed and so innocent, so full of hope, framed by the stiff white and black fabric. He saw her face now, framed in white, and it was as if she were young again, as if her whole life lay ahead of her while she slept on the high-tech mechanical bed, as if she were awaiting some kind of judgment, some decision—would she go on or would she be gathered home to God? He leaned across her again, kissed her, felt the soft skin. She was quiet, breathing softly, eyes closed, hands limp. He felt the tears on his face and let them come. If he couldn't cry for Elizabeth, then what point was there in being alive at all?

He sat on the bedside chair for a long time, saying nothing, watching her, thinking about what he had to do and how he could set about doing it. . . .

When he woke up, the television was on. A nurse must have turned it on for him—as company. The morning on which the news of Elizabeth Driskill's misfortune became widely known, a variety of events occurred in different parts of the world.

The head of the police garrison in the south of Mexico had been killed with a car bomb. A French airliner trying to land at the Mexico City International Airport had been blown out of the sky with 129 people aboard—a SAM had chased it across the runway as it attempted to land. Everybody died, of course. And from their HQ the revolutionaries claimed that this new stage of the civil war would be the last, would lead to their final, total victory.

He watched as a clip from a speech last night came on the news.

The audience in San Diego was rabid.

Sherman Taylor had always held a place within their pantheon of heroes. Many of them had been shocked at his defeat by Charles Bonner. Shocked and embittered to a degree that had caused concern among some of the more moderate Republican leaders. Taylor's fervent admirers were not true ideologues, they were worshipers at Taylor's eternal flame. Some of them had fought under him in Vietnam, and with him they had mourned what they saw as the government's refusal to let them win the war. They had fought with him in the Middle East and shared his moments of triumph. The medals on his chest were in a very real sense *their* medals. And they hated Charles Bonner deep in their bones.

When the former president spoke at Jack Murphy Stadium—the National League Padres were out on the road—the place was packed. San Diego and Orange County were Taylor country. But they came with one enormous question: Why had he deserted Price Quarles, who had paid his dues to the party and to the nation, in favor of, God forbid, a Democrat? What did such an act mean to them, the Taylor loyalists? What the hell was going on?

Taylor didn't leave them waiting for long.

"I have been asked again and again why I left the Republican Party and joined the campaign of Bob Hazlitt. Why did I turn my back on the party which I represented when I served in the White House? Well, let me say a few words about that."

He outlined once again why he believed Bob Hazlitt was the man to lead America, the man of experience whose values of hard work and loyalty to your country and whose clear vision of the future were what he, Taylor, had always tried to live by. He told the crowd that ideology was a thing of the past.

"We must, *must*, move beyond the old labels and the old ways of thinking. Democrat and Republican—those labels mean nothing anymore, that's the message I bring to you! We are Americans . . . we are all Americans! And we must decide on the man who should lead us to his view of what this country should be. Charles Bonner believes in an America that takes its anonymous place in the phalanx of nations, an America subject to the decisions of others . . . of foreigners who have no concern for all America stands for. Price Quarles was chosen to be my running mate because he carries out instructions, he is a competent and decent man who carries out policy, and as president he would carry out the orders and policies of *others*, whoever they might be. We must all realize that *it is the man who matters.* The man's integrity. The man's vision of America. The man's accomplishment. And I ask you, what must this man offer us? What do we need to see as his vision?" The words hung like a heady perfume over the crowd as they waited for the cry to glory. "America triumphant," he thundered at them, "an America that leads, that sits at the head of the table, an America others follow . . . America . . . triumphant!"

He hammered at them with this new message and then exhorted them to join him in his support of Bob Hazlitt. "He is . . . the . . . man! And we Americans, rising above the bondage of an outmoded party system, must support him!"

When they had calmed down, he went on.

"And now the President wants to get me safely out of the

way. He proposes sending me to Mexico to head a peace commission! He wants me to play a part in surrendering our leadership, our sovereign might, our destiny. Oh, I might go . . ." There came a shocked gasp of disbelief as he looked out over them, deadpan. Then he raised the volume: ". . . if we were sending an invading force to straighten things out down there!" The crowd went crazy. Sherman Taylor soaked up their adulation.

"It is a transparent, threadbare, partisan political attempt to deter me from supporting the candidate of my choice. If I, Sherman Taylor, am to be disenfranchised, stripped of my constitutional rights, it will take more than Charlie Bonner to do it!" He was pushing their buttons and they were responding like trained rats. Taylor went on: "I will not be suckered by this President who will stop at nothing to win an election and weaken our nation! I will not bow out of this campaign—not for Charlie Bonner, not for anyone! And I will see it through to the day Bob Hazlitt of Iowa takes his oath of office in Washington, D.C.!"

The crowd could barely control themselves.

Ben switched stations.

In Chicago workmen swarmed through the catwalks and ladders and hydraulic cranes that were part of the structure of the Ernie Banks International Convention Center that rose in splendid, octagonal grandeur on landfill extending seventy-five acres out into Lake Michigan. In an unhappy workplace accident an electrician had fallen three hundred feet to the floor of the hall but bounced off a bunch of vinyl-encased fiber-optic cable, tripped over thirty tons of AstroTurf, staggered to his feet, and fainted dead away on realizing that not only wasn't he dead, he had only sprained his ankle. When interviewed in a local hospital he remarked that he'd always been a Democrat and his survival would certainly keep him one. "God loves us Democrats," he'd called out but refused to be pinned down as to whether he was a Hazlitt or Bonner man. The next day he was back at work with an Ace bandage on his ankle. Giving autographs.

A home show was occupying half of the Ernie Banks

Center, but the rest of the hall was well into the process of being turned into the home of the Democratic Party for most of a week in what promised—according to the *Old Farmer's Almanac*—to be the hottest July in Chicago in fifty years. Thirty-six miles of electric cable was being laid, thirteen hundred Heartland computers with Pentium chips and more gigabytes of memory than Milton Berle were being installed, four hundred TV monitors and the largest indoor television screen in the world were being wired, more than half of the world's known supply of Phonovision units were being wired into the satellites and fiber-optic cables, thirty thousand seats were being painted red, white, and blue, and that didn't count the five thousand on the convention floor. Enough paint to do the Golden Gate Bridge twice was being applied to the walls and stage and podium that seven hundred union carpenters were in the process of building. Forty theatrical set designers were working on different aspects of the shows that would punctuate the week's more routine events. The stage behind the podium rested on four hydraulic lifts. Somebody said it would hold six individual productions of *Cats* simultaneously, though no one appeared ready to test the hypothesis. A special "environment" was being built for the actual party mascot who would be thrust into carefully controlled service from time to time during the week, including the final Sunday-evening gala when the retractable dome of the center would be opened for the fireworks show over Lake Michigan, a fireworks show that some clown at an observatory in California contended would be visible to the American space station circling Mars. The organizers of the convention had even gotten permission to use a limited amount of the fireworks inside, according to a spokesman. It was thought to be a sign that eight million dollars' worth of Bangers and Flowing Fire Tails and Cherry Bombs and Green Angels and Golden Antlers and Red Popping Nukes were bound to produce a very big fireworks display indeed.

It was going to be the convention to end them all.

Everybody said so.

Ben was sitting alone with Elizabeth. He was holding her hand, which was warm with life, which occasionally and he supposed reflexively tightened on his fingers. Could she be sending him a message of hope? He talked to her during those long hours he spent beside her bed, listening to the breathing, feeling her presence as he would if she'd only been sleeping. He told her the simple things he felt, how much he loved and needed her, how much he looked forward to the years left to them if only she could pull out of this. He told her he'd never love anyone else and he reminisced with her about how they'd met that wild night in Princeton in the aftermath of his sister's murder—his sister and Elizabeth's best friend. He moved back and forth through their life together, sometimes laughing aloud at something he remembered to tell her sleeping figure. Once a nurse poked her head into the room with a big smile on her face. "You two sure are having a good time in here!"

"That's us," Driskill said, smiling at her. "The laugh-a-minute Driskills."

"She's a lucky lady! Such a loving husband!"

"I'm here to tell you the luck all runs toward me."

It was while he was sitting at her bedside, his mind recapping the results of what he'd learned from his investigations—the piling up of information that tantalized him, made him believe he was taking the measure of the beast behind the curtain of lies and stories and self-protective ass covering—it was then that Nick Wardell finally ran him to ground.

"You're a hard man to find, Ben—tell me, first off, how's Elizabeth?"

"I'm sitting right beside her, Nick. She's sleeping like a baby. She looks pretty healthy." He tightened his mouth, clamped his jaw down to make sure he wasn't hit by a laser of emotion. "She just won't wake up."

"She's healing up, Ben. I knew a fella out here, now get this—this poor son of a bitch was in a coma for ten years . . . after an automobile crackup that killed his best buddy.

Ten years. And, honest to God, all of a sudden he woke up and a coupla weeks later he walked outta the hospital. No shit." Everybody had an encouraging story.

"Ten years is a long time," Driskill said. "I'm hoping for a shorter-term recovery."

"You miss the point. People do wake up, that's all."

"I appreciate it, Nick. Now why the hell are you looking for me?"

Nick Wardell said, "Ben, I'm not sure how to say this exactly, so maybe I'd better just come out with it. You remember Lad Benbow?"

"Not an easy man to forget."

"Well, he's done an about-face. Decided not to be such a hardass. I don't know why. It might be Elizabeth. Anyways, he says Varringer's girlfriend is ready to talk."

Driskill felt the little frisson along his spine. This could be the break. "That's good, Nick. She's the key to what Varringer was really thinking."

"Well, I don't know about that. I think we're sitting on a keg of dynamite here, Ben. And we're lighting matches to pierce the darkness. . . . And if it ain't dynamite, well, what have you lost? I know it's a tough time, though. Your choice, Ben."

There was a long silence.

"Ben?"

"All right, Nick. I'll see you in time for dinner."

Chapter 19

Wardell had picked him up at the little airport terminal again and driven across the river into Illinois, and curled down to the right toward Drover's Lake, which was in fact a kind of offshoot of the Mississippi with a channel that allowed the houseboats out into the river. The summer heightened all the scents of the lake and the wet earth, and you could just hear the music from a gambling boat moored nearby.

"You should be real glad the fish flies don't come until a little later in the summer. We have some mosquitoes here, we have some fish makin' funny little noises coming up out of the water, we have some little animals wandering around in the dark—but we ain't got no fish flies and you're one lucky man. I'm just trying to cheer you up, Ben."

Wardell parked the four-wheel-drive with the leather seats and the super sound system near the old wooden dock to which Lad Benbow's houseboat was tied. There were several docks, most of them newer and sturdier looking than this one. The night was full of the squeaks and rolling noises of the houseboats in the water, the sucking sound of the backwash licking the docks.

"Out of the way," Wardell said. "Lad is very nervous about keeping his client's identity quiet as the grave. Lad takes no more chances than he has to. Funny, Ben—I'm a little nervous about all this. I'm not much for houseboats and water and snakes and such."

It was a big old rectangular boat, no smooth and rounded corners, no fiberglass, nothing to indicate that it could move faster than a man could stroll. Wooden, well preserved, several windows or portholes or whatever you wanted to call them—Driskill wasn't a sailor. It looked like what it was. A little house that was sitting on a larger rectangle of wood that was a boat. So be it. He climbed on board.

Lad Benbow came out to greet them. He was carrying a glass. The ice tinkled.

"Driskill, glad you could come so quickly. You move fast. Let me say how sorry I am about your wife."

Driskill nodded. "Bad break," he said softly. "I'm afraid time is running out on us. . . ."

"Indeed it is. You can damn near hear the ruckus starting in Chicago and it's almost two hundred miles from here. Come on inside, get yourself around a gin and tonic."

"Is she here yet?" Driskill asked.

"In due time, in due time. I wouldn't get you out here on a wild-goose chase. Jesus, it's too hot to stand out here."

Five minutes later they were arranged in wicker chairs in the main room with doors leading off to a bedroom and an office. Lamps were on, casting a low yellow light, and a Zoot Sims recording was playing very softly on a compact stereo. It was fifteen or twenty degrees cooler inside and the humidity was lower but it was still hot enough to wilt the balls on a brass bulldog.

Nick Wardell was wearing green-and-white Adidas sneakers, leather, the three stripes, and above them Black Watch plaid golfing slacks from Orvis or Bean or someplace. The greens were a horrible match. His arms with their red hair bulged from the sleeves of the polo shirt, and his scalp shone pink, sunburned, through the close-cropped hair. He was sipping on a very tall gin and tonic. The lime floated among the ice cubes like a willing frog.

Lad Benbow sat in a white wicker wingback chair with his longs legs stretched out so his heels rested on the coffee table. He was wearing gray slacks and a white button-down-collar oxford-cloth shirt, unbuttoned at the front, and his Royal St. Andrews Old Course club tie hung over the back of the chair, fluttering from time to time in the blasts from the air conditioner. He was holding an equally tall, sweating glass containing gin, tonic and a large slice of lime.

Driskill briefed them, at Wardell's urging, on the events surrounding the President and the campaign during the past few weeks. He told them about his own perspective on the murders of Summerhays and Tarlow and as much as he knew of why Tarlow came to see Herb Varringer. He told them about Rachel Patton and how genuinely confused the President was by the LVCO stock story.

Wardell had told him that Benbow would expect a quid pro quo so far as information went. He wasn't just going to lie down and roll over: He had information of importance and Driskill had to earn it, Driskill had to lift the tent corner and give him a peek at the big show.

When Driskill's recitation of events had reached the present moment Lad Benbow thanked him for the guided tour. "There is no spectator sport as brutal as politics, I think we can all agree. My heart goes out to the President and his wife. But, on the other hand, nobody made him take the job. Why anyone should want it—in this atmosphere of utter corruption and dishonesty and moral depravity—is quite beyond my understanding. However, there's always someone, isn't there? Now, to the point . . . I have had several conversations with Herb Varringer's lover, who came to me with certain information which might be of interest to the authorities here in Saints Rest. Whether or not our law enforcement people actively want to take on some of the forces in this state, with their cadre of corporate lawyers, seems increasingly unlikely. I don't blame them. They would lose. In fact, the President and his people appear to us to be the only ones capable of using what you're going to hear tonight."

Nick Wardell stood up. "This is where I'm butting out, gents. I don't want to know a damn thing about Herb's private life. None of my business. Ben, when you're done here, why don't you just come on over to the gambling boat and look for me in the bar? We got you a room in a very fancy bed-and-breakfast you'll never find on your own." They heard him walking along the side of the boat and then the slight rocking as he climbed off.

Benbow said, "You ready?"

"Let's bring on the mystery guest," Driskill said. He was suddenly thinking about Elizabeth. He had to push her image out of his mind.

Benbow picked up a telephone, touched one number. "You can come on in now. It's just Driskill and me."

Herb Varringer's lover was a real looker. Almost six feet tall. Close-cropped natural blond hair. Large hazel eyes. Wearing slacks and sneakers and a polo shirt. A gold watch, a gold ring, and a gold earring in one ear.

"Mr. Driskill? How are you? My name's Chris Morrison."

"So, you can see why Herb was so obsessive about keeping his lover's identity—even my *existence*—out of the public eye." Morrison was a lanky man, in his midthirties, with a handsome but studious face. He was a professor of English at a small liberal arts college in Wisconsin.

"I'm hardly a raving queen and Herb was an old-fashioned in-the-closet homosexual. He knew people nowadays don't care all that much about sexual orientation. Still, the world of business is different even now and he was mainly concerned about the people in his generation, the men he'd done business with all his life, he would just have been so humiliated at the jokes people would be making behind his back. It was fine with me—and our relationship was mostly just companionable. Not entirely, but mostly. We'd meet places far away like Banff or St. Bart's or Europe. And when we met in public here Herb himself was perfect cover—nobody in their right mind would look at Herb and think he was within hailing distance of gay. So we kept it a secret . . . but he told me I was the only person he felt comfortable confiding in . . . and over the last few months the burden had gotten too big for him to bear, I don't mean our relationship, but all this Bob Hazlitt crap he'd been carrying around for years . . . so he finally just let it all out over a long weekend we spent in Evansville. Why Evansville? Because I think Don Mattingly was the best ballplayer I ever saw and we'd always talked about going down there and eating at his restaurant and stuff. So, it seemed like a safe place for us, just two men in different motel rooms holding a business meeting with a little baseball for background. That's when he told me everything that was eating him up inside. . . ."

Driskill said, "I share your feeling about the great Don Mattingly. Go on."

Over an hour, in painstaking detail, Morrison began to address the issue of Herb Varringer's concerns about the extent and power of Heartland's intelligence-gathering satellites, Heartland's effective control of the flow of highly classified intelligence, which included its accessibility to Heartland itself, the degree to which Heartland exerted control over the intelligence services and had a huge voice in the actual creation of foreign policy.

He described how incalculably rich the company was. He talked about how Herb Varringer and Bob Hazlitt had been friends since the early days, how Herb had taken his place on the corporate board as Heartland grew larger than anyone but those deepest inside it understood. He talked about how Herb had come to learn that Heartland satellites had reached the point where they could penetrate any and every telephone circuit on the face of the planet, how every telephone line was now compromised by Heartland, how every computer that used a modem could now be plundered by Heartland satellites from twenty-three thousand miles away in space.

He explained how Herb had come to believe that Bob Hazlitt was convinced he *was* America. And how Herb had expressed his concern to Bob Hazlitt himself . . . and how he'd come to realize that he'd gone too far, that in remembering a time when they'd just been friends, open and honest with one another, he might have signed his own death warrant. He described how Herb Varringer had come to understand that his life and fate had become inextricably interwound with an entity whose very size defined its power for evil.

When Chris Morrison had finished his remarks, Driskill felt as if he should leap to his feet and lead a standing ovation. Morrison had held the room spellbound with the low-key intensity and precision of his recitation.

Lad Benbow considered the glossy polish of his black penny loafers and the red socks and finally looked up at Driskill. His first words surprised Ben. "I'm famished. Let's order in some Chinese."

While they waited for the food to arrive, Driskill told them how Teresa Rowan had crystallized the crucial sticking point—if the intelligence budgets became public it would lead to the biggest scandal in the history of the Republic. With Morrison's additions, the situation's complexity increased. If the public knew that Heartland had access to all satellite-gathered intelligence intended for the government, that Heartland could therefore use whatever it chose to conduct its own foreign policy and bring pressure to bear on the government intelligence community—well, there was no way to know how dramatically the public would react. As a political charge it was the equivalent of a neutron bomb. The investigations would go on for years.

Lad Benbow said, "Heartland is it, then. Pandora's box. The real thing. Right here in Iowa." He seemed to find that at least moderately amusing.

"The AG is right, you know," Driskill said. "They *cannot* let it happen—Heartland cannot let those budgets be made public. And they can't let all these charges of Herb Varringer's go public."

"What are you saying?" Benbow was fiddling with a pipe cleaner.

"They'll have to kill the President if they can't defeat him. They may have to kill him anyway, just to be safe, and to warn anyone else so thoughtless as to try to carry out the plans put forth in January." Driskill felt the faint rocking of the houseboat as small waves lapped at its belly. "Unless somebody can get at Heartland . . . remove the head, the brain, the power . . ."

Benbow said, "The trouble is, we can sit here and theorize all night, and we can know pretty damn sure that it's all true, it's all figured out. We know why Bob Hazlitt is running for president—he wants once and for all to consolidate his and Heartland's position. Link the White House and Heartland *in one man*. Maybe it's just megalomania . . . but once Bonner made the State of the Union speech it wasn't megalomania anymore, it was essential that the President be stopped. We can theorize that the killer on the loose is somehow tied in to Heartland's wanting to keep their importance hidden from view—that he killed people who came snooping around Heartland, like that Tarlow and Herb Varringer, that he realized Tarlow knew too much and was ready to take it back to Summerhays and report . . . and we can be pretty sure that what Tarlow was reporting was all that Chris has told us tonight."

Driskill said, "There was a lot of money floating around deep inside the Democratic National Committee and the intelligence community. And that's where the scandal about Charlie had to come in. There was a lot of money from the DNC invested. Money was going to LVCO, I know for sure, and they thought they could use that against Charlie. I'm willing to bet a lot of it was going to and from Heartland, black money that's never accounted for."

Benbow said, "I wonder, did Tarlow know what the back channel you describe in the White House was really doing? Will *we* ever know what it was there for? Everybody's dead except your Mr. Sarrabian and the man we don't know, this guy who was supposed to be in the White House—which frankly sounds a lot like a red herring smells, Ben." The doorbell rang. The food was at hand.

Chris Morrison, who had talked himself dry telling his story, chatted about the general political situation while they ate. Finally, he stood up. "Look, you guys, I'm a little nervous about staying here and listening to you talk inside politics. Okay? I've tried to be a help but I think I'm done. If you need me, Lad, you know where to find me. And Mr. Driskill, it's been a pleasure to meet you. I'm not much of a political animal—up there in the academic ivory tower, so to speak." He smiled self-consciously.

"Just one thing, Chris," Driskill said. "I'd like you to take a look at something—see if it's anything you recognize." He took out his wallet and spread the wrinkled piece of white paper on the coffee table. "Here, does this mean anything to you?"

Morrison knelt down and peered at the squiggly line drawn across the page. He looked up, a perplexed expression on his face. "You got me. Is this a test?"

Driskill smiled. "I guess it is, in a way. But so far not a damn soul has the answer."

Lad Benbow looked up from his drink. "Thanks, Chris. I'll be talking to you soon, the will and all—I'll ring you."

They finished their drinks, heard the roar of Morrison's Corvette coming to life and kicking up some gravel.

It had begun raining when they left the houseboat. Benbow drove over to the gambling boat to find Wardell. He brought him back and suggested they all come up to his place for a last drink. Wardell said, "You're talkin' my language, Lad. You up for that, Ben?"

"I'm up for it, Nick."

Fifteen minutes later they had followed a couple of switchbacks up the limestone bluffs from downtown Saints Rest and pulled up in the circular driveway before a nineteenth-century Victorian mansion so perfectly turned out that it looked like it had gone up overnight. Cream and hunter green, a goodly amount of gingerbread along the roof's eaves and framing the perfect porch with its perfect swing. Standing on the porch out of the slanting rain, Driskill looked out over the town, the golden dome of the courthouse, the shadowy outline of the high arching bridge they'd just traversed, the train moving along the tracks clinging to the Illinois hillside across the river, its light poking ahead into the rainy darkness. Traffic lights flickered green and red, blurring brightly.

"Welcome to my home and my office. Come on inside."

The three men traipsed in and Benbow led them into a large octagonal room to the left of the front hall. Its windows gave onto the porch. The furnishings were, in the kindliest terms, eclectic. The only light came from a twenty-seven-inch television set that was displaying a Yankees–White Sox game from Chicago with the sound off. Benbow stepped on a floor switch and soft lights flooded the corners of the room. "Look, I'm ready for a Coke or something. You guys want any booze?"

They both shook their heads no, but Wardell said, "I'll have one of those Wild Boars you keep in the fridge. That's a soft drink, right? Lager is out where I come from."

"Five miles from here," Benbow scoffed. He went to get the drinks.

"Lad's not a bad guy. You're getting a better picture of him than you did last time."

Benbow came back with two beers and a Coke.

Driskill said, "Lad, you sandbagged me with Chris. You've been calling him a her ever since I met you."

"Well, you'd do the same thing in your client's best interests. I don't want to get this guy killed for knowing too much—he's an innocent bystander. All he ever did was bring a measure of happiness to the last years of Herb Varringer's life—that's not a hanging crime, if you see what I mean."

"True . . . but I damn near fainted."

"Well, I admit, I did enjoy my little surprise. I wish this thing were more distinct, more defined." Benbow took a sip from his Coke. "I've had cases like this. You know the general shape of the animal beneath the drop cloth, you just can't be absolutely sure whether it's a camel or an elephant or a rhinoceros. But you know there's something under there and it's got four feet and a mouth and two eyes and it's guilty as hell of something or other . . . but trying to prove it . . . now that's something else again."

Driskill said, "I want to call the hospital in Washington, check on Elizabeth."

"There's a phone in the hallway, Ben."

Driskill placed the call, waited. When he spoke it was to a floor nurse, who transferred him to a doctor who was checking on Elizabeth. It was past eleven o'clock in Washington. He listened carefully as the doctor told him that her vital signs were fine, no complications from the surgery, they had her hooked up and she was being monitored constantly, and no, she hadn't regained consciousness. But her response to deep pain stimulus had been encouraging—a slight jerking of one hand. Driskill felt his own heart racing as he listened and willed himself to calm down. He wanted to be with her. All he had to do was finish the job and he could go back where he belonged.

Once they'd talked themselves out—Driskill's mind largely elsewhere—he packed it in and insisted that he needed a walk back to his B&B down on Bluff Street.

The summer rain was still falling when he left Benbow's. He was carrying a borrowed umbrella, stood at the overlook from which he saw the pretty white bandstand in the park before the WPA post office building. The streetlamps cast their eerie glow through the rain. It was midnight.

He walked along the tops of the limestone bluffs, looking down on the great block of the newspaper building, standing to look at the library with the trees dripping rain and the breeze moving in the leaves. He was getting things straight in his mind and it was a hell of a job. Like nothing he'd ever imagined before. Worse. Yet everything he learned seemed to lead him back to the same spot. He now had a theory of the whole business . . . no, not the whole business, everything but Drew Summerhays's role. That was still beyond him.

Standing at the top of a long flight of stairs cut through the bluff, leading down to the library and the town surrounding it, he heard the sound of the rain coursing down a gutter etched into the limestone beside the steeply angling steps. He had walked back to a spot just below Benbow's house where a few lights still burned in the windows. Rain dripped steadily from the archway where the steps began. The only light below came from the far end of the tunnel covering the stairway. He felt for the handrail and began the downward trek toward the light. . . .

The light was shining in his eyes, it was so bright, driving like a scalpel into his eyes, the pain was almost unbearable, he shook his head and that only made it worse and he felt like he was upside down and all wet and he began coughing, and someone was bending over him mouthing words in some unknown tongue, or weird cadence, or something, his head was hurting so much he felt like throwing up and the voice was so far away and persistent and weird and he felt like he'd skidded a long way on his face. . . .

Thunder was rumbling over the bluffs and lightning crackled through the darkness overhead. It was raining harder without lowering the temperature. Benbow stood on the porch, an ear cocked, looking out over the town where the lights were blurred by the rain. He'd come out to check one last time on his town and he'd thought he heard something, a yell or a scream of surprise. The rain was bouncing off the street and making a big show in the light of the streetlamps.

He looked at the black hole cut into the top of the cliff where the stairway led all the way down to Bluff Street. Those damned stairs. People were always falling down. Slippery as a Washington lawyer. The cliff itself was dangerous, just grass and a big rock or two on top, and nobody had ever bothered to put up a railing. A couple of years ago a guy was sitting on the edge of the cliff fifteen or twenty feet from the entrance to the stairway and slid off— impossible to say if it had been an accident or a suicide— and broke his neck upon landing. Well, he had to get his flashlight and go look now for the silly bastard who had fallen down the steps in the rain.

Benbow found him near the bottom of the stairway, sprawled across the width of the stairs like a tree felled to block the way. Benbow grabbed the railing to save himself from the same fate and descended the steps slick as grease with a thin coating of silt and mud and bits of gravel, following the bobbing cylinder of light pouring out from his heavy-duty torch.

When he reached the body he saw that Driskill's face was rubbed raw on one side and his nose had been bloodied and he wasn't looking all that chipper.

"Driskill . . . give me a sign . . . are you in there?" He played the light across the face and the eyelids fluttered open and it sounded like he swore. "Wave to me, wave your hands. . . ."

For a moment he thought it was all over.

Slowly Driskill raised his hand and gave Lad Benbow the finger.

Benbow decided he'd live.

Lad Benbow looked across the rim of his coffee cup and surveyed Driskill's face, which was not in perfect order. The rain had gone and the morning sunshine was flooding the porch. The windows of the octagon room were thrown open to catch whatever breezes the day might offer. The temperature was already building. The courthouse dome shimmered through the waves of heat.

Chris Morrison was standing at the window holding a mug of his own, blowing steam away so he could drink it.

Driskill had slept badly after getting cleaned up. His face was scraped. He had a headache. But, as his Elizabeth remarked occasionally, he cleaned up real good.

"So, what happened to you?" Morrison asked.

"You explain, Lad." He felt like he'd chipped a tooth when he fell and hit the cement stair.

"After he flipped me the bird, he took my hand and got up," Benbow concluded after describing what Driskill had gone through with the attacker on the darkened stairway. "Then he told me I should see the other guy."

"Fucker ran away," Driskill had muttered. His blazer, which was cut to ribbons, lay in tatters now over the back of a chair. Same with the shirt. But no blood. He'd spent the night in one of Benbow's spare rooms.

Benbow was sitting behind the desk, his back to the bay window, puffing on a pipe, smoke wreathing his head. "Very lucky, our friend Driskill."

"I thought I was safe. I was in Iowa! I was halfway down those damn stairs. Then I heard this guy behind me. I looked back when I heard a noise, then he seemed to fall toward me—I guess he was jumping at me. He had a knife, but it was funny, it wasn't in his hand, I could tell that in the struggle with him . . . it came out of his sleeve or something. I was being attacked, I couldn't stop and ask him . . . the son of a bitch." Driskill was choking on his anger. "He brought it up at me, trying to get the blade into me so he could just pull up and empty my guts . . . he was so eager to slit me open. If he'd waited another second, until I was just a little closer—" Driskill shrugged.

"He'd have had you."

"He's the luckiest man alive, Lad. I'm bigger than he is and I'm probably just as strong. He was busy going at me with the knife but I was hitting him, I slammed his head against the wall, then he laid a forearm across my face and the pain blinded me for a minute. Jesus, it was a mess . . . and then I head-butted him and knocked him back out of the stairwell and he took off . . . and I slipped and fell down and landed on my face."

"Obviously he was watching you, knew your plans." Benbow shifted on the couch. "He's a killer and whoever's running him has decided that you've become too big a pain in the ass. Killing you and dealing with the PR results of that is less of a problem than having you dig around—once it was known you were going to Iowa they hit the eject button. You were getting too close. What that means for the rest of us I hesitate to speculate."

Driskill turned his stiff neck. "Chris," he said to Morrison, "I thought you wanted out, all the way out."

"I just had a thought once I got home . . . I called Lad."

Driskill looked at Benbow and waited.

Lad Benbow spoke up. "Chris . . ."

Chris Morrison answered from where he stood at the window. He was wearing chinos and a white button-down shirt with the sleeves rolled up on tan forearms.

"When Herb and I became close, Herb decided I needed some taking care of. I don't make much money, I'm not a businessman, my parents have both passed away . . . so Herb, being the kind of man he is, I mean *was,* asked Lad to act as his executor and help set something up that would provide for me the rest of my life. And Herb was getting pretty concerned about his own well-being these last few weeks. He told me about something that I didn't tell you last night. I wanted to speak with Lad again privately before I mentioned it. I guess I was being overly cautious, but it was the last thing Herb ever told me about and . . . and he was very upset about it. All it was . . . well, this is all it was . . . two words. *Earth Shaker.* He said Heartland was going to start up Project Earth Shaker and he didn't know how to stop them. I don't know what it was." Morrison shrugged his square shoulders and stuffed his hands down in his pockets.

"Go on, Chris. Finish it."

Morrison looked away, staring out into the sunshine. His voice was without emotion, far away. "Herb told me that he'd gone to Bob Hazlitt and argued with him about Earth Shaker. Tried to get him to stop it . . . and Bob Hazlitt personally told him that he was going to use Earth Shaker, that it was worth a few lives to help bring things to a boil—that was how he put it to Herb. Which was when Herb went to Drew Summerhays and Summerhays sent Tarlow out here. That's it. That's all I know . . . nobody has tried to contact me, or frighten me off, or hurt me, so I have to believe they don't know about me. And I've just tried to stay out of the way. Can't even go to Herb's funeral. . . ."

"Earth Shaker," Driskill mused.

Benbow leaned forward and opened a thin leather briefcase. "Ben, that piece of paper you believe Herb gave Hayes Tarlow. A piece of paper with a line drawn across it . . . Would you dig it out again?"

Ben went to the ruined blue blazer and extracted the small envelope from the breast pocket. "Right here."

"Would you put it on the table? Flatten it out. That's one piece of paper that's been through a lot." He chuckled softly to himself. "All right, there it is. Take a look at it . . . you'll never see it the same way again."

Benbow got his briefcase and removed a copy of *USA Today* dated a few days before. He opened it, laid it on the table, front page faceup, a map in color in the lower corner of the page. "Now take a look at the map, Ben . . . Chris . . ."

Driskill was the first to speak. A long, drawn-out "I'll be damned . . ."

Lad Benbow smiled slowly, shaking his head. "Right in front of us!"

The map was a detail showing the border with Mexico cutting across the southwestern United States.

The erratic line nearly paralleled the borders. Just inside Mexican territory.

It was an earthquake fault line.

Chapter 20

Could he tell the President what he was going to do?

If Rachel Patton had been right, if there was someone in the White House working for Hazlitt's side, was that how the killer had tracked him to Saints Rest? But had he told anyone? Had he mentioned it while he was rattling on to Elizabeth's still form on the bed? Had he mentioned it to the President? He didn't remember . . . but he didn't think so. But how else could he have been followed for the attack on the steps the night before? Wiretaps through the Heartland satellite systems? He hadn't told anybody what he was going to do. Still, there had been the call from Nick Wardell. There had been that one call. . . .

No. He couldn't call anyone. No White House for comfort, no Nick Wardell, no Lad Benbow . . . no allies anywhere.

He was going in alone.

Driskill arranged for a car rental and headed west from Saints Rest; away from the river, away from the bluffs, through rolling fields and forested hillsides with the shadows of the fleecy clouds racing across them. Then the land flattened out and the heat waves shimmered up off the highway, bending and twisting the endless fields of corn into something very like a seascape, waves of corn plunging and rolling and shifting in the heat and sun. He drove for three hours before he saw them. Then the car seemed to move irresistibly onward, as if drawn by a gigantic magnet.

There, rising through the heat waves, rising through the dust floating up from the landscape in the killing heat, rising up at first like a delusion, then slowly gaining definition, were the Heartland Towers.

Two eighty-story towers, each a city block square, rising up from the crust of the earth, with an eight-story walkway midway between top and bottom, covering the immense area between them, all to form an enormous H bestriding the horizon like nothing else in the world. It was the flatness of its surroundings that made the H so viscerally shocking. A hundred thousand people—and even that merely a fraction of all the workers marching under Heartland's worldwide banners, whatever name they might bear—worked in just these towers and in the subbasement laboratories deep beneath the incredibly fertile soil of the most fertile of states. It was a vertical world rising like two immense missile silos from the surface of Iowa, as if proclaiming a new and independent nation at the core of the nation's heartland. Before Heartland, before Bob Hazlitt, there had been no private concern as large as this anywhere in the country. And then, in a relatively short time, there was Heartland. The beating heart of the technological world of the twenty-first century.

He drove for forty miles, watching the towers grow clearer, larger, then another twenty, and he found himself inside the huge buildings' support system. The towns. Bob Hazlitt had built them with the latest developments in human engineering in mind—with up-to-the-minute schools, housing, recreation centers, the parking lots and the grocery stores and the department stores and the malls. Heartland, IA.

Deep in his belly he knew that Heartland lay behind everything he'd been involved with ever since he'd embarked on his errand of mercy to visit Drew at Big Ram. Heartland. And—he was only guessing, but he knew it was a good guess—Heartland would turn up somewhere behind LVCO, would emerge from the blowing smoky fog behind Ballard Niles and Arnaldo LaSalle and Tony Sarrabian, whether they knew it or not. Heartland lay at the center of it all.

But at the end of the day, who knew how many murders had been carried out in the name of the greater good of Heartland? Who knew how many people had been corrupted and then destroyed for the greater good of Heartland? Had the greater good of Heartland consumed a man like Drew Summerhays, who had been so incorruptible for so long? Was anything left of human integrity in the face of the Heartland appetite? Had Drew and even Charlie Bonner somehow been sucked in? That would seem to be the crucial question. Certain parts of the intelligence community were Heartland's tool now, certainly the ISO . . . and they influenced others.

And a great many of the computers and telephones that connected all the intelligence services and the secret police organizations throughout the world were probably now prey to Heartland's intrusion. . . .

How long would Heartland continue as the embodiment of the secret government against which Charlie Bonner had warned the world?

Could Heartland be stopped?

Watching the steel-and-glass towers rising above him, as if they were both newer and at the same time older than anyone could imagine, as if they might have once housed the ancient priests of other worlds, Driskill had a momentary sense of abject hopelessness. What could men do in the shadow of the monolith?

Well, the towers were only the work of men. What man can do, man can screw up. It was a basic law, like gravity.

The flaw inherent in Heartland was that it carried within it the spirit and brain of the robot. It had been calibrated to infinity, it could work as the result of computers that could make ten billion calculations a second without creating any heat, it could work for you; it could read a novel, it could sing a song, hell, it could write an opera. It could sure as hell make war and be Death Bringer to the world, and maybe it could even cure cancer and AIDS before lunch if you really wanted it to . . . if all that fixing and curing wouldn't louse up all the plans for the future of the world as human beings had known it.

But it was like the robot that—no matter how hard the scientists tried—simply couldn't walk down the steps and across the lawn and out onto the sidewalk and down the curb and across the road without falling down again and again and finally shorting out in a paroxysm of frustration. It was the walking that was the hard part, up and down, oops watch out for that pebble, oops here comes a seam in the sidewalk, ouch, shit, what the hell's this, it's soft, it's green, it's not a rug, what the hell is it, oh, I'm falling again . . . oh, shit, it's grass . . . and I can't get the hell up.

Heartland was vulnerable because it was the creature of one man.

Cut off the head and make it mind its manners.

After identifying himself at the user-friendly reception area and being greeted warmly by one of the great man's courtiers, Ben Driskill was whisked upward in an elevator that traveled at exactly the speed it required to analyze and x-ray and interpret everything about him, including the perspiration on his skin and the dilation of his pupils and his breathing rate, all of which might tip off Security to a bomb-carrying nut case come to see the wizard. Years ago they had once identified and isolated a gentleman who believed some of his inventions had been stolen by Heartland and had by way of retaliation turned himself into a human bomb—not with infernal devices strapped to his body but by swallowing a kind of experimental explosive, a derivative of plastique, which he could detonate by concentrating his brain waves on how much he hated Bob Hazlitt—thus, he was a suicide killer and in the end got at least half of his wish. The sensing devices that far surpassed anything at Langley or the White House picked this up but weren't quite sure how he was going to cause the explosion . . . but when he was escorted, very politely, to a room where he was told he could wait for his meeting with Mr. Hazlitt, and when he realized it wasn't a normal waiting room but some kind of *cell,* he got so worked up he did explode, doing over a quarter of a million dollars in damage to the room for the man who has everything. On two other occasions—involving a lone, utterly mad terrorist, and a vocally disappointed buyer of a Heartland software program—the holding cell was used, but Flying Bob figured the bomb swallower more than made up for the cost of the room's existence.

Driskill was greeted by a handsome woman in her fifties who had already read the computer SearchNet report that appeared on her screen while he was in the elevator. The elevator led directly into her office, which was done in cool shades of brown, sand, and steel. A very large Iowa landscape by the gifted master of the subject, Ellen Wagener, hung impressively over her desk. The side walls of her office were nothing but glass, which seemed to let the vast skyline in. There was a sense of standing on a window ledge and looking in the direction of forever. He felt like he was seeing the earth from a space station.

The woman came out from behind her desk with her hand extended. She welcomed him warmly, introduced herself as Mrs. Keating, told him how highly she had heard Mr. Hazlitt speak of him, and inquired with a good deal of sensitivity into Mrs. Driskill's health. She also hoped the flowers Mr. Hazlitt was having delivered daily to her hospital room were not a nuisance, but "he believes so strongly in the good vibrations of God's most beautiful creations, the flowers of the field, that he just knows they'll help her come back to us real soon." Driskill felt as if he had wandered onto a stage where a play was being performed by the inmates of an asylum.

"I was hoping to see Mr. Hazlitt," he said, emulating as best he could her wacky graciousness. "I came to Iowa to see him, actually—to thank him for his concern about my wife but primarily to speak with him before we all go to the convention. You can imagine what a madhouse Chicago will be once the contenders get to town."

"Oh, my, won't it be fun! I'm still trying to convince *himself* to take his faithful personal secretary with him but he hasn't decided yet. Tell me, have you come as an emissary from the President?" She smiled. It was the sort of place where she could refer to one of the most powerful men in the world, her boss, as *himself*. Like Mac referring to Charlie. You almost had to know: She wasn't in on it, she just worked there, dated from the good old days. A Heartland lifer who owed her soul to the company store and was damn glad of it. Just folks. Had she known about the worst of it, Hazlitt would have pulled the plug on her the way he had on Herb Varringer. . . .

She was wearing a blue business suit with a pretty flowered blouse. Her hair was cut short and flecked with gray. She reminded him of a political science teacher he'd had in high school. "Please, you may answer with complete confidence in my discretion. I am Mr. Hazlitt's last line of defense, so to speak." She smiled again. Very good bridgework. She wore several handsome rings on slightly reddened fingers, a good Iowa woman who'd been known to lend a hand around the house and do a dish or two.

"Well, yes, the truth is I have come from the President. Time is running out, isn't it?"

"In that case, I've been empowered to make a suggestion."

Driskill couldn't help smiling. "All this while I was in the elevator?"

"The speed of modern communications is truly incredible, isn't it? Of course, we are on the cutting edge here—if it exists, we've got it in the towers. I let Mr. Hazlitt know you were here. And his suggestion is that you join him and his family tomorrow at the celebration of his mother's one hundredth birthday—you'll enjoy yourself, I promise you, Mr. Driskill. Just because two men might be on different sides of the political fence doesn't mean they can't enjoy one another, don't you find that to be true? And his mother—that's Lady Jane, as we call her—is a joy! The big doings are out at Backbone Creek." She turned back to her desk and opened a folder. "I've even got a little map for you." She handed him the paper and pointed with one polished but unpainted nail. "You're here now. You can stay at the Flying Bob Lodge and make the drive tomorrow. It's only about forty-five minutes. He promised that he'd have time for a chat then. Really, he'll be so upset if you don't come." She was smiling a trifle imploringly.

"Of course I'll come. You tell him I wouldn't miss it."

"Oh, you're very kind, Mr. Driskill."

"It's very decent of him to take time out for me. Now, do you think that elevator can get me down to earth?"

"I'm almost certain it will," she said coquettishly. "We haven't lost anybody recently."

"That is a relief. Thank you for being so helpful."

"Just doing my job. Next time you pay us a visit, you be sure to stop in and say hi. I'll be real unhappy if I hear you dropped in and passed me by."

"Not a chance of it, Mrs. Keating. Just get me down safely and I'll be yours forever."

Assuming they were watching him, he ordered up a room service burger, watched a movie, soaked in a hot tub, felt some of the stiffness from the attack on the stairs fade from his war-weary body. Just before he went to bed he made another call to the hospital. Nothing had changed. Elizabeth was stable. They were thinking about moving her out of the ICU tomorrow. Maybe.

The morning came early to Iowa and from the deck outside his room—which he'd noted went for seven hundred dollars a night and was termed an executive suite—he could look out over a golf course green as a bottle of Tanqueray, stretched like a fabulous carpet dotted with snow-white sand traps and bunkers and in the middle distance, church steeples and tree-shaded curving streets of handsome, upper-middle-class housing with the blue disks of backyard swimming pools and jeeps and luxury cars and loaded pickups in driveways and at curbs. The golfers were already out, playing through the arcing sprinklers before the heat of the midsummer day began baking everything

SAINTS REST 333

dry and hard. Though Driskill knew that this golf course
and these green lawns never browned out, never hardened
up. It was obviously real, as real and palpable as anything
could be, but nevertheless there was an air of unreality, an
escape from daily reality. But, he reminded himself, what
the hell was wrong with that? It was what everybody
wanted, and who could blame them?

They weren't dealing with toxic waste, there wasn't
going to be a hell of an explosion or a meltdown some day,
there wasn't going to be a generation of little kids with no
arms and two heads . . . they dealt in communications and
information and satellites. It was a nice clean world.

Well, he was the serpent, he supposed. Welcome to Eden,
pal. He had to nail Saint Bob, and all that was left was the
Earth Shaker card. He was going to pound it in, like a stake
through the heart.

Driskill consumed the Farmer's Breakfast Works in the
lodge's coffee shop. He discovered their unique approach
to the meal. You told them exactly what you wanted—a
couple of eggs, a couple of strips of bacon, a couple of
pancakes, a six-ounce fresh orange juice. They brought you
four eggs, four strips of bacon, four pancakes, a twelve-
ounce fresh orange juice with plenty of pulp in it and it was
cold. The thing was, they brought you exactly twice as
much as you actually ordered. "That's what makes it the
farmer's works," the smiling girl said very seriously. "Big
appetites out here in the heartland."

"You're a local girl."

"I sure am. We're all local. Mr. Hazlitt guarantees summer jobs to all the kids from the ninth grade on up if they
want 'em. Caddies, greenskeepers, maintenance at the tennis center, parking cars, working on the town newspaper,
home health care aides for the sick or the elderly . . . it's a
great place to live."

"Your folks, what part do they play in the scheme of
things?"

"Dad's actually editor of the paper and Mom manages
one of the infant care centers."

"And you're a cheerleader—I'll put money on that."

"I guess I'm the type."

"I suppose everybody is pretty excited about Hazlitt's run for the Democratic nomination."

"Wouldn't you be? I mean, he's someone we know. And you can see he's done pretty darn well for the people around here, hasn't he?" She had to go attend to other customers and Driskill left her a large tip. Twice what he normally would. It seemed only fair.

He found the picnic ground at the park on the banks of Backbone Creek. No problem. There were several hundred cars and TV trucks and limos, media people clustered in knots as if awaiting the Second Coming. Driskill blended in easily with the crowd of people arriving for the party.

The sun was shining, the pale blue sky dotted with clumps of fluffy white clouds, the breeze off the plains rustling in the treetops. Willows dipped toward the water, water skeeters skimmed along the surface, and oaks and maples and cottonwoods and sycamores shaded the paths. A few rowboats moseyed along the creek. Driskill followed the flow of people along its banks and eventually came upon a bunting-draped speakers' rostrum. TV cameras were mounted on all sides and there were maybe a thousand folding chairs on a bright green carpet. Yellow ropes blocked off the chairs and security guards were unobtrusively ringing the area. A large hand-lettered paper banner hung between two tall locust trees. HEAR CANDIDATE BOB HAZLITT SPEAK OUT TONIGHT. He was going to televise to the country again tonight, a last cry to battle on the eve of the convention. Up on the speakers' stand the director was conferring with technicians to ensure a smooth transmission. Cables snaked away to a satellite control truck stuck back in the woods.

He made his way farther until he had passed through hundreds of people chowing down on hot dogs and ribs and pork barbecue and tons of fixings and Pepsis and Cokes and lemonade and then, in a glade up ahead, cordoned off by more security guards, was the point of the day's activities. The birthday party.

When Driskill reached the guards, who wore sports clothes and walkie-talkies and side arms badly concealed under floppy shirts, they gently stopped him and produced portable metal detectors. He identified himself. "Oh, yes, Mr. Driskill, I'm well aware of who you are." The tall black guard smiled down at him. "We've got special orders from Mr. Hazlitt himself to offer you every convenience and escort you into the family area." He pointed to a hooded TV monitor. Driskill's face filled the screen. "Been lookin' for you, Mr. Driskill. Come on with me, we'll get you inside and all taken care of."

The picnic tables with their red-and-white-checked tablecloths, the big pitchers of lemonade, the smell of the barbecue, the bowls of coleslaw and fruit and Jell-O salad, potato salad, the aroma of suntan lotions and baked beans—it was all perfect. There was a softball game going on, kids yelling, the sound of the bat striking the ball and the sight of kids dashing headlong around the bases. He stood and watched the scene unfolding before him and it all reminded him of Ray Bradbury, the great science fiction writer, creator of *The Martian Chronicles*. This was *The Martian Chronicles*, all over again.

He felt as if he'd stepped through a curtain, as if he'd followed a beckoning finger in a strange, time-bending bazaar, and now stood like a man out of time—in another time where he saw men playing banjos and a barbershop quartet singing "Down by the Old Mill Stream" and "Oh, Them Golden Slippers." He remembered Bradbury's space travelers coming upon the old hometown, Mom waiting for them, everything intact from their childhoods, a world of total comfort and care, a world free from worry where nothing had gone wrong, where all the small-town hopes still existed intact and in the end goodness and Mom's fresh baked bread and the smell of burning leaves late on an autumn afternoon and kids swinging on a tire hanging from a stout tree limb would somehow prevail. Mom would call to you from the porch that it was time to come in for supper and Dad would be sitting in the overstuffed chair with his copy of the evening paper and people were good, they wished you well because it was a good world and your life and the town's life were what mattered, not what was happening in Turkey or China or Siberia.

Driskill watched the scene playing out before him—the softball game and the smell of the grilling and the sound of the quartet singing—and it was good. He knew it was good, anybody with half a brain would have seen how good it was. It just wasn't real anymore. It was all being created and acted out for the benefit of the billionaire's greatly aged mother, a small tumbled-together sack of bones topped off with some wisps of snowy hair who sat in a wheelchair, wearing a kind of middy blouse and navy skirt and navy sneakers. She leaned heavily to one side and her mouth hung slack but her eyes darted here and there, the pale blue that in the very old can indicate exceptionally clear vision or near blindness. Her head moved fitfully like a bird's. Occasionally she opened her mouth and seemed to laugh. A banner was strung across a couple of towers of hay bales. *Happy 100th, Mama!!!* A nurse at her side was feeding her a cut-up hamburger and some Jell-O salad. Whenever the nurse got ahead of her she'd shake her head like an old bird, knocking the spoon or fork out of the nurse's hand and onto the ground. Then she'd squawk at the nurse, her voice dry and flinty and edgy, bossy, and then she'd look around and squawk for her son. "Bobby . . . Bobby . . . you get over here, your mother wants you, right now."

The camera crews were rolling as unobtrusively as possible, shooting the traditional family scene and trying to be careful with the batty old lady who must be seen to be appreciative of and doting on her mighty son. There were people Ben assumed to be relatives, by the look of them, hovering everywhere, and Hazlitt was chumming around with all of them, predominantly overweight men and women who doubtless worked for him or wished to God they did. They still wore leisure suits and they were sweating like hogs and the women in big skirts and peasant blouses busied themselves over the picnic fixings unless it was their turn to be whisked up to ritualistically touch the old woman's clawlike wrinkled hand, like a bird's foot, and lean close and kiss her forehead before she flicked them away with a swift movement of her withered hand.

Bob Hazlitt was standing off to one side, arms folded across his chest. He was wearing seersucker slacks and a white shirt and his face was reddened by the sun. He was watching the camera crews moving through the crowd, shooting stock footage—endless shots of his mother, from which only a few feet would be edited into commercials showing that in addition to everything else, Bob Hazlitt honored his poor old mom! He went to say something to his mother, leaning down by the hearing aid, and it was apparent that he couldn't keep from treating her as his mother, a memory, rather than as a very old woman who wasn't at all sure what was going on. He talked to her but her reactions meant nothing. He kissed the wispy white hair. Hazlitt was sweating and from nowhere a makeup woman appeared and toweled him off, then brushed some powder onto his forehead. It was a family scene you might have thought was from Horton Foote, but the truth was it was hardcore Tennessee Williams, the festering world where everyone lies and lies and lies and has lied so long they think they're telling the truth. Everybody was sucking up to Hazlitt as if he were Big Daddy in *Cat on a Hot Tin Roof*: He was, of course, Big Daddy and more; everyone at the picnic depended on him, on his mood, on his morality, on his whim. Driskill wanted to walk up to him and do Burl Ives. *I smell the powerful odor of mendacity. Do you smell it, Sister Woman?*

He was a widower, a condition of which he made much in his campaign, but he'd been keeping company with a fetching movie star in her late forties who was replacing a career that had pretty much turned into a dry hole with a relationship with Hazlitt that would keep her in the public eye and might get her to the White House as First Lady if she played her cards right. Her name was Marina Lavering and she was spending a lot of time with her arm linked through Bob's, trying to ignore the nutty demands of his mother.

Bob Hazlitt turned and saw Ben Driskill and slowly disengaged himself from her and casually made his way in Ben's direction, stopping on the way to laugh and comment and pat relatives on the back, getting ready to make his speech as the afternoon faded. He was fingering the folded papers of the speech, smiling, looking at his watch, holding out his right hand to Ben Driskill, containing his anger and irritation from the last meeting.

"Ben Driskill, just about the last man on earth I'd expect to see here today. But here you are. Isn't my Mrs. Keating at the office—Flora, that's her name—isn't she a wonder? Did you sleep well? Everything all right at the lodge?" He was mad but he wasn't ready to ruin his day.

"Yes, everything was fine and Mrs. Keating is just great and so far as I can tell most of the folks around here think you've got the nomination locked up."

Hazlitt shrugged. "Things are coming together." He was watching Driskill with a certain wariness. "It's going to be close. How's the President taking it all?"

"With his usual equanimity, of course. The fact that you're going to have to kill him if he gets the nomination hasn't gone unnoticed. You could say they're vigilant."

"You do say the damnedest things, Ben. If you're here to bring me a message . . . well, why don't you just get the hell on with it and leave us in peace. Is Charlie out? Is he going to withdraw? Is that why he sent you here? Does he want to avoid the licking I'm going to give him in Chicago? You want to apologize for your behavior at the Croquet Club? Is that it, did he send you to make amends? Or did you come on your own—wanting to change camps, maybe?" He smiled. It was a warm, empty smile that had produced a lot of results over the years.

"He wants you to quit the race, Bob. Go gracefully and nobody will ever know the truth."

"Oh, that's all, is it?" Hazlitt's face and voice were flash-freezing. His eyes swiveled to Driskill's. "He's either lost his mind or I'm going deaf. Which is it?"

"You're done, Bob. It's all over. You're going to quit the race and you'll make a speech at the convention pointing out that all you'd ever wanted to do was affect policy and after meeting with the President you feel that he gets it, that you and he are on the same wavelength, that you'll be serving as a special consultant to the President."

Hazlitt turned slowly to look at a man standing ten or twelve feet away. The man was watching Hazlitt and Driskill and he had wires coming out of his ears and headphones in place. For all Driskill knew Hazlitt was miked and this security guy was his personal bodyguard. He was one of those Secret Service types, a smaller version of Clint Eastwood. Eyes with a lean squint. He caught Hazlitt's glance and nodded. He walked with a shadow of a limp, as if it were a badge of honor, as if to say he'd taken one for the boss. There was also a tiny Band-Aid across the bridge of his nose. He wore a tan washable summer suit and perspiration glistened on his forehead above the dark aviator glasses. He had to wear the jacket because of the firepower it masked. The momentary passage with the bodyguard had taken just enough time for Hazlitt to regain his footing.

"Bringing threats to my mama's birthday party is bad form, Ben. You'd better explain yourself. Just hold on a minute." He turned and walked back to his mother, who seemed to have fallen asleep. One of the nurses was wiping her chin. Hazlitt knelt beside her, put his head near hers, whispered something, and one of the old woman's hands flapped slightly in her lap, dismissing him. When he returned he said, "You got a mama, Ben?"

"No, my mother died when I was a kid."

"Well, it's no picnic—pardon the pun, I guess—to have one reach a hundred. Poor thing . . . But she wants to live to see her little boy become president."

"Well, I hope you've got a brother out there in the weeds somewhere, Bob, 'cause it ain't gonna be you."

"You'll have to elaborate a bit before I just up and capitulate. I think you're blowing smoke, soldier."

Hazlitt led the way down a green-fringed path, away

from the crowd, down toward the gurgling stream with the cattails and the drooping willow fronds bending down to touch the water. The clouds had made their way eastward and the sky was a flat blue with the sun, even in its descent, burning like a laser. The bodyguard moved along behind them, listening intensely to his earpiece. Hazlitt had to be wired. He was probably being recorded as well. The music was fading and the buzz of insects replaced it. The path was dusty. Hazlitt was saying nothing, swinging a cattail ahead of him as if he hadn't a care on earth.

"I used to fish along here. My grandfather would take me in the summer—my mother's father, the one with no ambition. My dad was working at his engineering company, a little cement-block building on the outskirts of Edgewood. We used to take catfish out of this stream. Just load a hook with a worm, night crawlers . . . When I was a little kid I used to have a night crawler stand out in front of the house, I'd wake up after a night's rain, and there'd be night crawlers on the sidewalk . . . a penny a night crawler. They were way underpriced, now I think about it." He smiled at the creek streaming past, at the memories in its flow. "And now I'm going to be president. Only in America. Now, what were you going on about back there? You'd better tell me but, frankly, your desperation is showing. The President's bedrock strength is ebbing, we keep track of the delegates—every blessed one of them—twice a day and the tide is running my way. The people think he's giving away the store and the people are right. You'd better speak your piece and be on your way. I've got a speech to make here pretty soon." His eyes flickered over to the bodyguard, who was standing at ease, in the shade of a stand of locust trees.

"As I said, Bob, you're through. We know about everything. Where would you like me to begin?"

"How the hell should I know?" His impatience was showing now and he mopped his face with his handkerchief.

"We now know you had Herb Varringer murdered and we know why. You shot off your mouth to him once too often—and what he heard he didn't much like. He didn't like the control you had over the intelligence community with your satellites—"

"Nonsense. Herb was one of the big supporters of the whole satellite end of the operation. I've known him my whole damn life. And his father worked for my father. His death was a very sad day at Heartland, I promise you."

"He knew it was wrong for you to own the satellites and lease them to all the intelligence agencies. He knew you knew everything that was going on—you controlled what the agencies knew. Because you could tap into the entire world's intelligence-gathering sources. He didn't like the idea of Bob Hazlitt setting the foreign policy of the United States."

"You actually expect me to take these accusations seriously?"

"I don't really care, Bob. I thought it was only common decency to give you a way out. Otherwise, poof, you're gone whether you take it seriously or not."

"I'd bet you don't have one piece of evidence—speaking as an objective onlooker. You couldn't have any. Because you're making this up out of whole cloth. But don't let me stop you. It's an amazing story."

"We have chapter and verse on your influence over the ISO and a couple of other agencies. We know about the sweetheart deals on the satellites, we know about the blackmailing of foreign interests and the manner in which you moved in and took over the agencies here. It's all technology—you had it, you got to it first through government contracts so huge they make World War Two look like something that happened in a sandbox. The government let you do the development using their money at a time when everything was being turned over to private industry. The deficit had to come down, the politicians finally figured out how to do it—prime your pump and let you build your own fleet of satellites. Oh, America got a lot for its money—but they had to share it all with you." Driskill took a deep breath and asked silently for divine guidance.

He was playing a part and he could have used more rehearsal.

"Now you listen to me, you puffed-up son of a bitch!" Hazlitt had balled his hands into fists and his face was purple beneath the sunburn, his eyes on fire. Twenty feet away the bodyguard shifted anxiously, like a killer on a leash waiting for the call. "I don't know what you think you're doing, but accusing me of planning to assassinate the President—"

"Is the absolute truth, Bob. You cannot—repeat, absolutely cannot afford to let the budgets of the intelligence agents be made public. You've got to get Charlie out of office. They can cook the books all they want but the time will come when there will be questions in Congress about the billions that seem to have disappeared . . . and they all went to Heartland . . . and Charlie Bonner can prove it—"

"Charlie the stock swindler? I somehow doubt he'll be taken all that seriously, Ben."

"Fine. Let's find out. Because we've got the whole thing under a microscope. We know who's handling the destruction of the President, we know how it's going down—"

"You make me laugh, Ben! You really do."

"We've got so much crap on Arnaldo LaSalle that he won't have a choice—he'll break our stories on his show. He'll be turning against you in public. He was your errand boy and you got him the ratings with the lies you fed him . . . but now he'll screw you for a bigger, better story. That's life these days, Flying Bob. People just won't stay bought." He watched Hazlitt's face tighten along the jawline, watched him swallow. "Same thing with Ballard Niles. Balls in a vise."

"I don't actually believe any of this."

"And that's not all, Bob. You had your man kill Rachel Patton, a young woman who was quite innocently involved in the setup—"

"Setup? You've lost your mind!"

"We know you've hung the frame around Charlie Bonner's neck—this bogus stock manipulation deal. Did you enjoy the irony of using government money to set up the President? He wasn't buying stock—Tony Sarrabian was, and you rigged certificates to implicate the President. And then innocent people like Rachel Patton got involved. And when the fix was in place, you started killing everybody who knew about it—Hayes Tarlow and Drew Summerhays and Rachel Patton . . . and when word began getting around you made a helluva mistake—you had your goon try to kill my wife. She's in a coma and you call me a son of a bitch—"

He cut himself off, knowing he couldn't afford to lose control. He was throwing everything he could think of at Hazlitt, every crazy idea he'd had as he lay in bed in the Lodge last night. He was relying on a single principle: Some of it had to be true, at least true enough to get inside Hazlitt's defenses. He felt like he'd jumped out of a plane in a dream, no parachute, hoping for the best. ". . . and he tried to kill me in Saints Rest and yet here I am, giving you your last chance. We've got it all documented, sworn statements, taped confessions. And the President has sent me just to give you a way out. He doesn't want you disgraced because it will bring disgrace on the party and on America itself—at a time when the President is dead serious about ending your secret government and beginning a second American revolution—"

"You must be crazy, Ben. There *isn't* an American government without Heartland . . . and there's no Heartland without *me*. Ben, I have to tell you, you look sane enough but crazy you must be." Hazlitt had leaned down and now skimmed a flat rock across the stream, expertly, watching it skip twice and then land in the brush on the other side. "You come all this way, you make a bunch of wild accusations—"

"But you know they're not wild, Bob. That's the point. You know they're true. And it's not just me. It's the White House and the Department of Justice and it's evidence left behind by Herb Varringer which didn't come to light until the last couple of weeks. Herb left us documentation with every *i* dotted and *t* crossed—he was the worst enemy you could have, he was one of the true believers who'd been totally disillusioned. You can bluster all you want, you can deny it, but if you don't get into line here and now, it's all going to be in the papers and on TV because the President can't wait for you to fuss and fume. He'll have to take you down and it won't be pretty to watch. The indictment is ready and waiting for the attorney general to release it. The convention is gaveled to order tomorrow . . . and the truth about Bob Hazlitt will hit the papers and the TV in a couple of days. Think about it, Bob. You'll be arrested, the charges will be all over the papers and the airwaves. The nation and the world will see you as nothing but a war profiteer—only the war you were fighting was for Heartland, for yourself, for the control of the hearts and souls of the people—you didn't fight it in some foreign field against our nation's enemies, you didn't need courage and bravery in service of a greater good. I wonder what people who believe in you would say if they knew the truth—that you're just another man who's enriched himself while marching over the bodies of other, better men.

"The man who's out there killing for you—does he know what you are? Does he know you're just one more money-grubbing creep who wants the power to decide on life and death for others? What if your killer is a man of principle? Wouldn't that be ironic? He's probably crazy . . . so maybe he believes in you, in your fight to save the defenses of the United States, in your fight to keep the infidels from winning, in your fight to protect the old values that America stands for in his mind and the fight to keep your boot firmly on the neck of the lower orders. What's he going to think when he learns that all you wanted was the money and the power, that you're just another fucking politician willing to kill to get elected? Is that what America has come to? Jesus . . . it's so disgusting, you and your allies, men like Niles and LaSalle and Sarrabian."

Hazlitt turned to him with a slow smile, looked at his watch. "Your time is up, Ben, and I have to tell you, the bluff doesn't work with me. Maybe you can push other guys around and scare hell out of them but they're not Bob

Hazlitt, don't you see that? I am a warrior. I have fought for my country—"

"Better think twice, Bob."

"And I know the course this nation should follow. I can see the future and I know what we must do to meet it. And I have no idea what you've been talking about today. Killers out terrorizing the countryside? Rubbish. Indictments? Arresting me at the convention? I doubt it. You've played your cards and you can't bluff me out of the pot. So, I think you've made a wasted trip. I'll see you in Chicago." He began to move away, nodding to the bodyguard. "Let's go, Lieutenant."

As they fell into step with the bodyguard behind them Ben Driskill remarked casually:

"Ah, just one thing I forgot to mention—there'll be a charge of mass murder. An official charge . . . Bob Hazlitt charged with mass murder." Driskill smiled distantly. "My God, Bob, it's enough to make your blood run cold, isn't it? I think they're combing law books now for something appropriate, a way to couch the charge."

"I can't believe you're still talking to me, Mr. Driskill." Butterflies and grasshoppers and buzzing insects flickered before them; there was a constant buzzing kind of hum you heard in the countryside. Invisible life at work, out of sight, busy. "You're the one who's done. You and the President—I thought you'd come here seeking a way out for the President, a way to save face."

"Well, no, actually. You see . . . we know all about your big secret . . . Earth Shaker."

"I beg your pardon." Hazlitt stood stock-still. Sunlight filtered through the canopy of leaves along the stream. Driskill's senses had heightened. Sweat was running down his back, soaking his shirt. The buzzing was almost deafening, flies swirling in the sunlight with their myriad eyes glowing blue and green and black, and the dust hanging in the air with the sun filtering through, and the sound of the bodyguard breathing. He had some kind of allergy. His nose was plugged and he had to breathe through his mouth. "I beg your pardon?" Hazlitt repeated.

"Earth Shaker. Herb Varringer left us the whole story. You didn't get to him soon enough."

"*Earth Shaker* . . . Sounds like the dinosaur they just discovered, *seismosaurus*." Hazlitt had turned to face him.

"We know what it is and we know how you used it. Even if everything else I've said was just my whim, you must realize that since we know about Earth Shaker . . . well, inevitably then we know it all. The fact that LVCO is the corporate entity which benefits most from it and the fact that LVCO is where the President's money was supposedly invested—it's a wonderful irony that it should all play out like this. Was it intentional? Wasn't it just a little risky to bring LVCO into your plan for destroying the President? There's no point in denying that LVCO is controlled by Heartland—"

"Earth Shaker," Hazlitt repeated. "Would you care to explain it to me?" Hazlitt's lips had gone white and his face was streaming sweat. The redness was bleaching away. His voice sounded suddenly weak, like a man who is dehydrated and fighting for strength before he faints.

Driskill had gone over it countless times since the meeting in Benbow's office. He wanted to keep it simple but now, in the heat and the blistering sun with Hazlitt looking suddenly weak and tentative, he struggled to remember the exact words.

"You and LVCO, somehow you're connected—all your best satellite people within the very highest regions of Heartland and LVCO have created a satellite known as Earth Shaker . . . that was how it was known to Herb Varringer. It was what turned him completely against you. From thousands of miles away you can attack anywhere on this planet. Not just listen to everybody—those are the old satellites. We're talking about *attack satellites*. I don't pretend to know how the hell it works but the National Council of Science has been put on alert—when we tell them what we know . . . about the earthquake in Mexico— well, nobody has ever contemplated such an act before. You fired up Earth Shaker and used it to cause the Mexican earthquake—you used it to pursue political aims, to create a level of chaos which will make it nearly impossible for the United States to keep troops out. You're trying to wreck the President's peace initiatives. *That's* Heartland's foreign policy. When it all comes out and the President and the National Science Council announce that they have irrefutable evidence that it was you, Heartland and LVCO, who caused the earthquake—well, they're going to lay at your feet all the casualties, a slaughter of the innocents."

Hazlitt stared at him, mouth slightly agape, then slowly sat down on the bank above the creek. "You cannot reveal this, Driskill—it's one of the scientific marvels of all time, no one can be allowed to find out what Earth Shaker can do. We at Heartland have created a kind of ultimate weapon, we've disguised it as nature. It is the wrath of God, coming from the heavens and striking down our enemies. . . ." His voice dried out, cracked and lowered abruptly, as if none of it was worth the candle. It had happened so fast. The lieutenant, his bodyguard, moved to his side. Hazlitt sagged forward, his face ashen. "You don't know what you're doing. . . . Ben, you can't let this out, this is the one secret that must remain secret. . . . It gives America all the power over the planet. We can keep our hands clean and still punish evil, punish our enemies. Man has dreamed of such a weapon through the ages . . . Bonner must understand—"

"It's up to you, Bob. Get out of the race and save the world. It can't get much simpler than that. Give me the word tonight. I'll inform the President that you will leave the campaign and throw your support to him." Driskill suddenly realized that he was breathless, that he had almost reached the promised land. It was almost over. "You and he have had a meeting of the minds, blah, blah, blah . . . can you do that for me, Bob? I think I might need a piece of paper, signed by you, before I have the right to contact the President."

Hazlitt gasped softly, had trouble speaking. The bodyguard looked down at him, waiting.

Driskill stared. "Are you going to be all right?"

Hazlitt choked out a laugh. "Why not? You've just cut my heart out. What could be wrong?"

"It's a dirty game. Nobody played it dirtier than you. That's all. You never should have gone ahead with Earth Shaker. We might have held off on all the rest of it, taken our chances at the convention."

"I got some bad advice," he murmured. "Go back to the lodge. I'll let you know."

"Sherm Taylor will be mighty unhappy."

Hazlitt shook his head. "Sherm Taylor," he said softly. "You never know about Sherm Fucking Taylor." He looked up at his aide. "Lieutenant Bohannon . . . give me your hand." He clung to his bodyguard's arm and slowly raised himself. He'd gotten a lot older in the last few moments.

Driskill watched him walk slowly away, clinging to the strong arm of his handler, back toward his mother's one hundredth birthday party.

It had all turned out so differently than Bob Hazlitt had planned.

Chapter 21

Back in his room at the hotel Driskill waited. It hadn't yet wholly sunk in that his plan had worked. So much of it was bluff . . . and without Earth Shaker and the squiggly line it wouldn't have worked at all. The more he obsessed on the close call, the faster his heart beat. Had he done it? Had he really done it? Was Hazlitt finished?

Finally the news came through: The proposed televised speech Hazlitt was to deliver from his mother's party was being replaced with a video of a speech he'd made in an Iowa cornfield a few weeks before. Driskill watched it with the sound barely on, wishing he could call the White House to tell them what had happened out at the creek, to tell them that the battle was won. But he knew there was too big a chance the Hazlitt people would be listening, and you never knew what might happen next—he doubted it, but there was always the possibility that Hazlitt might change his mind, might try to take advantage of the Bonner camp being lulled off guard. So he sat and watched the speech and it was all the typical stuff and it was all just campaign history now. If Hazlitt kept his word.

Finally he called St. Peter's Hospital and got a nurse he knew by now. But there wasn't any news. He could hear the resignation in her voice. The idea of losing her was simply unspeakable, so he held to the belief that it wasn't going to happen. It couldn't happen. It was their life together. It had to turn out all right. . . .

The package arrived by messenger from the towers at eleven o'clock that night.

The man at the door was the fellow Hazlitt had called Lieutenant Bohannon during the afternoon. It was a simple transaction. "Mr. Hazlitt instructed me to tell you that he'll be flying to Chicago tomorrow. He'll try to get in touch with the President tomorrow and convey the message personally. But this empowers you to assure the President that the contents are an accurate reflection of Mr. Hazlitt's views." He handed the envelope to Driskill.

"Have you been with the campaign long?" Driskill asked.

"Long enough to know politics isn't for me." Was it a moment of humor? Or not? His face was expressionless.

"That's pretty much the way I feel. The costs are high."

"Yes, sir. May I say how sorry I was to hear about the attack on your wife?"

"You're very kind."

"I'm praying for her, sir."

"I thank you," Driskill said. He watched the man walk away down the hall. It was impossible to guess his age. Thirty? Forty? Fifty? One of those people. He took the envelope back into the room with him. It was addressed to him and he opened it.

It gave him the power to tell the President of the United States that Bob Hazlitt would not continue to seek the Democratic nomination for president. It empowered Driskill to tell the President that he felt confident in turning over the future of the party and the nation in the light of their substantive discussion of the issues. Simple. Bob Hazlitt was out of the running. Now was the time for coming together in Chicago, time for the triumph of a president.

Driskill was exhausted but also energized. He didn't want to stay all night in the shadow of the towers. He wanted to get away, like a man escaping from a radioactive field. His concern with Hazlitt had been replaced by anxiety about the killer, who was darting through his mind now, in and out of his fears as if they were shadows. He was still out there—the dog of war. The man who had tried to kill Elizabeth and had then come after him. Had he been called off? Or was he still there, watching, following?

He drove through the hot, moonlit night, bugs spattering the windshield, humidity pulsing from the wet earth. My God, it was all so crazy, in a logical world, to build the Earth Shaker with all of its malignant power, then use it to hammer a president into the ground, and then find it turned on yourself, as Hazlitt had. Politics skewed everything, every principle an honest man might live by. Here he was, hell-bent on getting the good news to Charlie Bonner—as if the creation and use of Earth Shaker were merely part of a political campaign, with no importance of their own. The fact was, the twenty-first century would now face the existence of a weapon far more devastating than any previous bomb. Earth Shaker could hold the world hostage: Control of it would produce a kind of ultimate sky bludgeon. The world would hate and fear one nation—even one group within one nation—and the inevitable result would be for terrorists to dare that nation to use its utterly preposterous power. Could anyone use Earth Shaker as a conscious weapon of policy? Bob Hazlitt had. Truly, mankind had taken unto itself the wrath of God.

And yet he went to sleep in a roadside motel wondering not about the consequences of living in a world with Earth Shaker but about Drew Summerhays, what he had been up to, why he would have partaken in a plot to set up the President . . . about the killer who was out there somewhere, loose . . . about Elizabeth as she slept so deeply.

Driskill drove on into Chicago with a brilliant sun overhead, through the rolling farmland past Fever River and the lazy little town of Oregon and the statue of Blackhawk by Laredo Taft and the Rock River and finally into the flatlands and then the city itself with its great towers and the haze beyond them over Lake Michigan.

The administration's advance guard was installed at the

new Marlowe Hotel overlooking the lake. The Ernie Banks International Convention Center rose like a great concrete balloon a few hundred yards on down the shore. The hotel had a grandiose, Las Vegas showplace quality about it, a kind of spiffy vulgarity. The architecture—notably the use of the pyramidal shape on so vast a scale—had turned heads among critics throughout the world. The *Times* of London's architecture man had suggested that "if some very important personage isn't buried under this thing, probably in his Rolls and with lots of butlers and footmen and equerries and mistresses, then some very important personage missed a hell of a bet." New Age philosophers had a field day with the shape and the extensive use of various crystal materials in public spaces. It was, they declared, an awfully powerful space, which was certainly true when the President had begun moving in. But so far as Ben Driskill was concerned, getting out of the car at one of the four equally important and powerful entrances, Chicago was just too goddam hot to be alive in. Like a blast furnace.

Nobody in the campaign party was expecting him. Nor had they known where he had been. The White House communications center patched him through from Washington to Ellery Larkspur. "Benjamin . . . the prodigal has returned. Come up, come up."

"Come down here and pull some strings for me. The way they're acting, you'd think somebody important was staying here. And I'll need some credentials. Give me the run of this whole town, okay?"

"As always," Larkspur chortled softly, "you come with the simplest of requests. Just tell me where you are."

Ten minutes later Larkspur was coming across the lobby with the huge pharaohs gazing down upon him. He looked as perfect and immaculate in his seersucker suit as he had that day in the concourse at Union Station in Washington when Driskill had come down to make his first report to the President.

"So where have you been?"

"Heaven."

"What the hell's that supposed to mean?"

"Iowa."

"Ha! What I remember about Iowa is Cokie Roberts on the air with Imus one day after the caucuses saying it's pretty funny, the way Iowa kills politicians."

"Hysterical. Our blade man tried to kill me in Saints Rest. How do you like that, Larkie? Twenty-four hours after he got Rachel Patton and Elizabeth. How the hell did he know where I was going?"

Larkspur scoffed. "In this day and age, I'm afraid there are a million ways. He's obviously well supported. Technologically speaking." They were in an elevator going up.

"The gang all here?"

"Mmmm. Well, Landesmann and Ellen are on the twentieth floor, one below me and the Presidential Suite, and the VP is stashed on the tenth floor where he won't bother anyone, we got a couple of the speechwriters, the PR folks, most of the communications staff . . . the usual suspects. Mac, of course. They're all up hanging about in Mac's suite trying to remember what they've forgotten to do."

"How do you think it looks, Larkie?"

"All our polling of delegates shows we're damn near to a deadlock. Hazlitt's gaining delegates but it's like the Chinese water torture. Slow. It's up to the undecideds and we're putting on all the pressure we've got. The LVCO thing lingers like mustard gas over the battlefield. We leaked a new Fairweather spot on the 'mysterious murders in Iowa' so we're getting lots of coverage. If we actually run it, we're going to have trouble with the Campaign Activities Act later. And," he sighed, "the perceived Bonner weakness on Mexico isn't doing any good . . . a lot of people have a bellyful. There were border raids into Texas and New Mexico last night—the bastards."

"I'm gonna change all that, Larkie."

"Right. Of course, Benjamin."

The suite looked out over Chicago in the afternoon heat, the haze akin to fog. A couple of news helicopters could be seen in the distance. As soon as the President was in the hotel the airspace would be bleached and cleaned, as they liked to say.

They were all there. Mac, Ellen, Landesmann, a couple of writers, a few others. Ben spoke to Larkie who spoke to Mac, and the nonessential personnel were dispatched to different rooms.

"All right, ladies and gentlemen. I can't go into details, it's a very involved story . . . but there is a bottom line and this is it." He watched their faces. They didn't know whether to be hopeful or afraid.

"It's all over. Bob Hazlitt is withdrawing."

He watched the mouths drop open, watched them looking at one another.

"Charlie Bonner is going to be the nominee."

They were sufficiently stunned to forget to embark on impromptu celebration. He confronted their almost disbelieving faces and told them that they couldn't give the slightest hint of the news outside of present company. "We're going to have to sit on this for a day or two . . . but, dammit, you guys deserved to know. I can't show you the letter because the President hasn't seen it yet. But I will personally hand him the paper written in Bob Hazlitt's own hand, guaranteeing his withdrawal. Once Hazlitt reaches Chicago his people'll make the announcement."

"Okay, wise guy," Ellen Thorn said, "what's this all about? How can you *do* that?"

"Well, I hate to sound conspiratorial—"

"Don't worry," Oliver Landesmann said, "it suits you."

"Ah, high praise from one who knows." There was a sense of silliness and relief in the room. It couldn't be denied. Things had come right in the end. It had all been worth it.

"Seriously—I've got to report to the President first."

They all booed him. But then came the questions about Elizabeth. Like Lieutenant Bohannon, they were all praying for her.

Fifteen minutes later Driskill ran into Nick Wardell down in the lobby among all the sarcophagi and date palms and coiled snakes and golden, solemn lions and what appeared to be the scattered remains of the Monogram Pictures prop department. They repaired to the fancy bar off the lobby, the Mummy's Walk, and Wardell leaned forward, punching a thick, stubby finger on the tiny table. "I hear rumors that Bob Hazlitt is dropping out. What do you hear, my highly placed friend?"

"I'd applaud his good judgment. And I hope your rumors are right."

"People inside the Hazlitt delegations are going nuts . . . but Hazlitt's spokesmen are swearing on a stack of Bibles it's not true. And Sherm Taylor is already here and what do you think he's doing? Parading around among Democrats for the first time in his life, very tight-lipped, very presidential. Very sober . . . You know what I think, Ben— let's face it, the campaign kicked into high gear once Sherm came on board. And now all the snap, crackle, and pop have gone out of Sherm. With his candidate looking good, Sherm would normally look like the best-dressed pig in shit in the known universe—but now he's looking pensive."

"Like the sphinx," Driskill said, tapping the small ceramic sphinx in the middle of the table, the one that was winking.

"Some people are writing it off saying he went directly from being a Marine general to being president and missed getting kicked around in the world of politics—and he don't much like it—"

"Hell, they must have forgotten four years ago. Charlie kicked him hard, about a fifty-six-yard field goal, I'd say."

Wardell nodded. "Well, I think something's up. . . ."

"Something always is," Driskill said.

The television cameras were on hand at the airstrip with the twin towers of Heartland forming a perfect background as Flying Bob in his old leather flying jacket and peaked cap with the scrambled eggs on the shiny bill and the white silk scarf made ready to leave for Chicago. He managed a laugh with the cameramen and told them to get the shot because it was too hot for this nonsense. Once the

photo op was concluded he stripped off the scarf and
jacket and did a walk around the P-38 Lightning, perhaps
the most distinctive fighter plane of World War II with its
twin fuselages and tails. A thing of great beauty. He said it
was the prize of his collection.

Hazlitt waited, leaning against one wing, facing eastward into the sun, while one of his aides loaded suitcases
and a duffel bag into the compartment.

"You get everything packed, Lieutenant?"

"Yes, sir. Ready to go."

"You've been a great help."

"Thank you, sir."

"You going straight to Chicago, too?"

"I'll be there tomorrow, sir."

"Well, I'm sure the general will be glad to see you. I'll
see him tonight, of course . . . and then I'll be addressing
the country the next night." He looked back at the luggage
compartment. "Everything there? Don't want to get there
and not have my tux or some damn thing."

"Right as rain, sir. I made sure and checked it twice."

Hazlitt climbed into the plane and closed the canopy. He
gave the photographers and cameramen the thumbs-up as
he began taxiing. Tom Bohannon saluted. The sleek tubu-
lar double-fuselage conformation made the plane look like
a prehistoric flying creature. As Hazlitt went past at full
speed, he waved and pulled back on the stick and it slowly
lifted off the tarmac, so graceful you could cry.

Tom Bohannon had put the encounter with Driskill on the
dark stairway out of his mind. Stupid. He couldn't believe
he'd failed, but it had been slippery, Driskill was a big
strong motherfucker, and it had just turned into a mess. He
lay back in his room at the Flying Bob Lodge, watching
television. He'd seen the guy who'd fallen three hundred
feet from the catwalk at the convention center and survived
with a twisted ankle. Amazing story. Absolutely amazing.

He opened a biography of Tom Paine, half-listening to
the Cubs playing in Pittsburgh on television. It was begin-

ning to rain in Pittsburgh, but the announcers thought they could get the game in. He liked it here. It was calm, it was easy, and everything was taken care of. He looked at his watch, then went back to reading about Paine in prison in France waiting to learn if he would be beheaded. The government in Washington had completely abandoned him, the official policy being that any American traveling in a foreign country was completely governed by the laws of that country. Poor bastard! Needing some help. But Tom Paine wasn't bitching about it. He claimed that he was a citizen of the world—not of any single nation—and he was willing to live by that principle. Bohannon had to hand it to Tom Paine. He liked to think of himself as sharing Paine's belief in certain basic principles, including the need to be absolutely true to yourself. Citizen Paine was only one of many heroes who occupied Tom Bohannon's personal pantheon. Patrick Henry had been just a kid, an amateur spy, but it wasn't his accomplishments that had lived down through the years—it was the manner of his death that had served as a standard for all those called upon to die for their country. And Washington. Tom Bohannon had a tough time thinking about George Washington without misting up. That such a man—a man who would disarm his nation's intelligence system and thereby render his nation helpless in the midst of a hostile, increasingly mongrelized world—that such a man would call up the memory of Ethan Allen and the Green Mountain Boys and call himself the founder of a new American revolution was a kind of blasphemy that made him choke on his own bile.

The announcer was screaming over the crowd and Cubs runners were dashing around the bases, their hats blowing off, kicking up dust.

There was a knock at the door. Bohannon checked his watch, got up, went to the door, opened it.

A bellhop was waiting outside.

"Mr. Clayton, sir. This just arrived for you, sir."

Bohannon took the plain business-letter-sized envelope. He felt in his pocket and handed the bellhop, a pretty girl with short blond hair who did credit to her uniform, a one-dollar bill. "Thanks."

"No problem." She flicked a little salute and hurried back down the hallway.

He opened the envelope.

Stand ready to move in defense of America.

He smiled slowly. He was always ready to defend America.

He left the hotel and walked two blocks to a pay telephone. Using a Sprint card issued to Andrew Clayton, he swiped it through the slot and called a long-distance number. He listened for the ringing and then a voice said: "St. Peter's Hospital."

"Hello, this is Bob McDermott calling from the White House. Could you put me through to the floor station where Mrs. Benjamin Driskill is located?"

"That would be Four West. Just one moment."

He heard the clicks and the ringing of the phone. "Four West."

"Hello, this is Bob McDermott from the White House. I'm just checking in for the President. All I need is a progress report on Mrs. Driskill."

"Oh, Mr. McDermott, didn't I speak to you earlier today?"

"I wouldn't be in the least surprised. Three or four of us here call just to stay up to the minute. How is she? Any changes?"

"This is Mr. McDermott?"

"Yes."

"I'm sorry. I can't give out any more information than I've already given today."

"Well, I guess no news is good news. At least it's not bad." He paused to think. "Don't forget prayer," he said.

"Oh, no, we never forget prayer. My guess is we nurses pray more than anybody else on earth outside of a church."

"The President is very pleased with all of you at St. Peter's. Good night."

When he got back to his room, glad to be out of the sweltering heat, he flicked on the television, surfed . . . and something very odd was going on. He was having a pee and came back into the room zipping his pants.

The correspondent on the television was going nuts. Somebody was dead.

Aboard *Air Force One* the President was playing poker with Arthur Finney of the *New York Times* and two guys from *Newsweek*, and Linda who had just taken the largest pot of the game with a full house. There was a good deal of laughter and joking, fatalistic self-deprecating remarks by the President about what he might do if he lost the nomination. The reporters thought he was in a remarkably good mood. "For a man who's thirty-five bucks down," remarked Larry Thorson, the AP man who had in fact been born and raised in Saints Rest, of all places.

Suddenly the copilot, affectionately known as Big Bill Posey, came back to the card players. He was a tall, burly man with curly hair and at the moment a slightly concerned expression.

"Excuse me, Mr. President. We've just received word from our people at O'Hare and from the security force in the air cordon around O'Hare . . . there's an emergency at the airstrip. Not exactly clear at the moment. But it's going to hold us up until they get a real tight grip on it. We'll be delayed. Nothing to worry about, folks, but it's just that little odd blip on the screen we want to stay far away from." He looked down at the table. "Speaking for America, sir, I want to congratulate the First Lady on her superior card-playing skill."

"Thanks, Captain," Linda said.

"Just more evidence of what a lucky woman she is," the President said. "Thanks for the update. Just keep us in the picture, Bill. What kind of delay are we talking about?"

"Half an hour or so. Maybe an hour. Can't be sure until we know what they're talking about."

"Okay, Bill, but remember we're on a tight schedule."

In the Bonner Command Center at the Marlowe, Driskill and McDermott and Thorn and Larkspur were awaiting the President's arrival, which would be covered on TV. It always made a good show, *Air Force One* with the seal and the flag swooping in and the President and First Lady alighting to the pomp and circumstance, the governor and the mayor and everybody who could get invited to the welcoming ceremony—it just made for a hell of a show.

While they waited they were watching the TV blimp's coverage of Bob Hazlitt's P-38 Lightning whisking across the sun-burnished surface of Illinois, over the little town of Oregon with the TV picking up the majestic Blackhawk statue, even going in for a close-up of Bob Hazlitt in the cockpit waving to the TV camera in the blimp.

When it happened it took a moment for the millions of viewers to grab hold and understand what they'd just seen. A lot of folks remarked later that it reminded them of the Gulf War back in '91 when it all seemed like a video game, puffs of smoke, bombs going down smokestacks, not quite real. Others, comparative old-timers, remembered the killing of John Kennedy and the murder of Lee Harvey Oswald a nanosecond of memory later, as if time was making the two events blur into one.

The P-38 was zipping along, shining in the sun, Hazlitt waving, and there was that sudden eruption of smoke, seeming almost harmless without benefit of sound effects, and then the flash and then, instantly, not in slow motion like the movies, the plane dissolving into flying debris that blew through the air and was gone almost before you saw it. It was then picked up again by the blimp-cam as it fell through the air and finally disappeared against the background of the earth below.

The TV camera swung violently this way and that as it tried to find something, the fuselage, a tail section, anything, a wing going past a cloud, any damn thing at all, but by then the wreckage, which was in very, very small pieces, was strung out on the ground over miles and miles of farmland and industrial parks almost to the edge of O'Hare itself. He'd been eleven minutes from landing. It would take five days until a kid whose family was returning from their summer vacation found Bob Hazlitt's left thumb in their dog Odin's dish. They had taken Odin on the vacation to the Wisconsin Dells and technically it was Odin who found the last remaining bit of Flying Bob. Luckily little Ike had arrived before Odin could consume the evidence.

More people watched the death of Bob Hazlitt than any other man in history, including Oswald, who was murdered, after all, in a much smaller United States when satellite links didn't take the pictures everywhere.

His mother was not informed of her son's demise.

$Air Force One$ arrived at O'Hare in a cocoon of almost unbelievable security. As the 747 had come in for its landing they had looked down on the bits of burning wreckage of the P-38 and then it was gone, behind them, and the enormous plane was settling down on the runway. Captain Posey had informed the President and his party that it was being reported as Bob Hazlitt's plane. Most of the nation was in a kind of shock, and the reporters were doing their best to hint that it could be some kind of insane conspiracy and if people didn't stay tuned they sure might miss something even bigger.

The President was hurried off his plane at the far end of a runway not in use. Two hundred police officers cordoned off the area, and an armored truck arrived to accompany the party down to the Loop. There were no speeches, no bands playing—at least none that the President could hear. A decoy team drove into town in PresLimOne, which had been flown in the day before by Air Force Cargo Transport along with eight other official limos. The motorcade surrounding the armored truck stretched three miles and featured armed troop carriers, police cars, SWAT motorized units, and several other unidentifiable but hugely impressive vehicles. Overhead helicopter gunships swirled about filling the news-network choppers' radio frequencies with the warning that they would be blown out of the sky if they did not peel off at once and go away. Far away.

The pharaohs at their mightiest would have loved the chaos outside the Marlowe.

Bands from the local high schools, grade school tumbling teams, mimes and jugglers of all known descriptions, cheerleaders doing their stuff with a flash of panties and cowboy boots—they were all doing their stuff for the arrival of the President and they weren't going to miss their big chance just because somebody's plane had crashed or blown up or whatever.

Word was filtering through the crowd and the mounted policemen and the vacationers hoping to get a view of the President and the delegates doing the same thing, word that there had been a terrible plane crash at the edge of O'Hare, word that an Air Force jet had crashed into the main United terminal with hundreds of casualties, word that a Northwest 727 had crashed into the Ameritech headquarters, word that Bob Hazlitt's plane had crashed and killed the candidate . . . nobody swarming outside the Marlowe knew the right story for sure, but they damn well knew that the President's plane was fine . . . or had burst into flames upon landing or had been hit by a SAM missile.

Then there was an eruption of security as the motorcade began to arrive and a flood of schoolkids with red, white, and blue balloons burst out of the hotel lobby and another bunch carrying the little flags with the AR2 logo on them and the Stockton, Illinois, High School marching band playing "In the Cool, Cool, Cool of the Evening" made way for the Stockton High School state championship football team and then they all got pushed and shoved out of the way by Chicago police, mounted and on foot, and Secret Service people, and there was a tuba gleaming in the sun falling with a clatter on the sidewalk and the President was climbing out of the armored truck, being hustled along by the Secret Service until he'd had absolutely enough of it and he stopped, subtly gave one of his bodyguards a shoulder and stopped the herky-jerky shoving parade hustling him along and those standing closest to him heard him say,

"Goddammit, what are you guys doing, you're knocking people down, you think these kids are gunning for me? Hey, miss." He moved toward the girl in the band uniform struggling to pick up the tuba, her fancy hat almost falling off, tears running down her cheeks. "Are you all right, miss?" He put his arms around her shoulders and grabbed the scowling Secret Service man who'd knocked her down and reporters had gotten close and there were seven or eight handheld roving TV newscams catching it all and President Charles Bonner said, "What's your name? . . . Julie? Well, Julie, these men that take care of me, like Dan here who sort of steamrollered you, they don't mean to run over people—do you, Danny?"

Danny shook his head, realized he was on TV, and began to smile slowly, had presence of mind enough to say, "The President makes it tough sometimes, Julie, but we all know it's just 'cause he likes to get close to the people. I'm real sorry." He looked at the President, who said, "Well, Julie, the United States government is going to get you a new tuba and you can bank on that. And thank you for a warm welcome, thanks for coming down to say hello," and he kissed Julie's cheek, leaving her beaming, and then waved to the kids and began to shake hands and work his way into the hotel, under the marquee. People engulfed him, an assassin's delight, and then somebody yelled from the crowd: "Didja hear? Bob Hazlitt's plane just blew up out at O'Hare!"

And the President pressed on into the hotel, pretending he hadn't heard a word.

The President met with Ben Driskill first.

Ben gave him the complete story of his meeting with Hazlitt. The President heard about Earth Shaker for the first time, as well as the attack on Driskill in Saints Rest. And after the recitation there was a long pause. The President massaged his eyes with his fingertips and stared out the window at Chicago, which wavered and wobbled in the heat.

"Earth Shaker," he said. "Ben, this is so crazy. Is it really true? No, wait a minute—that's all bound to come out sooner or later. Not in public, I don't mean that. You know what I mean . . . Jesus, I'm thirsty."

He sighed and looked around for a drinks table, poured a bottle of Diet Schweppes, then another. He handed Ben's to him.

"Ben, I'm not sure I can take in what you're telling me. You personally are inventing a new kind of politics. You haven't told these bastards the provable truth about one damn thing. Why do they just buckle under?"

"I didn't invent anything, Mr. President. I just learned how to play their game. The assumptions we've made have happened to be true. Hazlitt wasn't buying any of it until I told him I knew about Earth Shaker. When you've got the ultimate secret weapon and you've just tested it with results so horrible they were never contemplated—and then some asshole walks in on you and knows all about it . . . well, when he went, he went fast."

"He didn't have to consult anybody. He just figured that if you knew it came from his satellites there was no way he could get out of it. He must have felt lower than gopher shit."

"He didn't look too good, Charlie, I'll give you that."

Ellery Larkspur had quietly materialized from next door and was standing at the floor-to-ceiling window, which was blacked-out glass like a limousine. You could see out; the killers and goons couldn't look in. He was wearing a gray-and-white-striped seersucker suit. He might have been posing for a glossy advertisement.

Through the window he looked out at the apparition-like dome of the Ernie Banks Center, which seemed to rest on a cloud of humidity and construction dust and bubbling heat. His hands were in his pockets and his face was pinker than usual. He was frowning at the world.

The President said, "Give us your read, Larkie. Gut feeling. Hazlitt's out of the game. What does it mean?"

"We're still going to have to face the LVCO thing, especially now that the Mexican government's brought LVCO in to assess the earthquake situation. It looks as if you're *profiting* from their catastrophe."

He saw Ben's surprised look and said, "You're behind, Benjamin. It was on LaSalle's show. Now, we know that Tony Sarrabian is the largest stockholder in LVCO and it's all recent. The attorney general has got to go after him, really put the hammer down until the truth runs out. He's got to be at the heart of whatever's going on. Squeezing Sarrabian hard enough should provide something. Then the President's probably in the clear."

"Which," the President said, "leaves us to deal with Hazlitt's death."

Larkspur took a drink of iced tea. "Sarrabian," he murmured as if he hadn't heard the President. "Yes, we'll have to deal with him." He didn't sound optimistic.

"Unless somebody kills him," Driskill said.

Larkspur continued: "But who knows what the day and the night and the day will bring? Not this old veteran, I promise you. People are trying to get used to the idea that Bob Hazlitt, who was among us yesterday, is now only a memory. His delegates are swarming loose, looking for help. What do we do? Do we throw them a bribe to bring them on board—it's not like they have another candidate to go to. Should we try to reel them in? Will we look . . . insensitive? If we fail, it could all be very embarrassing."

"Like they might say no."

"Exactly, Mr. President."

"What the hell did Hazlitt think he was doing with this Earth Shaker thing? I mean, Jesus, sounds to me like he was seduced by technology and went nuts." The President was musing half to himself.

"Well," Driskill said, "they must have wanted to increase the chaos down there and make you look like a wimp for not going in and putting an end to the war."

The President said, "How long can we keep all this under our hats? Can we get through the convention without any of it coming out?" He frowned at them. "The Republicans will kill us with this if it gets out too soon. *Democrats Kill Thousands*—I can see the headlines now."

Larkspur nodded. "Oh, we can keep the lid on for quite a while. Until after the election. The guys who built it for

Heartland have no idea we know about it, they have no idea it's an issue in the campaign—an earthquake is an earthquake, shit happens. Because it's not an issue in the campaign, it's just between us and Hazlitt. There is no public side to this at all. It'll take a huge investigation and it can last forever—nobody's going to come running out of the woods saying they can start earthquakes. Nobody in their right mind."

"After the election," the President said. "We produce some evidence well into the second administration."

"If then, sir," Larkspur said. "Maybe we can just bury it altogether. Like all the UFO stuff. And we're still finding out things concerning the development and testing of the atom bomb. Years from now when it starts to dribble out we won't care—and your place in history as a peacemaker will be indisputable."

"Well, it makes me nervous." The President was smiling bleakly, not much pleasure in it. "But we can't leave those guys who fired off Earth Shaker to chance, and whatever we do by way of investigating, we absolutely cannot engage in a cover-up. But, for now, no one knows that thing in Mexico was anything but a perfectly normal earthquake. My bet is, the earthquake watchers will be the first ones to see something funny about it—believe me, they will, and we've got to be ready to respond up front. That's policy, as of now."

Larkspur, smoothing his hair back from the high dome with his large, liver-spotted hands, said, "I took the liberty, Mr. President, of speaking to the attorney general about this problem of the men at Heartland SatOps. I had no knowledge of the earthquake, of course, but I was just checking up on a few things. Heartland has stations all over the world—but I assume there's no reason why the Earth Shaker signal might not have been sent from SatComCent at the towers in Iowa—"

"SatComCent," the President repeated. "It sounds like WW Two."

"Well, we'd have ended WW Two a lot sooner if we could have hit Japan with a couple nines on the Richter scale. We could have put a stop to it December eighth, 1941. In any case, I suggest Attorney General Rowan get the FBI out to Iowa, to Heartland, to begin the investigation into Hazlitt's death—and we'll be briefed every few hours."

"Thank you, Larkie. Right on top of it." He sighed. "Okay. Hazlitt. What are they gonna do? Just scrape up a bunch of Illinois dirt and figure some of Hazlitt's in it?"

"Probably bury him," Driskill added, "in a pyramid with half his servants and all of his pets. You should have seen this bodyguard of his—Marine Corps poster boy. He'd have taken a bullet for Hazlitt. He even inquired after Elizabeth's condition when he brought me the letter from his master. The whole thing—the party for his mother, the restaurant where they double your order no matter what it is . . . His secretary could have been June Cleaver and Bob was the Beaver, the way she acted about him. The whole thing was surreal—I could never make you understand what that party for his mother was like." Driskill shook his head tiredly.

The President said, "What are we to do with the letter?"

"You mean, make it public or keep it to ourselves?" Driskill said. "We've also got to consider Sherm Taylor. Sherm's gonna want something to say."

"Yeah—well, I'd like to hear him say, *Fuck this, I'm going back to the Republicans!*" The President smiled hopefully. "I wonder if we could blackmail him into leaving our party?"

Larkspur shook his head. "We don't have anything to threaten him with. That's the problem. Oh, we could undoubtedly dig up something—but not in time to use it during this convention."

"It's his Medal of Honor," Driskill said. "He keeps thinking he has to live up to it."

The President looked from one to the other. "I think we should release the letter."

"To what end?" Larkspur inquired. "Do we want our people to think you were out making deals with Hazlitt?"

"Hell, Larkie, what else can we do to bring folks together? Maybe it works, maybe not—but it shows Hazlitt seeing the light. We can go on about how we had a long talk on the phone, he saw the virtues in what I was doing, I suggested a few areas where we might compromise, he agreed—and he decided to address the convention and ask for their support in withdrawing and throwing his support to me. I agreed to a major cabinet post if he wanted it . . . and he took off for Chicago. Blooey. That's the end of Bob Hazlitt. Doesn't that sound, ah, reasonable?" The President stood up, pacing around the gathering. "What the hell are we so down in the mouth about? Hazlitt's dead, for chrissakes, the nomination is ours! At least among ourselves, we ought to be cheering to high heaven!"

Larkspur said, "Well, it's never quite that simple, Mr. President. We're all in a state of shock—what we're talking about is how we spin it. We may not really have had time to realize what the bottom line is . . . your nomination. But better to restrain our enthusiasm—if we've learned anything, we should have learned that nothing in politics is reasonable."

"I don't want to be a wet blanket," Driskill said, "and maybe I'm just being a wee bit paranoid here—but what if somebody blew the plane up? What if it comes out over the next few days that he was murdered on TV in front of a television audience in the tens of millions—?"

"Are we really gonna get into this?" The President looked at Larkspur.

"Well, we should be prepared if someone else raises the question. But we don't think that there was really foul play, do we?" Larkspur was tapping his mouth with a presidential seal ballpoint pen, anything to keep from smoking.

Driskill said, "No, but we shouldn't ignore the possibility—and if somebody did kill him, who has the motive? The world's going to look at us, my friends. We're the ones who benefit—"

"God almighty, Ben," the President half shouted. "Give it a rest for just a moment. There's an awful lot to do without that. We'll have to keep very close contact with the FAA and the FBI boys on the scene. The first hint from them goes to us—I mean, they're dropping enough hints as it is. Larkie, can you get that word out to the FBI?"

"Of course."

"Then let's go forward with releasing the contents of the letter. Lemme think how we should go about that," the President said. "No mass release. Not first off. Maybe we should save it for the delegates themselves; I might even use it somehow. Gotta think about all that. We can release a photocopy of the letter, right? But we need to figure out when." He picked it up off the coffee table and glanced through it. "We'll vet it in the morning. Develop some final plan. . . . Men, I'm tired as a cat. Larkie, you work out something on the LVCO thing—one more denial from me about the stock stuff, but get your people working on Sarrabian. We need something solid. Let's say we meet here tomorrow at seven."

Chapter 22

The press conference went off at eight o'clock the next morning.

It was not held in the hotel's Ramses Room, which Mac had said denoted condoms and was too small anyway, but rather in the dramatic Memphis Ballroom, which was decked out with presidential trappings, huge paintings of Democratic presidents, crossed flags of presidents and the states from which they came, huge gilt mirrors, gold draperies, a polished parquet floor, everything. It was felt that using the Marlowe for their press conferences and briefings rather than electronic-friendly available space at the Ernie Banks Center itself gave the impression that the President—since the Marlowe was his headquarters for the convention—was personally concerned and involved with the efforts to solve the riddle of what exactly had happened to Bob Hazlitt.

Bob McDermott took the podium first and waited for the babbling to subside. First, from the administration, from the President personally, and from the Democratic convention he offered the deepest sympathy for the family of Bob Hazlitt and for all those who supported him so heroically. There would be a ceremony honoring his memory in the great Gathering Hall in Heartland, Iowa, on the coming Sunday night and the President and First Lady would attend. Final interment would be "at the family plot in the countryside near Heartland where he grew up and began the remarkable life that was cut short yesterday. Second, we have a major announcement to make of great significance to the Democratic Party, to the nation, and indeed to the world." He paused for that critical instant, then said, "Ladies and Gentlemen, the President of the United States."

Charles Bonner came out briskly, accompanied by Attorney General Teresa Rowan and his private counselor, Ellery Dunstan Larkspur. Ben Driskill stood watching with Mac at the side of the stage. There were roughly nine hundred reporters from around the world sitting on folding chairs. It was ninety degrees outside, which meant the temperature was going to crack a hundred. In the ballroom it was already edging toward unbearable.

"As you can imagine, I am greatly saddened by the death of my old friend and sometime opponent Bob Hazlitt. We salute his brave spirit. There will be a fitting tribute on the convention floor later this week. Now . . . I want to allay any fears and put to rest any rumors you may have heard. Everything I've been told by investigators at the FAA and FBI has convinced me that there is no evidence of foul play in the tragic explosion that cost Bob Hazlitt his life less than twenty-four hours ago.

"However, I am here to tell you something that has been until this moment a secret. You all know Ben Driskill," he said, looking over at Ben, gesturing in his general direction, "and you may have noticed that he's been absent from the campaign spotlight the last week or so—at his own insistence, so as not to distract from the serious business at hand—in order to investigate certain allegations made against him and against this administration. Mr. Driskill, one of my most trusted friends and associates, has been working behind the scenes to hold this great party together—honest differences of opinion between men of goodwill can sometimes be adjudicated and compromised by those who are pure of heart—and it was he whom I sent to Iowa to discuss the future of the party and the nation with Bob Hazlitt."

Driskill felt a slight smile spreading across his face: all

the bullshit, enough crap to choke a python. It was as if he'd never been accused of complicity in murder by LaSalle and subsequently the rest of the frenzied press and by Hazlitt supporters, as if some of the little problems were not a handful of murders, the framing of the President, the machinations of Sarrabian, LaSalle, Niles, and Hazlitt. It was rather as if a few problems had been overcome, problems among friends quite free of murder and blackmail and twisted arms, and now the world would go forth and do good. It was like one of Alec Fairweather's commercials, like the one he'd seen on TV this morning in which the events of yesterday, when Charlie spoke to the high school tuba player, had already been edited and gracefully shaped into a commercial for the best darn guy who'd ever been President of this great ol' country. The President was going on.

"It is to Bob Hazlitt's great credit that over this past weekend he and Mr. Driskill met in Heartland for intensive discussions of those issues that had divided us since his entry into the contest for the nomination. Ben went to the hundredth birthday party honoring Bob Hazlitt's mother." His voice caught briefly on that image; he couldn't resist the poetry of it. "He walked by the waters of Backbone Creek with Hazlitt in the hot Iowa sunshine and together the two men discovered an immense common ground when it came to solutions to the problems facing this great country of ours . . . and in the end Bob Hazlitt gave Ben Driskill a letter he was to deliver to me as a statement of purpose as we came together last night for our final talks before the convention came to order . . . and today Bob Hazlitt was going to join me in this very room to make a joint statement." The President surveyed the crowd of reporters. The cameras were humming, the reporters had begun that crazy buzz you couldn't see but could somehow hear. The President left them hanging, it seemed an eternity, and then he spoke again.

"Today Bob Hazlitt was planning to withdraw from the contest for the Democratic presidential nomination." There was a sudden intake of breath and rustling movement. Nobody could leave the room with Charlie Bonner speaking, but they wanted to be ready.

"And this great Democratic convention was to become a celebration of shared beliefs in the ways to combat problems and maximize opportunities and remain the strong leader that we Americans have no choice but to be, that we have no choice but to face together. Now that joint statement of our belief in the future will never be made. But I will be making the case this week for what both Bob and I believed in . . . and in the meantime"—he finally lifted the sheet of paper, handwritten and signed by Hazlitt, and waved it—"in the meantime we have this generous letter that Bob Hazlitt wrote in his own hand. We've run off Xeroxes for everybody here and will be faxing it, some three thousand copies, to journalists around the country as soon as we have finished here. You will see that Bob was ready to join with me in building a new America. Now, I realize this is big news and you're going to have a lot of work to do. You're going to be running all over this town and it's going to be a long, hot day. If you've got questions, please direct them to Bob McDermott and his assistants . . . 'cause frankly I've got work to do. Thanks for your attention." The reaction was intense.

"Mr. President, have you spoken with Sherman Taylor since the tragedy?"

The President was shaking his head no, his voice carrying only a few feet as he made way for Mac to reach the podium. "And now," Mac said, "are there any questions I can help you with? Scheduling, delegate events, event changes . . . Yes, Barney Clay?"

"Listen, Mac . . . how can you guys be so sure somebody didn't put a bomb on Hazlitt's plane?" Somebody else said, "Mac, is anybody safe in this campaign? Do you have any explanations for all the violent deaths that keep hounding this campaign?"

Mac smiled at the sea of faces, sweating, reddened, mouths open. Pencils were poised, cameras whirring. "What are we gonna do with you people? The two men contending for this party's nomination come to a meeting of the minds that saves the party from splitting in two, we agree on a candidate, and then one of these men dies in a tragic accident . . . and all you can think of is murder! Look at yourselves—what does it say about you?" But he was smiling. He knew them and they knew him. "I didn't load his plane—how am I supposed to answer questions like that? We only know what the FBI and FAA have told us."

"You're saying there could have been a bomb on his plane?"

"I'm saying that you now know what we know. We've told you what the investigators have told us thus far."

More questions spilled out of the mouths. The pot was boiling, steam was rising.

Mac mimed not being able to hear the questions and quickly caught up with the President's party. An assistant was left onstage to discuss various arrangements for the reporters, changes in schedules, and God only knew what else.

Mac caught up with Driskill. "Went okay, right?"

"TV should love it. Ratings'll be through the roof."

"All you gotta do is give 'em what they want. A thriller."

Driskill was right. TV coverage had maxed out since the plane exploded. Since that defining moment the convention had become the most continuously watched political event in recent history. But that was the least of it.

Overnight a kind of miracle had happened.

By that afternoon the crammed, sweltering streets of Chicago as well as the vast sweep of the "Convention City" area were suddenly decked out in signs proclaiming that the People had a new candidate for the Democratic Party. The party and the nation must turn to him in this time of crisis. . . .

Sherman Taylor.

The Marine general. The former president of these United States. The winner of the Congressional Medal of Honor . . . who had bowed to the tireless efforts and determination of Bob Hazlitt to reach the White House, but who now was willing to serve his country again in its highest office.

His face looked out from shop windows, and the crowds, tens of thousands, milling around the Ernie Banks International Convention Center were already carrying signs and wearing paper hats with his likeness on them and for twenty bucks at a vending center you could buy a handsome all-wool pennant with a picture of Taylor looking out at you, visage grim, ready to take on anything for America. Color portraits of the great man appeared as if by magic, the stern no-nonsense face, the flag, the Medal of Honor, the gleaming Marine sword. . . .

Late in the afternoon he called a press conference at the media center about fifty yards across from the convention center itself. The asphalt was gooey and beginning to bubble underfoot, but the reporters were making do. Crews were laying down some kind of composition material that reduced the inconvenience. Flung across the open spaces was an archipelago of man-made islands, sandy and covered with palm trees and picturesque shaded bamboo huts where refreshments were to be found. Somehow it all blended in with the yachts anchored nearby and the endless expanse of Lake Michigan beyond.

Tom Bohannon stood at the back of the room, scanning the faces. He watched the ebb and flow of reporters' interests as the moments dragged while they waited for the former president to face up to the reality of his own support. Sherman Taylor came into the room with several people joining behind him. He wore a dark blue suit with a very thin pinstripe and his deeply tanned face was set in stone; the deep lines on either side of his mouth appeared to have been left there by an acetylene torch. The crowd of reporters and the TV crews grew still and he waited until it was quieter yet and he waited until it was dead silent.

"I don't have a great deal to say, ladies and gentlemen. I am greatly saddened by the death of my friend Bob Hazlitt. Seldom have I known a man so full of life and energy. This country of ours is a lesser place without him in it." He waited with his hands clasped on top of the rostrum, looking at the reporters as if willing them to believe him, every word he said. All you could hear was the occasional click of a shutter and the whirring of the tape machines.

"You may have noticed this heartwarming show of support for me outside the convention hall and in the streets of Chicago. It shows, I think, that Americans are political animals and a very resilient lot. However, beneath the signs and banners they're waving, they are grieving for Bob Hazlitt, just as I am. But they also know that the machinery of political life, once started as this was many months ago when I went to snowbound Iowa and sat down and visited with Bob Hazlitt and urged him to offer himself to the country—they know that the machinery can't be stopped. It's going to keep grinding onward toward some conclusion or other. For better or worse. Bob Hazlitt would be the first to acknowledge that the nominating system of the Democratic Party is in high gear and is going to produce a nominee.

"We will mourn Bob Hazlitt but we will also choose a candidate to take his place. Let me say here—I am not now nor have I ever been a candidate for this nomination. I have spent my post-military career affiliated with the Republican Party. I became a Democrat in order to demonstrate my commitment to the candidacy of Bob Hazlitt. I can offer no encouragement to those of his followers who have labored through the night to produce the posters and banners with my name and face on them. I appreciate their efforts but I must tell them, I am not your candidate for the presidency. As young people say, I've been there, done that." A small respectful ripple of laughter.

"We must turn our attention over the next two days, two days without sleep because it is a large job and little time, to the men and women we know well in this party. We must consider once again President Charles Bonner and the intelligence policies he espouses, we must look long and hard at David Mander, his vice-president, we must consider the career and the capability of Attorney General Teresa Rowan. We must look at the leaders among the Democrats in the Congress and in the statehouses and we must look to those who are not presently in government but whom God created to hold high office. But I ask you not to look too long nor too hard at Sherm Taylor. I sought nothing from my relationship with Bob Hazlitt, nor do I want any glittering prize by default now that he is gone. But I will give my thoughts to anyone who seeks them. I will counsel and discuss the possibilities of candidates with anyone who asks me to do so . . . but you must understand I am not seeking this nomination. Now, if there are questions, I'll do my best to answer them."

"Mr. President, how do you—"

"Please, I'd appreciate your referring to me as *General* or *Mister* rather than as Mr. President. We have a president and I feel he alone should be addressed that way. Now, please go on."

"General, how do you account for the fact that these signs all over Chicago and the convention center appeared so quickly? It seems like a concerted effort, very well financed—printing companies expect to be paid, people have to be organized to get this kind of material out so quickly—"

"To tell you the truth, Sam, I've just heard about the placards. I don't know who put them up, I don't know anything about them. I just found it a touching demonstration of loyalty to an old familiar face. I'm sure they're Hazlitt people who want a place to go—that's the decision facing us all over the next day or so. There isn't much time. There's no margin for error—tragedy has made hostages of us all."

Margaret Bondurant from the *Chicago Tribune* was on her feet, her voice piercing the cacophony of voices from the reporters. "What do you make of the President's handing out the letter from Bob Hazlitt? Hazlitt was taking himself out of the race—so his death made no difference from a political point of view. You'd all be looking for another candidate even if Bob Hazlitt were here . . . unless you agreed with him and made it unanimous for Bonner."

"That letter," Sherman Taylor began. "I don't know about that letter. Seems like it's awfully convenient for the

President, doesn't it? Quite a stroke of luck for the President. I was not privy to the conversations the letter alleges took place between the President and/or the President's representative, Mr. Driskill, and Mr. Hazlitt—I knew nothing about them. That alone wasn't characteristic of anything Bob did these last few months—we really were a team. He valued my advice, I was proud of his courage, his willingness to say what needed to be said. For him to suddenly go off and have secret conversations with the other side and cave in as completely as the President alleges . . . well, I don't know what the President said to him. I don't know if these talks even took place. One man says they did and the other man is dead. We'll never know for sure, I suppose."

Al Folger from the *Miami Herald* said, "Sounds like you're calling the President a liar and a scoundrel, General. That's pretty strong, isn't it?"

"I'm just saying that we've got to be sure of what and whom we believe. Then we can make a choice for a candidate we'll be proud of—that's all I'm saying and nothing more. We need to find out the truth behind these last few days . . . what was Bob Hazlitt up to? What happened to his plane? When we have those answers, we'll be in a much better position to move forward. Now you'll have to excuse me, I've got some engagements—as you can imagine, there's a lot to do."

"What kind of a timetable are you on?"

"Well, it speaks for itself, doesn't it? Tomorrow night I'm going to address the convention. A film is being put together now, honoring Bob Hazlitt, and I'll be presenting it to the convention. It's going to be a truly historic occasion. The President is going to speak as well—first time ever a sitting president has addressed the convention before the balloting. Next night the balloting and the nomination. And on the final night the nominee of the party will address the convention . . . it's a pretty simple timetable. Now, please, excuse me." He turned away.

Margaret Bondurant's voice sliced through the murmur that had started to build. "Are you saying flatly that these overnight supporters of yours are wasting their time? Are you saying that you will under no circumstances accept this party's nomination for president? Are you telling us the door is closed and locked and nobody's home?"

Taylor turned and smiled slightly. "No, Margaret, that is not what I'm saying. I am saying that under no circumstances will I seek this nomination. I will not lobby for it, I will not cajole delegates, I will not compromise my principles with private interests—"

"But you are open to persuasion? You would accept a draft?"

"The delegates must be left free to work their will. Now, thank you for your attention, ladies and gentlemen. I really must be going."

As Ben Driskill was leaving the media hall he bumped into a reporter from Baltimore, red-faced and rotund, tie loosened, collar open, sweating like everybody else. "Sounded like Groucho Marx, 'Hello, I must be going.' Well, that sonuvabitch Taylor is in the race, Ben. Standing right on the remains of Bob Hazlitt."

"Looks that way, Jack."

"Goes without saying."

Pushing his way toward the doors Driskill found himself shunted to the side by a group of delegates arriving for a state press conference—Democrats from the great Commonwealth of Massachusetts coming together to meet with their home-state press. He watched them with their pins and pennants and hopeful sweating faces, shirts soaked through, hair plastered onto foreheads, ID tags hung lopsidedly around their necks. He waited for the herd to pass and then turned and bumped into the man standing next to him.

"Well, this is a coincidence," he said.

He was staring into the face of the lieutenant who had been Hazlitt's bodyguard, chauffeur, aide-de-camp.

"I hear tell there's no such thing as coincidence, sir." He put out his hand and Driskill took it. "It's logical to see you here, when you think about it. I'm on General Taylor's staff. He had me working for Mr. Hazlitt this past week."

"I'm very sorry about Hazlitt," Driskill said.

"So am I. But politics is war, that's what the general says. There are bound to be casualties."

"A harsh view."

"In war you have to get used to it. Any new word on your wife, sir?"

"Not really. The longer she stays under . . . well . . ." He caught himself confessing his concern to the lieutenant as if they'd known each other forever, were intimate friends.

"Don't give up hope, sir. If there's one thing I've learned in life that's it. Never give up hope."

"I'll remember that. I don't think I will give up hope." They were walking toward one of the great doorways to the outside world. Nearer the door it was hotter still. "How long have you been on Taylor's staff?"

"Oh, I was one of his people a long time ago. Then I was out of commission for quite a long while. But when he needed me—he remembered me. He never forgot about me. I can hear him now—" The eyes were glazing over just a bit. The military mind, Driskill thought. The lieutenant was wearing contact lenses. One eye was tearing, over-flowing. "When the time came, he used to say, *Get me Tommy!* I don't know how many times I've heard people tell me that story—overseas, I mean. Tough job needs to be done . . . *Get me Tommy!*" Suddenly the solemn face broke into an almost boyish smile. Driskill wondered again how old the man was. Sometimes he looked twenty-five and others he might have been twice that. "It's a great pleasure to serve a man like General Taylor. Now, if you'll excuse me, I'm supposed to be working for him right now." He was wearing a Marine Corps officer's uniform and he snapped a smart salute.

"He decided he'd support Bob Hazlitt and he said, 'Get me Bohannon,' is that it?"

"I guess he knew there'd be plenty for me to do, sir. I certainly have been busy. Now, please excuse me, sir."

"Absolutely. We'll probably bump into each other again. Convention like this, it's a surprisingly small world."

Stepping outside into the wet smack in the face of the

heat, with the sun setting, burning through the layers of pollution hanging like a shroud over the towers of the city, Driskill took out his cellular phone and punched up a number. He looked through the haze at the Marlowe Hotel and with a practiced eye picked out a certain window. The phone was ringing. The President's party had taken over six floors of the hotel, four that were full of people, and two that were full of Secret Service—not quite people, after all, he thought to himself. Then he heard the voice say, "Yes?"

"Archangel here," Driskill said.

"You don't say." It was Larkspur. "How are things out there in the real world, Archangel? Hot enough for you?"

"Fishercat's question. I have the answer."

"And what is that answer?"

"Yes. He's going to run. He's already running hard as hell."

"Well, we need to put our heads together. Come on upstairs."

"Is the President really going to address the convention tomorrow night?"

"He thought he might drop by."

Tom Bohannon pushed his way through the supporters with the placards and banners to reach the cordoned-off area of elaborate mobile homes only a few feet from the back of the convention center. Normally there was plenty of room for headquarters operations within the center, but for the sake of superior air-conditioning the mobile homes were the preferred resting places for the candidates and assorted high-rollers who needed places to rest and plot and soak up the small-batch bourbons and single malts and horse around.

The general was right behind him, surrounded by uniformed Marine officers—when a former president and Marine general calls the Marine Corps commandant, you really can't quibble with him about providing a security guard of Marines. Bohannon knew that among equals he was far more equal. Closer to the great man himself. They'd been to war together. But now he was worried.

He went into the trailer and the rest of them waited outside. Standing beside the door, holding it for the general, Bohannon felt a moment of disorientation. The huge esplanade had been turned into a bunch of desert islands. It didn't make much sense but it was pretty. He'd read that ten thousand tons of sand had been brought in and shaped into the mounds and pathways with a thousand perfect palm trees swaying gracefully in the breeze beneath the hellish sunshine. Far away on the watery horizon of Lake Michigan yachts and gigantic sailboats sat quietly and, nearer in, resting by the piers, were the yachts of the mighty: supporters of the party; the big spenders, the men like Tony Sarrabian whose yacht had been *flown* in by way of a giant leased transport plane; the corporations that employed the lobbyists who created at a very great cost a world that no one needed; the movie stars who'd attached themselves to the party, to the President; the foreign powers who wanted technology and weaponry and needed very good friends in high places; and anyone else who wanted an edge in the corridors of power. If you had a yacht, this was the place for it to be, and most of them had been sailed by their expert crews all the way from California or back east at Martha's Vineyard, all the way to Chicago for a week of partying and self-indulgence and showing off. Bohannon found himself reminded of the Wizard of Oz—none of it bore any relationship to a reality he could understand.

He thought of Abu Dhabi and the palace of the sultan of Brunei and other places he'd been, in Hong Kong and Tokyo and Damascus, where the powerful rich merely said what they wanted and it was there. Nothing real about that, either. But then he'd spent most of his life in places so unreal, doing things so preposterous that they defied description—which was just as well.

He went into the trailer and sat down to wait while the general took yet another shower. He poured himself a glass of tonic over ice and sank back into the chair wishing he'd been less friendly with Driskill, but among other things the contact confirmed that Driskill didn't recognize him as anyone but Hazlitt's bodyguard—he was safe. He could stop worrying about Driskill. That was the only thing General Taylor didn't like about him—a tendency to think too much, to worry about things that were worryproof. "Otherwise, Bohannon," the general was fond of saying, "you'd be the perfect weapon." Well, he'd never stopped thinking or worrying, not when he hadn't been allowed to see a light for three months and had been virtually blind when he came out, blind and afraid of noises and afraid of the movement of the blankets in the night, as if the rats and snakes he'd lived with in the fetid darkness for so long were back, bursting through the membrane of his imagination. All that had kept him even partly sane was his ability to think, to conjure up images and ideas and spy stories—if only he'd been able to remember all the stories he'd invented in the darkness. He could have been a writer. Or sold his ideas to the movies. But whenever he'd taken a long hard look at the plots they'd always sort of fallen to dust.

He'd learned about double and triple thinking, twisting ideas until they begged for mercy. And now he was thinking about the general and those damn sunglasses, how you could never see where his eyes were looking; he'd be standing there telling you something that was so crazy you'd try to catch whether or not it was a joke, or a lie, and all you ever saw was those flat darkened disks, though sometimes he'd smile at you. . . . Once he'd told Bohannon to kill a man in Beirut—they were standing right there, the general and Bohannon and the guy who'd let them down. And Bohannon had said, here? Now? With what? He didn't have a gun. And the general looked into the face of the guy who was already a dead man and said, Oh, hell, Tommy, kill him with your bare hands or stomp on his throat or some damn thing 'cause I've got this bad back, now get to it. And the man had looked at Bohannon like, was this real or was this guy nuts, and then Bohannon had killed him. Slammed his head against a stone wall until his eyeballs were on the ground and he had pretty much stopped breathing or resisting. But he hadn't been able to see the general's eyes. What if he'd only been kidding around, just to see if Tommy would do it? Well, it was all a long time ago and there was no use crying over spilt milk. Anyway, the double- and triple-think thing was coming up in the back of his mind; there was something about Ben Driskill that made him wonder if he, Bohannon, knew the real plot of the story or if he was just the general's tool.

The general hadn't been too talkative because he was still angry about the screwup on those slippery steps in Saints Rest. "I don't want to hear any more about it, Tommy. I understand, you're getting older, you're not as fast as you once were, you probably got some arthritis developing you're not even aware of. You've been damn good, Tommy, but when it starts to go, it starts to go, and there's no stopping it. Maybe you've even lost your taste for it—who the hell can blame you? Well, we get through this, you've earned a nice long vacation and a change of jobs . . . more administrative stuff, not so much in the way of field ops. And, anyway, Driskill is a big son of a gun, he's a hard man to take down, always has been from what I hear. . . ."

Bohannon found himself reflecting on the general's words. Reading between the lines. More administrative stuff . . . And he began to wonder. Still, he wished he hadn't gotten quite so friendly with Driskill at the media center. It was showing off, seeing how close you could get to the other side without them knowing it. . . . Showing off, for God's sake. It was a little late in the day for that.

The meeting between the President, Ben Driskill, and Ellery Larkspur lasted less than an hour. When it was over each man believed that the defeat of Sherman Taylor was assured—give or take. They called it *Operation Second Place*.

The President had already called the Council of National Science Advisors into a top-secret meeting to work on the

Earth Shaker thing with Heartland's head of engineering, who had quickly discovered from Secret Service messengers who arrived during the night that refusal was not an option. Two separate groups under airtight security would meet at Duke University and the University of Washington. "And," the President said with some feeling, "we've got to come to grips with the stock certificate thing, Ben. The Republicans are gonna put it right back on the national agenda, maybe even before this convention is over. We'll be needing some real hard answers."

Driskill said, "Mr. President, there's only so much we can do about it in two days. I've been to see Sarrabian. He denies it all. I'm working on one more possibility. Give me time—"

"*What* time?" the President said.

"Right now," Larkspur said, "I think our Operation Second Place takes precedence."

The President nodded shortly. His temper was losing the battle with his nerves.

The day ended when you couldn't keep your eyes open, when the adrenaline finally gave out and you had to sleep. And before you knew it, night had blurred into morning and there was a thick haze outside the window and all the newspapers outside the door and the breakfast tray with lots of orange juice was coming in, ready or not.

Once he'd cleaned up and switched to his other suit, Driskill headed from the Marlowe in search of the attorney general, who was rumored to be in the offices at the center. Lightning and thunder were cracking off to the west over the great city. The Sears tower and all the other towers were blurring in the haze that promised rain.

By midmorning the Ernie Banks Center was throbbing and pulsing with life, the great heart pumping people and rumors and excitement and depression in all directions at once. TV cameras panned the esplanade between the Marlowe and the center, famous faces had staked out their own territories and were doing their stand-ups for the all-day spot coverage, crowds standing about watching them intently, hundreds of Bonner supporters waving placards and banners emblazoned with his warmly handsome face and the *AR2 Taking Back Our America* logo, hundreds of others chanting "We Want Sherm!" and carrying huge banners with a photograph of the general and the words emblazoned in blood red, *Taylor . . . Again.*

Schoolkids dressed like corner newsies of the thirties were everywhere hawking the newspapers that Alec Fairweather's people, ferried down from Minneapolis during the night, had created during the hours since Driskill's meeting with the President and Larkspur. Operation Second Place was the creation of two convention papers, the *Convention Chronicle* and *The Trib,* each pushing hard on the headlines that trumpeted *Taylor Asks Pres for 2nd Place???* and *General for VP? He Wants It!* New editions of the paper appeared every two hours, which showed what you could do with an unlimited budget. The six o'clock edition of the two phony papers featured a full-color computer-created picture of the President with his arm around Taylor's shoulder while the President beamed at the crowd and Taylor looked adoringly at the President. The headlines read *It Looks Like a Twosome!* and *President Writes a Ticket!* The newsboys shouted, "Getcha papuh here, free to everybody, getcha papuh, Bonner picks Taylor for VP," and every two hours fifty thousand more papers arrived.

Inside the convention hall, where day and night had become outmoded concepts, thirty thousand people waited, a third of them connected to news-gathering and production operations around the world. The seats were all taken, the bands dueled constantly with "In the Cool, Cool, Cool of the Evening" versus a hastily convened Taylor band playing "The Marine's Hymn" from the halls of Montezuma all the way to eternity. Uniformed Marines seemed to be everywhere, apparently called on by Taylor to handle security for him, each wearing battle ribbons and decorations of all kinds. It was a madhouse: The word was out that both the President and Sherman Taylor would speak to the convention in an entirely unprecedented event.

In front of the blocked podium, convention business had been going on ever since the delegates were gaveled to order by Jess Holyoke. After his moment in the sun Jess had passed the baton to Sandra Mainwearing of Peoria, thirteen-term congresswoman, who was the permanent chairperson. She was even yet presiding over endless platform fights, endless speeches by congressmen who wanted their moment of convention broadcast time, speeches droning on virtually unheard by the delegates on the floor talking and squabbling and trying to get over their hangovers. Enormous battles had been waged over the issue of dismantling the intelligence community, and the attorney general had addressed the convention on the subject but delegates already knew where they stood and one group from California had walked out of the convention and their replacements had had to have their credentials okayed. The only thing most everyone agreed on was they were interested in the death of Bob Hazlitt and what it meant for the average delegation.

Driskill found the attorney general on the convention floor finishing up an interview with CNN. When it was concluded he drew her aside.

"Teresa, if you ever loved me—"

"Oh, boy, here it comes," she said.

"I want you to skip all the usual channels, okay? I want you to run a top-priority computer check on a Marine called Tom Bohannon, who served under Sherm Taylor in Special Forces or whatever the Marines called it. Maybe fifteen years ago. More or less. We need everything we can find on him."

"Who is Tom Bohannon?"

"I don't know. That's why I need this check run. Check everything . . . even the files that have been scrubbed. Okay? You are the attorney general. I need to know who this guy is."

———

TV shows were revving up with any politicians and pundits they could find, dragging them out of caucuses and meetings with the reporters from back home and arm-twisting sessions with representatives of the candidates. For the media there was one primary subject—Sherman Taylor. Which was just the way Charlie Bonner wanted it.

No matter who was being interviewed, the questioning began this way: "Tell us, this Sherman Taylor business—is he running hard for the top spot, as it seems to many, or does he really mean he's not a candidate?" It was inevitably a two-part question: "Has he already accepted the second spot on the Bonner ticket? Lots of people, insiders, are saying it's a done deal. What do you think?"

And then the politician or pundit moved into high gear and held forth. Nobody knew any answers for sure. But Charles Bonner looked on in good humor, and when a reporter spotted him passing through one lobby or another fired the VP question at him, Bonner only smiled and said, "Dream ticket, right?" He said it with a laugh, but it was the dominant news of the early morning.

When the fax came in, Ben Driskill had bailed out of the center and was sitting alone in the President's campaign room in the suite at the Marlowe, drinking coffee, nibbling a chocolate doughnut.

Thomas Bohannon had begun in the Marine Corps, then been seconded to a Special Forces Group WI and served for a time under Gen. Sherman Taylor, who had been famous for his commando strikes with small groups bent on doing maximum damage to secret installations or rescuing hostages or carrying out political assassinations. The W indicated "wet," which meant kill-at-will missions. I indicated "insurrection," which meant the group was frequently deployed to aid or destroy revolutionary, or for that matter governmental, groups in foreign countries. These were the super-high-risk black-bag jobs that most people preferred to believe happened only in the movies. It was felt he could "become" other people in the name of disguise almost at will. A series of photographs were also faxed through, each purporting to be Thomas Bohannon. He stared back at Driskill in several guises . . . none of which were the man Ben had just seen on the floor.

But the records the attorney general had accessed reported something else.

Lt. Thomas Bohannon had died in captivity during a mission within Nigeria seventeen years ago.

Ben Driskill was dealing with a ghost.

Inside the Ernie Banks Center, music blared and there was TV everywhere, cameras poking like hungry, snuffling snouts at him. Driskill had Bohannon's number now, marveled at the coolness of all the contacts Bohannon had instigated over the past few days, living on the edge of discovery yet avoiding it, pushing at fate, testing to see if Driskill remembered him, twice referring to Elizabeth and his concern for her.

Was killing the President the kind of challenge now awaiting Tom Bohannon? Could he possibly have killed Bob Hazlitt? He had stalked Rachel Patton—that was all Driskill could be sure of. Eyes of two different colors . . . But what else had he done? You could guess, you could think you were right. You couldn't prove it. And this time real, true proof was what you needed.

Driskill felt like the maze he'd walked into was now closing around him, and the exit was no closer than it had ever been.

He had told Larkspur, for God's sake, don't let the President come to the center tonight, keep him safe until we find Bohannon, it's so unnecessary to make an appearance ahead of time. The party—which *is* the President, bottom line—controls the convention, he'd said. Have Mac inform the Taylor camp that there'll be no appearances by candidates on the night of the Hazlitt tribute, period. But he was voted down by the only vote that counted, the President's.

"Ben, I'm not backing away from this," he said. "We're playing chicken here—it's too good a chance for me to grab this nomination for me to back off. I'm not going to give Taylor an excuse to say I'm railroading the convention, running it my way. We're going to go ahead, we're going to take this nomination and tonight, with luck, we can settle it for good."

As the afternoon wore on, eight thousand people were milling around on the floor of the convention and twenty-five thousand more filled the galleries, and somewhere in there was Tom Bohannon—or whoever the hell he was. A killer, a man whose brain might be turning to fiery, burned, and smoking mush, for all Driskill knew. What did the killer think was going on . . . did it all make sense to him? Did his mind take in anything outside the boundaries of his mission? He was a killing machine, and what good would he be once the killing was over? Would he be with the general for the whole ride? Or was it all going to stop?

The big lies that had worked to bring the President down from his apparently unassailable position as leader of a majority party and into a contest with the challenger from within his own party, the big lies had now been turned on the challenger, and there might be no time left to recover. Taylor's great hope was to bring the convention to its feet tonight with a speech for the history books, a clarion call that would make him the logical candidate, the beneficiary of Hazlitt's movement. Was there such a speech? Was there a mind to devise and write it?

The afternoon was grinding to a close with a floor fight over whether or not Two-Gun Tony Granado, the governor of New Mexico, would be allowed to address the convention since both the President and Sherman Taylor were preparing to do so. Granado's supporters never intended to win the floor fight: They were positioning their man for a run four years hence. What it did was hold up the convention for an hour and a half and provide the Granado forces with priceless television time.

Outside the hall, the Granado caravan had drawn up and the candidate was speaking—or *plain* speaking, as he'd have put it. He was pointing out that Sherman Taylor was a sham, a liar, just another politician in it for the chance to line his own pockets, that after all his support of Hazlitt and all his fine speeches and waving Old Glory, what did you have? Just another guy wanting to climb back on the gravy train. It was a terrible comment on America, Tony Granado proclaimed, when men like Hazlitt and Taylor would just cave in to that man in the White House when the going got tough. Why, Jesus Christ, they'd had Charlie Bonner on the run, they'd piled up charges against him like no other president had ever had to face. He wasn't any more fit to represent the Democratic Party than . . . than . . . and he wasn't half the man Tony Granado was. . . . The TV cameras were eating it up.

Driskill wore all the credentials of the Bonner campaign in the hall that night. He came in the back way with the campaign, back on the team, smiling for all to see. In the holding room behind the stage they were all there. Ellen Thorn and Linda Bonner were whispering to one another in the corner; Mac was using his cellular phone, checking with delegate counters stationed around the floor. Ellery Larkspur was huddled with the President, who was sitting in a makeup chair having some antisweat goop patted onto his face. Larkspur was talking swiftly, determinedly into his ear, his face a mask of concentration. Ellen Thorn left Linda and joined Mac, working the cellulars. Assistants stood at the ready charting the votes, the ever changing totals.

Oliver Landesmann saw Driskill and came over, wearing one of his sour grins. "All is madness," he said. "How can they keep track of anything?"

Driskill said, "It gives them something to do. How does it stand?"

"Ellen tells me the undecideds are just huge. All these Hazlitt people—poor devils are just in shock. I hear the President has got an idea about taking advantage of the confusion and making 'em vote on the nomination to-night."

"I'm not sure that's a good idea. It could take a hundred ballots."

Landesmann and those like him, in the campaign but not at its absolute heart, knew nothing of Bohannon's presence or what it could mean. But the President's head of security had fanned sixty special agents out into the crowd looking for him, watching for him, though the description they had could not really be relied on. Ben supposed there was little else he could do, and the fact was the hall was overflowing with men who could be Bohannon.

Driskill walked out to the floor, stood at the edge of the immense stage, staring out into the crowd with the spotlights playing across the thousands of faces and banners and milling delegates. There were hundreds of Marines in uniform acting as a kind of phalanx for Taylor. If Bohannon was still in uniform . . . Oh, Christ, there was no point in speculating.

On the gigantic screen above the stage a movie about what was happening in Mexico had begun. It was narrated by Linda Bonner and dealt in humanitarian terms with the agony. While it filled television screens across the nation and throughout the convention center, the delegates and press and onlookers paid it no attention whatever. The floor of the convention seemed to writhe and move as if it were alive. The deal making was in full cry, but no one knew quite what deal to make. Bonner operatives moved through the crush making sure that everybody understood that there was only one real representative of the party now, that Granado was an upstart without qualifications, Hazlitt was only a memory, and Sherman Taylor was a Republican in Democrat's clothing, and besides they'd heard from reliable sources that he was trying to talk Bonner into giving him the second spot on the ticket. The problem they were running into was widespread. Delegations committed to favorite sons, wanting to wait it out and see what happened, were more firmly lodged in cement than ever.

The movie about Mexico was too heart-wrenching for many of the TV directors, who switched to live coverage of their correspondents interviewing people on the floor.

Late editions of the real newspapers were arriving on the convention floor. The *Chicago Tribune* bannered *Taylor Says "It's a Lie!"* The *Sun-Times* replied with *What Did Bonner Have on Hazlitt?!* In every conversational knot of delegates the subject was the same—what could you believe? Did anybody know the truth?

Driskill made his way to the Iowa delegation and found Nick Wardell displaying a Bonner pin of modest proportions in the lapel buttonhole of his seersucker jacket. Sweat streamed down his sunburned forehead. "Ben, for God's sake, we've got a lot of Hazlitt people here, they're mourning. Jesus, what are we supposed to tell these people? Is that letter the real thing, scout's honor?"

"On my mother's grave, Nick, it is exactly what it purports to be. Bob Hazlitt was getting out of this race and throwing his support to the President. He told me so to my face."

"Hey, folks, listen up!" Wardell was gathering the Iowa delegation to himself. "Now I know that many of you had very strong feelings for Bob Hazlitt. And you had good reason to hold them. I can't think of another man who did as much for our state. But . . . but . . . I'd like to introduce you to Ben Driskill, who spent much of this past weekend with Bob Hazlitt. You even went to his mother's hundredth birthday party, didn't you, Ben? And you had a long, long conversation with him . . . and you came to Iowa wondering if there wasn't some common ground you could discover between the President and Mr. Hazlitt, ain't that right, Ben? And you told him that the President was not wedded to some of the ideas that Bob found so troubling—right?" Driskill nodded, glad that Wardell was the one trying to make himself heard over the continuing roar all around them. He wasn't entirely sure how far he should go with lying outright before the delegates.

"Well, the President wanted to make it clear to Mr. Hazlitt that he never intended the United States to face a frequently hostile world with a weakened intelligence capability. Different, yes, but not weak. Mr. Hazlitt surely agreed with him on that. It put to rest his greatest fear about the President's reelection. And he absolutely agreed that in the end, a campaign against a sitting president could be disastrous for the party."

Nick was nodding and squeezing his arm. "Thanks, Ben, I know you want to speak to other delegations, thanks a million," and he moved away, telling the Iowa delegation that it was time to count noses yet again.

The film about Mexico's horror had run its course, and somewhere a band was playing "Happy Days Are Here Again." The Red Cross and Chicago Health Office began to appear here and there, battling their ways through the nearly impenetrable crowds, trying to get to those who were fainting and collapsing and dehydrating and vomiting from overindulging, and the rumbling continued, coming up through the soles of your shoes and he began to wonder, yes, it had to be the motors straining to run the generators and the air-conditioning units and, yes, there was more, feet beginning to stamp rhythmically on the floor of the convention center, and he thought they were impatient for the air-conditioning to come back on . . . and then the chanting began to register. . . .

WE WANT TAYLOR WE WANT TAYLOR WE WANT TAYLORWEWANTTAYLORWEWANTTAYLORWE WANTTAYLORWEWANTTAYLOR . . .

And it occurred to Driskill that just possibly these delegates didn't want Charlie Bonner after all, they wanted a change, and if it couldn't be Bob Hazlitt it might just as well be Sherm Taylor.

STOCK SCAMMER . . . STOCK SCAMMER . . . STOCK SCAMMER . . . HE'LL NEVER BEAT TAYLOR AGAIN . . . CAN'T BEAT TAYLOR . . .

He'd heard about things like this happening at conventions, a deadlock blown apart by a sudden freakish surge by the supporters of a single candidate, like a virus getting loose in the crowd, the uncommitteds get a whiff of it . . . and they had to follow, they didn't quite know why, they just knew they had to follow . . . WE WANT TAYLOR! WE WANT TAYLOR! WE WANT TAYLOR!

Tom Bohannon stood in the mobile home with his back to the crowd trying to move in on Taylor. There were lots of uniformed Marines to hold them at bay. The general led the way into the back room of the trailer home and indicated a bottle of bourbon. "Have a drink, Tommy. Generators are blowing out everywhere—just too damn hot in old Chicago."

"I reckon we've seen worse, General."

"Well, you can say that again." He put his hand on Bohannon's shoulder and looked him in the eyes. "You've been there when the going got tough. You've earned a vacation."

"What's next for me? I'm not done yet, am I?" He'd heard it before. He didn't like it.

"You've earned a rest, Tommy. Win or lose, I think you've earned a nice retirement. You want to go to Florida? Or back to France? You've earned a long rest, Tommy."

"You wouldn't put me out to pasture yet, would you, General?"

"That pasture's pretty nice, the villa on the Riviera. Course if you prefer, there's a lodge in the Sierra Nevadas—it's yours if you want it."

"That's generous of you, General."

"Couldn't have done this without you. Tarlow, Summerhays—Jesus, it must have been crazy on Shelter Island that night, in that storm. You're the best, Tommy, that's what it comes down to."

"And now you figure I'm done."

"Well, you know . . . that problem with Driskill on the stairs—the thing is, I don't want something to *happen* to you, I don't want someone to *kill* you . . . that's not how it should end. You've done great and terrible things for your country and for me, Tommy, you deserve a real life now."

"Sad thing is, I've only really known the one life, General."

"You were the best, Tommy."

Tom Bohannon could see that the conversation was beginning to make the general uncomfortable. He read it in his eyes and he read it in his body language.

"Well, General, I think I'd better get out there and make sure our people are tending to business. The idea is you want the mass of them to charge toward the stage when you and the President are there together, you want them shouting 'We want Taylor, We want Taylor'—like that?"

"Exactly."

"Well, General, I won't see you until after the festivities tonight . . . let's hope everything goes right."

"It's gonna be a wonderful night, Tommy. Everything we've worked for."

"What if you don't win the nomination, General? I was just wondering . . ."

"The way I see it, I'm positioned exactly right to take the second spot on the ticket and he'll sure as hell have to offer it to me when he sees my strength among the delegates—he'll have to offer it and I'll take it, and . . . let's just say I won't be the traditional VP." He laughed. The steely eyes, the etching of the lines around his mouth. "I'll be inside the administration and I've got ways, I've got people . . . I'll be President before the term is up, one way or another. I was a good teacher, wasn't I, Tommy?" He threw his arms around the killer he'd created and held him tight.

"Semper Fi, Tommy. Always faithful, Tommy."

"Semper Fi, General."

And then Tom Bohannon turned and headed back out into the crowd, ready to face his destiny and do what he'd been trained to do. He had learned what he came for. He knew what had to be done.

Chapter 23

The fervor of the crowd backing Sherman Taylor had begun to send out shock waves during the Hazlitt film. It was impossible to gauge their numbers, but the visceral nature of their demonstration stemmed from the Marines who clung together, a mighty surge of loyalty to the general. The pounding, the stomping, the chanting—it grew and grew, as if it were alive, determined to take over the convention.

Driskill was pushing his way through the hot, sweating bodies to the area behind the stage, hoping to get to the President's holding room. It was nerves: He wanted to see the familiar faces, he wanted to see that Charlie was all right. There was something so unsettling about the crowd, about the countless Marines somehow forcing their will on the convention. Something was going to happen, but what? The rumors that the entire convention was being compressed, that party officials had discussed the issue with both Bonner and Taylor, the rumors were everywhere. But everyone he'd spoken to personally said no, it could never happen, there was too much to do. But what if Charlie wanted to roll the dice now?

He was being pushed along by the crowd, and when he came to rest he was outside Sherman Taylor's trailer, which had been pulled inside the center, about thirty yards from the back entrances to the stage itself.

Tom Bohannon came out the door to the trailer, stood,

and stared up at the huge television monitor where the Hazlitt movie was driving toward its climax. Clips of film showing Flying Bob as a young businessman representing the chamber of commerce, shaking hands with some former president, Bob during the building of the twin towers in Iowa, Bob on a trip to meet the Russian president, Bob with his mother riding in an Iowa parade . . . Bohannon stood transfixed, watching, didn't seem to hear Driskill calling his name, then slowly turned and melted into the crowd before Driskill could make any headway toward reaching him. He was gone.

Workmen were shoving past wheeling a huge display into place at the foot of the ramp leading up to the stage where the movie was still heading toward its climax. It looked like some kind of flag that didn't make any sense to Driskill, who caught the eye of the security chief guarding the door to the trailer and nodded. On impulse, Bohannon in his mind, he said, "I'm coming from the President, Jack. Urgent."

Jack Barlow, the Secret Service man seconded to Taylor, opened the door, spoke with someone on the inside, and waved Driskill up the little stairway and inside. A senior aide pointed to the far end of the trailer and went back to speaking to his deputies. Driskill found the general buttoning up the full-dress uniform coat, watching himself in the mirror. "Come on in, Mr. Driskill, take a load off. Crazy out there, isn't it?"

"Crazy's the word, General."

"Well, get to it, Ben. What do you want now?"

"We hear you're going to accept the number two spot. If it's offered."

"I've thought about it. But . . . this crowd." He smiled at himself in the mirror. "They might not stand for Sherm Taylor settling for second place." He cocked his head, listening. "Hear that? Sounds to me like they're out for some red meat . . . and the veep is not red meat. I can't ignore the people, Ben. We'll just have to see. I've got a feel for people, a feel for the men, I've always had it . . . I'll know when I get out there." He picked up the Medal of Honor from its velvet-lined case. "Did you ever see one of these things up close?" He held it out to Driskill. "Go ahead, take it."

Driskill looked at the medal nestling in his hand. The Congressional Medal of Honor. It was the general's talisman, the enduring proof of the sacrifices he'd made for his country.

The general said, "I wonder if any man becoming president has had one of these. . . . I'll have to check." He took the medal back from Driskill's hand.

"Why don't we just cut the bullshit, too, General. Listen carefully. We know everything about Earth Shaker. We know what you sanctioned. You were running Hazlitt—"

"What the hell are you talking about? Earth Shaker?"

"You're just wasting time—we know all about Tom Bohannon. We've got him tied to you with bands of steel. You know it and I know it. In fact, he just left here—"

"Y'know, Driskill, it would give me so much goddam pleasure to just run your ass. You have no idea of your place in things, no idea of just what an insignificant piece of shit you are—God, I feel better just saying that." He smiled at the thought. "Earth Shaker," he said scornfully. "Tom who? . . . Jesus, Tommy Bohannon . . . where did that name come from?"

"Oh, you know where it came from. You never can quite clean everything away, General. You know where it came from . . . and you know damn well we're not bluffing."

"I knew a man named Tom Bohannon a long time ago. He was a hero. He's been dead for years. I heard he got it in Beirut back when it got real bad there. Or somewhere in Africa. Brave man. More guts than brains, as they say. Believe me, what Tommy Bohannon has to do with me, is just egg on your tie. Nothing. You're just talking to hear yourself, that's all it is."

"Yeah, well, he was at Bob Hazlitt's birthday party for his mother and Hazlitt addressed him by name."

"Maybe Bob Hazlitt was mistaken. Maybe he got it wrong—or you did. How should I know?"

"Sure. He also tried to kill me the other night."

Sherman Taylor stared back into the mirror at himself, then slowly, carefully raised the Medal of Honor over his head and lowered it until it settled around his neck. He adjusted the medal in the mirror, centering it.

The general laughed. "As I remember the lieutenant, if he'd tried to kill you . . . you'd be dead. Good-bye, Ben."

"Listen to me, you son of a bitch!"

"No, you listen to me, Driskill. I'm tired of you. Go away. And I'm going to tell you something. If there is such a thing as Earth Shaker, I'll shove it down your throat and yank LVCO out of Charlie's asshole . . . because I'm going to tell you a little secret. If there is an Earth Shaker, the boys at LVCO, not Heartland, built it, and your boy is up to his neck in LVCO—the same boys Charlie Bonner's in bed with."

"That's your version, General."

Taylor turned back to the mirror, enjoying the view. "You try and prove I'm wrong by tomorrow, Driskill. And good luck to you. Now get out of here. It's over for your boy."

"You poor bastard," Driskill said.

"And why's that?"

"At your age, you should know . . . *it's never over.*"

The film ended with one of those shots of Hazlitt walking away across an Iowa field, heading into the sunset alone, a visionary, with Aaron Copland trumpets playing for this uncommon man, and Sherman Taylor's voice almost cracking on the soundtrack as he said, "I find it hard to believe . . . we shall never look . . . upon his kind again." Then the music morphed into "America the Beautiful" and was overwhelmed by tumultuous applause ricocheting around the gigantic enclosure, cheering for the memory of Bob Hazlitt and chanting for the coming of Sherman Taylor. Finally, the crowd quieted for the minister of the largest Protestant congregation in Chicago, a black guy with a lot of matinee idol in him, and he asked for a moment of silent prayer for the fallen leader, then launched into a spoken prayer of his own for the souls of our departed leaders. His resonant voice filled the center, holding the raucous delegates silent and at attention.

When he was finished and the lights on the podium went up again, the item Driskill had seen being wheeled up the ramp had come center stage and seemed to be exploding. It was like an enormous Fourth of July entertainment, a huge flag of the United States with Bob Hazlitt's face at its center and around it, the burning and popping of small explosions, brilliant colors, smoke drifting away. Somebody had decided that Bob's official send-off shouldn't end with a minister but with a series of moderate bangs that left people staring with their mouths open at the garishness of it. The colors weren't fading, kept exploding as Bob's white scarf seemed to be floating out behind him. The shouting and hooting and applause drowned out everything else.

Driskill could barely move in the crush of people, staring up at the podium some twenty feet above the crowd with the great slabs of bulletproof glass protecting the speaker from whatever overly excited homicidal maniac might have gained entrance to the big party. The laser-projection unit was hidden beneath the stage but projected the speaker's speech onto the slabs as well as onto the screen built into the podium directly before him.

Painstakingly he made his way through one delegation after another, his eyes roving across the crowds, concentrating on the clusters of Marines. The Iowa delegation, the Indiana delegation, Kansas, Kentucky, Illinois . . . And then, there he was again, suddenly in front of him, in full uniform, looking more than ever like the Marine poster boy. His face was pinkish with health, no disguises, an expression of confidence and youth spread across it. He seemed to be leading a cadre of Marines who surrounded Sherman Taylor as he prepared to march to the stage. Then he was slipping back into the crowd. Taylor's procession was slowly moving past him, toward the exploding flag. . . .

Bohannon.

Driskill was trapped, couldn't reach him with any speed, tracked him as best he could as Bohannon moved like a phantom among the Marines, and if there was one man in the hall who might murder the President of the United States it was this man, the true believer, the man who knew he was right, and Driskill had to keep him in sight.

Driskill pushed his way past a knot of delegates, keeping him in his sights, and suddenly Bohannon turned as if he'd been warned and scanned the crowd behind him, his gaze passing over Driskill, who ducked his head, looked down, and when he looked back up, Bohannon was looking right at him; Ben saw the luminescent eyes, felt the steely madness of them, was sure Bohannon had made him right then and there, but then Bohannon's gaze swept on across the crowd. The eyes . . . his eyes had been watering, Driskill remembered that, the eyes bothering him out in Iowa— he'd had the contact lenses in, and they must have been bothering him. Now he'd taken the contacts out and it was almost as if Bohannon just didn't give a good goddam anymore . . . here I am . . . come and get me.

Bohannon was moving through the crowd, his uniform blending with all the others, moving like irresistible fate. The lights were still very low in the hall, red and white and blue spotlights sweeping rhythmically across the scene. Driskill was having a hell of a time keeping him in view, trying to close the distance between them. Jesus, which Marine was he, there he was, but Driskill couldn't seem to close the gap; Bohannon kept surging closer to the stage, and then something was going on up there on the stage, the delegations had broken out of their areas, at least some of them had, and they were pushing forward, mingling with the Marines, and then an enormous cheer exploded somewhere behind them and cascaded down across them. The President of the United States had slipped onto the stage without an introduction, waving to the crowd, smiling the huge smile with the gleaming teeth in the tanned face, running his hand back through his blond-streaked hair, perfect in his navy-blue suit, somehow so much more accessible than a president normally was. Now he was just another celebrant at the big Democratic Party convention, almost one of them, one of the folks in the crowd. Almost.

Driskill felt the enormous hold he had on them, a fact, a truth that was so easy to forget in the rough and tumble of others trying to take his job away from him. He waved conspiratorily, winked at the crowd, smiling as if he'd just invited everybody over for an evening in the family room. The band struck up "In the Cool, Cool, Cool of the Evening" and the crowd was swaying and singing the words . . . "*tell 'em I'll be there.* . . ." And there was a kind of rock star recognition of their guy, his charisma reached out and stroked them, and after several minutes he slowly let his smile fade and raised both hands to quiet the cheering.

Bohannon was still pressing forward and Driskill had gained a bit, trying to get close enough, not sure what he was going to do when he reached him but he'd do something, anything, when suddenly he began to make his move, and the President had begun to speak and Driskill knew time was running out, any moment now. It would be Bohannon's last kill and he wanted to make sure. . . .

"You know, I'm not supposed to be here tonight—" Bonner was interrupted by thunderous applause. "But— this is a special moment for me, and don't worry—the rumors you've been hearing are true, we've made some changes in the convention schedule. We're going to get to the nominating speeches tonight and the balloting, however long it takes . . . and tomorrow your nominee will come to this hall and address you . . . but I just had to come here tonight to pay my respects to a fine American taken from us far too soon, a worthy adversary, a man I could always respect for his forward thinking and his willingness to break new ground, take risks, make the big decisions." He was disarming the Hazlitt loyalists, drowning them in sincerity and fellow feeling. Driskill thought: He is sooooooo good.

"You've all heard by now that Bob Hazlitt and I—out of our love for this great country and this great party of ours—buried the hatchet over the past weekend. He was never more alive than when I spoke with him by telephone—he'd enjoyed his talks with Benjamin Driskill representing me and he informed me that he was looking forward to working with me during the coming months as we prepared for my second term. We discussed the possibility of his joining me on the ticket while that great American David Mander would become our ambassador to the United Nations. We planned to explore that idea further this week . . . and then we lost him, destiny claimed him."

The crowd of Marines and Taylor supporters was growing restless, had begun to chant and stomp their feet for Taylor. The President put his palms up to calm them. "Now you may also have heard that General Taylor has approached us about taking Bob Hazlitt's place on the Democratic ticket, to bring us all together. . . ."

Driskill was amazed at the extent to which Charlie had grasped the power of the simple lie, the creation of confusion, the power of uncertainty in the minds of listeners. The crowd had begun breaking apart, Taylor supporters waving and shouting and Bonner's chanting *"Bonner more than ever, Bonner more than ever,"* and a band somewhere playing "Happy Days Are Here Again." Somewhere up ahead of him a punch was thrown and a scuffle broke out and security officers were swarming as best they could into the thickness of the crowd.

The President was undeterred. "I know you've all been wanting to hear from General Taylor . . ." People were screaming, shouting, applauding, shaking their fists in the air. Driskill hoped to God the President knew what he was doing. ". . . and in the name of party unity, on this unprecedented night in American political history, I want to personally welcome him as a new member of our great Democratic Party, I want to give you the opportunity to hear him for yourselves. So, now joining me before you, I give you the former president . . . General Sherman Taylor!!"

The cheering and yelling and the music swept like a tidal wave toward the stage, and the fight on the floor was turning into a brawl in the Ohio delegation as the President looked toward the wings. The music was ever louder, half a dozen bands playing from different places on the floor. This was a sudden explosion, the triumph of total chaos, the swelling music that had no discernible tune, the spotlights in the catwalks spinning without any idea of where they should be pointing, the animal throbbing of the struggling air-conditioning units and the lights dimming, the gigantic speakers bellowing sound one moment and fading the next, hundreds of correspondents with their microphones stumbling and pushing and trying to get to the fight or to somebody who could comment on the fight, everybody jockeying for position to see the huge monitors hanging on the walls all around the convention floor, the gigantic Diamondvision screen above the stage showing close-ups where somebody's nose was as big as a Cadillac and you couldn't hear any of the sound that went with the pictures and suddenly something, a truncheon, a fist, a forearm, fell across the Cadillac-sized nose and blood gushed out as if it were going to spurt from the screen and soak the crowd, and up on the stage the President was looking anxiously into the wings and then in a spotlight that miraculously found him there was the general in a dark blue suit with a white shirt and a plain burgundy necktie, with the Congressional Medal of Honor on its wide baby-blue ribbon hung around his neck, standing with his arms outstretched as if to embrace them all, looking out at the crowd, smiling in a formal, solid, imperial, fatherly way, and the roar of the crowd somehow managed to increase and the fight going on in Ohio had managed now to slop over into Nevada and Oklahoma and Driskill, looking up at the Diamondvision, thought maybe five hundred people might be involved, enough for a significant bloodletting but only a small number in so huge a crowd on the floor.

Driskill's eyes were still on Bohannon's back, then on his face as he turned around to survey the crowd. He had continued working his way toward the stage through the packed thousands where no sergeants at arms could possibly do anything to control the crowd. Driskill saw the eyes again as a light swept past Bohannon's head, saw him blink for a moment and shield his eyes, and then Driskill felt the eyes squarely on him and there was no doubt that Bohannon had seen him, now knew that Driskill was following him, and he plunged onward into the crowd down close to the stage—Alabama, Connecticut, and Colorado.

Up on the stage as the ovation continued Sherman Taylor finally broke the pose and snapped a salute, mouthing the words *"I salute you all,"* which nobody could actually hear, and a band somewhere broke into the "Marine Hymn" and a few bars were heard before some other band somewhere else burst in with something else and the burned-out fireworks flag was being removed and the President was holding his hand out, whether presenting the general or attempting to shake hands it was impossible to tell, and near the stage some huge banners were suddenly unfurled, *Bonner and Taylor, A Ticket for the Future* with their faces in profile staring toward one another. Then Taylor was advancing on Bonner, shaking his hand without a smile in sight, and for just a second Driskill had fixed his gaze on the stage and couldn't find Bohannon when he looked back and his heart skipped several beats. He rammed his shoulder through a knot of delegates, yanking others out of the way with his huge hands, and there was Bohannon ahead of him, standing in a group of Marines, maybe thirty of them, part of Taylor's key security guard, Bohannon looking back over his shoulder—he knew he was being followed but he wasn't sure why. Driskill saw the unholy eyes slide across him, searching the crowd, my God . . .

Bohannon was looking for someone else!

Someone else was following *him,* but who? Who knew he was there? He was the general's creature. Now the general had pulled away from President Bonner and had a microphone in his hand and he was waiting for some kind of break in the cascading river of sound to allow him to speak and finally it came, the lights dimmed a bit further and there was a convergence of spotlights on him, and he was speaking.

"It's true that I come here tonight to honor the memory

of my great friend and inspiration Bob Hazlitt." Thunderous applause like an avalanche on a mountainside. The Marines up ahead were applauding, shouting, and Bohannon's head remained stock-still. "But I am also here to set the record straight. I am here tonight . . . to ask for . . . your support . . . as I seek the office of . . ." The sound level had decreased to a point where you could almost hear yourself think, and the general's voice came out strongly through the dozens of speakers; the news anchors in their elaborate booths, which dangled from the mighty I-beams in the suspension of the roof, leaned forward; the engineers cranked the power on their headphones and hoped to God it was going out along the network satellite feed and the cables.

Then Driskill saw a flurry of movement in the semilit darkness ahead of him—only ten people between him and Bohannon now. It was impossible to see what was going on. Bohannon lunged forward with something in his hand as he reached upward toward the two men. Driskill's eyes flickered back upward to the stage and there, as if he were a puppet, the general had stiffened up and was then falling backwards, great gobs of blood spouting forth from the hole in his lower throat where the Medal of Honor had been, blood pouring out and spattering the bulletproof angled slabs of glass that had failed to save Sherman Taylor, and then there was a concentrated intake of breath that sounded so loud in the enclosed hall you'd have thought it would have sucked the stage and all the people thereon down the collective gullet, and as Taylor went down the President leaped forward to catch him and there, kneeling on the floor of the stage, with the blood-soaked body of Sherman Taylor in his arms, he looked out into the vast howling crowd with an expression of such anguish that the whole world saw what came to be called ever after the single greatest historical photograph in the history of the United States of America. . . .

One president drenched in blood and dying, in the arms of another.

Driskill never knew how many seconds he lost looking at the tableau on the stage, straining to make sure that Charlie, who was sprayed with blood, was all right. The cops and security people were dashing out from the wings and Mac and Oliver Landesmann came across the stage and went to bend down to help President Bonner. Landesmann slipped in the blood, went to his knees, and Driskill looked back and Bohannon was gone and then in the crush, no one knowing just where the bullet had come from in the darkness and the density of the crowd, a Marine was facing Driskill, his eyes staring, and then his shoulder rammed into Driskill's chest and an arm swung up pushing Driskill out of the way and in the hand was a bloody knife, a slightly undersized bowie knife, and then the man was gone and Driskill was falling back over the chairs of various delegates, taking the delegates with him in a screaming pile, and he saw the Marine with the knife swallowed by a mob of enraged delegates, saw the knife clatter to the floor and skitter along beneath stumbling delegates, saw the Marine's fists flailing in the crowd, saw him dragged down again, and Driskill couldn't figure out what the hell was going on. Taylor hadn't been killed with a goddam knife, he'd been shot and the shot had come from among the Marines. And then he saw hurtling through the crowd four Marines, Bohannon white-faced and dazed, yelling and pointing up one of the aisles, telling them the killer had just run up the aisle. People were screaming and pointing, and the three other Marines went pushing and pulling in the direction Bohannon was pointing and Driskill knew something had gone wrong, Bohannon had killed the general all right, and as he tried to get up Bohannon was on him, pushing him back onto the floor, crying, *"Stay down, stay down, he's got a gun,"* and everybody hit the deck again and Driskill reached for his leg and got kicked in the face for his efforts. Then Bohannon was off into the crowd and Driskill was struggling to his feet, swearing, going after him. . . .

The crowd was so vast, so individual, so confused and terrified and grief-stricken and simply shocked, that security was an illusion. The aisles were clogged, the TV cameras were everywhere, the lights were playing across the mayhem on the floor, the monitors and the Diamondvision were deluged with images of the nightmare that were simultaneously flooding outwards across the nation and the world. . . .

The President was helped to his feet, the body of Sherman Taylor stretched out on his back, eyes staring up into nothing, arms thrown out to the side as if he'd been crucified, a pose that Alec Fairweather and his cameramen would love, and the President was at the microphone, his face and shirt covered in blood, and he was calling to the people to be calm, to remain in the hall, *Please, I beg of you, remain where you are, the doctors must be able to get through to General Taylor,* as if that was going to resurrect the bastard, and Driskill was plunging into the maelstrom in the direction Bohannon had gone and when he'd reached the outer corridor of the center and stood alone, watching humanity pour back inside, then he saw Bohannon, outside the building, standing all alone in the trucked-in sand, leaning against one of the palm trees so far from home, gasping for air, vomit dripping from his mouth, his hands on his knees, his head shaking from side to side.

Driskill stood in the shadow of the towering statue of Ernie Banks with his bat in the air, ready to hit one all the way across Lake Michigan, ready to play two and hit one to Indiana, and the sound behind him was fading away and sirens were screaming from police cars speeding across the parking lot, taking the fire lanes. But the sirens were far away, too, everything was far away, *reality* was far away, and somewhere back in the cavernous building a former president was dead or clinging to life by a thread and Charlie Bonner, who didn't duck for cover, Charlie Bonner, who moved forward into the line of fire to keep his enemy from falling to the floor, Charlie Bonner, who caught him and held him and knelt beside him when he fell, Charlie Bonner was living out the opportunity to perform a heroic act, and he was doing it as well as a man could and he was ensuring his place in the hearts of his countrymen and the history books. . . . And out here Ben Driskill seemed to be the only one who knew that the assassin was standing under a palm tree throwing up. The cops and the guards didn't get it at all, they had no idea, they didn't even see the guy puking over by the palm trees, and Driskill wondered what the hell had happened to the other Marine, the one with the bloody knife in his hand, but he pretty well thought he knew, he didn't understand but he knew, he knew what that guy had been doing in the hall, he was beginning—in some very labyrinthine way—beginning to figure it out and it was just the way it had been in his old days, with the Church, with all the plotting and screwing around with people's minds, the secrets and the passing of power and the hoarding of power. It was all the same damn thing, this was the same damn thing, and he began to walk toward Tom Bohannon, but in his mind he was seeing other people, he was seeing other places—Charlie in Vermont, demanding that he produce Rachel Patton who was soon to die; he saw Drew Summerhays, lying dead in his greenhouse while the storm raged in off the Atlantic; he saw Teresa Rowan warning him not to trust the President and Ellery Larkspur shaking his head and advising caution at all times and never turn your back; he saw the President in the shadows of the National Cathedral in the middle of the night telling him he needed him on the team; he saw Bob Hazlitt's ancient mother in the terrible heat and Bohannon standing with his hands clasped behind his back while the insects buzzed and the willows dipped toward the stream; he saw Bob Hazlitt's old P-38 disappearing, disintegrating in a puff of smoke with wings and tails falling off; he saw the bubbling red hole in Sherman Taylor's throat and the President not hiding but reaching out to catch him as he fell; he saw Elizabeth at last beckoning him back to her and he tried to pull himself back to the present, and he walked toward Tom Bohannon. . . . It all came down to this, he was trying to catch a man who had died long ago, trying to catch a ghost.

And as he approached he thought Bohannon waved to

him as he straightened up, leaning against the curving trunk of the palm tree, and he waved back tiredly. Then he saw that Tom Bohannon had a gun in his hand and was pointing it at him and it was wavering in his hand and then he fired it and some sand puffed up about ten feet away, but the sound of the gun caught the attention of the guards and cops back by the hall and Bohannon said, *"Sorry, didn't mean that, went off by accident,"* and Driskill nodded and said, *"Are you losing a lot of blood?"* and Bohannon said, *"What are you talking about?"* and Driskill said, *"No need to bullshit me, I saw the guy with the knife and it was all bloody,"* and Bohannon coughed, tried to laugh, and said:

"The guy the general sent to kill me?" He coughed. "A little fucking late, wasn't he? He always called me Warrior One. Never told me he had . . . Warrior Two waiting."

Driskill was standing close to him now and he could smell the blood.

"I feel like I'm a million miles away. I'm dying very slow, it's a . . . a . . . process. No pain. Like getting very tired."

"The general brought you back to work for him, isn't that right?"

"Ah, the old general . . . and then he actually sent this guy to . . . kill me and I didn't know it until it was too late . . . until I felt the shove of the knife going in . . . I thought I was the only one he trusted."

"The crowd got him," Driskill said.

"Serves him right, the bastard."

"I thought you were going to kill the President."

Bohannon coughed, looked over Driskill's shoulder, brought the gun up and didn't have the strength to hold it. His chest and belly and legs were soaked with blood. "I've killed so many people . . . well, if this is dying it's not so bad."

"But why did you turn on him? Why not just fade away? He'd have taken care of you."

"I got to thinking that it was about over, me and the general, I'd done what I could for him . . . and I knew what he had to do. I'd done it myself out in the field. With the general, once he used people up, then they became a luxury you couldn't afford . . . but then I realized he was going to do it to me, and I . . . it was a shock."

Slowly Bohannon looked out toward Lake Michigan and the boats with the bright lights tied up, the yachts of the mighty. He wasn't going to make it to the lights, to the water, he wasn't going to get away. "The general used to tell me when we were off doing some god-awful wet work of some kind, killing some hostages so they wouldn't talk, or rescuing some guys, or trying to go unnoticed in some hot buggy sandy place—he used to say to me, Bohannon, you're gonna die in a shootout somewhere and there won't be a soul left alive to mourn your passing and I said to him, you too, you bastard, and he said bullshit, I'll die a hero of the nation, you just watch . . . and he said, you'll be dead, you'll never know. . . . Well, he was right, I am alone with no mourners and he's a hero. I got him right in the old Medal of Honor . . . some shot, Driskill . . ."

"Why? Why did you have to shoot him?"

He gurgled softly, a bloody laugh. "It's a . . . Marine thing." The blood was thickening now, coming from his mouth.

There were lights shining on them now because the TV people had found them, and with all the new lenses Driskill knew they were shooting close-ups but they couldn't get any sound, Bohannon was just whispering as his strength went. His hand lay outstretched in the sand and the fingers no longer clutched the gun. Blood was pooling all around him where he sat, and Driskill knew there was no point in calling for medical help and at this point the warrior deserved to be carried out on his shield. All the people he'd killed for the ambition and drive and betterment of Sherman Taylor. "Who'd've thought it would all turn out like this—it was supposed to be the fucking White House. . . ."

He didn't say any more.

By the time the cops and the TV cameras reached them Driskill was leaning against the same tree with Tom Bohannon beside him. He was too tired to explain it all to them; he said he just came out to see who this guy was . . . and they got to talking and he thought, Jesus, he just shot Sherman Taylor.

While he waited for the cops and the TV people and the ambulance and the Secret Service and the inevitable hassle about who had jurisdiction, while he waited to get freed up to go back in and see how the President was doing, while he fought the nervous exhaustion that was whipping him, driving him into the sand like a tent peg, he heard a telephone ringing, and he looked around and thought, what the hell, and then he realized the ringing was coming from his jacket pocket. He was soaked with sweat and the warm evening rain that was slowly drifting down on them and his hand was shaking and slippery when he got the phone out of his pocket. "Hello?" He felt like a fool, given the circumstance. Maybe it was news about Elizabeth, they had his number . . .

But it was someone else.

And he listened.

Driskill

Former president General Sherman Taylor, thought to have died within seconds while cradled in the arms of President Charles Bonner, was still alive. As dawn broke he was still in surgery and on life-support systems, but he clung doggedly to life. He appeared to have been saved by the Medal of Honor that hung around his neck. The assassin's bullet glanced slightly upon striking the medal, thereby providing that fragile lifeline to which he held so stubbornly. People around the world who thought they'd seen everything with the Kennedy assassination now had to pause and reconsider.

A Marine who, according to government records, had died in Beirut or somewhere in Africa either ten or fifteen or seventeen years ago depending on which news source you were hearing, had apparently fired the one shot at General Taylor just as he was about to speak to the Democratic convention. The bullet had found the perfect seam between the slabs of protective glass. Not luck. Skill. The whole story of the would-be assassin was giving them a little trouble. The Marine's name appeared to be Tom Bohannon, who would have been forty-three or forty-six years old, if he hadn't already been dead. He was an orphan who came from either Florida or Oklahoma, according to records, or just possibly from the state of Washington. Tom Bohannon had been assigned to General Taylor's Special Forces unit on several occasions and had served with great distinction, surviving severe torture while a prisoner of terrorist regimes and, indeed, escaping after killing most of his captors. Little was known about his personal relationship with General Taylor beyond some letters of commendation the general had long ago written to help him get some decorations. But, of course, the man who murdered General Taylor couldn't have been Tom Bohannon since Tom Bohannon was long dead. And in any case, the assassin was now dead as well, whoever he was. The general feeling was that he was, in fact, Tom Bohannon, whose records had been scrubbed for some obscure government reason. But, then, maybe not.

Another Marine, identified as Floyd Marmot, had killed Taylor's assailant in an attempt to save the general—this was how the media and the government spokesmen analyzed the situation, which, admittedly, was highly conjectural—and had then been beaten and stomped to death by a swarm of delegates who presumably thought he was involved in the killing of General Taylor. It should also be mentioned that in the hall that night fully half of the people queried assumed that the attack had been on Bonner and that Taylor had been killed by mistake.

The *Sun-Times* said it all that morning.

TAYLOR ATTACKED—BONNER THE LONE SURVIVOR!!

What exactly the general had been intending to say was lost to history. There were two immediate schools of thought on that score, those who believed he was intending to impress on the convention that he was indeed running for the *presidential* nomination, replacing his own candidate Bob Hazlitt, and those who felt just as strongly that he was accepting President Bonner's invitation to take second place on the ticket.

The *Chicago Tribune,* under the photograph of the President cradling the wounded general that was used in virtually every paper in the world that day, declared: IT'S BONNER . . . BY DEFAULT!

It looked as if the convention were headed now for a single nomination for the office of the presidency and a vote by acclamation, and Charles Bonner would be ready to fight for a second term. He would address the nation either that night or the next.

I took a shower and read the newspapers sitting in front of my air conditioner and then I called my old friend Ellery Dunstan Larkspur.

He answered by saying, "Oh, who could it be now?"

"It's me, Larkie. Can I come up and see you?"

He paused. "Anything special, Benjamin?"

"Pretty special."

"All right, then. Of course. Come now."

Larkspur, befitting his seniority and closeness to the President, was quartered on the presidential floor. When I knocked, one of his secretaries who was just leaving opened the door. "Hi, Ben," he said softly. "Did you ever see such a night? I watched you on TV out there under that palm tree . . . it was positively surreal."

"Positively," I said. "How's Larkie coping?"

"Let's just say he has great reserves of acceptance and resilience. He's much the same as if last night had gone by without incident. He's really incredible."

"Or possibly nuts," I said.

"I forgot that possibility." Grinning, the secretary slipped past me into the hallway.

I went into the spacious suite with all of its glass looking west to the lake and south toward the Ernie Banks International Convention Center and the towers of the Chicago Loop. The heavy white drapes had been pulled back and all the windows rolled open and a wonderful breeze blew through the two rooms. The Marlowe fountain was gushing far below and there was a kind of afterimage of the night and morning's mist hanging in the sky. The clouds looked thick enough, creamy enough, to cut with a knife. Sailboats slid along the surface of the lake. I stood in the open window leading onto his deck. A palm tree hung gently over the white table, the great leaves moving in the breeze.

Larkspur was wearing a pristine, cream-colored robe of incredibly soft terry. There was a navy-blue crest on the breast pocket. It was knotted at his waist. Bare feet beneath and another cream towel around his neck. His hair was freshly barbered, combed back close to his skull. He wore dark glasses, the big black-framed kind that Mastroianni wore decades ago in *La Dolce Vita*. Some things just never went out of style. The white table was covered with newspapers, including the flown-in *Washington Post* and the *New York Times* city edition. There were covered silver serving dishes, a cart of used plates and goblets.

"Benjamin. Sit. You look more than a little wrung out from your exertions of last night. Eat. You name it, it's on this table or that serving cart. I felt in an expansive mood when ordering. When the bottom falls out of the world you know, the best thing to do is make certain of your own existence. Prove to yourself that you're still alive, that you're among the survivors."

"Well, Larkie, I don't know quite how to say this. I don't quite know what I'm going to do. . . ."

"Come, come, Benjamin. No need to be shy with your Larkie. We push on. We heal the American people, we build a great second term for Charles Bonner—and we do our best to keep the past from growing sick and diseased and infecting the present. We are political men."

"I know it was you. *All you.*"

Larkspur leaned forward and carefully poured me a cup of coffee and warmed his own. He pushed the cream and sugar and sweetener toward me. He smiled like a professor dealing with a good student who worries too damn much about ephemera. "I'm afraid you'll have to be a little clearer than that. What was *all me*?"

"When Rachel Patton told me about the back channel operating in the White House she held out two names—the man of mirrors and the man in the White House. I figured out that Sarrabian was the man of mirrors, no great credit to me . . . but you may remember I came up empty, we all racked our brains over it, we couldn't figure out who was in the White House working to set up the President, didn't even know if he existed. I finally decided it was a figment of her imagination—and then someone called me just last night . . . with the name of the man in the White House. The name was Larkspur."

"Aha, I see, I see . . . and you believe this someone, is that what's troubling you?"

"Yes, I believe him, Larkie. He's got proof. Tapes . . ."

"Well, I'll be damned, Benjamin—what an amazing fellow he is!" He sipped his coffee and looked from me to the view out over the city. You could feel the heat now, riding on the breeze. It was going to be murder as the day went on. The newspapers flicked in the wind. "Tell me, did he know about my relationship with General Taylor? Did that come into it at all?"

I didn't answer. It was time to listen.

Larkspur said softly, "Must be Tony Sarrabian, of course. Trying to cover his behind. Can't say I blame him."

"I pretty much figured it out by myself. Building on a hint here, a hint there. If you were behind the back channel, then it stands to reason that you were involved in all the efforts to bring Charlie down. I don't know how. I sure as hell can't imagine why . . . but you were there. I used to think you were a lot like Drew Summerhays, but now I think that you were, rather, the exact opposite."

"Well, Benjamin, you're a pretty cool customer, sitting here and saying all this to my face—I applaud you. But what if I have a few of my hired thugs run in and pitch you over the balcony railing?" He was grinning at me. The signet ring on the little finger of his right hand caught the sunlight and shone like buried treasure.

"Not your style, Larkie. I'm surprised you haven't thought of the big question—why don't I just pick *you* up and throw *you* over the edge? OLD INSIDER LEAPS TO DEATH—BETRAYED PRESIDENT BONNER. Really, Larkie, I could do it . . . I'd avenge everybody, starting with Hayes Tarlow and Drew Summerhays and Rachel Patton. . . ."

"Oh, they'd still be dead." He was buttering a bit of toast plucked from a silver toast rack. "Sometimes I think we're all just playing our roles in a drama that was written a long time ago. Sometimes I think that maybe we don't have free will after all. But, I'm not a philosopher, am I? It's just a stray thought—it all seems ordained to happen the way it does. Maybe there was never a way to avoid it." He smiled to himself. "Sherman Taylor never got over his loss to Charlie, you know. He believed in America, he believed he knew what America should be, and he believed that Charlie was taking it in the wrong direction, that all the work that he had done with Bob Hazlitt and others to build up America's defenses privately and ensure her supremacy would be revealed. It all began with that bloody speech Charlie wouldn't let anybody see beforehand—that set everything in play, don't you see? He brought it on himself, didn't he? All that talk about making the budgets public . . . Taylor saw in that the seeds of destruction. All he believed in would be destroyed totally. And he wouldn't let that happen. So he came to me. The next day, Benjamin. *The next day* . . . We'd known each other in the old days when he was up to his neck in the blackest jobs I've ever heard of. He had a nugget, an idea that *could* become a plan . . . he needed me to create the plan. He had Bohannon, of course, who became a critical part of the plan—struck me that they'd make a pretty lethal pair. And they did, didn't they?"

"I'm sorry but I can't connect these dots. The back channel and the whole Taylor-Bohannon-Hazlitt nexus . . . it's always seemed as if they were two different spirals which might twine around each other but never actually touched—"

"That was because you didn't know about me, dear boy. I'm the point where they touch, don't you see?"

I shook my head. I didn't get it.

"Oh, perhaps you're one of the slower students, Benjamin. I began to have some doubts about Charlie's presidency . . . he was turning out to be rather a softy, or so I feared. I love the man . . . and I'm so proud of him now. He's proven he can be a scoundrel, his political instincts take my breath away, I wouldn't have believed he could have survived this primary campaign and the subsequent struggle—but at the beginning, after that godforsaken State of the Union speech, I agreed with Taylor." This was all carefully thought out. His voice was gravelly when warmed up and he had a habit of pounding something with his forefinger. At the moment it was my knee. "Now, take Sherm, Ben . . . I'm not including Taylor among these presidents who are asleep at the wheel, of course. He saw what Heartland was up to a long time ago, he helped Hazlitt do it, he was allying himself with Hazlitt while he was in the Oval Office himself. Hazlitt was doing what was good for the US of A and good for Sherm Taylor in the long view."

He saw me wince and withdrew his forefinger from my knee. "I'm sorry, Benjamin. But I get rather frustrated when I think about the way this all worked out. Now, follow me closely. . . . Eventually Charlie began to realize that someone *owned* the intelligence communities, he just didn't know who, and Charlie knew he had an issue if he could make it work for him—he'd been threatening to blow those budgets into public view for a long time, but he didn't know just *how* compromised the intelligence services had become. And since I found myself in agreement with Brother Taylor, I kept trying to calmly dissuade Charlie from going off on his white charger against the folks at the intelligence agencies. But then he got all this secret government stuff into his head. He was threatening to expose large parts of our entire national security system, make every penny have to be accounted for! And you can't do that in the real world. But you know Charlie . . . he gets an idea and he won't let go, he wouldn't let anybody else see his speech—talk about a red flag to us!

"I had to figure out a way to rid ourselves of Hazlitt and his incredible inside power, not that I minded one man having it—Bob Hazlitt was just the wrong man in my view . . . he'd taken government money to develop his satellites and worked with Taylor, and after *using* the money to build the satellites he had all their power . . . and all the information they collected *belonged* to him. And who the hell was he? Really? Nobody. Just a businessman who'd fallen into the right latrine and come out covered with gold. He didn't know a damn thing about running this country or the world . . . he was simplistic, if you get right down to it.

"So . . . I decided the best way to get rid of all our problems was to have Sherm support the grassroots populist billionaire for president and at the untimely death of the populist billionaire our former president, untouched by the mud of the campaign, would be there to raise the fallen banner and claim the nomination in a fury of emotion. But to make a long story short, we had not counted on the fact that the faithful Bohannon would tumble onto the idea and realize he now knew too much and Sherm was going to have him put down. Maybe we could have prevailed on Sherm to just file Bohannon away to Italy or France or wherever the hell it was . . . but maybe not. Bohannon thought he was going to get it in the neck and struck back first. Well, we'll never know for sure what ran through his mind last night. And Warriors One and Two are dead. Old Sherm, if he lives, may not choose to hash it over on TV with David Frost or write his kiss-and-tell memoir."

"For the record," I said, "Bohannon knew the general was going to put him down. He'd finished using him up and now he was going to have to get rid of him. That's what the general brought in this Marmot for, to do Hazlitt and Bohannon."

"Well, don't you have the answers, Benjamin! I thought as much—he couldn't let Bohannon just wander off—he'd have been a time bomb. Well done, Ben, I must say." He finished the bit of toast and it was so good he decided to have another. He carefully buttered it and dabbed it with Chivers orange marmalade. He took a deep breath. "I must say, it's good to have all the duplicity behind us—don't you agree? And, in the end, we got the best possible president. Odd, how things work out."

"Charlie?"

"Yes, Charlie. Of course, Charlie—who else? The way he's handled it all—and then this final masterstroke, the story that Sherm was about to take second place on the ticket! It gutted Sherm's chances, *whatever* the hell he was going to say to the convention—none of it mattered anymore, he'd peeled off enough of Sherm's support to do the job. He'll stand up and do the right thing now. He'll be so relieved he's got a second term locked up. Don't you worry, Benjamin. I can handle Charlie."

That sent a chill clear through me. I stood up and leaned on the railing, looking down at the convention center and the parking lot and all the police cars and the sawhorses blocking things off as if there was still some big doubt about who had killed who. I was taking in all Larkspur had said but I wondered how everything fit in. Yet I felt stupid having to ask. I was having breakfast with a prominent, honored American, about whom historians would one day write glowing biographies that would contain nothing of what he had told me that morning. Men like Ellery Larkspur didn't leave a trail. Maybe someday a conspiracy theorist would analyze the astonishing events of this campaign and would come upon something somewhere that would show Larkspur involved with Taylor many years before the campaign and an indication in some paper chase that Larkspur just might have known Bohannon, and the historian would begin to put pieces together and he might find a clue to something at LVCO that would lead him to the Mexican earthquake and a note in somebody's diary about Earth Shaker, and this historian might think, *"Holy shit, I'm onto something here."*

"What are you thinking, Benjamin? Shocked, are you?"

"No, not shocked. Horrified that I'm sitting here having breakfast with you and chatting as if this is just politics as usual . . . while by any conceivable moral standard you're going to burn forever in a fiery pit. You're the killer I told Bob Hazlitt he was. You're worse, Larkie."

"Well, I am different, you know. I'm alive and in fine fettle."

"You're the spirit of . . . evil."

"Well, there are no innocents, are there, Benjamin? We must know the laws of politics. The first law of politics is to attain power and the second law of politics is to rule in such a way as to retain power. I believe in the old rules, the old ways."

"You're an old-fashioned kind of guy, is that it?"

"Most of the best ones are."

"It doesn't make you any less guilty."

"So, what were you thinking? You were a world away, Benjamin—"

"I was thinking about Kennedy. The assassination. All the theories that developed over the years."

"Well, I'm hopeful that you won't be offering any help in that area."

"Are you kidding? Did you ever read the list of people who might have given information to investigators on the JFK assassination and just happened to die in the years right after it? I'm not a fool. . . . I might have been born at night, Larkie—"

"But it wasn't last night. I know."

"The only thing left I don't understand is . . . Drew. Drew's role in all of this—how could he have turned against the President? Are you telling me that he thought like you?"

"Not at all, Benjamin! No, Drew Summerhays was the master of us all. He knew how this game is played. Drew was the smartest of us all . . . he figured out what was going on and he figured out that to make it work, we, the bad guys, had to set up Charlie as part of it, to take a big fall. Drew sent Tarlow out there to nail down the Hazlitt end of things, the murder of that old pal of Hazlitt's who got on his high horse. And he knew my feelings about Charlie giving away the store to Hazlitt . . . he *said* he agreed, something had to be done about Charlie . . . and he convinced me he was one of our happy band. Well, he was eight or nine moves ahead of us. It was Drew who set up the back channel and got the stock thing going—he made purchases, he made sure I was up to my neck in it . . . *and then he informed me that he'd been setting me up, through the money transfers . . . he had a complete record of everything and he pointed out to me that unless I scrapped the whole Taylor/Hazlitt fandango he was going to 'his girl,' Teresa Rowan, turn everything over to her and she'd destroy me. And none of it would ever touch the President.* Well, it was too late for me to throw away Taylor and Hazlitt, obviously, even if I could have. The general sent Bohannon to Shelter Island to speak the truth to Drew, to point out that we were moving ahead. They spoke, and Bohannon killed him and made it appear at first glance to be a suicide. It's sad, all very sad, but Drew had already had a far better run than any of us will get. . . .

"In any case, Ben, Drew Summerhays didn't let you down, he was as brilliant at the end as he'd ever been—but he didn't quite realize that underneath it all, I'm not quite a gentleman. He was. The age of the gentleman is, I'm afraid, a thing of the past. Politics nowadays is too much a place without values, without morality. Ironically enough, I think you had a lot to do with making Charles see that the truth doesn't matter anymore, that it's the lies that count, it's the lies that decide the outcome. When Charles went on the counterattack against Hazlitt, when he turned you loose and then decided what he would do with the information you turned up, when he hired Alec Fairweather to do his commercials—then it all began to turn. He was going to fight back . . . he was taking the gloves off, he was putting his boot in the groin, he was turning his back on the age of the gentleman. It was the making of Charles Bonner."

"The making of Charles Bonner . . ."

"Yes, of course."

"And the weapon, Larkie . . . Earth Shaker?"

"Oh, that's been on the drawing board forever. As far back as the Star Wars days with Reagan. During Sherman Taylor's administration the technology began to fall into place. It just happened to come to life . . . now."

"You know what you are, Larkie?"

"Of course I do. I am what is called a kingmaker, a power behind the scenes."

"You're a common murderer. You tried to kill Elizabeth—"

"No, no, never that. That was all Taylor's doing, he's the one who would speak with Bohannon. I was shocked, horrified when I realized Elizabeth had been involved . . . that never was the plan, you must believe me, Benjamin. I adore Elizabeth—"

"Well, you certainly are reassuring."

"Ah, well, perhaps not just now. I'm sure you'll find that time heals everything." He shrugged the rounded, sloping shoulders. "But as long as you're a grown-up and not thinking of doing anything rash . . . you won't wind up like all those people after the Kennedy assassination." He took my arm, smiled slowly. "Just kidding, Benjamin."

I had nothing left to say to Ellery Larkspur. It might take me the rest of my life to think of just the right words. Larkie was woven deep into the fabric of American life, the kind of guy who set the big agendas and made sure they were carried out, one way or another. He was the essential American. No one would thank me for bringing him down, even if it lay within my power. I knew also, in one of those moral breaking points, that Larkie would take good care of Charlie Bonner, would see him through his presidency. I think Larkie actually loved Charlie. The idea of assassinating Charlie never entered the scenario. Yet Charlie was the reason it all happened. He didn't think Charlie was strong enough to run the country. A lot of other people died, but not Charlie. . . . I stopped as I was leaving and looked back at him. He was watching me go, curled inside his soft white robe, the haze of the morning burning away behind him. I don't know what he thought he saw in the expression on my face. I'm not sure what I was thinking at just that moment. But he looked at me and spoke again.

"Really, Benjamin. *Just kidding*. You're one of us . . . and they weren't, in the end, were they?"

"I'm going to the President." Yes, he'd known what I was thinking.

"As you wish, Benjamin. But don't set your expectations too high. Sarrabian's proof won't stand up. He's so suspect himself. And it will reflect badly on Drew and the dear old firm."

"I'll take my chances."

"Of course, and I'll take mine."

Then he said something else. "Cheer up, Ben. It's show business—you must see that. We are like everything else, just another branch of show business." He smiled. "It's enough to make a man laugh, isn't it? We take ourselves so seriously." He waved to me. "On your way, Ben. Go live your life and be well."

The President made time for me later that afternoon. He was going over final changes in the text of his acceptance speech. It had been decided that the convention needed some catharsis. Tonight they would declare Charlie and David Mander their nominees, Mander would speak briefly, primarily introducing him, and then in the wake of all the deaths, Charles Bonner would address the nation and gather its various people to him, bind them irrevocably to him.

"Ben, you've been my pal for a long time. But the service you've done me this week . . ." He suddenly choked up, something I'd never seen him do before. "I've never thought I'd deserve that kind of friendship . . . and maybe I don't. But you gave it . . . anyway. I've learned a couple of things this week, Ben. I've learned that I'm a politician through and through. Boil me away in the fiery furnace and that's the residue . . . pure politician." He rubbed his nose with a snowy-white handkerchief. We were alone. "And you . . . you're a great man . . . and I've only known two. Drew Summerhays and you. That's all I can say, it's probably all I'll ever say about it. But I'll never forget what Archangel did for me."

You see how he did it? He had me. I was his. He'd reached inside and pushed the right button in my chest. He knew the truth about himself and he gave it to me without frills and made me think just maybe, however much I said I didn't see it, he might be right about me.

"I won't argue with you, Mr. President. But I'm not a great man and it seems to me I have a helluva time even being a good man. I'm having a tough time now. There are some things I believe I should tell you . . . but honest to God, I don't know why, I don't know what difference any of it would make . . . you are what you are and you've pretty well pulled it off and there's no taking any of it away from you. I'll never forget seeing you lunge forward into the line of fire to catch Sherm Taylor as he fell. I wonder if there's another man in public life who would have done that, who would have overcome every instinct to take cover and gone to comfort his stricken enemy." I was so near tears myself that I felt like a sap. I was biting my lip. "I just wonder . . . what were you thinking? What was going through your mind?"

"You really want to know, pal?"

"I do."

"I don't know entirely, but one of the things I was thinking was what a fucking great photo op. It would follow me through history." His eyes crinkled a little at the edges and he gave me that movie star smile, like somebody in *The Wild Bunch*. "I swear to God. I'm telling you, I'm a shallow son of a bitch, Ben." He was putting the old con in.

"There are things . . . I really should talk with you, Charlie."

"Come to me in Washington. After the convention. I'm a little distracted right this minute." He looked at me, waving to the papers on the table. "Then there's this election to win . . . I finally did a smart thing, Ben. I just put Larkie in charge of the campaign. He's a natural."

"You're right, Charlie. And I'm going home. I've had enough."

He laughed. "Well, you've had plenty, I'll give you that." He stopped and said, "Oh, by the way, there's a call for you here—" One of his secretaries had come in and motioned to him. "This is for Mr. Driskill, is it, Jan?"

"Yes, Mr. President. Mr. Larkspur just put it through."

He pointed to the phone on his desk and then he went to look out the window, his speech in his hand, giving me privacy.

"Hello? This is Ben Driskill."

I listened for a few minutes. Tears were running down my face and I could barely speak.

"Elizabeth," I said. She was okay. She'd come back.

When I hung up the President stuck out his hand in that characteristic gesture. I took it and we stood there for a long time and when I left I stood in the doorway and looked back at him and gave him some advice for the evening.

"Make 'em love you, Charlie."

By the time I got to O'Hare the darkness of midsummer was encroaching and there was a heat haze lingering over the runways and it was stifling everywhere. Thunderheads were piling up to the west. The temperature still hadn't dropped below ninety. Chicago in the summer. I wandered down a corridor toward my gate and still had more than an hour to wait. The airport was crowded with vacationers and I could hear snatches of conversation but most of it was husbands and wives and kids. Not a damn thing to do with politics.

I saw an empty stool at one of the little bars where you could kill some time and I went over and sat down. Miraculously it was quite comfortable at the bar and I felt myself letting down. I ordered a beer, and the bartender pushed some peanuts my way. On the TV over the bar the nominating speeches were over and they were getting ready for the vote by acclamation. It looked much like any other convention of recent years. Huge by the standards of my own youth and early manhood, but pretty much like others of recent years. It was all perfectly stage-managed by Ellery Larkspur and the rest of them, with Mac and Ellen in the forefront. They would all be gearing up for the campaign. And for the moment it was a pulsing sea of support for the President. A visitor with no knowledge of the week's events would have thought there was nothing peculiar about any of it. Resilient, those Americans.

Bands were playing and people were dancing and waving banners and that was when I tuned in on the guys sitting next to me, sucking up brews and munching on cheese fish and nuts. One guy said, "The thing of it is, it doesn't make a damn bit of difference who wins the election. Fuckers are all the same. Kills me, the way they try to make us think there's any difference. Democrats, Republicans.

Maybe a nickel's worth of difference between them. The Republicans make my tax bite a little easier, the Democrats make it a little worse. And they didn't even talk about any of that this time. . . . It was all 'you're an asshole' and 'you're a bigger one' and 'you're a murderer' and 'so are you, shithead.' Political discourse." He was fed up.

"All this crap about junking the CIA and all those other agencies. Talk about a load of it! It's business as usual. Always. You think we're gonna get along without an intelligence community out there spying on everybody and trying to overthrow the bad guys and keep track of terrorists and nerve gas? I don't fucking think so. So Hazlitt was responsible for murdering somebody, whoever that guy was in the river . . . in the commercial. So what? I work for a company with over a million employees worldwide, the value of the stock is the only goddam thing that matters—you want me to believe they never killed anybody who got in their way? It's part of doing business, am I right?"

"There are always problems that can best be solved quickly, and that's the quickest way. It's a corporate world. They play by corporate rules. Or we play by their rules now. I'm damned if I know which came first. . . . But Bonner gives a good speech."

They were reducing the sound and the fury of the campaign to its essentials, making it simple. Because in the end it was simple. "And, let's face it, the economy is okay. Bonner's kept taxes under control. Both of my kids have got jobs. I don't live in the inner fucking city somewhere and neither do they . . . we're exporting more to Japan. India. China. Not half bad, when you get right down to it. We're so saturated with drugs it's pretty well topped out. The wife and I are going to take a golfing vacation to Arizona. Camelback."

"And they spend the campaign talking to us about the intelligence community! Bonner's selling us down the river. Jesus. We own the river. We own all the rivers, if you know what I mean. Terrorists—they're a problem. But have they blown up Chicago? Evanston? Hell no! What do they think really matters, anyway?"

"Well, it's the vision thing, isn't it? You get caught up in the Washington crap, you begin to think it's important. . . . Well, my advice is, get real. Everything's gonna be okay. It's tough to keep America down. We're on top, we're gonna stay on top. A few people getting killed—America survives, count on it."

"Goddam right. The banner yet waves, my friend."

"I'll drink to that. The banner yet waves!"

The President was about to speak and the two guys slid off their stools, having made their toast, and laid some money on the bar. Then they began talking about what brand of tractor-style lawn mower was the best, laughing over what kind of mileage one guy was getting. The President's face filled the screen.

"My fellow Democrats . . . I accept your nomination."

That set off another demonstration, balloons, music, the works. I watched for a while and had another beer and then went to find the men's room. When I came out the President was still talking. "Of course we must maintain a strong intelligence arm of government. I never suggested anything else . . . but it must be better than what we've had, it must be better than the old way. And toward that end . . ." He was still talking and so were the guys at the bar and I was missing it but it didn't make any difference. The camera's eye was picking out Teresa and the First Lady, and they were beaming and there was Larkspur in the VIP section nodding sagely at one observation, smiling broadly at something clever. Larkie was looking younger and healthier than he had in years. He was back at the core of things, the adrenaline of the nation was flowing in him again, as if youth had paid a return visit. His face radiated confidence and an acute understanding of the nation's needs. My job had just gotten a little harder. Larkspur was the kind of man you instinctively trusted.

The applause was loud and prolonged, the faces in the crowd smiling and cheering and feeling better about things, getting ready to go out there and win an election. Already the memory of the loss of Taylor and Hazlitt was beginning to fade. It was surreal, the speed with which the flood of media, the power of the President's face on a million television screens, swept you and your life and death into the past. It felt like the nature of time was being explained in words of one syllable and each word was the right word. Ellery Larkspur's name was already pushing past their names—he was alive, after all, still in the game, and in the case of those two, out of sight and out of mind was not an entirely bad idea. The truth about Taylor and Hazlitt was going to seep into the public consciousness like a moderately unpleasant virus, one best gotten rid of quickly, without too much analysis because the truth might be something you really didn't need, or want, to know. The public was preserving itself, choosing to know more about the present, the quick, not the dead, and pondering the future, not the past. It was, on the whole, the best way to go. In the end, you had to do what you could do with your own life, whether you were the President or Tom Bohannon or Elizabeth Driskill. Or me. Sooner than you could imagine the tide would come running, it would find you and you'd be swept back into the past as if you'd never lived, and I supposed that was why so many people discovered faith in something else as they sensed the approaching tide. I finished my beer and saw myself reflected in the mirror behind the bar. I was smiling. Just a little. The bartender had been watching and he turned to me. "Easy come, easy go."

I nodded in agreement. It was amazing, all right.

Charlie was making them love him.

I wondered if there was any point in trying to do the right thing. The odds weren't so good. . . .

I picked up my briefcase and set off in the self-absorbed crowd of people hurrying down the endless corridors toward their planes, wrapped up in their own lives, which was how it was supposed to be, turning away from whatever enjoyment they'd derived from the week's political soap opera. It had had everything and the ratings had been very high and sooner or later we'd all found out whether it had any particular meaning for our own lives.

I felt myself being lost in the crowd, just another American who loved his country and knew it would somehow forever remain a mystery. As I stood before the last television screen before entering the walkway to the plane I looked up and felt the tightness in my throat as I looked at my old friend, his face calm and reassuring and his eyes telling everybody that everything was going to be all right, and I swallowed hard because I knew by heart, as did every American hearing the call to order and to action, the words that were to come. I watched his face through slightly blurred vision, trying to keep my face from betraying the emotion I was feeling. I was the kind of guy who always felt a tear when the flag went by, there was nothing I could do about it. And I heard the words and I saw my dear Elizabeth first of all, and I saw Rachel Patton and Hayes and Drew and Varringer and Nick Wardell and Chris Morrison and Lad Benbow and all the rest of them, I saw them listening and watching, I saw them all and I heard the words and I clenched my jaw against the silly, overpowering emotions that were bred in the bone and were beyond my control. . . .

"And now we must take stock and prepare ourselves for a great campaign that will make us all proud. . . .

"We must remember the principles of freedom and democracy for which through the years Americans have died. . . .

"I accept your nomination humbly and I will devote all the efforts of my body and soul to be worthy of your trust. . . .

"And now it is time for me to bid you good night with the words that are written so deep in the heart of every man who has held this office. . . .

"God bless and keep you all . . .

"And may God bless America."

New York City
Washington, D.C.
Sugar Bush, VT
Shelter Island, NY
Dubuque

About the Author

THOMAS GIFFORD is the author of *The Assassini, The First Sacrifice, Praetorian, The Wind Chill Factor,* and other novels. He lives in Dubuque.

From the *New York Times* bestselling author

THOMAS GIFFORD

THE ASSASSINI

"A monumental thriller, Gifford's masterpiece."
—Ira Levin, author of *The Boys from Brazil*
____28740-0 $6.99/$8.99 in Canada

THE WIND CHILL FACTOR

"Thunders along at breakneck speed . . . a blistering
novel of suspense."—*The Hartford Courant*
____29752-X $6.50/$8.99 in Canada

PRAETORIAN

"[*Praetorian*] is filled with excitement, passion and drama
. . . an achievement rare in contemporary thrillers, let
alone historical ones."—*The Washington Post Book World*
____56502-8 $6.50/$7.99 in Canada

THE FIRST SACRIFICE

"Conspiracy on a grand scale."—*Chicago Tribune*
____57217-2 $6.50/$8.99 in Canada

FREDERICK FORSYTH

THE MASTER OF INTRIGUE

___29742-2	**THE DECEIVER**	$6.99/$8.99 in Canada
___26630-6	**THE DAY OF THE JACKAL**	$6.99/NCR
___26490-7	**THE DEVIL'S ALTERNATIVE**	$6.99/NCR
___26846-5	**THE DOGS OF WAR**	$6.99/$8.99
___57242-3	**THE FIST OF GOD**	$6.99/$9.99
___25113-9	**THE FOURTH PROTOCOL**	$6.99/$8.99
___28393-6	**THE NEGOTIATOR**	$6.99/$8.99
___27673-5	**NO COMEBACKS**	$6.99/$8.99
___27198-9	**THE ODESSA FILE**	$6.99/NCR
___10244-X	**THE SHEPHERD**	NUSR/$6.99
___09128-X	**ICON**	$24.95/$32.95

Ask for these books at your local bookstore or use this page to order.

Please send me the books I have checked above. I am enclosing $ _____(add $2.50 to cover postage and handling). Send check or money order, no cash or C.O.D.'s, please.

Name _____

Address _____

City/State/Zip _____

Send order to: Bantam Books, Dept. FL, 2451 S. Wolf Rd., Des Plaines, IL 60018
Allow four to six weeks for delivery.
Prices and availability subject to change without notice.   FL 2C 1/97

PSALMS
A GUIDE
TO PRAYER
& PRAISE
Ron
Klug

15 inductive studies
for neighborhood,
student and
church
groups

Harold Shaw Publishers
Wheaton, Illinois

CONTENTS

Introduction

The Psalms are some of the most widely read and best-loved portions of the Bible. For thousands of years these songs of faith have spoken to the hearts and minds of people in all lands. Literary critic Mark van Doren has called the Psalms "the supreme lyric poems of our world." Like all great literature, the Psalms reveal their full meaning only to those who are willing to study them and make them their own.

Keeping in mind a few basic understandings will help you as you begin your study of the Psalms.

Basic Understandings
1. *The Psalms are songs*.
The Book of Psalms was the hymnbook of the Old Testament. The word *psalm* comes from a Greek word which means "songs sung to the accompaniment of stringed instruments." The Book of Psalms is sometimes also referred to as the Psalter, which comes from a word for a stringed instrument or songs accompanied by stringed instruments. So if we think of the Psalms as being like our contemporary folk hymns, sung to the strumming of a guitar, we are not far off.

The Psalms were sung in the Jewish temple in Jerusalem and later in synagogue worship. Since New Testament times the Psalms have also been at the center of Christian worship. In the form of Gregorian chant they became the basis for the worship and prayer life of religious communities. At the time of the Reformation, hymn writers like Martin Luther turned the Psalms into hymns to be sung by the congregation. Especially in the Calvinist churches the Psalms formed the core of worship. Throughout history composers have turned to the Psalms for inspiration, using the musical forms and styles of the time. In our day composers have set the Psalms to folk or jazz or rock music.

2. *The Psalms are poetry.*
C. S. Lewis wrote: "Most emphatically the Psalms must be read as poems, as lyrics, with all the licenses and all the formalities, the hyperboles, the emotional rather than logical connections which are proper to lyric poetry. They must be read as poems if they are to be understood, no less than French must be read as French or English as English. Otherwise we shall miss what is in them and think we see what is not" (*Reflections on the Psalms,* New York: Harcourt, Brace & World, 1958, p. 3).

But don't let the word "poetry" scare you. The poetic devices used by the psalm writers are easy to understand. As you read and study the Psalms, watch especially for these techniques:

Parallelism
Almost all psalm verses are divided into two parts. Often the second half of a verse repeats the thought of the first half, but expresses the thought in a slightly different way. A few examples will make this clear:

> He who sits in the heavens shall laugh;
> the Lord has them in derision.
>
> *Psalm 2:4*

> The earth is the Lord's and the fulness thereof,
> the world and those who dwell therein.
>
> *Psalm 24:1*

Sometimes the second half of a verse, rather than repeating the thought of the first half, offers a contrast:

> For the Lord knows the way of the righteous,
> but the way of the wicked will perish.
>
> *Psalm 1:6*

Other times the second half merely completes the thought of the first half:

> The law of the Lord is perfect
> converting the soul.
>
> *Psalm 19:7*

Imagery
The Psalms are rich in picture language. The vivid images drawn from everyday life are often what make a psalm meaningful and memorable. Watch for devices like these:

> Simile (comparisons with *as* or *like*): "He is like a tree planted by streams of water."
>
> *Psalm 1:3*

"As the hart longs for flowing streams,
so longs my soul for thee, O God."

Psalm 42:1

Metaphor (direct comparison): "The Lord God is a Sun and Shield."

Psalm 84:11

Hyperbole
To avoid misunderstanding, watch for *hyperbole*, in which the writer
exaggerates his point to "get through" to you:

"All night I make my bed to swim;
I water the couch with my tears."

Psalm 6:6

3. *The Psalms are prayers.*
Dietrich Bonhoeffer, the Christian pastor exterminated by the Nazis in 1944,
called the Psalms, "The Prayerbook of the Bible." The Psalms are unique
prayers, for in them God speaks his Word to us, and we, in turn, can use the
Psalms to speak his Word back to him in prayer. Used in this way, the Psalms
can inform, broaden, and enrich your prayer life. Perhaps the most important
thing for you to do as you study the Psalms is to identify those verses which
express your feelings of praise and thanksgiving, your anguish and longing,
and your faith and love for God.

4. *The Psalms are God's Word to us.*
The Psalms are more than beautiful poetry and lovely songs. For thousands
of years people have heard in them the Word of God speaking to their human
situation. The Psalms tell us the truth about ourselves, our nature, our
troubles, our hopes, our frustrations, our pain. And they tell us the truth about
God—what he is like, what he wants of us and for us. And perhaps more
than any other part of the Bible, the Psalms speak of our relationship with
God, the intimate personal knowing that can happen between a human being
and the God who is Creator and Lord of All.

Like all the other parts of the Bible, the Psalms are the Word of God expressed
in the words of men. God used human writers in a variety of situations to
express his truth. Almost half of the 150 psalms are attributed to David,
Israel's great king and her "sweet singer." The superscriptions or headings
also mention other authors, and about 50 of the psalms are anonymous.

Through these writers God speaks his Word to many of the basic human
problems and situations in life. There is no finer introduction to the funda-
mental ideas or themes of the Old Testament than the Psalms.

Approaching the Psalms

Like a modern hymnbook, the Psalms contain songs by a variety of authors, written over a long span of time. Unlike a modern hymnbook, the Psalms are not arranged in any logical groupings. The present book of Psalms seems to be a collection of smaller collections. Therefore, if we begin with Psalm 1 and read through to Psalm 150, we come against a bewildering variety. This makes it hard to "get a handle on" the book of Psalms.

Scholars have recognized that the Psalms can be divided into various literary types. Some of the main ones are:

> a hymn of praise
> a lament (a cry of pain, from an individual or group)
> a song of thanksgiving
> a song of trust
> a penitential psalm (asking for forgiveness)
> a wisdom psalm (expressing truths about life)

One helpful way to study the Psalms is by learning well one psalm of each literary type, then referring to and reading other examples of this type. This is the method we shall employ in this studyguide.

Hints for studying the Psalms

1. If possible, *sing* the Psalms. They were meant to be sung, and singing will help you make the psalm your own. If you use this studyguide in a group, perhaps one member could be responsible for bringing a recording or leading the group in singing some musical setting of the psalm being studied. Parts of many of the psalms have been set to music in volumes such as *High Praise* (Harold Shaw Publishers, Box 567, Wheaton, IL).

2. Because the Psalms are poetry, they should be *read aloud*. To help bring out the parallelism, the Psalms may be read antiphonally; that is, with the leader reading the first half of each verse and the group reading the second half. Or divide the group and have each subgroup read half a verse.

3. Remember that the Psalms are Old Testament scripture written before the time of Christ. As you study a psalm, you should first ask: "What did the writer mean to say to the people of his time?" Then ask, "What is the Holy Spirit saying to me through this psalm?"

4. This studyguide is based on the *Revised Standard Version*, widely accepted as an accurate translation. You may find it helpful to read the Psalms in the older *King James Translation*, a model of seventeenth-century English style which brings out much of the stately beauty of the Psalms. Or try one of the newer translations such as the *New International Version* or the *New English Bible*. Or you may gain some insights from one of the freer paraphrases, such as *The Living Bible* or Leslie Brandt's *Psalms Now*.

5. In order to use the Psalms in your own life of prayer and praise, you may want to memorize a few verses or an entire psalm. Choose those parts of a psalm which especially express your own thoughts. You can memorize them, using spare moments when you are doing routine work. If a verse or verses have been set to music, you can memorize them even more easily. Then, throughout the day, you can speak or sing to God in the words of the Psalms.

6. When you study as a group, the members should first study the psalm on their own, meditating on it and answering the questions in the studyguide. Then, when you come together, begin with prayer and by reading the psalm aloud. Then work your way through the questions, sharing your insights and discoveries. Some questions will direct your attention to what is being said in the biblical text. Others will ask you to think about the meaning of the text. Still others will ask you to apply the Bible teaching to your own life.

7. Keep a careful check on the time. Begin and end the study at the agreed hour. The leader's responsibility is to keep the group on target. The target is the Psalm being studied. Keep the discussion moving along so you can complete the study in the time alotted. Tangents can be time consuming. Unless they are relevant to the discussion, suggest tabling any tangents for later discussion.

8. Encourage everyone to participate in the discussion. Stress that the answers to the questions in the studyguide lie in the text. Occasionally a series of questions will be followed by an illuminating quotation or an explanatory note.

9. Stick to the Psalm being discussed. Let the passage speak for itself. If additional background is needed the studyguide will give you the cross references. However, as the study continues it will become natural and helpful to refer back to psalms discussed earlier because then the group members will have a common frame of reference.

10. For further information on the dynamics of group study, read Gladys Hunt's *HOW-TO HANDBOOK*, available from Harold Shaw Publishers, Box 567, Wheaton, Illinois. It is recommended that all group members read the *HOW-TO HANDBOOK* for a good understanding of how an inductive study works.

PSALM 8: Praise to God as Creator

If you have not already done so, please read the introductory material on pages 5-9. Begin your group discussion by reading this psalm aloud. Try reading it antiphonally, with the leader reading the first half of each verse and the group responding with the second half.

Psalm 8:1, 2
1/Psalm 8 has been called "Genesis 1 set to music." As a background to the study of this psalm, read the creation account in Genesis 1.

What is the theme of Psalm 8, as stated in the opening and closing verses? What do these words mean to you personally?

_____

_____

note: *"Among the Israelites the name was understood to be an expression of the nature or identity of a person." Bernhard W. Anderson* Out of the Depths: The Psalms Speak for Us Today *(Philadelphia: Westminster, 1970).*

2/Verses 1 and 2 are the most difficult in the psalm. Read them aloud in another translation like the *New English Bible* or *Today's English Version*. Do these translations shed any new light on these verses?

_____

_____

3/Even though God is so "majestic," who is able to comprehend and express his greatness? Compare Matthew 11:25. Why may children be able to perceive God's glory more readily than adults? Have you seen this happen in your own experience with children? Give examples.

_____

_____

4/Who might be the enemies of God? How could the praise of children be a defense against these enemies?

_____

_____

Psalm 8:3, 4

5/What may the psalmist have been doing when he was inspired to write this psalm? When he contemplates the moon and stars, what question comes to his mind? Why might the stars make a person feel small or insignificant? Does our modern study of science add to or detract from this human feeling of insignificance?

_____

_____

_____

6/What answer does the psalmist give to his own question, "What is man?" or "What is man's purpose on earth?" Think of other answers to this question which might be given by scientists, philosophers, or the man on the street.

_____

_____

_____

7/Verse 5 says, "Thou hast made him a little less than *elohim*," which can mean either *God, the gods,* or *the angels*. Which translation makes the most sense to you?

_____

8/How does God intend man to be related to nature? In your own words, what does it mean that God gave him "dominion"? How do you relate verse 6 to current problems of ecology, pollution, the energy crisis and the use of earth's other resources? In view of floods, hurricanes, drought and disease-bearing organisms, can it be said that man now truly exercises dominion over nature? What insights do you find in Romans 8:18-25 regarding man's relationship to the creation?

_____

_____

_____

_____

_____

9/Read aloud Hebrews 2:6-9. To whom does the writer apply the words of Psalm 8? Can you think of any times when Jesus exercised dominion over creation? Psalm 8 is also quoted in 1 Corinthians 15. What do verses 27 and 28 say about Jesus' dominion?

_____

_____

_____

Psalm 8:9
10/After describing man's exalted role in the universe, to what theme does the psalmist return? Why does he stress that the God of creation is _our_ Lord?

_____

THINK IT OVER
11/Psalm 8 teaches that the creation is good and that man has a very high position, "a little less than God." Do you know anyone, Christian or non-Christian, who takes a low or negative view of man or the creation? What can be done to help that person gain a more positive view?

_____

_____

12/Does this psalm give you any insights into the purpose of _your_ life? What do you see as the purpose of your life right now?

13/Write on the lines below the words of any verses of Psalm 8 you wish to memorize and use in your own prayer and praise. You may also wish to begin making a mini-file of index cards with verses from the Psalms to memorize or you may display each week's verse or verses in a prominent place and suggest that your family participate in this memorization program.

_____

_____

_____

_____

_____

FOR FURTHER STUDY
Another good example of a psalm which praises God as creator is Psalm 104.

PSALM 19: Praise to the Lord of World and Word

Have your group read the psalm aloud, with some reading the first half of each verse and the others the second half.

Psalm 19:1-6
1/What is the psalmist affirming in verses 1-4? What features of God's creation does he especially mention?

_____

note: *At the time the psalm was written, "the firmament" was thought to be a solid dome arching over the earth, separating the waters in the sky from those on earth.*

2/According to verses 3 and 4, the created universe cannot speak in words. How then is it capable of "telling the glory of God"? What is the *them* referred to in verse 4? What two pictures does the writer use to describe the movements of the sun? Why might he have chosen the sun as a special focus for describing and meditating on the glory of God?

_____

_____

_____

3/What can we learn about God from the world of nature? Why doesn't everyone, then, believe in God? Read and compare Romans 1:18-25.

_____

_____

Psalm 19:7-11

4/After describing how God is revealed in the creation, to what does the psalmist turn? In verses 7-9 what six synonyms are given for God's law, his written revelation? What does God's Word do for us according to each of these verses? Which adjectives are used to describe the Word of God? Where do we find the Word of God today?

_____

_____

note: _some scholars believe that "fear" in verse 9 should read "word."_

5/In verse 10 what is the psalmist's ultimate conclusion about the value of the Word of God? What concept does verse 11 add concerning the purpose of the Word of God?

_____

_____

Psalm 19:12-14

6/According to verse 11 there is a "great reward" for obeying God's law; yet what problem does he refer to in verses 12-13? How does he want God to help him in this?

_____

_____

7/What two kinds of sins are mentioned? (Look up "presumptuous" in a dictionary if you're not sure of the meaning.) How does God deal with our hidden faults? With what result?

_____

_____

8/In conclusion, what does the writer ask God in verse 14? What is the significance of the words he uses to describe God? When might this be a good prayer for you to use?

_____

_____

THINK IT OVER

9/Ray Stedman writes that Psalm 19 "tells us that the knowledge of God has been written for us in two volumes, and that it takes both volumes to know God. There is the revelation in nature, and there is the revelation given in a Book, in the written Word. Both are essential to the knowledge and understanding of God." (*Folk Psalms of Faith,* Glendale, CA: Regal Books, 1973, p. 33.) Do you agree?

_____

10/What is your present attitude toward the Bible? How does it compare with that of the writer of Psalm 19?

_____

11/The poet Elizabeth Barrett Browning wrote:

> *Earth's crammed with heaven*
> *and every common bush aflame with God;*
> *but only those who see take off their shoes,*
> *the rest sit around it and pluck blackberries.*

How are her words a commentary on Psalm 19:1-3?

_____

12/In the space below, write out the verse(s) in this psalm that you wish to memorize.

_____

_____

_____

_____

_____

_____

FOR FURTHER STUDY

If possible, listen to a recording of the magnificent chorus, "The Heavens Are Telling" from the *Creation* oratorio of Franz Joseph Haydn. If you don't own one, try your local library. Another psalm which praises God for his creation is Psalm 148.

Sing #8 in *High Praise*.

3

PSALM 33: Jehovah: Maker and Monarch

Begin your group meeting by having this psalm of praise read aloud.

Psalm 33:1-3
1/What commands or invitations are given in these verses? To whom are they given? Who *are* the righteous and upright, according to your understanding?

_____

_____

2/What characteristics of religious music are given in verse 3? Does this verse suggest anything about our use of music in church?

_____

_____

Psalm 33:4-9
3/What is the significance of the word "for" in verse 4? According to these verses, what reasons do we have for praising God? What does the psalmist teach us about God in these verses? Do the metaphors in verse 7 add to your understanding? How did God create the universe? What should be our reaction to the creative power of God?

_____

_____

_____

_____

Psalm 33:10-17

4/To what subject does the writer turn in these verses? In contrast to the obedience of nature as seen earlier in the psalm, what is true about man? How is that illustrated in verse 10? What does God do about man's disobedience? How?

_____

_____

_____

5/What is the positive side of man's relationship to God, as given in verse 12? Is our country a "nation whose God is the Lord"? If not, how could it become that?

_____

6/According to verses 13-15, how is the Lord able to control history? Note the repeated emphasis on the word "all."

_____

_____

7/What sources of false trust are warned against in verses 16-17? Are we guilty of this superficial attitude as a nation? as individuals?

_____

_____

Psalm 33:18-22

8/What promises are made in these verses? What are the characteristics of those whom God delivers? From your own experience, give examples of how God has kept this promise.

_____

_____

_____

_____

9/What response to the God who controls creation and history is described in verses 20-21? What does it mean to "wait" for the Lord? Can you truthfully make statements like these?

_____

_____

10/After speaking *about* God, what is the psalmist's prayer directly *to* God in verse 22?

_____

_____

THINK IT OVER

11/The writer of Psalm 33 was convinced that God not only created the world, but that he now controls its events. Do you share this conviction? Why is it sometimes hard to believe this? If we do believe that God is in charge, what effect should this have on our reactions to circumstances?

_____

_____

12/List all the reasons why we can trust God with our lives, according to this psalm.

_____

_____

_____

_____

13/In what area of your life do you find it hardest to "wait for the Lord"? How do you plan to change this?

_____

_____

14/Write down any verses in this psalm which you could memorize to help you build trust in the God who is "Maker and Monarch."

_____

_____

_____

_____

_____

FOR FURTHER STUDY
Other psalms which praise God as the Lord of history are Psalms 146 and 147.

PSALM 46: Praise to the Lord of History

Have your group read this psalm of praise aloud antiphonally.

Psalm 46:1-3
1/With what great statement of faith does the psalmist commence his psalm of praise to God? What does it mean for you right now that God is your "refuge"? your "strength"? your "help in trouble"?

_____

_____

_____

2/What do the word pictures in verses 2-3 suggest about the world we live in? How would you restate verses 2-3 in contemporary terms: "therefore we will not fear, though. . . ."?

_____

_____

_____

3/How does fear make any bad situation worse? What antidote to fear is suggested in these verses?

_____

_____

note: *The Word* selah, *which appears in many psalms, is somewhat of a*

24

puzzle to scholars. The best guess seems to be that it was some kind of musical signal directed to the singers. Always remember that the psalms were meant to be sung.

Psalm 46:4-7
4/These verses referred originally to the city of Jerusalem, the religious center of the Jewish people. They thought of the temple there as God's dwelling place. How might we apply these verses to our situation? What, for you, is the city of God, the habitation of the Most High?

_____

5/What might the river symbolize in verse 4? Read aloud and compare Jeremiah 2:13 and Revelation 22:1-2. What suggests the presence of hostile forces surrounding the city of God? What assurance can God's people have despite them? What kinds of hostility do you face in your life? What confidence can you have?

_____

_____

_____

_____

6/What are the names of God given in verses 4-7? What does each mean to you? Someone may want to review the high points of the story of Jacob recorded in Genesis 25-49.

_____

_____

_____

note: *Verses 5 and 7 are good examples of the parallelism typical of Hebrew poetry.*

Psalm 46:8-11
7/What actions of God are described in verses 8 and 9? Are these verses to be understood literally or figuratively? Are these "works" of God occurring on the earth today? When might these actions be completely fulfilled?

_____

_____

_____

8/Who is speaking in verse 10? How would you restate this verse in your own words? Does this verse help explain why we sometimes fail to hear God speaking to us? How might you change your lifestyle in order to have more time to "be still"?

_____

_____

_____

9/How does verse 11 sum up the message of this psalm? What individuals are referred to in this verse? How are the past, the present and the future linked? What confidence can you draw from verses 10-11?

_____

_____

_____

THINK IT OVER
10/Popular books such as _Future Shock_ by Alvin Toffler point out the difficulties of living in a time of rapid social and technological change. What are some unhealthy ways in which people respond to this rapid change? How can we find the faith to cope with a world which, in many ways, seems to be falling apart?

_____

_____

11/Have there been times when your world seemed to be falling apart around you? Did you experience God as your refuge and strength? How?

_____

_____

12/What can you learn from this psalm about how to face fear and anxiety?

Which verses should you memorize to help you?

_____

_____

_____

_____

_____

FOR FURTHER STUDY
Verse 1 of Psalm 46 inspired Martin Luther's hymn, "A Mighty Fortress Is Our God." Your group may wish to sing this powerful expression of trust.

You also may want to sing #20 in *High Praise*.

Other psalms which express confidence in God as the Lord of history are Psalms 113 and 117.

5

PSALMS 42-43: The Personal Cry

Most scholars think that Psalms 42 and 43 were originally one psalm. As you read these verses aloud, note how a chorus is repeated in Psalm 42:5, 42:11, and 43:5. This is an example of a *lament*, a personal cry to God in time of trouble.

Psalm 42:1-5
1/What vivid picture does the psalmist use to express his longing for God? Have you ever experienced this thirst for God? Are you experiencing it now? Look up and read aloud John 4:7-15 and John 7:37-39. What does Jesus say is the answer to our thirst for God? Can a person know God and still thirst after him? How can we "behold the face of God"?

_____

_____

_____

_____

_____

2/In Psalm 42:1-5 the writer mentions two reasons why he is "cast down" or depressed. What are they? Who do his enemies seem to be?

_____

_____

3/Faced with his depression and the mocking of his enemies, what does the writer do? Do you have any memories of profound worship or other religious experience? Does it help you to recall them?

_____

_____

4/What question does the psalmist ask himself in verse 5? What does he encourage himself to do? What is the basis of his hope?

_____

_____

Psalm 42:6-11
5/Where was the psalmist when he expressed his thirst for God? Why is his location significant? (Locate Mt. Hermon and Mt. Mizar on a map. In these mountains there were waterfalls like those mentioned in verse 7.)

_____

6/When the writer feels depressed and overwhelmed by life, what does he remember? How constant is God's care? What does verse 8 mean to you? You may want to look up this verse in several translations.

_____

_____

7/What questions does he then hurl at God? What problem is again mentioned in verses 9, 10? To what theme does the writer return in verse 11? Of what is he confident?

_____

_____

_____

Psalm 43:1-5
8/List the three things the psalmist asks God to do for him in verse 1. What is the meaning of *vindicate*? What questions does he again ask of God in these verses? Do you think God is pleased with questions like these?

_____

_____

9/The writer expresses two needs in verse 3. Why are these important to him? What is meant by God's *light*? by "thy holy hill"? What promise does the writer make? Do you see any evidence that the writer's attitude has changed during the psalm?

_____

_____

_____

THINK IT OVER
10/Why does God sometimes seem to be far from us? How can we experience more fully the presence of God?

_____

_____

11/Do these verses offer any practical suggestions for handling depression? What does the psalmist do when he is depressed? How do you handle feelings of depression?

_____

_____

_____

12/Are there any verses in Psalms 42 and 43 that you wish to memorize and use in your own prayer life?

_____

_____

_____

_____

_____

FOR FURTHER STUDY

More than 40 of the psalms can be classified as laments. Among the finest are Psalms 31, 38, 57, 71, and 77.

Sing #18 in *High Praise*.

PSALM 22: The Cross and The Crown

Psalm 22 can be seen both as a personal lament and as a messianic psalm (one which finds its ultimate fulfilment in Christ and his reign). When he wrote, the psalmist was speaking of his own condition—himself. But at another level, the psalm expresses Israel's deep longing for a messiah or savior. For the Christian, the psalm paints a vivid picture of Christ crucified.

Psalm 22:1-8
1/What is the psalmist's emotional climate at the beginning of this psalm? What is his attitude toward God? Have there been times when you have felt like this? What caused those feelings?

_____

_____

_____

2/What is the significance of the word "yet" in verse 3? In verses 3 and 4, how does the writer attempt to handle his feelings of being forsaken by God? According to verse 6, how does the record of God's help toward others make _him_ feel? What else adds to his feeling of despair and forsakenness?

_____

_____

_____

_____

Psalm 22:9-18

3/How is verse 9 similar to verse 3? Despite his own feelings and the mockery of others, what does the psalmist realize in verse 10? What is his prayer in verse 11?

_____

_____

_____

4/In these verses, what metaphors does the writer use to describe his personal enemies? his own physical condition? Because his physical condition is so serious, according to verse 18, what are his enemies about to do? In one word or phrase, summarize the psalmist's situation.

_____

_____

_____

5/When in his own life did Jesus quote verse 1 of this psalm? (Compare Mark 15:34.) Which other details in these verses vividly describe the crucifixion of Jesus? (You may want to review the accounts in Matthew 27, Mark 15, Luke 23, or John 19.)

_____

_____

Psalm 22:19-31

6/In verse 19, what suggests a change of mood and thought? What four pleas does the psalmist utter? Who or what is represented by the dog, the lion, the wild oxen?

_____

_____

7/In anticipation of God's help, what promise does the writer make? Where is this to take place?

_____

8/What is the relationship between verse 22 and verses 23-31? What reasons does the psalmist have for praising God? How would you summarize his personal testimony? What will be the results of this testimony?

_____

_____

_____

_____

9/What is the psalmist's vision of the future in verses 27-31? According to your present understanding, when might this vision be fulfilled? How does this vision of the future compare with your own?

_____

_____

THINK IT OVER
10/Psalm 22 begins in a mood of despair and ends on a note of triumph. How is the psalmist enabled to move from despair to positive affirmation?

_____

11/How do you account for the similarities between Psalm 22 and the accounts of the crucifixion of Jesus? Read aloud and compare 1 Peter 1:10-11, John 19:24.

_____

_____

note: _"In fulfilling the Scripture, then, Christ sometimes took the human experience of the Old Testament saints, lifted them up to a higher level, carried them over into a new sphere, poured them into a fresh container, and brought them out into a perfect fulness. It is_ in this sense _sometimes that the Scriptures are fulfilled." Walter C. Wright,_ Psalms, Vol. I (Chicago: Moody Press, 1955), pp. 65-66.

12/What clues does this psalm give as to what we can do when we ourselves are suffering or experiencing a feeling of being forsaken by God?

_____

13/Are there any passages in this psalm that you wish to memorize or use in your own prayers?

_____

_____

_____

_____

_____

FOR FURTHER STUDY
Other messianic psalms, expressing Israel's hope for a savior, are Psalms 2, 16, 45, 72, and 110.

7

PSALM 90: God Our Dwelling Place

Although there are among the psalms many personal laments expressing the distress of an individual, in Psalm 90 we have a *community lament*, the cry of a people, a church or a nation. Begin your group meeting by reading the psalm aloud, antiphonally.

Psalm 90:1-2

1/With what great affirmation of faith does the psalm begin? Moses is traditionally recognized as the writer. Consider his life and then think what it would have meant for him to call God his "dwelling place," or home. Read aloud and compare Acts 17:26-28, John 15:4-7 and Hebrews 13:8. What do we learn about God and his existence from these verses?

_____

_____

_____

_____

_____

Psalm 90:3-6

2/According to these verses, how is man radically different from God? How is God's view of time different from ours? Compare 2 Peter 3:18. To what are a thousand years compared?

_____

_____

_____

36

note: *In biblical times the period between sunset and sunrise was divided into three watches, so that a watch was the smallest unit of time.*

3/What is the cause of a person's death according to these verses? What pictures does the psalmist use to portray the brevity of our lives? How do these similes make you feel?

_____

_____

_____

Psalm 90:7-12
4/Have these verses read aloud. What seem to be the key words? Why is God angry? How do you react to the picture of God as angry? Is this the picture commonly presented today? What might be the effect of emphasizing God's love without also declaring his anger at sin?

_____

_____

_____

5/According to this psalm, what is the relationship between God's anger and the shortness of our lives? How would you characterize the description of our lives in verses 9-10: optimistic, pessimistic, or realistic?

_____

6/What should be our reaction to the brevity of our lives and God's anger over sin, according to verse 12? In the light of the rest of the psalm, what does "a heart of wisdom" mean to you?

_____

_____

Psalm 90:13-17
7/The psalmist asks God to perform seven actions in these verses. In your own words, what does each of these actions mean? Which of these requests seems the most important to you right now?

_____

_____

_____

_____

_____

8/Why does the psalmist ask God to return? Has God been away? If God seems absent from your life, how would you feel about his return?

_____

_____

9/Which prayer request is emphasized by repetition in verse 17? When you think of the work you do in life, what would you especially like God to "establish"?

_____

_____

THINK IT OVER
10/Make a list of all the things you learn about God from this psalm.

_____

_____

_____

11/Is God your "dwelling place" in life, the place where you live? If not, what could you do to make this more true in your life?

_____

12/This psalm is often read at funerals. What comfort does it offer?

_____

13/Do you feel that you have come to terms with the prospect of your own death? How could this psalm help you?

_____

14/Which verses from this psalm do you wish to memorize?

_____

_____

_____

_____

_____

FOR FURTHER STUDY
Read or sing Isaac Watts' stirring rendition of Psalm 90, "O God, Our Help in Ages Past."

Other psalms of community lament are Psalms 12, 44, 80, 85, 94.

8

PSALM 51: A Prayer for Forgiveness

Psalm 51 is one of the finest examples of a *penitential* psalm, in which the believer freely admits his shortcomings and sins and asks God for mercy and forgiveness. Begin by reading the psalm aloud.

Psalm 51:1-5
1/According to the superscription (title) of this psalm, David, King of Israel, wrote this psalm after being confronted by the prophet Nathan. (Read the story of this encounter in 2 Samuel 12:1-14.) What four things does the psalmist ask for in these verses? What does he admit about himself? What is his attitude toward his wrongdoing? What deep conviction does he express in verse 5?

_____

_____

_____

note: *"In the first three verses the psalmist uses three different words: transgression, iniquity, sin. To change the phraseology we would use rebellion, crookedness, failure. Rebellion, or wrongdoing, in connection with the moral government of God; crookedness, perversity (from the verb to bend) in connection with a straight course of conduct; failure, or missing the mark, in connection with a divine ideal."* Walter C. Wright, Psalms, *Vol I, (Chicago: Moody Press, 1955), p. 120.*

2/What gives the psalmist the courage to come before God and ask for forgiveness and cleansing?

_____

40

Psalm 51:6-12

3/List the eleven imperatives or requests in these verses. What is the writer asking God to do for him in each of these prayers? Is it enough for God to forgive us by merely cancelling the penalty for sin?

_____

_____

_____

note: *Hyssop is a plant, the branch of which was dipped into water or blood and sprinkled on a person as a sign of purification (See Exodus 12:22, 23).*

4/How do you understand verse 8? How might God "break your bones"? Why does salvation bring joy (verses 8, 12)?

_____

_____

5/Look back over verses 6-12. When we ask God to deal with our sin, what negative actions should we ask for? What positive actions?

_____

_____

Psalm 51:13-19

6/As his response to God's forgiveness and renewal, what does the psalmist promise in verses 13-15? How can a forgiven sinner effectively teach transgressors God's way?

_____

_____

7/Verses 16-17 point out the shortcomings of a religion based only on ritual, such as animal sacrifices. What kind of sacrifices does God want you to make in your life? What is the right attitude in which to make them? Read aloud and compare Hebrews 13:15-16.

_____

_____

note: *Some scholars think that verses 18-19 may have been added so that the psalm does not have a completely negative view of sacrifice or religious ritual.*

THINK IT OVER

8/What is your understanding of sin? Is sin a concept we would be better off without? Are you personally more in danger of underestimating your sins or overestimating them? What is God's cure for each of these problems?

_____

_____

_____

9/In addition to confessing our sins to God, is there an advantage in confessing our sins to another person? Under what conditions do you think it is helpful to confess to the person you have wronged? Are there times when it is not advisable?

_____

_____

10/Discuss the statement: "Purity as well as pardon is the desire of the true penitent." Irving L. Jensen, *Psalms* (Chicago: Moody Bible Institute, 1968), p. 68.

11/Which parts of this psalm will you memorize to use in your own prayer life? Write them down.

_____

_____

_____

_____

_____

FOR FURTHER STUDY

Sing a musical setting of this psalm, like Richard Redland's "Lord, to Me Compassion Show." You also might want to sing #32 in *High Praise*.

Another fine penitential psalm is Psalm 32.

PSALM 103: Blessing the Lord

So far in our study of the psalms we have looked at examples of psalms of praise, personal and community laments, and a penitential psalm. In Psalm 103 we see an example of the song of thanksgiving. Be sure to have your group read this psalm aloud.

Psalm 103:1-5

1/To whom is the psalmist speaking? What two things does he urge himself to do? What does it mean to "bless the Lord"? How can humans give blessing to the sovereign God?

_____

_____

_____

_____

2/Note the five verbs the psalmist uses as he enumerates the benefits God has given him. What are the results of these blessings?

_____

_____

note: *"The Pit" was another name for* Sheol, *the place of the dead. "Redeem your life from the Pit" suggests God's rescue from an experience of despair or destitution approaching death.*

3/The psalm writer David seems to be speaking in these opening verses from personal experience. From your knowledge of the story of David what personal reasons did he have for thanking God? At this point in your life what are the main "benefits" for which you wish to bless God?

_____

_____

_____

_____

Psalm 103:6-14
4/After thanking God for personal blessings, what does the writer remember? How does the history of Israel show that "the Lord works vindication and justice" for "the oppressed"?

_____

_____

5/Is there a contrast between God's revelation of himself to Moses and how he made himself known to the children of Israel? You may want to review some of the events in Exodus chapters 1-20.

_____

_____

6/What do you learn about the nature of God from verses 8-10? Define the words "gracious," "chide," "requite". In verses 11-14 what three comparisons or pictures are used to demonstrate God's love and mercy?

_____

_____

_____

Psalm 103:15-18
7/How does the writer contrast God and man in these verses? According to this psalm, who experiences the love of God? Define "covenant." How can you keep God's covenant in your life?

_____

_____

_____

Psalm 103:19-22
8/After recalling his personal blessings in verses 1-5 and the wider blessings to Israel, how does the psalmist further enlarge on his theme? Do you really believe that God "rules over all?" If so, how will that show in your life?

_____

_____

_____

9/Whom does the psalmist invite to share in his thanksgiving and praise? What reasons do *you* have for joining this hymn of praise? (Notice the effective use of contrast between verses 20-22a and 22b, and the sense of completion and unity produced by ending the psalm with the same personal note of praise on which it began.)

_____

_____

THINK IT THROUGH
10/How do you express your thanks to God for the benefits he has given you? Are there any new ways in which you can "bless the Lord"?

_____

_____

11/As a nation, what blessings do we have to be thankful for? How can our nation express its thankfulness?

_____

12/What additional blessings, beyond those of the psalmist, do we have as Christians who live in the New Testament?

_____

13/Which verses of this psalm can you use best to express your thankfulness?

Write them below and memorize them.

_____

_____

_____

_____

_____

FOR FURTHER STUDY
Perhaps some member of your group can find a recording of one of the many musical settings of this psalm.

Your group might want to sing #31 in *High Praise*.

Other psalms of thanksgiving are Psalms 82, 116, and 118.

10

PSALM 107: A Pilgrim's Song of Thanksgiving

Some of the psalms are known as *pilgrim songs*. It is believed that they were sung by groups of pilgrims traveling to the Temple in Jerusalem for one of the great religious festivals. This pilgrim song is also a psalm of thanksgiving. When your group meets, read the psalm aloud with part of the group reading the refrain sections: verses 6-9, 13-16, 19-22, 28-32.

Psalm 107:1-3
1/To whom are verses 1-3 addressed? In your view, what kind of people are these? What does the psalmist urge them to do? Why?

_____

_____

Psalm 107:4-9
2/Each of the following four sections of the psalm describe a special group of pilgrims who were delivered by God from particular evils. Which group is spotlighted in verses 4-9? What was their problem? What did they do in the face of their difficulty?

_____

_____

3/Discover where else in the psalm verse 6 is repeated. In each case, what do the following verses describe?

_____

_____

4/What are the hungry and thirsty wanderers encouraged to do in verse 8? Where in the psalm is *this* verse repeated? What additional thought is found in verse 9?

_____

_____

Psalm 107:10-16
5/Who are the "some" in verses 10-16? Why have they been imprisoned? What did God do for them? Describe bondages other than physical imprisonment. What is God's goal for all who are bound? (See Isaiah 58:6.)

_____

_____

Psalm 107:17-22
6/On which group of people do these verses focus? What cause does the psalmist see for their illness? Is there any connection between "sinful ways" and sickness today? What did God do for those who were sick? How did he do it? According to verse 23, how can they express their thanks?

_____

_____

_____

_____

Psalm 107:23-32
7/Who are the "some" in these verses? What vivid pictures do you have of the dangers they underwent? What did God do for them? Compare this with Mark 4:35-41.

_____

_____

_____

Psalm 107:33-43
8/How does God deal with the wicked? By contrast, what does he do for the upright? According to verse 42, what are the results of this double action?

_____

_____

THINK IT OVER

9/This psalm expresses the thanks of four groups of pilgrims: the wanderers, the imprisoned, the sick, the storm-tossed. With which of these groups do you most clearly identify: Has there been a time when you were a wanderer through life? When you were imprisoned by some habit or attitude or situation? When you were sick—mentally, physically, or spiritually? When you were battered by the storms of life?

_____

_____

_____

_____

10/In what ways have you experienced God's deliverance in situations like these? In what ways do you still need deliverance?

_____

_____

11/How does the message of this psalm compare with the popular saying: "God helps those who help themselves"?

_____

12/What verses of this psalm would you like to memorize to use in your life of prayer and praise?

_____

_____

_____

_____

_____

FOR FURTHER STUDY

Let one or more members of your group find and share a hymn or song which especially expresses his or her feelings of thanksgiving.

As a group you may want to sing #22 in *High Praise*.

Other psalms of thanksgiving are Psalms 118, 124, and 138.

11

PSALM 23: A Song of Trust

Because Psalm 23 is one of the most famous portions of the Bible its very familiarity may make it more difficult for us to appreciate the richness of its meaning. As the psalm is read aloud, try to imagine that you are hearing it for the first time. Try to picture in your mind the shepherd caring for his sheep in the fields of Judea.

Psalm 23:1-3
1/Verse 1 states the theme of the psalm. Why is a shepherd a good picture of God? What are the characteristics of a good shepherd? Why do sheep *need* a good shepherd? Can you say with confidence, "The Lord is my shepherd; I shall not want"? Why, or why not?

_____

_____

_____

2/Leslie Weatherhead says of this psalm: "It strikes a positive note. It is not beseeching God to be something or to do something. It is stating positively that he *is* and *does* all that is required by man." *A Shepherd Remembers: Studies in the Twenty-third Psalm* (New York: Abingdon, 1938), p. 20.

According to these verses, what four things does the Lord do for us? What does each of these actions mean to you in your life right now? Be specific!

_____

_____

_____

_____

3/How does the shepherd lead his sheep (Read John 10:3, 27)? How does God lead us today? How do you seek the guidance of God? What are the still waters and green pastures in your life?

_____

_____

_____

4/Why does God do all this for us? How would you paraphrase the expression "for his name's sake"?

_____

_____

Psalm 23:4
5/What scene in the life of a shepherd is the psalmist painting in this verse? Why can the sheep feel safe even in the valley of the shadow of death? In what sense can _you_ say, "I fear no evil"? Does this mean that nothing bad can happen to a Christian? What is the Christian's hope and comfort in the face of evil?

_____

_____

_____

6/What does God's rod signify in your life? his staff?

_____

_____

note: _The rod and staff were standard equipment for shepherds. The rod was a short club with a heavy knob at the end, used as a weapon against wild animals or marauders. The staff, a long stick sometimes curved at the end, was used to guide the sheep and to pull them back when they began to stray._

7/Read John 10:1-18. How does Jesus fulfill the description of the good shepherd in Psalm 23?

_____

_____

_____

Psalm 23:5-6

8/Many scholars think the picture changes in verses 5, 6 from God as the *good shepherd* to God as the *gracious host*. According to Middle-Eastern custom, a man pursued by enemies could gain protection from his host. No enemy would dare violate this code of hospitality. In verse 5, how does God act as our gracious host? What do these actions mean to you? Who or what are the enemies in your life? How does God help you to feast in their presence?

_____

_____

_____

9/What confidence does the psalmist express in verse 6? Discuss the meaning of "goodness" and "mercy". What does it mean to you to "dwell in the house of the Lord forever"?

_____

_____

_____

THINK IT OVER

10/How do you account for the popularity of this psalm? Why have so many found in it a sense of strength and comfort?

_____

11/The psalm uses the picture of a shepherd and his sheep, imagery which may not be personally familiar to us. If you were to choose a picture or comparison from your own experience to express God's care for you, what would it be? (One teen-age boy paraphrased this psalm, "The Lord is my parole officer," identifying the person on whom he could most depend.)

_____

12/If you have not already committed this psalm to memory, you may wish to do so now.

FOR FURTHER STUDY
Find some of the beautiful musical settings of this psalm, like the hymn, "The King of Love My Shepherd Is." Sing it or listen to a recording of it together.

Other psalms of trust include Psalms 63 and 121.

12

PSALM 27: Light and Salvation

As you read this psalm of trust, note the shift in mood between verses 1-6 and 7-14. Some scholars think these were once two separate psalms: a *psalm of trust* and a *lament*. Others see in this psalm an expression of two different moods in the life of the same individual. Either way we read it, this psalm will stir us to trust in God and his help.

Psalm 27:1-3
1/What three pictures of the Lord does the psalmist mention in verse 1? Discuss these metaphors. What does each mean to you? What is the result in the psalmist's life of his positive perception of God?

_____

_____

_____

2/What types of trouble does the writer describe in verses 2 and 3? How does he respond to these situations? Why?

_____

_____

3/While we may not be facing a host of human enemies, we may apply the words, "though a host encamp against me, my heart shall not fear," equally well to the battlefield of the heart, where enemies like doubt, despair, jealousy, fear or depression may be arrayed against us. What assurance does this psalm give? How does Jesus fit the picture of the Lord in verse 1?

_____

_____

_____

Psalm 27:4-6

4/In verse 4 the writer states the focus of his life, his central purpose. In what three ways is this purpose shown? Restated in your own words, what does each of these mean? How does the psalmist's aim in life compare with your own?

_____

_____

_____

5/In verse 5, in what three ways does God provide protection for David? These metaphors spring from the wilderness setting which David knew so well. How would you translate them into today's culture?

_____

_____

_____

6/As a result of the gratitude he feels for God's presence and protection, what three promises does the psalmist make?

_____

note: _The reference to a tent is a reminder of the time when the people of Israel wandered in the wilderness of Sinai, using a tent or tabernacle as a portable chapel._

Psalm 27:7-12

7/How is the mood of verses 7-12 different from that in the first six verses? What is the writer's situation? How does he feel?

_____

_____

8/What does it mean to "seek the face of God?" How can we confidently come into the presence of God? Compare the promises of God found in

Deuteronomy 4:29 and Jeremiah 29:12-13 with the encouragement of Hebrews 10:19-22. How do *you* seek the face of God?

_____

_____

_____

_____

9/List the ten ways in which the psalmist asks God to work on his behalf in these verses. Briefly explain what each one means.

_____

_____

_____

_____

10/Do you know of any situation in life where these words of verse 10 would apply? How is God a better parent than any human mother or father?

_____

_____

Psalm 27:13-14
11/What is the mood of these last two verses? On what is this attitude based? To whom is verse 14 addressed? What is involved in "waiting for the Lord"?

_____

_____

_____

THINK IT OVER
12/Do you recall a situation in which you had to "wait for the Lord"? What was the outcome?

_____

13/Which enemies—physical, mental, emotional or spiritual—do you most fear in your life? How do you handle that fear?

_____

14/How can the message of this psalm help you handle your fear better?

_____

15/Which verses of this psalm do you wish to memorize?

_____

_____

_____

_____

_____

FOR FURTHER STUDY
Other psalms of trust include Psalms 73, 128, and 139.

Sing #10 in _High Praise_.

13

PSALM 73: The Problem of Evil

This is a wisdom psalm which explores the problem of evil and the meaning of life. Begin your group meeting by reading the psalm aloud.

Psalm 73:1-3
1/What basic conviction about life does the psalmist state in verse 1? Then, as he observes the world around him, what does he notice? How does he react?

_____

_____

Psalm 73:4-14
2/List the chief characteristics of "the wicked." Which of the writer's words or expressions do you find especially fitting? Name some individuals or groups in the world which fit this description. How do you feel about such people?

_____

_____

_____

3/Because the wicked in the psalmist's world are so prosperous, what is the attitude of the general public toward them? toward God? Is this true in our society?

_____

_____

4/When he sees the success and popularity of those who scorn God, what conclusion does the psalmist draw in verses 13 and 14? Have you ever shared this feeling?

_____

Psalm 73:15-22
5/Faced with the paradox that the wicked seem to be better off than the good people, what does the writer first try to do? What was the result? Where does he then go to look for an answer?

_____

6/What answer does he find? What metaphor does he use to express the precariousness of the wicked person's hold on life? Can you think of any recent examples from our society that illustrate this?

_____

_____

7/As the psalmist looks back on his period of doubt, how does he feel about it?

_____

Psalm 73:23-28
8/After realizing how brief is the success of the wicked, the psalmist reminds himself of the blessings of the believer. Make a list of these blessings. How are they different from the "blessings" or advantages of the wicked?

_____

_____

_____

_____

9/Verses 27-28 summarize the contrast between those who ignore or rebel against God and those who love and obey him. Paraphrase these two verses in your own words.

_____

_____

THINK IT OVER
10/One commentator has titled this psalm "The Great Nevertheless." Why is this an appropriate title?

_____

11/"God blesses the good people and punishes the wicked." Is this an adequate description of what happens in the world? What conclusion does the writer of Psalm 73 come to? Is there any connection between obedience to God's commands and human success?

_____

_____

12/Psalm 73 shows the writer working through his religious doubts and questions. Do you have any doubts? What do you do with them? What can you learn from this psalm about how to handle doubt and bitterness?

_____

_____

_____

13/Choose those verses from the psalm which you can memorize and use in your prayer life.

_____

_____

_____

_____

_____

FOR FURTHER STUDY
Psalms 37, 49, and 63 also deal with the problem of evil.

PSALM 139: Facing Your Enemies

Psalm 139 can be seen as a *lament* or as a *wisdom* psalm. It may be helpful to read this psalm in a contemporary translation or paraphrase.

Psalm 139:1-6
1/To whom is David speaking here? What basic conviction does he express in verse 1? List the seven ways in which God shows his understanding of us.

_____

_____

_____

2/How does the psalmist react when he realizes how completely God understands him? How do you react?

_____

Psalm 139:7-12
3/David has described the omniscience ("all-knowingness") of God. What attribute or characteristic of God does he explore next? List the possible escapes from God which the psalm writer considers. Why would each of these fail? How do people try to escape from God today?

_____

_____

_____

_____

note: "There is a vast difference between the experience of God for one who is in heaven and for one who is in Sheol or hell. In heaven we shall experience to the full the love, compassion, glory and warmth of God; the positive of God. In hell it is the other way around. There men experience the absence of God's love, the dark side of it, the wrath of God; the negative. But it is still God, that is the point. God runs his universe and there is no escaping his presence." Ray Stedman, Folk Psalms of Faith (Glendale, CA, Regal Books, 1973), p. 310.

Psalm 139:13-18
4/How far back does God's knowledge of you extend? What phases in the development of a child are described in verses 13-16?

_____

5/What does verse 16 suggest about our lives? What is the writer's reaction in verses 17-18?

_____

Psalm 139:19-24
6/What mood change occurs in these verses?

_____

7/What does the psalmist ask God to do? Why does he want people destroyed? How do you react to this idea?

_____

_____

8/To what request does the writer's logic lead him in verses 23-24? Why is it wise to make a personal application of a general observation? Can you echo the longing for purity which David expresses here?

_____

_____

THINK IT OVER
9/Discuss the paradox of verses 19-22 of Psalm 139 as contrasted with Jesus' words, "Love your enemies, bless them which persecute you, bless and curse not"? How can these two attitudes be reconciled? Read also Acts 4:29-31. How are we to respond to our enemies?

_____

_____

_____

10/C. S. Lewis said, regarding *imprecatory* (or cursing) psalms like Psalm 139: "If the Jews cursed more bitterly than the Pagans, this was I think at least in part because they took right and wrong more seriously." *Reflections on the Psalms* (New York: Harcourt, Brace & World, 1958) p. 307. Is there a legitimate hatred of evil?

_____

11/Summarize everything you learn about God from this psalm. How should this understanding of God affect your life?

_____

_____

_____

_____

12/Which verses of this psalm are so meaningful for you that you wish to memorize them?

_____

_____

_____

_____

_____

FOR FURTHER STUDY
Other *imprecatory psalms* are Psalms 137, 69, and 109.

15

PSALM 91: Living in God's Protection

Psalm 91 is an example of a *wisdom psalm*, one which teaches some basic principles for daily living in the presence of God. Begin your discussion by reading the psalm aloud antiphonally.

Psalm 91:1-4
1/Where is "the shelter of the Most High"? Does the parallel phrase "the shadow of the Almighty" help you clarify this? What kind of person can live as close as this to the Most High God? What kind of relationship can that person claim? Do you have that kind of closeness?

_____

_____

_____

2/In verses 1-2 the psalmist makes a general statement about God's protection. How does he speak more specifically in verses 3 and 4? What does it mean to you to be delivered "from the snare of the fowler"? from "the deadly pestilence"? Have you ever experienced deliverance like this?

_____

_____

_____

3/What two images of God are shown in verse 4? Which means the most to you? Have there been times in your life when you have felt covered or shielded by God?

68

_____

_____

Psalm 91:5-8
4/What results from the promise of God's protection? According to the psalmist, what four things do we not need to fear? What does each one mean to you?

_____

_____

5/What additional promises are made in verses 7-8? Have you ever experienced protection in the face of danger? Are Christians always protected from harm in war or in daily life?

_____

_____

Psalm 91:9-13
6/What is one means by which God protects us (verse 11)? Do you ever think of angels protecting you or your family? Why, or why not? When did Jesus claim the promise in verses 10-11? (See Matthew 4:6 or Luke 4:10-11.)

_____

_____

Psalm 91:14-16
7/List each "I will . . ." in these verses. Who is saying it?

_____

_____

_____

THINK IT OVER
8/List all the great promises made in this psalm.

_____

_____

_____

_____

9/What conditions or requirements must be met if we are to receive the benefits of these promises?

_____

_____

10/How would you have to change to be open to receive these promised blessings? What keeps you from changing? What would help you to change?

_____

_____

11/Which verses of this psalm do you wish to memorize?

_____

_____

_____

_____

_____

FOR FURTHER STUDY
Other _wisdom psalms_ are Psalm 36, 37, 45, 112, 128, and 133.

Sing #24 in _High Praise_.

WHAT NEXT?

If you're like most Bible study groups, your question now is, "What shall we study next?"

To help you with that question, we've developed the chart below so that you can find your own level and area of interest. If this particular studyguide matches the pace and depth of analysis that your group needs, chances are that other Fisherman studyguides in the same level will be right for you as well. Simply pick one of the many studyguides that are available at your appropriate level.

Later On

When you finish your next studyguide, we recommend that you move on *in a sequence* by selecting from either the same subject area or the next numbered group. Continue in order from there. Many Bible study groups have a high degree of cohesiveness that extends over a period of time. By using studyguides in sequence you will:

  a. Grow in maturity as a group,
  b. Cover the major areas of Christian life and belief in a systematic and balanced manner,
  c. Learn to study God's Word in depth through the inductive method.

	Learning about God	Personal growth in Christ	Living out our faith
Level 1 *Beginning*	**1** Mark Ecclesiastes David: Vol. 1	**2** Proverbs and Parables Higher Ground Psalms	**3** Acts 1-12 Letters to Thessalonians
Level 2 *Inter- mediate*	**4** Genesis 1-25 John David: Vol. 2	**5** Genesis 25-50 James Guidance and God's Will	**6** Acts 13-28 Building Your House on the Lord Ephesians
Level 3 *Advanced*	**7** Romans Hebrews	**8** The God Who Understands Me Let's Pray Together	**9** Letters to Timothy Revelation

Available at your local bookstore or from the publishers.

Harold Shaw Publishers, Box 567, Wheaton, IL 60187